LOOKING AT
THE STARS

LOOKING AT THE STARS

IAN PATTISON

BLACK & WHITE PUBLISHING

First published 2006
by Black & White Publishing Ltd
99 Giles Street, Edinburgh, EH6 6BZ

ISBN 13: 978 1 84502 103 0
ISBN 10: 1 84502 103 7

A CIP catalogue record for this book is available
from the British Library.

Typeset by RefineCatch Ltd, Bungay, Suffolk
Printed and bound by NordBook A/S

I would like to thank Robert Kirby and Sara Starbuck at PFD; Patricia Marshall at Black & White Publishing; also George Kosinski.

'All of this happened while I was walking around starving in Christiania – that strange city no one escapes from until it has left its mark on him . . .'

Knut Hamsun, *Hunger*

CHAPTER ONE

There's one street in Tucker and one store and the man who runs it has one leg – it's what you might call taciturn. We live a few miles east of Big Sur, my partner and I. If you were to see me heading for that store in my checked Marlborough shirt, my Levi's blue jeans and my Rockport ranch boots, you might take me for a native of these parts but you'd be wrong. The man in the store calls me Shane and when he does I say, 'Aye, that'll be right – Alastair Shane maybe or Dougal Shane.' But he doesn't get it, having no Scottish in his disposition or genealogy. Sometimes, when I forget to modify my accent, he looks at me blankly, like I've cleared my throat, not spoken. He knows teeth, though – I'll say that. He knows every orthodontist from here to Fresno. He's an authority due to bitter experience. I guess that's why they call him Muley.

When I first bought this spread, the first thing I set to doing was fixing up all the broken fences that bounded my new-found acreage. After a few weeks of lonely, inexpert toil, it dawned on me there was no creature on the outside that was bursting to get in, nor any on the inside that that was dying to get out, so those fences might as well go ahead and mend themselves – I'd sit on the porch and read. What do I read? Books mostly, I admit it. It's a hard habit to break. Like smoking, some things just can't be helped. In my experience, whatever hunger is at the back of the mind will, sooner or later, come to the front – which is how I came to be here.

You'll bear with me, I hope, while I take you back a few years – to Glasgow where I never quite belonged.

In a few weeks' time, I was going to hit another birthday – my forty-first. If I was still a nobody on that date, I was going to do something about it, something drastic, trust me, no messing.

Don't tell me you've never thought of suicide – I won't believe you. The basic proposition of life is this – once we realise we're never going to be a somebody, can we delude ourselves that being a nobody can still be interesting?

I remember standing in the bar of Xenia in Ashton Lane, swaying benignly. In a few spritzers' time, being versatile, I'd sway truculently. I suppressed the thought of my impending birthday the way I drawered and cupboarded the piles of unread scripts in my makeshift office. Some critics moan that we've lost the art of storytelling. But stories are everywhere. What we've lost is the art of truth-telling. The lies start with ourselves and ripple outwards. How often has something shaming happened to you, some minor humiliation where you've come off second best? What's your instinct? Same as mine, probably – to rewrite the script in your head by obsessive degrees so that, by the time you come to recount the tale, you've turned into the finest verbal swordsman in all Europe, the hero of his own pathetic fiction who first lacerates then skewers the enemy with a few deft verbal strokes. So don't tell me we don't know how to tell stories. But the truth, ah, the truth is a different matter. 'Genius,' as the old Christmas cracker aphorism has it, 'is seeing things exactly as they are.'

Take this pub I was more or less standing up in – everybody in Xenia wrote scripts, except, of course, for its writers. It goes without saying that these scripts were worthless, even the good ones. But

writing and reading them gave us all something pleasantly maso-
chistic to do, aside from the daily unpleasant masochisms of
earning a living, looking for love and even, God forbid, finding it.

What I'm telling you, apart from the fact that I was drunk and
contemplating suicide, is that it was Friday night and I was looking
for a woman. Of course racial memory told me that to actively
look for a woman would automatically preclude the possibility of
finding one and the percentage shot was that I'd stagger home to
my Cecil Street garret with my penis draped, metaphorically, over
my arm like an unwanted umbrella. Nevertheless, there was still
the humid promise of perfume in the air and what I didn't want to
do was fritter away valuable debauchery time.

That's why, when I felt a tap on my shoulder, I began fumbling, in a pre-emptive sort of way, for the little wad of business
cards I kept in my top pocket. I'd made eye contact with Walter
Urquhart accidentally when I'd come in and he'd given me one
of those bright selfish smiles that told me he'd be over at some
point to mutter the dread earnest phrase, 'Have you had a chance
to read my script yet?' Urquhart was a tall man of forty-five with
a standard-issue shaved head and denim jacket. He was an
unsuccessful accountant who'd quit to become an unsuccessful
writer. Basically he'd traded in one uniform for another and now
scraped by doing odd jobs and living on the yield from his small
private pension. I took out a card and focused my contact lenses
– 'Blockbuster Video'.

Wrong card. I dug again – 'Terence Gifts, Script Consultant'.
This wasn't my real name, I should tell you. Along with Ivan
Rugg and Mick Hamsun, Terence Gifts was one of a number of
noms de guerre I used for various purposes, mostly avoiding
shame. I wanted to keep my real name for my writing work –
should I ever be writing again. In my few years as a script-reader
– sorry, 'consultant' – I'd never handed anyone a business
card without feeling shifty and bogus, convinced that the mere

act of proffering one tainted both me and, by extension, them, these innocent strangers. Except that usually they weren't strangers and were no more innocent than myself. Anyhow, here I now swayed, Terence-Bogus-Gifts with a double hyphen. Urquhart tapped me again and, having no choice, I turned and we did the obligatory little 'Hi, pleased to see you' pantomime.

'I saw your father this week,' said Urquhart.

'Oh yes?' I said, taken aback.

'Yes, I'm helping him with some old tax matters.'

'Wear gloves so's not to leave prints.'

Verging on truculence, I took a sip of my spritzer, only it was more of a glug than a sip, and I wiped wine and soda from my chin and shirt. I risked a glance to the far side of the bar, just below the stairs to the small gallery. The petite, delicate-featured brunette was still there. A small bear in a leather blouson was attempting to entertain her. He had a pint lager glass in his hand – not a smart move on his part. Xenia only sold Furth on draught, the kind of heady, thudding brew that required you apologise for your later behaviour in advance. The whole art of eye contact is not to make eye contact. The lightest of approximate brushings is all that's required to register, or impart, an interest that may or may not prove to be mutual.

I'd spotted her when I was at the bar, ordering. She was small, dark, sexy and soulful – the type I was weak for. She'd received my overture – or rather underture – with good grace. Which is to say she'd ignored it without the faintest flicker of apparent interest. Crucially, she hadn't vomited outright or fetched a bouncer. I leaned my weight on to my right leg so I could manoeuvre a discreet, watchful position over Urquhart's shoulder.

'Anyway, he sends his regards.'

'My father does?'

'Yes,' Urquhart continued, 'he says he has an important message for you.'

'Does he have a terminal illness?'

'Not so far as I know.'

'Then he's got nothing to say that could interest me.'

Urquhart laughed so there'd be no awkward silence. I was irritated. I wanted an awkward silence. I wanted to drop a hint the size of an anvil that would make him go away. But we both knew that wouldn't happen till he'd hit me with it. So he hit me with it. 'Have you had a chance to read my script yet?'

I nodded vigorously to imply that I had. But my mouth said, 'It's at the top of the pile for Monday.' I could see the clock. Ten forty-five. I was relaxed about the small bear. Apart from anything else, he'd made his move too soon. The place was licensed till one because of the West End Festival – he'd never make his chat last that long. Most men have what? Maybe twenty or thirty minutes' worth of the sort of sprightly, semi-improvised shite and onions otherwise known as charm with which we hope to entertain the drawers off a woman. Beyond that lie the lands of Repetition and the Awkward Pause.

'You said that last week,' said Urquhart, trying to hide his disappointment behind a matey chuckle.

'I know,' I said, 'and I'd meant to but I've been busy with a script of my own.' This was a partial truth. Hacking impotently through the jungle of desperation, I'd stumbled upon a stray idea. In no time, I'd sedated it and dragged it back to my office. Here, I'd expertly beaten the life out of it, shorn it of hoof and fur, then crammed the resultant cadaver into the blender, so that it had came out pappy, bland and pithless in the modern television manner we all know and loathe.

I was excited by my idea. It was just as lousy as everybody else's – it must be in with a chance. What was it? I won't bore you or me with the details but do you remember the pitch for the film *Alien*, said to be the greatest pitch, if not the greatest film, of all time? Reputedly, it consisted of just three words – 'Jaws in space'. Well, how does this grab you? – 'Proust in Paisley'. No, me neither. But, like the fool that I am, I persisted. By the way, I should also explain that I'd grown used to using terms like 'pitch' and 'heat' and 'water-cooler moments' without blushing. I think I'd grown too ashamed to blush.

Anyway, here is the gist. Celia Proust is a medium. Following a bang on the head, she's now a bedridden invalid but has developed these strange psychic powers . . . I should explain that the word was out at the time that STV was looking for a successor to their cop show *Taggart* and a nervous BBC was looking to stymie them by coming up with a Scottish cop show of their own. Anyway, all the known world was, it seemed, gagging for yet another cop show. I'd noted that *Taggart* had taken its name from a well-known chain of car showrooms around the West of Scotland and that this precedent had been set with a bunch of successful books based on a cop called Laidlaw, also the name of a big local car chain. So who does Celia Proust meet and strike up a friendship with while recuperating from a bump to her dainty cranium in hospital? Why, none other than recovering alcoholic, small, dark, yet still soulfully beautiful, WPC Wendy Fiat. OK, it sounds like shit when I give it out straight like this but, with hard work, I knew it could be transformed magically into piss. It would keep me alive, justify my continued existence and promote me from being a nobody into an anybody, while I looked for the big killing – the movie script I would one day write and that would succeed beyond my wildest – no, better than wildest – my most ardent, sacred dreams.

When that happened I would be a somebody. If I was a somebody, I wouldn't have to kill myself through pure self-disgust – that simple.

Those are the details I wasn't going to bore you with and, by the time I'd got through not boring Urquhart with them, he was shifting his weight from Caterpillar boot to boot and his little squirming eyes were screaming, 'Me, me, talk about me!'

So we talked about him and, as we did, I looked up to watch the dark-haired girl. Except that she wasn't there any more – just the bear and his friend, a potbellied guy with a lank fringe and black jeans, who'd thoughtfully absented himself while the bear had made his play. The bear was looking all pleased with himself and laughing uproariously so I knew he'd been dumped and that the girl hadn't just gone to the toilet. I caught his eye and he caught me catching it. I'd have given him one of my wry smiles, foiled cocksman to cocksman, but, on my snidey little face, they tend to come out as smirks and, with the bear being raw, it would have been asking for trouble. When married guys envy their single pals, they only think in terms of conquest, not of the interminable nights when you draw in your hook to find nothing on the end of it, not even the bait. The single man is his own bait. If women reject his hook, they reject his very being.

'G'night, Urquhart.'

'What'll I tell your father?'

My slack mouth mumbled something, I don't know what. As Urquhart said, the man was my father. What in hell are we supposed to say to those sorts of people?

Outside, across the lane, bouncers in windcheaters and using two-way radios herded outdoor boozers within a narrow strip of licensed drinking area. A stiff breeze gusted, whipping drizzle on to the backs of hardy, defiant young revellers who had turned, shoulder on, to shield their Buds and Breezers from the elements. It was a typical summer night in Glasgow. On nights like these, there was nothing else for it – you went home with your hard-on and a bag of chips from the Philadelphia, as I now did.

The lights were out again on the landing and I climbed the stairs in darkness. I lived in a large single room on the top floor of a tenement building occupied for the most part, but not exclusively, by students. They had all scattered home for the summer to comfortable middle-class houses in Guildford and Cheadle, leaving only the occasional Neanderthal like myself to rattle around the long, spooky lobbies like so many abandoned Boo Radleys. I clumped along the bare lino of the hall, unlocked my door and turned on the light.

Sixty watts' worth of bulb, all the wiring could accommodate without snapping in Blimpish protest, struggled to illuminate my living space. The effect was not so much to dispense light as to smear it around the middle of the room, skipping the corners like a lazy cleaner. There was enough, though, to startle a mouse which darted out from the scullery recess and into the junk cupboard to its hole behind the gas meter. Nobody could work out why I chose to live like this, least of all me. I knew it was tied up with guilt, insecurity and, in some bygone literary way, idealism. After all, proper writers lived in poverty, didn't they? Sure, but only when young. If they were still unsuccessful by the time they hit my age . . . well, you already know my feelings on that one.

Not that I could be classified as impecunious, I had an income of sorts – enough to keep me in spritzers, even at west end prices, and I could enjoy the odd brunch meal in the Cul de Sac. But man does not live by ciabatta alone. I'd set out to be a writer and I wasn't writing. I remembered the opening line of a Raymond Carver tale I'd read. It went something like this: 'I was between stories so I felt despicable.' Actually, I think he used the conjunction 'and' but, to me, 'so' is stronger so I've script-edited him. Feeling gloomy cheered me up and I put on a Leonard Cohen CD with the intention of slouching against the window frame, watching the drizzle and croaking along to 'Tower of Song'.

Tomorrow would be Saturday. I'd rise early, make a pot of coffee – the shagging coffee, not the instant coffee – and sit at the table. I'd remove the Daddies Brown Sauce bottle and plough dutifully through some of the scripts I'd brought home from the piles that were clogging up my office. I say 'office' – I had a Portakabin out back of the Alba Media Corporation building where I worked as a script-reader. I say 'worked' – through sloth, I'd allowed those piles to grow to unmanageable and alarming levels. I had become obliged to start lugging some home with the intention of worrying them down to acceptable levels – acceptable to me, that is, if not to my employers or the authors concerned.

I stood by the kettle, feeling centred and all-seeing. 'I needed so much to have nothing to touch,' sang Leonard, 'I've always been greedy that way.' I'd read that he sometimes retired to a Buddhist retreat on Mount Baldy in California, to study at the feet of his tutor, Roshi. I found this lifestyle seductive but I knew it would never work in Scotland. While you were sitting cross-legged on Ben Lomond, trying to meditate, small junkies would be battering you with Irn-Bru bottles and stealing tins of Spam from your rucksack.

The light was winking on the answering machine. I tried not to get excited – I was on Mount Leonard, above all that herd mentality stuff. All the same, I stepped over my bulging script bag and pressed play.

'You have two messages. Message one.' Message one was, as usual, a dreary query in a ponderous, self-conscious delivery from one of life's serial no-hopers – in this case, my mother. 'I was just wondering . . . you're not in . . . What would you prefer . . .?' The gist of it was 'What do you want for your birthday?' – as if I cared. What did it matter? I could ask for anything – a Porsche Boxster, the return of my wasted youth – but I'd still get the same thing she gave me every year – a book token. Sadistic old crow. My tin kettle wheezed asthmatically through the dust on its whistle. I pressed 'delete' and crossed to the cooker.

'Message two.' At first, I thought it was some sort of atmospheric prelude to a Leonard track I hadn't noticed before but, unless Aiden Lang was doing backing vocals with Jennifer Warne, I had it wrong. I could hear a melee of voices and pinging tills that was so arch it might've come from a Beeb Sound Effects Library. Through it all I could hear a plonking piano that was trying hard to tinkle wryly and, over the piano, Aiden's voice was shouting to be heard from his mobile. My ears gathered in a couple of nouns and a name and, from those, I was able to deduce the rest. Lang was in the Melba Room, yahooing with Denis Rourke. If I got this before twelve, for God's sake come along. 'End of final message.' I looked to the clock by my bed. Eleven thirty. Leonard moaned from the sideboard; the kettle crackled, cooling; the pile of scripts meandered across the table like a fractured Manila tombstone. I washed my cock, brushed my teeth and was there in twenty minutes.

The Melba Room was a favourite place for over-thirties to go when the pubs shut. It stayed open late and was located on the outer edge of the city centre so that, if you couldn't get a taxi, it was a walkable distance back to the west end. A condition of its extended licence meant that alcohol would only be served if the patrons also bought food. This kept the worst of the free-roaming bears away.

I paid off the driver and walked up the steps to the concrete concourse. The gusting wind had dropped so that the rain was now falling vertically which, all in all, was as close to a balmy summer's evening as the Glasgow weather gods were likely to bestow. The doorman let me in like he was doing me some sort of grudging favour – which, as it happened, he was. I'd been involved in an incident a couple of weeks before. It had involved, of course, a woman. Whose name I never learned. And a man, a ginge, whose name I can't recall, but with whom I'd been locked in deadly verbal jest for the woman's favours. Witticisms had flashed like Stanley knives then, as the blades dulled, the crude chair legs of open insult had been brandished and, well, you can imagine the rest – you've been in pubs, you know what petulant office workers look like when they try to pummel each other with their soft, white hands.

The delicious fug of stale air and fresh noise wrapped itself around me like a big welcoming arm. The piano sounded less plink-plonky now and I could make out a few pretentiously retro bars of a Cole Porter tune before it twittered to an unsteady halt. A big girl in a black party frock was leaning over Henry, the piano player. Her pals were flanking her, goading her on. She was wearing a big cardboard sign that read 'Getting hitched'. To what, it didn't say – a covered wagon or a plough, possibly. I could hear her shouting at Henry, 'Play it, you baldy wee swine! Play "As Time Goes By"!'

I felt the big welcoming arm morph from mere metaphor to become two real, bony hands around my neck. 'How goes it, Denis?'

'Get them in,' mumbled the mouth of Denis Rourke from his flushed face. He thrust an empty wine bottle and a crumpled twenty at me. 'Going for a pee.'

I called for a cheeseburger and a bottle of red as instructed, put fifteen more to it and ordered a bottle of white, with soda, for myself. I was in the mood. You know as soon as you walk in whether you and the pub are sympatico or not. Jostled by the throng, I wobbled one-legged, scanning the bar. Where would they be sitting? Ah, but of course. Aiden Lang waved from a table near the ladies' toilet – a favoured hollow for the seasoned quim hunter. After all, every woman had to take a leak – two sometimes if she wanted to run further checks, en route, on some guy she might later be intending to snare.

Speaking of which, who was that who'd just stepped out of the ladies' and was making her way back to her friends in the corner booth? Why, it was the dark-haired, soulful mystery babe from Xenia. I decided, if given half a chance, I'd make a move. And, if I wasn't given half a chance, I'd make one. I locked the wine bottles by the neck in the fingers of one hand, balanced the cheeseburger on a side plate with the other and negotiated a ponderous, bumping slalom towards Aiden Lang. By the time I made the table, Denis Rourke was already back, slouched against the mahogany partition, lighting a Marlboro Lite. You'll appreciate I'm speaking of a bygone age, when lighting up wasn't an action that caused mass panic in bars and didn't send rosy-lunged citizens rushing hatless into the streets in search of law enforcement officers.

Lang was a writer who didn't write and Rourke an actor who didn't act – I felt comfortable in their company.

'Champagne!' cried Aiden Lang, pouring a glass of the house red. 'It's celebration time.'

'Double celebration,' said Denis Rourke, sweeping up his change from the table.

'What's the occasion?' I asked, all innocence.

Aiden handed a generous glass to Rourke. 'He's got a *Taggart*,' he explained, 'and I've sold a screenplay.'

I was smiling but I felt that sickening jab to the nervous system that only comes with the success of our dearest friends. 'Well done,' I heard my mouth say.

'Cheers,' said Denis Rourke and he took a big glug of wine.

Shelving the more deadly matter of the screenplay, I proceeded to *Taggart*. 'All three episodes?'

'Two and a half,' said Denis. 'Then I'm a corpse.'

'Not bad for *Taggart*,' said Aiden.

I agreed. 'If you'd been London-based, they'd have killed you quicker to save on the subsistence allowance.'

We all nodded. I liked Denis Rourke. I enjoyed his joie de vivre and admired him for the intensity of his depressions. Most of all I respected him because, as an actor, he'd resisted spelling

'Denis' with an extra N or a Y to make himself 'distinctive'. He was also an indiscriminate cocksman of renown. Legend had it that, in the old days, he'd cupped the breasts of two thirds of Banarama when they'd stayed at the Albany and once, when accused of having taken a blow job from a man, he'd replied, 'So what? A mouth's a mouth.' I'd heard that story before I'd even met him – it had tickled me, being so un-Scottish a sentiment it might almost have been written by Burns. I could imagine Moira Anderson and Kenneth McKellar singing it on some ancient, putrefying Hogmanay show yet to come, 'For a' that and a' that, a mooth's a mooth for a' that.' But, for all that, Denis was still an actor. If his west-end flat was ablaze from cupola to hash stash, he wouldn't emerge till he'd draped a Cashmere sweater over his shoulders and rescued his Ryvita.

'I haven't done a telly since I was a fishing boat captain in *Heartbeat.*'

'A *French* fishing boat captain,' recalled Aiden Lang.

'With a Paisley accent,' said Denis and he went on, 'I knew I only had one speech so didn't even bother my arse opening the script the night before and instead got pissed with Billy Givens. Next morning, I looks and sees the whole thing's in fucking French.'

I laughed, accommodatingly. I'd heard this story several times but was happy to feed off it yet again till life dealt us some new ones.

'Anyway,' Denis continued, 'I says to Colynne Foxxe, who was playing Man with Bike, One . . .' And Denis told his story. And we laughed, Aiden and I, but not too loudly because we were both thinking the same thing – loud laughter on a Friday night speaks to women of drunkenness and drunkenness is the enemy of fleshly promise.

Denis, all storied-out, made his back comfortable against the partition again and cast a roaming eye around the room. 'Givens said he might be in but it doesn't look like it.'

'Pity,' I said but I was relieved. There's a law of media physics which states that, whenever two actors are gathered together in a room, any third person shall receive no oxygen.

'What have you spotted?' asked Aiden.

'Don't look,' I said. 'The dark one.'

'They're all dark,' said Aiden, 'especially the blondes.'

'The one with the eyes,' I said.

'Ah, well now,' said Aiden, 'they haven't all got eyes . . .' and his own little glittering stones beadied around the place. 'Got her.'

I looked. He had. 'Do you know her?'

'No,' he said.

'I know her,' said Denis.

My heart sank. 'You haven't?'

'She's a solicitor,' protested Denis in an innocent tone, intended further to beguile our interest. Which it did – mine at least. 'Don't make out you never get lucky with solicitors.'

'You did a dentist,' Aiden supported. 'If you'd do a dentist, you'd do a solicitor.'

'I tried with her once but no go. Anyway, I was too pissed to perform.'

'Didn't she offer legal aid?' said Aiden.

'You've a specific effect on women,' I told Denis. I was pointing – it was the drink. 'Either they run towards you or away from you. You remind them of those guys who pushed them round on the waltzers at the shows when they were fourteen.'

'That's a myth,' said Denis. It wasn't but, by declaring it as such, he was hoping to nurture the possibility that it might become one. 'Isn't there something else you want to ask me?' he said. 'Apart from whether I slept with her?'

Aiden and I looked at each other.

'Oh, yes,' I said, 'what's her name?'

'Chloe.'

I lifted my glass. I thought about her name. Chloe – it made the ice cubes tangy in my tepid drink.

'What do you know about her status?'

'Not much,' said Denis. 'Somebody told me her life story once but I wasn't listening.'

'That's because you weren't in it.'

'There was some guy but I think something happened.'

'Metaphorically or actually?' asked Aiden.

Denis shut one eye and did pensive acting. 'Why can't the actual be metaphoric?'

'If the actual were metaphoric,' said Aiden, 'then they'd be synonymous. And a synonym is not a metaphor.'

We were in danger of crawling our way down a tedious semantic pothole. I gave a stout tug on the conversational rope so that the benefit of the drink might not be squandered. Like the best heroic gestures, it involved monumental self-sacrifice.

'You haven't told me about your screenplay deal, Aiden.'

The moment was upon us. Aiden was immodest enough to scratch his head bashfully. I watched him take a deep breath while he struggled to find words – specifically the four or five in the *Oxford Dictionary* that wouldn't be required in his retelling, 'brevity' and 'terse' being chief among them. But he was brief or, if not brief, its seductive cousin, interesting. He kept his ego in check, the facts scrupulously before him, and he was sensitive to my own presently luckless status. In short, he was a bastard.

Basically, he'd sold an idea for a romantic thriller to a prominent Hollywood film actor, of Irish origin, who had better remain nameless. I'm not sure why he needs to remain nameless so let's call him Liam Neeson. He'd had dinner with Neeson in London and interesting points of view had been put to him. As a result of these interesting points of view, Aiden had now raised his head fatefully, perhaps forever, from the narrow trough of heather, coke, bile and envy that constituted the staple diet of the Scottish creative classes. 'Plan A,' announced Aiden, 'If this works, I'll go to Los Angeles.'

'What if it doesn't work?' I asked, encouragingly.

'Plan B, I'll go to Los Angeles.'

Dinner with a film star had persuaded Aiden of what he and others had come to suspect – that the dull, old Scottish knee-jerk deference toward London was disappearing, to be replaced by a bright, new Scottish knee-jerk deference toward Los Angeles. Why, went the argument, should Scottish talent go cap in hand to London, when London then had to go cap in hand to Los Angeles? Why not go straight to the top, cut out the middleman and receive your rejection straight away? That way, a promising young film-maker could be embittered, disillusioned and back working behind the counter in Blockbuster within six months where otherwise it might take him three years. I'm paraphrasing but that was the general thrust.

Through the miraculous emotional laxative of drink I soon found myself contributing to the discussion with phrases like 'The trouble with LA . . .' and 'If Liam's ever in Glasgow . . .' without blushing or beating myself with my own shoe. Denis, listening quietly, said little. He had friends in California – actor friends who'd gone out there during the Great *Trainspotting* Gold Rush of '96 and done well. Which was why he couldn't visit them. They'd only ask him why he was still scrabbling around for *Taggart*s when they were meeting producers in the bar of the Mondrian and driving the Pacific Highway to Malibu for the weekend. At least that's how Denis imagined them – probably the reality was different; probably they took the bus to Santa Monica and scoured the malls looking for square sliced sausage and Celtic videos. When they were all again equals, which is to say failures, they could be friends once more. I was simultaneously elated and crushed. The fact that Aiden could come within touching distance of an entree into Filmland was heartening but, at the same time, his success threw my own sense of failure into relief.

'If I go out, come and visit me,' said Aiden.

'I will,' I said. But I knew it wouldn't happen – if Aiden was to be successful, I wouldn't want to go out there and, if he wasn't, he wouldn't want me to come. He was just spreading a little dutiful emotional largesse around, as even I might have done. The time was approaching for me to make my move on Miss Dark and Soulful. Desperation had cooled to recklessness – so what if she rejected me? I'd been rejected before – why, in only a few mere decades, I'd be over it.

'Excuse me a minute,' I said, rising.

'Where are you going?' asked Aiden.

'Nowhere,' I said, sitting again.

'Careful – remember time's wingèd chariot,' said Denis.

'You're right,' I said, standing again. She was still over in the corner with her pals. I'd managed to make out two rings on the hands of her friends, one engagement, one wedding. But the pal with the engagement ring wasn't wearing it on the designated finger – hmmm. As every man knows, an engagement ring buys you a couple of years but, after that, you'd better come through with the lifetime goldie or you're history. He must've broken it off, the guy, not her, otherwise she'd have removed the ring herself as one of those slavish statements of empowerment that modern women love so much. Nothing on Chloe's hands. Good omen. I wiped my mouth, checked my fly for damp patches and turned to Denis. 'Do you mind if I use your name?'

'Why not?' he shrugged. 'I do.'

And with that, I went over.

Next morning I was awakened by a strange intimate droning. I opened my eyes to find Leonard still playing. This gave me the first mysterious reference point for the day or, more importantly, the events of the night before and I struggled to give memory a handhold on the wet moss of lost time. For a few perky seconds I inspected my sensations and, finding no untoward symptoms, declared myself to be free of hangover. This was to prove merely the brief and false euphoria that seduces the alcohol abuser into attempting ambitious feats of physical accomplishment such as rising and going for a pee.

I muttered and sniffed my way to the sink and stood, dozily, trying to relieve myself. The morning hard-on intruded on the task and a mug and a couple of side plates on the draining board received a brief, pungent hosing before my aim could be revised.

As I stood, swaying numbly, the distant traffic hiss from Byres Road told me two things – that the day was well under way and that it was raining. I staggered from the sink and looked at the clock. Eleven o'clock. On the windowpane, two fat blue-bottles buzzed and squabbled like fighter planes in a dogfight against a grey familiar backcloth of cloud. I wanted to vomit but, being unwilling in the cold to subject myself to the protracted ritual of leaning, gagging and groaning, shivered back into bed and pulled up the covers. No matter – a crusting mosaic on the floor by my discarded trousers told me the task had been partially undertaken. I chastised myself, felt my disgusted spirit depart for a more worthy vessel and shut my eyes, ready to face the day.

I could hear faint, tinny applause. I still hadn't turned off the mini hi-fi. Leonard's voice droned on in an endless CD cycle of eternal recurrence. I asked myself whether it was worth a second struggle out of bed or if I should sit tight and hope to sleep through it. 'I greet you from the other side,' sang Leonard, cheerily, 'of sorrow and despair . . .'

And that's when I remembered the previous night, and Chloe.

'Hi, I understand you're a friend of Denis. We were wondering if you'd like to join us for a drink?' I was having to shout my laid-back invitation above Henry's piano and the hen night who were giving it the Waterboys' 'Whole of the Moon'.

'Thanks but I'm with friends,' the future icon known as Chloe said.

'They're welcome too.'

I wondered if it was a polite brush off. 'Of course, if you'd sooner not . . .' Nice touch play from me, I thought. Manly. I can take you or leave you.

'Let me check with my friends.'

She turned to check with the friends, leaving me standing, smiling inanely and tapping my foot along to Henry's cheesed-off, approximately tinkled Waterboys. From the corner of my eye, I could make out a brief, intense negotiation. Wedding Ring wasn't the problem – Wedding Ring was smiley, seemed open to suggestion, up for fun – but Engagement Ring remained sullen of countenance. Maybe she wanted to be coaxed – maybe she was still pining for Mr Engagement and hoping he'd show up, having realised what a fool he'd been to reject this sullen, hatchet-faced doormat who adored him.

Chloe turned back to me, smiling apologetically. 'We're having a problem,' she said.

'I can see that,' I said. 'Tell her to come over – she can make him jealous.'

'Who?'

'Whoever it is that's spoiling her life and your night.'

'It isn't that simple,' said Chloe. 'Just a second.' She touched my arm. When she touched it, I felt a thrill run from the tips of my ears, down my cock and out through my toes. I bet that thrill hit Greenland and is still running. I watched as Chloe nodded, her dark, well-cut hair bobbing expensively. She turned back to me. 'Majority wins,' she said. 'We'll be right over.'

'Good,' I said. With masterly restraint, I avoided doing handsprings back to the table.

'They'll be right over,' I told Aiden Lang and Denis Rourke.

'Well . . .' drawled Aiden.

'Indeedy,' said Denis.

I wheeled a couple of chairs from other tables and Aiden hastily bulldozed the crisp crumbs and chomped arcs of burger bun with a beer mat on to the floor. From here on in, it would be every man for himself.

In a straightforward handsomeness contest, I would come a plucky second behind Aiden – I knew that. One factor in my favour was that Chloe hadn't seemed the type to be beguiled by actorish celebrity. If she had, then Denis would have beguiled the drawers off her already and he hadn't managed that. This narrowed her choices – if choice she wished to make – down to two. I hoped that Aiden would home in on the married one but this was a forlorn prospect – experience had taught us both always to play the percentage shot. Married women loved to flirt, sure, often doing so in a heavy-handed and direct way, but, once they'd drawn your interest, they usually turned cowardly and headed off in a closing-time taxi. Then they'd spend the coming Monday washday in dreamland, feasting on the weekend banquet of attention you'd provided for them, free of charge. Of course, there was always Engagement Ring but she seemed less a gurgling fount of joy than a dark plughole down which our bubbling spirits might drain.

'Hi, Denis.'

'Hi, Chloe,' said Denis, extending a hand with studied laziness. 'This is Aiden.'

'And this is Sam and this is Morag.'

Wedding Ring, all breathless, proffered a hand and a 'hi'.

Engagement grunted, like she was inspecting train tickets, and clutched her handbag tighter.

'Sit down,' said Aiden, gallantly proffering the chairs that I'd scrounged and begged. I'd decided that my best chance lay in allowing Aiden free rein to win, as quickly as possible. For Aiden was never content in victory. Compelled to press on, he would pulverise a woman with charm and wit until gradually it dawned on her that, rather than being the object of his ardour, she was in fact a mirror upon which he could adore himself. As this realisation became plain and her interest withdrew, so charm would turn to desperation, then boastfulness and soon names would be flourished, only to drop, clanging to the floor. An address book might be produced, with telephone numbers of the rich and famous, displayed for the purposes of validation and admiration. These actions, to watchful women, held another mirror to Aiden – one which pleased or didn't, according to taste or whim.

'What brings you guys in here tonight?' asked Chloe, just to set us off.

'We're celebrating,' I said, pouring them wine. 'Aiden here's sold a script to LA.'

This was of course a nasty little pre-emptive strike, concealed within a gesture of magnanimity. I wanted Aiden's triumph acknowledged, discussed and disposed of right up front so the subject might be exhausted and the conversation moved on to a less exclusive topic, one that might hopefully involve myself – failure perhaps or, to dress it up in its Friday night finery, 'The Heroic Struggle of the Artist'. Caught unprepared, Aiden's eyes met mine, registering both gratitude that I had yielded him his soliloquy and resentment that it had come at the start of the first act, rather than at its climax, where I felt sure he had intended to place it. For a few moments, he laboured, struggling to recover his earlier note of monstrous humility, but gradually he found his rhythm and the self-effacement had flowed like fine wine.

'Where do you get your ideas from?' asked Sam.

'If I knew where they came from, I'd go there,' replied Aiden, employing a trusty aphorism from the Writers' Tool Box that we'd all utilised at one time or another. Appreciative tittering ensued. But only from Sam and Chloe. Morag, bearing an air of martyred boredom, gazed stonily at the door. I began to warm to her.

'As a lapsed Catholic, I love movie-making,' declared Aiden. 'There's a built-in accommodation for bad behaviour – it takes our worst excesses and turns them into cash.'

Movie-making. Suddenly he wasn't just another Jock scribbler – he was the third Coen brother. Again Chloe smiled, more freely this time, and stroked her glass. She was warming to him. Was she warming to him? Shit – *I* was warming to him so she must be. I told myself to relax – it was just the wine. As if that somehow diminished the possibility of amorous entanglement between the two; as if seven eighths of all the romances in all the world, since the beginning of time, hadn't kicked off with a few glasses of vino on a Friday night. Just the wine – what a hee-hawing ass.

When I heard Aiden use the terms 'heat', 'up to speed' and 'ball park' all in the same sentence, I decided it was time to bring down the interval curtain. I turned to Denis. 'Want to tell us about your *Taggart*, Denis?'

Denis did an 'oh, am I still present?' with his eyebrows. 'Why?' he said. 'Is Liam Neeson in it?'

'Everybody's been in *Taggart*,' said Sam. 'They filmed in my mum's conservatory once.'

Denis nodded. 'If your mum's conservatory got subsistence allowance, I want the name of its agent.' Denis lit another Marlboro Lite. He was morose and stood teetering at the gate of Denisland, a distant realm located far away, behind his eyes.

'We're losing the benefit of the drink,' I thought to myself, as if the moment was a patient on a table, hovering critically, between life and death, which of course, it was. Having made my diagnosis, I wrote us all out a prescription of good fellowship. 'How are you, Morag?' I said, turning to her. 'Are you enjoying yourself?'

'Does it look like it?' She smiled in a smug, victorious way to herself as if this somehow constituted a witty riposte and not just simple bludgeoning rudeness. Having uncorked the bottle of her contempt, she was unwilling, unable, to staunch its flow. 'You all think you're so smaaaart,' she said, drawing out the word and giving a little dismissive turn away of her head on its completion. Sam and Chloe seized the opportunity to make discreet, apologetic faces.

Aiden shrugged. 'Only comparatively,' he said. His rebuke was considerate, allowing the implication to hang unspoken in the air.

'But you're not smaaaart,' Morag continued, 'you're all just saaaad.'

There was an awkward silence while we all struggled to fix this ugly rip in the backcloth of our lives that had allowed reality in. I looked at Aiden. He looked back at me. He'd done his bit, his look said – he was the evening's star turn, he couldn't be caught scrapping with a dissatisfied fan, so to speak, by the stage door.

'Never mind sad,' said Denis, 'we're all doomed.'

Aiden and I perked up. Sad was pathetic, doomed was glamorous.

Aiden leaned on his elbow, glass in hand and gave Chloe what letching drunks hope is a ruthless, yet strangely tender, penetrating gaze. 'Have you ever been to Los Angeles?' he said.

'Yes,' smiled Chloe, 'once.'

'Did you do the Universal Studios tour?' I asked, elbowing my way into the conversation.

'No,' said Chloe. 'We went to Warner Brothers, though, just over the back lot.'

The sentries at my ears were alerted and presented arms –
'We? Who's "we"?'

'My brother and I. He wrote a film in his gap year. They
invited him over for the test screenings.'

I watched Aiden from the corner of my eye. I felt that, if
I tapped him with a tiny ornamental hammer, he would have
shattered into a thousand fragments.

Miraculously, Denis perked up. 'Your brother?' he said. 'You
never mentioned . . .'

'Why would I?' explained Chloe. 'Unless it's your own
achievement, it's a wee bit naff to boast.'

'And, if it is your own achievement, that's even worse,'
pounced Morag, gloatingly, looking for once directly across the
table.

Aiden laughed, deflecting, as best he could, this small
unpleasant missive.

I asked Chloe her brother's name.

'Eric Ross.'

Good. Now I knew her surname. I dimly recognised the
brother and connected him to a video in a Blockbuster sale bin. I
recalled a couple of big-name British comics who, suffering from
the tragic delusion that they could act, had helped compound
the whole sorry enterprise.

'The film was called *Deadbeat Romance!*'

'I remember,' I said, nodding. 'The exclamation mark in the
title killed it.'

I aimed a rueful smile at Aiden but he wouldn't meet my eyes.
We were both thinking the same thing – it didn't matter how bad
a movie it was, it had been green-lit and made and, worse, it had
been some pimpled seventeen-year-old who'd dashed it off in a
few bored moments between backpacking to Phuket and blowing
his student loan on Rolling Rock and scrotum rings. Aiden's face
had looked set and determined. As for me, I felt the drunk man's

tears of perplexed self-pity well up in my eyes. I took a careful sip of my spritzer. I was down to a small tilted arc in the glass.

'What's your brother writing now?' asked Aiden.

'Nothing,' said Chloe.

'Good,' I thought, generously, 'an old-fashioned, one-turkey wonder – well at least that's something.' And it was something. It was a stick to beat us with.

Chloe continued, 'Yes, an agent in WeHo . . .'

'West Hollywood,' explained Aiden, quickly, for my benefit.

'Fixed him up with work. There was talk of a first-look deal with Warners but Eric turned it down. He's put everything on hold for now to pursue his studies.'

Maturity. Everywhere you looked, it jumped up to thumb its nose at you.

'I'm taking out my mobile and I'm dialling a specific number,' said Denis, doing just that.

'As opposed to a general number?' inquired Aiden.

'Quiet!' ordered Denis. He pressed his palm to his other ear. 'I'm ringing a taxi. We need to move on before we lose the benefit of the drink.'

'You read my mind,' I said. I turned to Chloe. 'You're coming, aren't you?'

'Well . . .' She raised her eyebrows, inviting me to anticipate the problem of Morag.

'Where to?' asked Sam.

'Anywhere,' said Aiden. 'Arta! Let's go to Arta!'

'Arta!' instructed Denis loudly, into his mobile.

'Wait a minute,' said Aiden, 'There's six of us. Taxi only holds five.'

Morag shook her head. 'I'm not going.' She glanced from Sam to Chloe, looking for reaction. They nodded. The same stoical look appeared in the eyes of both women. Noticeably, neither of them made the slightest effort to change Morag's mind.

'It wasn't meant as a hint,' assured Aiden.

Morag shrugged heavily, moodily. 'That's neither here nor there. I'm not going – that's all. I'm going home. I'll get my own taxi.' But she didn't move.

'That'll be you away then?' I said. I was sick of her.

'I'd really like to come,' said Chloe.

I immediately squeezed her hand. 'I completely understand,' I said. 'Just give me your phone number and we'll say no more about it.' She turned away. She hadn't heard me. Had she heard me?

'You all take the taxi,' said Aiden, 'I'll follow on.' He was doing his best. He didn't want to be blamed for having raised the numbers issue. Morag was already on her feet. Chloe and Sam were following suit, reluctantly pulling on their coats.

I stood up quickly and began helping Chloe into hers. 'Will you give me your phone number?' I whispered, aiming for a tone of twinkling mischief but unable to keep the miserable hint of yearning from my voice.

'No,' she said.

'Then put on your own coat.' I didn't stop helping though. I watched as she fastened three big retro-60s girly buttons, from the bottom up. On the third, she said, 'But you can give me yours if you like.'

I gave her my card. She didn't even look at it as she dropped it into her bag. Morag began blowing her nose. As a hurry-up signal, it had all the subtlety of a shipyard siren. I positioned myself in front of Chloe so Morag couldn't hear what I was saying. 'What is it with her? She's been looking at the door since she came in. Can't she forget this drongo, whoever he is, for just one night?'

Chloe smiled, wanly. 'Bit difficult when the guy who stole her away from that drongo is sitting right next to you.' She raised her eyebrows. The penny dropped. How big is a penny? Not this one – it clattered to the floor like a bin lid.

'Well, cheerio,' said Morag. 'Nice to have met you.' She split her face to Aiden, then to me. The cow. Now that she'd got her own way, she was all smiles.

'Bye,' said Chloe.

As they walked to the door, they seemed to me like the three most alluring women in the world – probably because one of them was. The other two had got lucky by proxy. It dawned on me that I'd no idea which card, in my haste, I'd given to Chloe. Who was I now in her eyes? Terence Gifts? Ivan Rugg? Blockbuster Video?

Aiden was going round the bottles, trying to wring an extra thimbleful of anything, red or white, into his glass. It was that time of night.

'You . . .' I said. I looked at Denis, fumbling for le mot juste. I found it – 'You, *you*, you.'

Denis sighed. 'It was only a weekend shag fest but she got serious,' his voice was all sheepishly beatific. 'Still, I suppose I should've let her down gently.'

'Taxi,' announced Aiden.

And in Arta, with its expansive spaces, tight dresses, plush settees and lurid Glasgow parody of classical opulence, I felt the poet's urge to seize the mystery of the moment – to gouge it open and, climbing inside, to claim it for my empire. And at eight quid entrance and three quid a shot for spritzers, those were the kind of feelings I was entitled to. I wanted to be carried aloft on my kingly chair of alcohol, borne at each corner by four sturdy bottles of Soave. I wanted oblivion – otherwise known as freedom from failure.

But that was then and this was now. And on this, the morning after, the King lay abed studying the vomit on his moleskin trousers and the King must yet choose weightily between sleep and Leonard Cohen.

And Leonard won. And the King slept on.

The King was awakened later by a knock at the door. Trying to open his eyes, he found he could not. After a long moment of fluttering panic, the King realised he'd fallen asleep with his contact lenses in again. He fumbled on the duvet for his ermine robe, which was not in the strictest sense ermine nor, for that matter, a robe – it being, in fact, a dressing gown that lacked a belt and which was made from towelling of the finest terry.

Through his terror, His Majesty was bemused. He wondered how it was that his eyes had not gummed shut through the long night but, instead, had waited till the shorter broken sleep of the late morning? The King had no answer to this – not for himself nor for his people who lived inside his head and who beat its echoing walls with their fists and ploughshares. The knocking grew louder. Blundering from bed to wall with hands out-stretched, His Majesty led himself by touch to the door and, finding the handle, twisted it. He heard a voice say, 'Good morning. I was just wondering . . . have you had a chance to read my script yet?' He recognised this as the voice of his landlord, Mr Provan. He stopped being a king and reverted to his familiar disguise as tenant of a rented bedsit in Cecil Street. This was inconvenient, as it meant he could no longer refer to himself in the third person. Regrettably, it also obliged him to think and to feel and to suffer once more.

'No, Mr Provan,' I said, 'I'm afraid I've . . . gone temporarily blind.' I couldn't help turning away in embarrassment as I said this. We both knew I was cravenly offering up the drama of the moment as an excuse for my ongoing neglect of his script.

'Dear God,' he said, 'let's have a look at you.'

In the silence, I smelt his stale smell of tobacco and old wardrobes and heard his breath whistle through his nose as he had a gawp at me. Satisfied, he took me by the elbow and guided me down on to the bed. I let all of this occur without resistance or awkwardness for I too was entering my own drama. I heard the tap run.

'Has this sort of thing happened before?' asked Mr Provan from the scullery.

'Only when I've been overworking,' I said, my lying voice thin and brittle. I remembered the vomit on my trousers and grew afraid. And there had been – had there not? – a urine incident involving innocent mugs and side plates? Who knew what horrors lay in my sink? Which was to say, his sink.

The kettle was on, its dusty aluminium creaking in the heat of the shushing gas. Mr Provan clumped and coughed, busying the air as we waited for the water to warm. My unseeing eyes saw through his camouflage and I sensed his proprietorial gaze alighting on items and areas of doubtful hygiene. I heard the kettle being lifted from the gas and the gas being turned off.

'Do you have a cloth?' asked Mr Provan.

Ah, yes, I remembered my cloth. I recalled of old, the piquant awfulness of its stench the last time I had encountered it. 'On the pipe under the sink,' I said, praying that the desiccation of underuse would have subdued the worst of its bacterial threat.

'Ah, yes,' said Mr Provan, in a tone that told me he shared my disquiet. 'How about kitchen roll?'

'Sorry, I'm out of kitchen roll.' I was out of kitchen roll the way I was out of Roquefort cheese or a cleaner for my swimming pool.

'I'll use this then.' The air was swiped near my knees as he picked up 'this' and then quickly unswiped, as he said, 'No, I won't.'

I heard a mannerly knock at the open door and then Mr Provan's sister say, 'Oh, my God! What's happened here?'

Mr Provan counselled calm. 'He'll be fine,' he said. 'He can't open his eyes.'

'That would explain a few things,' said Mr Provan's sister, now in the middle of the room.

'You go on down, dear,' said Mr Provan, with a tone. 'I'll deal with this.'

'There's mince on the ceiling. How does anyone get mince on a ceiling?'

'You go on down,' urged Mr Provan again. 'Please.'

I heard a pained matronly sigh, a rustle in the air, a floor-board creak and she was gone.

'I'm sorry about the mince on the ceiling,' I said to Mr Provan.

'I'm less concerned about that,' said Mr Provan, injecting a note of compassionate levity into his tone, 'than I am about the vomit on the carpet.' He dabbed at my crusted eyelids with what I took to be the sleeve of my shirt. 'Most of us enjoy a wee refreshment,' said Mr Provan, 'but there are limits.'

I knew from his tone that my limits were not his limits and that his were the ones that counted. 'I'm sorry,' I explained, 'but it was a special occasion – a friend had just sold a film script.' By the unscrupulous mention of scripts I wished to divert his attention from the sordid world of mince, crusty eyes and vomit. In a qualified way, I succeeded.

'Who to?' asked Mr Provan.

'Americans,' I said.

'Ah yes,' said Mr Provan, 'them.'

Thin Cecil Street light broke through the bars of my upper right eyelid. Picking off tiny gunk crystals between thumb and forefinger, I blinked. 'Thank you, Mr Provan,' I said.

'You're OK?'

'I'm OK.'

'You'll manage the other eye?'

'I'll manage the other.'

He toyed with my damp shirtsleeve in a feigned, absent sort of way. If he put it down, he knew he'd have to go. He stood looking around the room. As he'd looked around the room plenty over the last few minutes, I knew he was doing it because he wanted to prolong the conversation. I watched him through my now one and a half good eyes. I wanted him out. I needed peace to tease down the trapped contact lenses that had lodged themselves, God knows where, in my eye recesses. These things can rattle around in your head for decades, like jettisoned rocket sections through space – you have to get them out pronto. Mr Provan wasn't having that. His gaze rested, as I knew it would, on the unsightly Manila pile on the table.

'Are all those scripts?'

His voice, despite his will, carried a coy note, wistful and heartbreaking that I found mildly repugnant. Here, spread before him like doubloons in a pirate chest, lay the glittering world of media – that wondrous realm he dumbly longed to join – a land of shitty telly and crap novels, of original proposals that were pale imitations of mass-produced ideas that should have died and gone to hell but instead stuck around to haunt the airwaves and clutter the bookshops in ever newer, tackier clothes. 'Yes,' I said.

'Is mine in there?'

'Yours is at the top of the pile.'

He gave a little gleeful snicker. I knew that snicker. I'd used it myself ten years previously when I'd received my first rejection slip from the Glasgow Citizens' Theatre. It was as if just being in the race was the same as winning it. And it was. To be in the pile was to be at the starting line – at the starting line, anyone could win. To Mr Provan, I was the man with the starting gun which made me an object of both resentment and deference – a combination further complicated by the fact that he was my landlord.

'I'll get back to you next week without fail,' I said. 'Promise.'

Mr Provan told me there was no hurry but everyone said

that. He continued to hang around and, when he took out a pen and began clicking and unclicking it, the original purpose of his visit dawned on me. I found my rent book and reached gingerly into my crispy trousers. Loose change normally makes a chinking noise in the morning pockets. When it makes a chunking noise instead, you know you've had a big, bad night out.

'Will a cheque do?' I asked.

Mr Provan allowed himself a little martinettish intake of breath before issuing his judgement. 'It's not a practice I encourage but, from yourself, yes, a cheque would be acceptable.'

I wrote out the cheque and gave it to him. I'd like to add at this point that he left but I can't because he didn't.

Instead he said, 'Now isn't the time to tell you about my book.'

I was about to agree.

'But I'll give you a brief flavour. It's a sort of guidebook. To this little corner of the cosmos we're presently living in.'

'Really?' Now I don't know about you but I'm petty – once I give somebody rent, I can't help wanting payback so I suspended the usual human considerations, including civility. This was a mistake on my part. Silence was a blank canvas on which Mr Provan sketched the wordy cartoon of his future opus. 'Of course, when I say guidebook, that isn't strictly true. I suppose it's more of a pocket history actually.'

'Interesting,' I said. To anyone normal 'interesting' is code for 'I have now entered a light doze and require that you depart' but not to a prospective author.

'I'm glad you think so,' said Mr Provan. 'The west end of Glasgow is rich in architecture and art. As you'll see from the present condition of my manuscript, I'm still at the early stages.' He stopped talking and smiled, all bashful and humble and pleased with himself. His silence was a prompt for me to applaud or burst into song.

'I look forward to reading it,' I said, rising to my feet. And, just in case he interpreted this as a three-dot pause rather than a full stop, I proffered my hand and added, 'and thank you very much for your help.'

'Not at all,' he said and he gave the room a last sly, scanning look, as if he were storing up images for future evidence or as a fund of gossip or both. At the door, he said something that disturbed me – all the more so since it was kindly meant. Mr Provan said, 'Forgive me but perhaps you might want to change the life you lead.'

I was taken aback. So much so that, when he left, I didn't even shut the door. I just lay on the bed in my kingly towelling robe and thought, as instructed, about the life I lead. But, after a few moments, disgust set in then anger and I thought instead about the life he led – sixty-five years old and tucked away with his widowed sister in a ramshackle basement flat with nothing but a tousled patch of garden and Classic FM to punctuate the humdrum day. I considered the way Mr Provan lived and, as I did so, a kind of pang took hold of my chest and shook it.

I realised that I envied him.

Yes, something had to change.

When I woke up, it was evening again. I washed and had dried myself down to the knees before I realised that, because my towel had been damp, I was now smellier than when I'd started. I made a mental note to douse myself down with deodorant. I asked myself why I needed to consider such a thing when my clear intention was to spend the entire evening script-reading at my table and putting my business affairs in order – after all, I was going to kill myself on my birthday, remember? That's if *Celia Proust* was rejected, which of course it would be. This being my pessimistic conviction, I'd concluded that a posture of calm diligence would create an admirable effect for posterity – the West of Scotland branch anyway. You know the kind of thing: 'He never let on . . .', 'worked right on up to the end . . .', 'the man was an enigma . . .' – 'Yes, I can't think of a better word for him, can you?'

So I bowed my enigmatic head and read these stinking sitcoms so that, in death, I might be thought of as what I could never be in life – a somebody.

I read and made dutiful notes on three separate scripts in rapid succession. One, from a vicar in Ormskirk, was about the zany, dreary life of a vicar in Ormskirk. The next, from a plain-looking female journalist – I'd seen her byline photo – in Edinburgh was about a pretty female journalist in Edinburgh who is, by turns, wisecracking and scatterbrained, yet possessed of a laser intelligence, and who, at all times, holds in scathing contempt all the males in her office who, nevertheless, uniformly adore her. The third was from a woebegone duffer in Nuneaton. An accompanying letter in red pen on yellow paper told a cautionary tale. It began:

> Dear Sir or Madam,
> Please forgive the shakiness of my handwriting but I am wheelchair bound and the arthritis in my hands [both] makes even letter writing a struggle. I hope you like my script. It would be a great fillip to disabled people everywhere if you would find it suitable for . . .

I screwed up the odious filth and threw it in the bin. No, he didn't deserve to be in a wheelchair. He should have been under one, the oozing, wheedling maggot.

I deleted him and the vicar from the book of sitcom life but placed an elaborate question mark in pencil on the title page of the female journo's MS. This I did for reasons of mischief. Middle-aged male executives in television companies – like Skipton, my boss – liked to advance young women, especially ugly ones, as it displayed in their eyes a scrupulous aloofness from sexual temptation whilst, at the same time, affirming their commitment to all things youthful and sisterly – these being in television, as in most media professions, the twin bedrocks of career enhancement. Indeed, many middle-aged execs had survived for years, feigning respect for young womanhood before an intemperate Christmas party lunge or sexist bark alerted enemies above and below and sent the bowling ball of change trundling inexorably toward the skittle of dismissal – or Independent Production as it is nowadays more commonly called.

The great irony cull of the mid nineties had accounted for many of these Grey Men, good and bad alike. Having grappled with and mastered the manuals of political correctness, they'd found themselves outflanked and then skewered on the kebab stick of laddishness. How women could demand to be treated as equal, yet willingly acquiesce to being shackled and anally rodded whilst answering to the name of Fuck-Bitch, was a glitch of fashion that had bamboozled the greys and exposed them as irredeemably square.

A few, the professional survivors, recognisable in their uniform of shaven head, rimless specs and black shoulder bag, still clung desperately to mainstream power by cunningly devolving that power to a plethora of youthful lieutenants. Skipton was one such. Skipton worked for the Alba Media Corporation and was Head of Production for whom I read scripts. I found it expedient to display the eternal vigilance of my script reader's eye by marking out the occasional piece of self-regarding guff from time to time for further consideration. The female journo would do nicely.

I rose from my table, feeling cleansed by my dirty work. I boiled the kettle and treated myself to a cup of shagging coffee. As I sipped, I looked over at the table, where the three reported-upon scripts were satisfyingly back in their A4 envelopes.

Well done, thou good and faithful servant. I knew, from my reserves of will and energy, I could manage another couple of scripts but no more. Five is the maximum number of sitcoms any sane person can read and respond to in a day without rushing weeping into the streets. 'Well, that's decided then,' I thought. 'I'll do two more then reward myself with an early night and a maybe a chapter of a novel – Patrick Hamilton perhaps, or a touch of Gerhardie.'

From tonight, life would be different. I'd taken the first short step on a new, straighter path. If I read what? Five scripts a day? Well, not five – three scripts? No four, make it four – four scripts a day – well, I could have that pile on the table read and disposed of by what? A week on Tuesday? Then I'd be free to tackle the backlog in the office. I'd make it a point of honour to quit this earth, if quit I must, with an empty in tray. Yes, how ironic that I should display such clarity of purpose now, just as the curtain was about to fall. Nothing became him so much in sitcom as his leaving of it.

I smiled indulgently to myself over this pebble of ancient truth I'd picked up, dusted off and polished. Where was that copy of *The Slaves of Solitude*, by the way? As I rummaged in the wardrobe, I could hear laughing voices in the street below and remembered, with a start, that it was Saturday night. Well, let them laugh – a few hours from now they'd all be blind drunk and spoiling for trouble. And, in the morning . . . well, the mornings didn't bear thinking about. Where was that book? An open holdall slumped in the corner of the wardrobe rang a distant bell. I unzipped the bag half expecting to find a treasure trove of forgotten memorabilia rescued from my succession of relationship break-ups. An odd hour of random nostalgia seemed appropriate to my situation and I alerted my finer feelings and had them lined up like guests at a premiere ready to receive the warm handshake of the forgiven past. Not for long. What I saw shocked me. A bagful of unread scripts – perhaps thirty or forty of them.

I scrabbled frantically around. Other bags – Oddbins bags, Victoria Wine bags, Thresher bags – held similar ghastly finds. What had I been doing? How could I have been so remiss? The answer, of course, was 'Easily'. As usual, I'd been substituting wish for achievement – I take scripts home therefore they are read. How easy to defer guilt by filling a bag with good intentions. And it wasn't as if I hadn't meant to read them. It was just a case of bag down, telly on, feet up and . . . let's do it later, after a spritzer – or two – or three. Christ, at this rate, I'd be ninety before I could kill myself – I'd have to pant on grimly to the Sunset Home just to clear the wardrobe.

I leaned my head against the wall, uselessly. All that night's work was for nothing – just pissing in the wind – or sink, according to taste. From the flat next door, a steady thumpity-thump started up, then shouts, squeals and the crash of glass. Now I knew why they call it a party wall. What to do? I looked at the script pile on the table. I looked at my shoes in the hearth. Their dark hollows beckoned like the mouths of sirens. 'Come to us,' my shoes sang. 'Remember that quiet thrill of expectation every time you step into us?' That quiet thrill spoke of freedom, however temporary. I sauntered over to my shoes. 'That's the spirit,' they said to me. 'Don't be scared.'

I told my shoes I wasn't scared.

'Go on,' they said, 'put us on. Try us for size – see if we fit.'

I did as I was told. I tried on my shoes. They fitted me. Taking it as a sign, I pulled on my jacket and headed for the door. 'Why not?' I thought. 'I'm a potential suicide – the balance of my mind is disturbed. I'm entitled to some fun.'

Saturday, being couples night in Xenia, wasn't as hectic as Friday. The fug of tobacco stung eyes and sullied clothes before rising to the oak-beamed ceiling, once white, now stained fungus brown. But I wasn't complaining, this is what I'd come for – myself and others whose eyes I caught, male and female but mostly male. They held a rueful smirk, those eyes, self-conscious yet sharing a common shame – the look of flies compelled to feast from the same small, dried-up dog turd. A drunk, a bald man of about fifty, was about to slide off his bar stool. 'They're all mad,' he said to his non-existent companion. 'They think they can tame me but they can't.'

A rough-and-ready code prevailed – if you stood to drink, male or female, you were up for it, part of the herd and sharing the blind urgency of its desires; if seated, you had declared your-self apart from, if not above, the pressing sexual drive. But this line, like all lines, was made for blurring and exceptions were fashioned according to the mood of the moment or, more usually, on who was doing the asking.

'Dry white wine and soda!' My shout joined the blizzard of orders flurrying around the heads of the bar staff. They were, in general, a good decade younger than the customers they served and their faces wore, like a uniform, a collective expression of restrained tetchiness. I felt that they pitied us. If so, they showed a fellow feeling that was more than our due for, if I were in their shoes and not my own dear, racy, peppy, sweet-talking shoes, I should have despised us all.

'Cheers.'

I paid for my spritzer and lifted it over the sluggish heads of the hardened bevviers who hogged the counter. With the first magical sip, I felt my shoulders slacken and my heart lift. I looked around the room. Who were these people? How did they get here? I could answer these questions easily enough. In their twenties, west-end people hung out in Brel down the lane. They'd meet, marry, then twenty years later they'd be divorced and hitting this place. A fifty-yard gain in two decades – not a result that had you swelling with the pride of achievement.

A frumpish girl in a belted jacket was standing next to me, trying to order a round. I made a couple of joshing remarks to get my mouth moving. Sometimes the longer you went without speaking, the harder it became to initiate a conversation and, before you knew it, you'd settled into the role of unloved pub loner for the evening.

I felt panic when I thought of the monstrous cache of unread scripts and a curious sense of powerlessness came over me. Curious because the solution lay in my own hands – all I had to do was read them. But so many and from so long ago – many months, judging by the postmarks. Usually, when someone rang up to enquire about the progress of a script, I cited the heaviness of the daily mailbag, my involvement in 'other projects' and urged patience. Almost always this lazy fiction was accepted.

Huddling moodily in the space vacated by the fallen drinker, I sipped my spritzer. Nobody is interested in writers, apart from other writers. We work in the illusion business. The illusion, by definition, happens before your eyes, not behind them. Acknowledging the writer is like going to the movies then turning your seat round to watch the projectionist. Movies. Aiden. How awful if he were to win an Oscar. I'd have to corrupt my nature with generous thoughts. I'd have to place my insincerity on full display for him to see through and exult in – all in all, a wretched double whammy.

'Hi, there.' Someone had spoken. The bleak, tall form of Walter Urquhart was at my side. 'Quiet tonight,' he said.

'I'm sorry,' I said. He had flustered me out of my thoughts. 'I still haven't read your . . .'

'No, no,' he interjected. He looked a little hurt and embarrassed. 'It wasn't that, I just . . .'

'Yes?' Realising that he wanted company, I eased down my drawbridge – just a crack. I was still of a mind to make something happen.

'I got a visit from your father,' said Urquhart.

'Yes, you told me last night.'

'No, I mean this morning. He asked whether I'd seen you.'

'Uh-huh. What did you tell him?'

'Nothing.'

By 'Nothing', I knew he'd repeated, word for word, every tiny detail of last night's exchange – or, more likely, it had been ground out of him.

'I sort of feel I'm caught in the middle,' he said limply. 'Anyway, he has another message. He says to tell you he's terminally ill.'

'What, since last night? How convenient.'

'That's what he said you'd say,' said Urquhart, reaching into his pocket. 'He said to show you this.'

He showed me a grubby medical card, folded in half. It was an outpatients' card for the Southern General – or the Suffering General as the locals call it. A rubber stamp was marked 'Oncology Department'. I felt Urquhart, as if under instruction, closely studying my face for expression.

'So what should I tell him?'

I felt hemmed in – he'd come to me bearing the twin horrors of scripts and family, things I guzzled costly spritzers to forget. I became aware of a growing tightness in my head. Brain tumour? Maybe I'd be joining the old man for a rollicking family day out down the Oncology Department.

'Your father,' persisted Urquhart.

Your father – demands, always demands. 'Tell him to die quietly and give us all peace.'

Urquhart shrugged. 'I tried.'

I huddled over the bar uncivilly. Turning back, momentarily assailed by guilt, I watched Urquhart not so much fade back into the crowd as be engulfed by it, as it brayed around him. I felt conspicuously alone. I thought about going back to my room but knew I'd be overwhelmed by a sense of gloom so resolved, at once, to stay out. 'Sod it,' I thought. Affecting an ethereal air, I moistened my lips and pouted like a cherub.

Turning to the nearest attractive female I said, 'While you're waiting to be served, would you like me to recite you a poem?' This was the most shameless approach in my grubby locker – aiming for the drawers by way of the heart – but most women, however hard-bitten, have a weakness for shit soufflé so long as it's well cooked. She had tumbling, russet-coloured hair and a wistful look in her sad grey eyes. They looked at me.

'You're fuckin' kidding, right?' she said.

Ah. I took a hasty step to the right and encountered a grizzled blonde with a mottled neck whose gin-laden eye-bags looked like battle scars from several heavyweight encounters in the Divorce Courts.

'Hello,' I breathed. 'My name is Owen Consumption and I live in a garret. Would you like me to recite you one of my poems before I die unloved in the gutter?' For some reason, I'd garnished my voice with the subtlest, if that's the right term, hint of Oirishness.

The grizzled blonde smiled, like she'd found water in a desert. 'Oh, how sweet,' she said. 'That would be lovely.'

I lilted out the opening line of 'Do not go gentle into that good night …' and chuntered on euphoniously. I preferred Larkin to Thomas but felt that 'Love again: wanking at ten past three' lacked the desired inclusiveness. A finger dug at my shoulder. I turned to find Ms Tumbling Russet giving me a look of peeved hostility.

'I only asked you if you were fuckin' kidding – I didn't say no, did I?'

'No,' I agreed.

Turning back to the blonde, I said, 'Will you excuse me?' But there was already a hastily vacated space where she'd been standing. Sensing trouble, the blonde had shrunk back into the safety of her respectable mixed-group gathering. Armani jeans and Prada tops eyed Ms Tumbling Russet warily.

I turned back to my new companion. I realised she was drunk. 'Buy me a bloody drink,' she commanded.

I bought her a bloody drink and another three. Then she bought me one – only some of which survived the buffeting of swaying torsos as she returned from the bar and the sloshing caused by her own gesticulating arms as she remonstrated, noisily and at length, with the buffeters. Her name was Karine. 'With a fuckin' E, right?' I suggested that if she ever wrote her autobiography, she might take that sentence as its title.

Karine was from the south side, over the river. She'd come west with a group of friends but had jettisoned them following a row over the payment of a bill in a pizza joint. 'You've seen me – I pay my way, do I not?'

I acknowledged that she paid her way. One round in four – that was a fair female average, in my experience. We were getting on fine. We were swaying in harmony. As the drink went down, I grew less embarrassed by her loud, grating voice and more enamoured of her energy and lithe slim body. We made each other laugh, once or twice, as we got the hang of one another or maybe what we were saying wasn't funny and it was just the healing communion of the drink. Whatever, I was prepared to do whatever it took to disenfranchise her from her drawers. And the scripts in my room and in my office? What scripts? What office?

I asked her what she did for a living. Her face twisted and she swore at me in irritation – but then she swore at me anyhow so I kept right on asking and it became a little battle of wills before she surrendered and told me about the bookie's shop in Shawlands.

'Do you like it?'

'Sweaty punters with stumpy pens. Wee burnt grooves on their lips from their roll-ups – that's my life. I hate my life. I hate everything.'

'Me too,' I said.

She paused for a glug of wine and a sway. 'What about you?' she said. 'What brings you into this shit hole?'

'The fresh air,' I said. 'Let's go somewhere else.'

She gave me the drunk woman's gaze, for show. Her face was first stonily severe then quizzical, as she vetted my character for potentially homicidal flaws.

'Relax,' I said, 'I'm a nice chap.'

'I'll be the judge of that. Let's go.'

She drained her glass and let it fall where she stood. We were out of there before it hit the floor.

Sunday. I was abed yet again and hung-over. No consoling sounds stroked the air – not even from Leonard. All sounds were crowds in my head, even the familiar murmur of that inner voice, purporting to be mine. Who was this lodger who slept under my scalp? Did he speak for me or I him? When I picked up my keys, I locked him in this room; when I returned, he climbed back inside my head. Though I was he, his ways were not my ways and tolerance chafed on both sides, his and mine – but especially mine since it was me who paid the rent.

A sudden panic – I consulted my eyes. Were they still seeing? Yes, affirmed both ocular departments; for verification, they showed me myself in the dressing table mirror. I was fuzzy looking back at me – part hidden by uncapped lotions and solutions, the nightly apparatus of the contact lens sufferer.

My arm was numb, I'd been sleeping on it during the night. The night? What night? Ah, yes, last night, Saturday night. I rose to pee, disturbing a dim yet vivid memory of having vomited in the sink. Never mind, with luck, I'll hose it clean with effing piss.

Why effing? I swore a lot last night. Effing, I said. Ah, yes. Her. Karine. Say it loud and . . . well, let's not say it loud, shall we? Soft then. Say it soft and . . . only you can't say it soft, can you? It's hard. And shiny black. Kar-ine. Not coal black. Taxi black. That taxi. Ah, yes, ah, yes . . . She'd taken me to some party. I recalled the stopping hackney – me with tottering steps and wine bottles chinking perilously in my carryout bag.

We went in the close and up the stairs, drawn by the thump of music. A door opened and it was Planet Speed, Buckfastland, Crack Corner – no wine with couscous here. It was home-made scars and too much Versace, all swirling yellows and zippered reds. Wee drug-dealer hoodies with glittering eyes and Stanley knives in the birds' handbags.

'Who brought this?' Our hostess removed Chardonnays from our Oddbins bag and looked at me with piteous curiosity. I felt like a well-meaning charity worker gifting Enid Blytons to the prison library at Rampton.

Karine tugged me away by the jacket. I resisted till I was fortified by a tumbler of white wine with cork croutons. Stepping, more or less, over the feet of seated guests, we occupied a romantic corner of the dance floor, by the canary cage. A fresh tune started. I was in luck – an oldie that I knew. Karine flailed her arms wildly, lost in a private, immediate surrender to Deacon Blue, the patron saints of drunk Glasgow women. Myself, I pottered spastically beside her, feigning relaxed animation.

'Dance!' yelled Karine.

'I *am* dancing.'

'I thought you were stubbing out a fag with your shoe.'

Chastised, I'd jettisoned my minimum-risk West of Scotland bum shuffle and cajoled my doleful limbs into furious activity. Until, that is, an adventurous elbow movement jarred the canary stand, rocking its axis and sending it toppling on to the wall where it had rested at an angle. The chrome door askew, the cage's yellow inmate had scooted from his cell in a whirring blur of 'Sod this, I'm off', startled cheeps and feathers.

Momentarily sobered by embarrassment, I remarked a slight seated figure, his feet in the hearth of the fireplace, his head lost in a private aromatic cloud. He was watching me from under the furred canopy of a green snorkel parka. He too had brought a pair of glinty eyes to the party but his glint was light not cruel and a light glint I realised, in my humbled state, is braver than the merely cruel since it has the courage to empathise with the object of its amusement. The wispy man tugged down his hood, expelled a breath of sour dopey air and grinned. Thinning fair hair lay matted across his scalp in tangles. Were those pyjama trousers he was wearing – a curiously familiar shade of blue. Hospital blue? And such genteel footwear – Ecco perhaps, or Mephisto?

Having accorded himself the status of all-seeing eye, a position I'd reserved entirely for myself, I decided his friendliness was a challenge. Yet shouldn't two all-seeing eyes see better than one?

'What are you looking at?' I'd intended it as an amused enquiry but he'd wrong-footed me so it had come out all grouchy – like Mr Gorbals-Ringworm, circa 1930, razored-up, yearning to be insulted.

'You,' said Parka, unfazed, 'you look interesting.'

'Interesting?' I felt flattered. 'In what way?'

'I don't know,' he said. 'Maladjusted. Unhappy people are usually interesting.'

I stopped feeling flattered. Woozily, I wondered if I ought to punch him, just to prove how happy I was.

His soused head wobbled on its neck plinth before he looked up suddenly and asked, 'Do you read?'

'Read what?'

'Never mind.' He'd weighed me up and discarded me. 'I like

to read,' Parka said. It didn't feel like a conversation. I happened to be eavesdropping on an interior monologue. He adopted a mock poetic tone of hopeful misery. 'I am moved by fancies that are curled around these images and cling – the notion of some . . .'

'Infinitely gentle, infinitely suffering thing.' When I finished the line for him, he looked at me, surprised. His eyes narrowed. I looked back, holding his stare. I sensed we were hovering on the brink of an ugly West of Scotland quoting brawl.

He reached for his free verse baseball bat. 'In a minute there is time for decisions and revisions . . .

'Which a minute can rever . . .'

'Jesus!'

The canary krrrped past my head then covered the room in a holding pattern, seeking out the open skyways. Alas, his universe had proved quickly finite, the living room door marking its outer limit. The canary's proud wee beak crashed against the heavy wood, propelling him in a plumb line to a hero's grave on the oatmeal carpet. Still dancing, but with restraint out of respect for the dead, I informed his mistress of her grievous loss.

She took it well. Her swaying arms held aloft, with a lit fag in one hand and a can of Red Stripe in the other, she declaimed 'Don't worry, they're ten a penny – I've had dozens.' Like the rest of the room, she was awaiting the great orgasmic swell of the coming chorus. Eyes clamped intently tight, she'd ride its crest on her trusty surfboard of alcohol. The floor trembled, the room swayed and then braced itself . . . And here it came . . . 'Real . . . gone . . . kid . . . dun-dun . . . dun-da-da-da-da-dun . . . WEE-OOO-WEE-OOOWEE-OOO-WEE-OOOO . . .!'

I felt the grip of Karine's hand in mine, firm and sinewy like the rest of her. I'd had a face once but now it was in her mouth. I felt a tap on my shoulder. A small dangerous object had manifested itself beside me. He had a Tommy shirt and a plaster on his forehead, from which seeped a trickle of fresh blood.

'I know you,' he said.

'Oh yes?' I armed myself with a disarming smile. 'Where from?'

'Your old man's pub.'

'Of course.' Not that my old man had ever had a pub. He'd had a shoe shop, though. And he and an assortment of reps and fellow tradesmen would refresh themselves at leisure in the rear office.

'Every alky in Partick used to congregate in that shop,' said the small dangerous man. 'I'm surprised he ever made any money.'

'He didn't.'

'Me and my mates,' needled the wee man, 'we used to go in there regular and milk the place dry. One time we walked behind the counter and picked up the till. We had to step over him on the way out.' The wee dangerous man craved a reaction – laughter or the taking of offence, either would do.

For a moment, I remembered from my youth the unpaid bills, the squalid fights, the moonlight flits, the empty plates at teatime. I chose laughter or at least a rueful approximation thereof. 'Yes,' I agreed, 'he was a character.'

The tug from Karine's arm and I was steered away. And she with me. I recalled huddled running through rainy streets, with Karine always ahead, searching out then finding the glow of her tenement burrow. And had it been worth it? My stolen night, my tawdry neglect of literary duty in pursuit of common bliss and low adventure? Yes, I say again, yes, it was – for I didst dip her, most intently, with my dipping thing. Did I mention protection? Forget it – a standing cock knows neither conscience nor prudence. And did I mention my hands? They might've been bandaged and in boxing gloves for all the sensitivity I was able to experience and doubtless impart, as I plumped, stroked, doyonged and pinged at the undraped goody bag of her body spread out on her living-room floor. The drunken pain in my head had been intense but on I pumped, with chivalrous intensity. In fact, all that had stalled my attempt to render unto Karine new and hitherto undiscovered peaks of sexual ecstasy was the noise of her snoring.

She had a pet mutt that sat, with its tongue out, watching me. 'What's your name?' I asked. But the mutt didn't answer. What would she call her dog, I wondered. Scotty? No, not Karine – Effing Scotty, more like. I rose to my feet and stood, swaying. I needed the taxi fare. I checked my wallet. I was skint. Karine's bag lay by her sleeping body. I gathered up the dusty fireside rug and spread it over her. Then I helped myself to her last twenty quid.

Feigning upright sobriety, with Karine's score note wafting in the air, I hailed a taxi under the Angel at Paisley Road Toll. The cab smelled of other people's drunken breath. Sprawled on the back seat, I watched the drizzle make cubist streetscapes on the windows. Behind me, in the cleared halo of the windscreen wiper, single figures walked purposefully, hoping not to be stabbed before that last cup of tea and the exhausted curl under the enfolding duvet. 'God help us all,' I said. The driver eyed me in the rear-view but didn't speak. 'God help everybody, except you.' A pothole made my stomach lurch and the pre-froth of vomit gathered in my throat. God helped me though and I didst not boak my load. A last wooze of yellow sodium from the street lights and I found myself perched, cross-legged and with lolling head, on Denis Rourke's moving magic carpet.

'I tell you what, that reminds me of Sinclair Neath – remember Sinky?'

'I remember Sinky,' said Aiden. 'Totally off his chump.'

'Great roaring bull of an actor,' agreed Denis, 'even in *Private Lives*. They called him "Under" Neath.' Denis turned to me.

'Sarcasm.'

'God rest him,' said Benny Lawrie, toasting with an empty glass.

I lay on the floor, elbow to head, trying to keep my eyes open. We'd been through the guitar phase. We'd all joined in with 'Losing My Religion'. Well, they had – I'd mimed – and, when the neighbours had threatened police action, old acting vets had started trading battle stories of rep and panto. There were still one or two women who hadn't drifted away but they were stalwarts and loyal to Denis.

'Sure, sure, God rest him,' said Denis, tetchily. He continued. 'Anyway mad Sinky's doing *Peter Pan* in Inverness . . .'

'The Eden Court? I know it – nice space.'

'The space is irrelevant, Benny,' said Denis. 'Do I interrupt your stories?'

'He hasn't got any stories. He never works,' said Sheila Something, a Denis groupie with tired tits and a 'Porn Star' T-shirt.

'Life is about choices,' said Benny Lawrie, with a sanguine slur.

'On you go, Denis,' said Aiden.

'I've lost the notion now,' said Denis. But he hadn't lost the notion – he'd just been just buying time while he tongued a Rizla paper.

The silence tempted me. I fell. I offered my chin to Aiden and invited him to hit it. 'Heard any more about the screenplay?'

'Yes,' Aiden said, 'I got an e-mail from Liam today. I'm finished with Scotland. I'm going to LA next month.'

I felt my stomach hit the canvas. As Aiden's arm was tugged aloft, I heard an imaginary Brooklyn voice boom out, 'And the non heavyweight screenwriting champeen of the world is . . .'

Benny fed his glass then mine from the last gasps of a half bottle of Grouse.

'I chose life. But I chose the wrong life.'

'Benny, shut up,' instructed Sheila Something.

'Anyway . . .' Denis continued with his story, expelling a deep breath of dope with practised ease. 'Sinky's playing Captain Hook, waving his cutlass, scratching his arse with the hook and in general bawling out the weans coz he hates doing matinees, when he hears this alarm go off in the car park. And he's giving it "A thousand curses on 'ee Peter Pan!" when he thinks, "That's my fuckin' car." So he belts offstage, leaving Peter to tap-dance or hump Tinkerbell or whatever and he's straight out the wings and screaming into the street, to lay into two of the most surprised-looking would-be joyriders you've ever seen in your puff. Stabs one with the sword, gores another with the hook and the best of it is Sinky's the one that gets warned for assault and causing an affray.'

We'd all marvelled dutifully at the surreal injustice of the incident.

Benny then spoke for actors everywhere. 'What were his reviews like?'

'Oddly enough, quite favourable. Pan was fuckin' livid.'

When I awoke, I was on the hearthrug and the only person in Denis's living room. Light was streaming on to my face and I could hear church bells. I felt for my forehead. It was still there – always a bonus. En route for the street and noticing his bedroom door ajar, I peeked in on Denis. He was asleep on his side with Sheila Something strapped to him like a backpack. By her head, I noticed a third pair of feet – ones with painted toenails.

'Do you mind?' said a scraping voice from the wrong end of the bed.

I looked. Morag was sitting wide awake with her hands clasped in front of her like she was waiting for a bus, or a coffin.

'Sorry,' I said.

'This isn't what it looks like.'

'No,' I said. But it was what it looked like. Two female leeches vying for the plump, fat rump of Denis Rourke.

'Chloe and Sam think I'm mad,' Morag said, 'but I'll win, you'll see. I'll get him in the end.'

'Sure you will,' I said.

It was musical cocks round here.

In the street, the sober world had been loud and smug. Retired Christian drivers, eager to pray, hogged Hyndland's gutters for their shiny Audi saloons. Strolling citizens with semi-skimmed milk and inky wedges of fresh broadsheet played the role of contented men. Life was good, meaning it paid them well. Even in Glasgow you could make a living out of natural soap or feng shui. You could buy a house for three hundred grand, spend twenty doing it up, put it on the market, then sit back and watch as the bidders fought each other for the right to make you rich. God might be dead but we'd all been beneficiaries in the will. The city fathers boasted Glasgow had cafes the way we used to have pawn shops. Unemployment was down. That's because the poor were now skivvying in those same cafes for four quid an hour. The poor didn't protest their poverty – they were too busy saving to buy trendy, torn, baggy jeans. If socialism came back with a Hilfiger logo, they might've bought that too.

Thinking these things as I headed back to my room, I came to a forced halt by the church in Cresswell Street. I saw him heading toward me and groaned. There was nowhere to run.

'Hello, Mr Provan, you're out early.'

He'd looked at his watch and arched his eyebrows . . . well, archly. It was as if his whole life was an end-of-season production by Perth Rep. 'Eleven o'clock – that's early?'

Without touching it, I felt the overnight stubble on my unwashed face and the grey bags under my eyes. 'I've been working,' I said.

'Me too,' said Mr Provan, 'on my book – you remember?'

'I remember, it's next on my list to . . .'

'Oh, no matter,' he said, brusquely. 'I've already been down to Clarence Drive to take photos of the railway station.' He held up a small camera to verify his industry. 'I love doing research – it's as if, well, as if the past is a kind of treasure I'm allowed to keep.'

I shrugged and nodded, dumbly.

'Well, cheery-bye.' And off he trotted.

He was writing. All credit.

Good luck to him.

May he choke on my jealous bile.

CHAPTER TWO

For the next month, I kept my head down in my Portakabin office. It's no exaggeration to say I slaved obsessively over *Celia Proust*.

You know when you're getting it right. The structure clicks into place and, as the characters move through their scenes, they seem to speak mysteriously for themselves. I'd upgraded Wendy Fiat to the status of fully fledged detective and reinforced the ineffable bond of sisterhood she and Celia had forged in adversity by allowing them to poke gentle fun at Rick, the gay resting actor who doubled as Celia's home help.

There was a love interest, of course. Wendy now had a boyfriend, the devoted yet headstrong Jack, who had renounced a privileged inheritance in Suffolk to come up north and be close to Wendy. This Jack guy worked with poor kids from the wrong side of town. The basic idea was that, in every episode, the psychic Celia would have some blinding, yet tantalising, flash of insight that would cause her to moan and clutch her forehead or else say a little coded something that would both give the astute Wendy the clue she needed to crack the case, while being oddly helpful in keeping her relationship with Jack on track.

I couldn't tell you how many hours I'd worked on this script. All I can safely say is I'd written like my life depended on it – which, of course, it had.

A somebody. Do or die, remember?

'Morning, Joan.' I was holding the swing door open for Joan, Skipton's secretary. Normally there'd be a spot of mild banter but I was too absorbed with Celia.

'Hi, how's the script coming?'

'It's coming,' I said.

'Must be good, to judge by that smile.'

'I take nothing for granted.'

'Writers always say that when they know they've hit a winner.'

She passed me, giving off a little waft of her fragrance, 'Crunchie' by Rowntree. She was thirty-two and it hadn't happened, which is to say it had, but the guy was a twice-married dud who couldn't forget his two exes, financially or emotionally, and now Joan's consolations showed on her hips.

'Hi, mate.'

'Oh, hi Rufus – good to see you. What are you working on?'

'A feature on the colour black – I'm shooting it in Guam.'

'Best of luck. Drop me a card when you've a transmission date.' It was a good idea to keep in with the Rufuses. In a few short years, all the sturdy old names, the Jims, Mikes and Grahams, would all be gone and the Joshes, Jasmines and Rufuses would be running the whole shebang. Thanks to Celia, I'd been tempted to start thinking in future tenses.

'By the way,' Joan said, 'Ally wants to see you.'

'Now?'

'Yes, before he goes out on location. And bring your script reports.'

'Why?'

'I don't know – better ask Ally.'

'Ally' Skipton was a year older than me but had pulled off the difficult trick of appropriating a youthful-sounding nickname.

The main office was empty as I stepped through on my way into Skipton's. Everyone was out filming a tribute to a

much-loved Scottish comic whom everybody hated. He was
rumoured to have a wasting illness. The fervent hope was that
he'd croak before the New Year and the show could go out as a
Hogmanay special. Skipton folded the flimsy 'Media' section of
The Guardian and threw it down on to the fresh pile of daily
papers.

'They never learn.'

'Who? What?'

'The stats people. It's not audience mass that counts with
ratings these days – it's share. But will they change their mindsets?'

'No,' I said, handing him my reports, 'they won't change their
mindsets.'

I arranged myself on one of those unfeasibly deep, armless
office chairs that, when pushed together, form an unfeasibly
deep, armless couch. Skipton ran his hand absently over his
stubbly head as he skimmed my reports. I was excited. I wanted
to tell him about Celia.

'Harph!' Skipton had made a snorting noise, signifying
mirth.

Scripts sat wearily on his coffee table like old copies of *Hello!*
in a dentist's waiting room. For show, I busied myself with an
unreadable novel. I knew it to be unreadable because I'd read it,
every last page, a couple of months earlier, at Skipton's
command. Trouble was time had passed and, before I'd managed
to construct a letter of detailed rejection, I'd forgotten what the
hell I'd thought of it. 'There's no need to read that one,' said
Skipton, 'it's dealt with.'

'I know,' I said, 'I dealt with it.'

'No,' said Skipton, 'you read it. Emma dealt with it.'

'Emma? Who's Emma?'

'New script reader at drama. Don't worry about it – not a
problem.'

'You gave a drama script reader a comedy script to report on?'

Skipton peered at me over his Varifocals. 'It's a novel, not the combination for the joke safe – lighten up.'

'It's a novel that I read.'

'That you read and didn't report on – correct.'

'I thought it wasn't a problem?'

'Not a problem for me, no . . . but then it isn't my job to write reports.'

Gently said but a rebuke. I did indignation acting and bristled for effect. 'You mean like the ones you're reading now?'

He didn't answer. He kept reading, head down. Skipton was a short, nervous figure with narrow eyes, a big nose, a lot of forehead and a devious mind.

Unlike most at Alba who declared themselves 'loyal to Scotland', Skipton had actually been invited to work someplace else. In the late eighties, some fellow regionalists, linen-suited, shoulder-bagged, Men of Vision, had been agitating to make Redditch a 'Centre of Light Entertainment Excellence'. 'Why should the regions be subjected to the bad decision-making of London despots,' they had argued with cold logic, 'when bad decisions can be made right here, by local despots?' They'd invited Skipton to lead the insurrection. He'd thought about it long and hard before coming to a firm decision – he'd hesitate. In the hiatus, the ringleaders were rounded up, summoned to London and warmly congratulated for their stimulating insights. Some were promoted and became broken men. Others 'went independent'. Some are so independent that, to this day, they speak to no one all week and earn no money. They became the kind of people who hang around the BBC Club saying things like, 'I know where the bodies are buried.' And so they should. They're usually under the floorboards themselves, with the rest of the corpses.

It wasn't going to happen to me. I'd rather be dead than a corpse.

'So what do you think?' I asked, mildly. Following my reverie, I'd forgotten I'd been indignant.

'These are good reports,' said Skipton, 'Witty, cogently argued – I'm enjoying reading them.'

'Thank you.'

'But then I enjoyed reading them the first time.'

'What?'

'These are old reports.' He closed the folder and slid it across the desk. 'You think I don't notice the dates? You give yourself away, matey.'

'What'd you mean?'

'The jokes – I remember your jokes. Take a tip, if you want to pass off old reports in future, keep them dull.'

'I am dull – my stuff's as dull as anybody's.'

'I know that – I was among the first to celebrate your dullness. But save it for your memoirs – it's wasted on your reports.' He tilted his head back and looked at me. 'How long is your contract?'

'I don't have a contract – you know that. We have an understanding.'

'It's on the brink of becoming a misunderstanding.'

The tips of my ears tingled with alarm. 'I'm writing again. I've been working on a script.' It hadn't come out the way I wanted. I'd wanted it to be cavalier in tone – a throwaway, not this wretched whine.

'Yeah, heard it.'

'No, I'm serious. It's a pilot for a series.'

He fixed me with a look. 'Drama?'

'Comedy drama. Thriller.'

'You believe in covering your bases.'

'They're your bases too.'

He treated me to a faint smile. 'Every script you receive you log and file, yes?

'Yes.'

'By the end of the month, I want a report on every script in your possession. This department has a bad name. That bad name is your name. Either change your ways or I change you.'

He held open the office door. There were people now in the outer office, people with eyes and ears and mouths.

'Remind me, before you go, in front of witnesses, what I want from you'

'End of the month,' I mumbled, 'script reports.'

'Fresh ones,' he said. 'Keep it new. Keep it new.' He looked up. 'Scobie!'

A big comedian was sitting in a little chair. A couple of the office girls were cooing around him. I remembered Scobie from when he started out. He was going to change the world. Instead he changed his wife, cars, houses and accent.

'Hi, boss.' He called everybody boss. It was his way of showing the world he'd remained humble.

'Come on in.'

I narrowed myself to allow Scobie through. I knew my face was crimson though it felt like it should be ashen.

Like a good secretary, Joan feigned oblivion and busied herself with a letter.

When I'd first stumbled into the television blender, I'd naively assumed any programme that didn't conclude with the arrest of the producer to be an artistic failure. The cynical part of me, which is to say the idealistic part, still believed that. Television, like politics, is the art of the possible. People think there's no censorship because you can see tits and willies and occasionally someone says 'fuck' but there are other, perfectly effective safeguards against the inconvenience of free speech. When telly people tell you there's no censorship, what they mean is that most of its practitioners lack the will, the knowledge and the imagination to test the boundaries of what is permissible. Just like you, we wear the same clothes and think the same thoughts. We're myopics who assume that, because we can see no boundaries, none exist.

I comforted myself with these thoughts as I sat in my Portakabin office. My hands were shaking. I opened up the file on my laptop marked 'Scripts Received'. Five hundred and twelve scripts were registered. I felt sick. I closed the file and summoned up 'Celia Script'.

I had to redeem myself – to do or die. To stave off an ignominious death, I needed a blistering return to form that would silence the doubters and have them queuing at my Portakabin door begging me to offer them the secret of fire. Put another way, what I'd actually needed was to read and report on five hundred and twelve scripts – but where was the glory in that?

I tapped out this:

DAY 4. Sc. 28. INT. NIGHT. CELIA'S HOUSE.

I stopped tapping.

In a few days, I'd be forty-one. Death stood by my elbow. Fate knocked at the door.

'Come in.'

This being a small office, death hopped aside to let fate pass.

I had my head down, trying to look creative, as Joan entered.

'I forgot this,' she said.

'Hmm?'

Joan proffered a yellow Post-it that was stuck to her thumb. 'There was a call while you were in with Ally.'

She stuck the Post-it on the rim of my computer screen.

'You alright?'

'Yes.'

Joan didn't look convinced. 'Sure?'

I stared at her coldly and she left, looking hurt. The truth was, if I'd started talking, I'd have ended up sobbing into the great soothing pillows of her breasts.

I peeled off the Post-it and read it. 'Chloe rang. Please call back.' On the back was Chloe's mobile number.

You could say I was grateful.

I went to bed dog-tired. At around one-thirty the phone rang. 'It's Denis.' With only those two words to go on, I already knew he was drunk from the roots of his hair to the ends of his toenails.

'Hi, Denis, how goes it?'

He did that drunk man, heavy breathing silence thing, while his brain tried to patch up a couple of grubby words and send them forth, respectably dressed, out into the sober night air. He slurred something.

'What's that, Denis?'

Repetition clarified a tetchy, impeccably pissed, 'Come on over.'

I told him it was late.

No matter. It was still, 'Come on over.'

Something clattered and I had a mental flash of the brass umbrella stand he kept by the hall phone smacking the parquet flooring. Then he moaned.

This unsettled me. I was cold and naked. I looked around for a shirt.

'How's the *Taggart* going?'

Nothing.

'Denis?'

'They canned me.'

'Who?'

'*Taggart* – they binned me. But I don't care. Come on over.'

'It's too late – I'm in bed.'

'Forget bed – come on over.'

'No.'

'Please.'

I felt bad. Friends, especially bar friends, don't say 'please'. But then bar friends aren't real friends, like you make in the playground when you're ten. Bar friends are really just accomplices to take the bad look off you, so you don't have to stand around, looking eerie, as you try to chat up women on your own. I used his silence to haul the duvet from the bed and wear it as a cloak.

'*Please.*'

'No.'

He started to cry. It horrified me.

'Denis?' The phone clattered. I heard him slide down the wall. I'd slid down walls myself, I knew what it sounded like.

There was another sound, which may or may not have been a howl.

'Hello, Denis?'

I couldn't hear anything. Silence. Maybe he was dead? I should have gone round to check – he didn't live far away. To check on a friend, even a bar friend, would be the right thing. But I didn't do the right thing. Instead, I did this thing. I hung up the phone. I sat down at my table, huddled myself tighter in the duvet and wrote:

Sc. 40. INT. DAY 5. INT. DAY. WENDY'S FLAT.

I knew it wasn't humanitarian but I couldn't be dealing with other people's despairing animal noises – I was too busy struggling with my own. Thinking these thoughts, I wrote grimly on.

And on. Till the dawn light broke and I was so stiff I couldn't stand up.

Sc. 50. EXT. NIGHT. DAY 6. THE COLD LONG ROAD TO THE SEA.

And, by eight a.m., it was finished.

Later that morning, giddy, elated, tired, I'd handed an A4 Manila envelope over to Joan.

'Your script?'

'Yes.' Not only my script, my fate.

'I'll make sure he reads it as soon as he can.'

'Thank you.'

That was it. All I had to do was wait for judgement day.

To pass the time before I killed myself, I rang Chloe and visited my mother.

'You're never happy for long, are you, son?'

I was sitting in my mother's house, peering at her through the stagnant palls of fag smoke. It was a duty visit in case I croaked. I waited for her to add, 'Just like your father.'

I'd lived at my mother's following the break-up of my last relationship. Like all women, my mother worked to a secret code of sublimation that left you to deduce her true wishes and intentions. After a few weeks, she'd begun to express dark doubts concerning the validity of my status as a paying houseguest. The council were 'cracking down' on this sort of arrangement. If uncovered, I would be required to leave and she might have her housing benefit suspended, pending investigations.

'Are you saying you want me to go?'

'No,' she'd said, doing pained astonishment, 'just be careful.'

We'd struggled on with our miserable arrangement until one morning soon afterwards when, preparing to seat myself at my improvised work desk in the box room, I'd noticed that both chair and work desk had disappeared – upped and gone during the night, leaving only a stark gap at the wall before which I'd stood, cup of tea and pencil in hand, feeling stunned and foolish.

Within the hour, I was prowling the windows of newsagent's shops in Byres Road searching for a safe haven to rent. Within the week, I was resident at Mr Provan's.

'You're awful jumpy,' my mother said suddenly, making me jump.

'Hmm?'

'Is it the drink?'

'No.'

'The drink gives you bad nerves. Your father had bad nerves.'

It was rare for her to mention him. Maybe I'd wrong-footed her by saying something breezy. If you said anything jaunty to my mother, she'd damp you down quickly, like you were a chip pan fire.

'Did you know he has cancer?' I asked.

'Yes.'

'How did you find out?'

'People tell me things. I have ears.

'What people?'

'Ordinary people – not like you.'

'Or him?'

'He wasn't always twisted. He took a wrong turning.'

'Wrong for you maybe – not for him.'

'I wouldn't say that.' She looked triumphant. 'He wants me to go and see him.'

'Oh, yes?'

'Aren't you surprised?'

'No. He wants me to see him too.'

'Oh. Will you?'

'No. You?'

She didn't answer directly. She proffered a plate of Jaffa Cakes. Perhaps expecting me to read them like runes.

When my father left home, he'd given neither my mother nor myself an explanation. He'd offered no cryptic note or message – just pulled on his old gaberdine mac and walked.

Over the next few weeks, bills had arrived and the occasional policeman, followed by creditors, who'd wanted to satisfy themselves that my mother wasn't in on some scam. There'd been reported sightings of my father staggering in and out of pubs in Partick and Maryhill but you get a lot of shoeless men in those parts and the claims could never be verified.

'More tea?'

'No.'

My mother returned from the kitchen and sat down. I watched her light a cigarette from the still smouldering butt of the last one.

It had occurred to me I might never again have the chance to ask her, so I asked her. 'Why did he leave?

'Leave what?'

'You. Us.'

'Who can say what's in that man's head? I'm not like him, I've not got horns.'

'Did he have horns when you married him?'

She didn't like my chirpy tone. 'He had a breakdown,' she said sourly. 'That's what led to the break-up.'

She took a deep drag at her fag and had a messy cough. 'Mind you,' she said, 'his birthday might've had something to do with it.'

'What birthday?'

'His fortieth – he left the day after.'

I looked at her. She seemed taken aback. 'You didn't realise that?

'No.'

'Yes, the very next day.'

We fell into another smoke-filled hole of silence.

'What age are you this birthday?

'Forty-one'

'So you are,' she said. 'Imagine that.'

So we did. We imagined that. Me and her. And possibly him too, my father. If he could be troubled to keep count of those coffin nails we call birthdays.

These and similar reflections went through my mind as I sat downstairs in Rogano, waiting for Chloe and our first date. Though it was only a nice neutral lunch, I'd wanted a special venue because I had a feeling she merited it.

Upstairs at Rogano is more expensive than downstairs, which was a complication. Although downstairs is still nice, if you took a woman there, she knew where she stood and would adjust her expectations accordingly. The danger of this was she might also adjust her responses. And you could've seen her point. You'd invited her to a Division A restaurant but you'd offered her a Division B menu. There's nothing wrong with Division B – that's where most of us live and generally women are quite happy with Division B – but, and here's the rub, only if you hadn't flaunted Division A before her eyes en route to the table. I was confused. Scheming bitch – she had me over a barrel already and we hadn't even snogged yet.

'Hi, there. Sorry I'm late.'

'Don't worry – hi.'

She stuck her face out to be kiss-kissed. I had a problem with that stuff. Apart from anything else I never knew which cheek to peck at first. So we'd started with a most un-chic collision of breathing apparatus as a prelude to lunch.

'I'm nervous,' said Chloe.

'Me too,' I said. And we both laughed. 'Have you been here before?'

She nodded. 'Twice,' she said, a little self-consciously. 'The first time two years ago – the night I got engaged.'

'Ah.' Doom. She was spoken for. 'And the last?'

She'd switched her smile to full radiance and looked me flush in the face. 'A year ago – the night we broke up.'

'Ah.' Terrific. She was broken-hearted.

The waiter trickled red into my glass.

'Would you like a glass of wine, Chloe?'

'Yes, I'd love a glass of wine.'

'Would you like to taste, sir?'

I wasn't concentrating. I was still looking at Chloe – drinking her in. I'd put in a bad few days between arranging our lunch and sitting across from her and here she now was – my lovely reward.

'Sir?'

'No,' I said, 'just pour, just pour.'

Remember those words. I'm going to come back to them.

Here's what happened in the days between that lunch and my planned suicide.

The day before my forty-first birthday, Aiden Lang had flown out from Glasgow Airport to Chicago. From O'Hare, Aiden had then caught a connection to Los Angeles. At LAX, a car was waiting, ready to waft him up to Wiltshire Boulevard which, as you and I both know, sits atop the Big Rock Candy Mountain, otherwise known as Success.

It had been raining when Aiden left. I knew this because I'd turned up at the airport to say my farewell. Unfortunately, Aiden's parents had been there, also an elder sister with assorted nephews and, well, I didn't think I'd blend with the moment, what with me being coloured envy green and having the fiery red dots of jealousy for eyes and all. So I'd slunk into WH Smith's and started thumbing the best-sellers masochistically until the telly screens had flashed a gate number and Aiden had climbed the ramp with his boarding pass, script case and expression of benign vindication aglow on his soon-to-be prestigious countenance.

I could have cadged a lift back west with one of the lesser Langs but I'd have been required to explain both my presence at

the airport and my absence from Aiden's farewell at the departure gate. The fact was that a trudge through Paisley in the
pouring rain had seemed no more than I'd deserved for having
committed the foolish crime of harbouring unrealisable dreams.

Walking home, I'd thought of how I'd set out years earlier to
write verse. About how, unfairly hampered by my tin ear, I'd
turned to the novel – well, a novel. When that had failed to find
a publisher, I'd taken up drama. When my plays had failed to find
a producer, I'd slid right down the literary pole, deep into the
Hell's Kitchen of sitcom.

Perhaps you'll recall my finest hour. For who among us can
forget *His 'n' Hers*, a perky pre-watershed two-hander, featuring
the Bodells, a thirty-something couple who remained partners in
a bathroom fixtures business after their divorce? You may
remember, like me, a sparkling single-series run or perhaps, like
others, you recall a screaming turkey that crawled down its own
bathroom plughole towards an ugly bloody demise?

As I walked, I imagined mocking tabloid headlines. 'Lonely
Death of Plughole Man.' I heard the insights of those who had
known me – 'He had grown strange,' said Plughole's close friend,
award-winning screenwriter Aiden Lang. 'He came to the airport
to see me off but he didn't say anything – just hung around the
bookshop squinting out from behind the Ken Folletts so my
family and I decided not to embarrass him by waving.' 'I blame
myself,' added handsome millionaire Lang, squeezing the hand
of actress girlfriend Liv Tyler, as they paused en route to Cannes.
'I feel there's more I might have done.' Lang revealed he was
planning a screenplay based on the life of his former friend to be
entitled *Bubbling Under*. In this work, Plughole Man is to be
portrayed as 'an odd little loser with slitty green beads for eyes'.
Lang described it as 'an affectionate tribute'.

Standing out of the drizzle under the hood of Dixon's, I
watched Jonathan Ross do a trailer for an indie film special from

Montreal. My mobile rang. It was Joan. Skipton was back from location. He'd read my *Celia Proust* script. He wanted to see me tomorrow.

With a mighty effort, I made my mouth move. It said, 'Thanks.'

Next morning, I woke to find myself forty-one. Lodged in the letterbox was a single card – from my mother. As usual, the card had doubled, sadistically, as a book token – for a fiver. Even if I wanted to flagellate myself by buying a book – which I didn't – I'd have to add another few quid of my own for the privilege.

The birthday was my day of judgement, as I've explained. Yet I would fear no evil. For God was with me – and me, I was with me too. And better than either God or me, a drawer in my garret hovel containing twelve packets of twenty-four Nurofen Extra – they were also with me. So you see, not only would I fear no evil, I would also fear no ill for, lo, I had the cure.

And the cure was called Death.

Or Glory.

So I sat in the outer office, heart racing, not so much ignoring as being oblivious to the squawking small talk around me. The phone on Joan's desk chirruped, I remember that much, 'Right-o.' She looked at me. 'Ally's ready for you now.'

And so he was – as was the girl who was seated by him with my script on her lap.

'Do you know Emma?' asked Skipton.

'I do now,' I said, offering my hand.

'I asked Emma to read your script since it's basically a drama piece.'

'Comedy drama,' I corrected.

'The genre abbreviation is dramacom,' said Skipton, 'which suggests a basic bias toward drama.'

'It's not a bias,' I said, correcting his correction, 'it's just that comdram's too cumbersome to say.'

'Whatever.'

Skirmish point to me, I thought, as I perched myself on the rim of the settee crater.

'Well . . .' Emma began.

During the brief moment of silence that elapsed as she tidied her thoughts before speaking, I somehow regrouped and experienced an inexplicable surge of strength. You see, I'd remembered how good my script was. All those still nights, labouring by singing light, this was where it would all pay off. I knew in my head, I had it right. I knew in my heart, I had it right. More than this, I knew in my guts, my instincts, the crystallised essence of all my knowledge and writing experience, that this, *this*, was my moment.

'Go for it, Emma' I said.

So she did. She went for it.

Around four minutes later she stopped speaking.

I uncrossed my legs and said, 'I see.' I unbuttoned then re-buttoned my jacket, absently. 'Thank you.'

'You won't forget those reports, will you?' said Skipton.

'No,' I said, 'I'm on to it.' I picked up my heart which had lain slashed and throbbing on his desk and tucked it back inside my shirt.

'Sorry,' said Emma.

'Me too,' said Skipton. 'But it's just not right. Not the premise, not the characters, nothing.'

'Better luck next time,' said Emma.

'Or maybe it's best you don't waste your time,' said Skipton, adding pointedly, 'it takes you away from what you're good at.'

I avoided Joan's glance on the way out. But she was compassionate and had already avoided my avoided glance first. I might've known. She was his secretary – of course she'd have known the verdict in advance.

I stood in the corridor in a sort of daze, looking up and down. People with careers in television, with shoulder bags and fashionable specs sidestepped me, passing quickly up and down. I had a question for them all to which I urgently required an answer.

What happens to us when our ambition outruns our talent?

What happens to the forty-year-old – sorry, forty-one-year-old – loser in the word war? Well, didn't I have the answer already? Twelve packets' worth of answers, in my Cecil Street garret?

Except . . . except, as you'll have realised by now, I didn't kill myself. Nope. Sorry to disappoint you. Can't even offer up a subtle plot twist or a stunning time loop to find me writing this from Heaven's gate. Nothing. Just plain couldn't do it. I'm all talk, I know. Too cowardly to take the coward's way out. But, from what I've told you, are you surprised?

Instead I went home. I fished the pills from the drawer and, fearing an attack of heroism or cowardice, depending on your point of view, I instantly binned them.

That settled, I went out on a date.

This date. Here, in Rogano. With Chloe, lovely Chloe. Except we wouldn't, as I'd dreamed, be toasting the acceptance of my major new cop-show dramacom *Celia Proust*.

'Just pour,' I said to the waiter, 'just pour.'

There. Didn't I tell you I'd come back to those words?

And we watched him pour, Chloe and I. And, strange to admit, how good that glugging tinkle had sounded in the glass.

'Cheers.'

'Cheers.'

And, when we'd sipped, how consoling, only brief hours after failure's bitter tang, had been the full-bodied flavour of the moment.

'Eric's always saying someone should base a film on me and my friends.'

'Eric?'

'My brother? The screenwriter?'

'Oh, yeah. What's he doing now?'

'He's a junior doctor.'

'Uh-huh.' Of course. What else would he be? Doctors were always becoming writers. Hodge, Hill, Laverty, Mercurio, Chekhov. Just add Ross and stir.

'You and he would have a lot in common.'

'You think so?'

I pictured this Eric. I saw him in a Berghaus anorak, with a Ewan McGregor haircut and an iPod, watching the rugby sevens at Melrose with his medical pals.

'And he's stopped writing you say?'

'So he maintains. But when I visit, I still catch him working on his laptop or making notes sometimes in his room. He still gets phone calls from his old agent in LA. Maybe . . .'

'Yes?'

'Maybe he could, you know, help you.'

Tugging this well-meaning barb from my flesh, I steered Chloe on to Celia. Covering my nakedness with the lies of wishful thinking, as if it might still happen, this stillborn turkey, this dodo. And, as I talked, I knew I wanted Chloe, not only physically but also for the solid, stolid, reassuring, middle-class idea of her. She came from a world of stable backgrounds and educated siblings, a mythical realm of dry sherry, wet suits, Espace people carriers, first-class travel, second homes and three-piece suites that are bought *as an investment*. In a word, she offered me shelter.

'So would you like to meet him?'

'Who?'

'My brother.'

'Love to.'

I looked at her again. After my meeting with Skipton and Emma, I'd found myself gasping, adrift in life's icy waters. A shamed suicide standing at the sink, clutching pills. In Chloe, I recognised the only piece of wreckage afloat on the cold indifferent ocean of my life. Instinctively, I decided to reach out and cling to her. And why not? Another girlfriend, another year – what difference would it make? If I killed myself now, at forty-one, what would I have to look forward to at sixty?

After kiss-kissing Chloe goodbye, I took a taxi in the direction of the Alba building. My intention had been to hurtle into the Portakabin, strap on my yoke of endeavour and begin working diligently toward the reward of a new and wholesome life.

At the top of Byres Road I paid off the cabbie. I was feeling bruised and dazed from recent events and crossed the street to the Grosvenor Hilton. Fine living is a quick-forming habit and I required a further brief injection of solid splendour to steady myself from my recent rigours. Pushing open the gleaming mahogany doors, I promenaded up the thick endless carpet toward the discreet bar on the right of the far horizon. The afternoon atmosphere of the Grosvenor bar was that of a staid cruise liner during the off-season. After the rupture my nerves had suffered, this was exactly what I required. Not actors, not directors – which, unfortunately, was what I got. A film director, interviewing actors, right there, if you please, in the bar. Our bar. The cruise-liner bar. And not just any film director but a particular one, Sir Common, His Ordinariness, Ken Loach.

'Dry white wine and soda please.'

I helped myself to some nuts and tried not to watch. Other drinkers tried not to watch too.

Uni lecturers on shifty trysts with students, legal beagles puffing and scribbling, enslaved salesmen on initiative courses – in short, the horribly real and gruesome world of work, all scant reward and no appreciation. I'd served in that world once. I'd rather be dead than do so again. By the looks of them, so too would these actors. Ken actors – which is to say not actors at all. Shop girls, minicab drivers, student deadbeats, the whole mana-cled, skint and pimpled, stoically stupid world of Kendom Come. A small, nervous man sat next Ken, looking out of place, self-flagellating and vulnerable, obviously the writer. A vivacious young gel was smiling brightly, reeling off her intimate personal details while a waiter gathered glasses close by.

'Yes, I did the Diploma Course at the RSAMD. My special skills include singing, fencing and horse riding . . .' Forget it. You could sense Ken's shoulders sag. If she'd listed her special skills as housebreaking, having brown babies and selling crack rocks on the Broomielaw, she might've been in with a chance.

Taking a sip of spritzer, I tried to relax and adopt a pose of amused superiority. Why I did this, I didn't know. Which is to say, I knew exactly why.

It was the writer – Laverty. I couldn't wrest my eye from him. The green light of jealousy lurked therein. Word had it that he and His Kenness would make three films up here. One, two, three – which was one more than two and three more than my own then current total of nil. How alert he looked. Gaunt, wiry, bright, energetic, that sickening cocktail of eagerness and energy that would have him spurting a thousand usable words a day down his right arm, into his gleaming laptop and back out again into actors' mouths, prior to that magical call of directorial bene-diction, 'Action!'

I put my drink down. It tasted sour in my mouth – it wasn't chilled white wine any more but another slurp from the tepid gruel of failure.

Stepping out into the traffic blast, I met Denis coming in. He was dressed in interview black and his hair had been carefully moussed and mussed. His eyes, though, were pinched and bloodshot. He grasped the nettle while I pretended there wasn't any nettle to be grasped.

'Did I phone you the other night?'

I attempted vagueness 'No, I don't think so.' Never act to an actor – it compounds any offence.

He fixed me with a determined look. 'I don't want the world knowing I was canned by *Taggart*, OK?'

I blinked and shrugged. 'We'll never mention it again.' Leaving a brief pause for respect, I added, 'Why'd they can you?'

'Artistic differences.'

'Ah,' I said. I could imagine the heady to and fro of the discussion. They'd said Denis was pissed. He'd disagreed. They'd differed and booted his arse out the door, artistically of course.

'Matter of fact, I never even phoned you, OK?'

'OK, OK.'

He relaxed. 'Do you know the writer on this effort?'

'Name's Laverty,' I said. 'I hear he used to be a doctor.'

'Didn't they all?' said Denis, brushing dandruff from a lapel. I blame Chekhov. Should move the hospital beds into Shepperton – the fuckers could whip out appendixes between rewrites.'

'Appendices.'

'Appendixes.'

'Are you sure?'

'Whatever,' said Denis.

And he went in.

First canned, then Kenned. It was that kind of time.

A couple of days after our Rogano lunch I telephoned Chloe at work. She was cool towards me, even prickly – hurt perhaps that I hadn't made contact earlier and had been playing the usual dating games. Still, better overcautious than overkeen.

'I thought maybe I'd failed the test.'

'What test?'

'The first date test.' She said this with an uncharacteristically sour snicker, as if she'd borrowed it for the occasion. I guessed she'd been talking to Sam and Morag.

'Let me take you out tomorrow night and explain.'

'Tomorrow night I'm busy.'

'How about Saturday?'

Silence.

'Chloe? Hello?'

'I heard you.' Shorter silence. 'OK.'

It dawned on me I wasn't the only person in the world with feelings. Apparently there were two of us. And we had found each other.

The following Monday, first one of the month, as promised, Skipton summoned me to his office.

'How are you?'

'Resolute. I salute my own strength, courage and indefatigability.'

I stood before him like a surly stranger, determined to make him invite me to sit. He looked up from a faxed overnight ratings sheet.

'Oh, it's like that, is it?'

'Like what?'

'Me got petted lip. *Celia Proust* rejected. Me not sit down till asked.'

'You're the boss.' I sat.

'I'm sorry about *Celia*.'

'Forget *Celia*,' I said. 'You've read my reports?'

'Yes.'

'And?'

'There's no and. Why should there be an and? You write them, matey, I read them – that's how it works.'

'Good.'

'I didn't say it was good – I just said there was no and.'

'So what are you saying?'

He took the blue script folder from a desk tray, pulled out my sheaf of reports and leafed through it. He let the split sheaf waft in his hand like the wings of a sick white A4 dove then said, 'Sixty?'

'Sixty.' I said. I gave a light shrug and blinked like a man who didn't know what his boss was driving at.

'In three months?'

'Yes.'

'That's all the scripts you've received?'

'Correct.'

'In the old days, we'd get a hundred a month.'

'The old days? That would be the old days before you took over the department?'

'Yes and appointed you as script-reader. Don't forget that.' Skipton remembered we worked in the laff business and narrowed his already slitty eyes. 'You try my patience, Meester Bond,' he said.

I stood up. 'Is that it?'

He ignored me. 'I hear you've cleaned up your act.'

'It wasn't an act.'

'No kidding? The roaring boy writer at your age – how quaint. Still, you've a nice healthy gut on you for a starving artist.'

'Department issue. Comes with the job.'

He patted the paunch under his Paul Smith casual and allowed himself a smirk. 'She must be good for you.'

'Who?'

'Miss Lunch. What's her name – Chloe.'

I sighed. 'Can I go now? We seem to be straying into the personal.'

'To the true artist, there's no such thing as the personal.'

'I wouldn't know.'

'What a sad admission.'

'Do you mind?' I said, 'You're taking me away from what I'm good at.' I opened the door.

'Who's Kevin Thwaite?' Asked Skipton.

I stopped opening the door. 'What?'

'And Alice Mold? Alan Prion? Dave Thurso?'

'What do you mean?'

'Sixty scripts. And four of these unknown writers have places for surnames.'

I shuffled a bit. 'So have you.'

'Exactly. That's why I'm alert to the phenomenon.'

'Four out of sixty? That's a phenomenon?' I laid on the scorn. 'If you take another look you'll find a Catriona Salter and an Andreas Peppiat. Does that constitute a conspiracy of the condiment races or should we wait till we get something in from Alan Sugar?'

'OK.' Skipton did 'I surrender' with his hands. 'It's odd – that's all I'm saying.'

'So it's odd,' I said. 'Life is full of odd people.'

And with that composed little nip, I left.

All the same, my shoulders had dropped about a foot when I hit the corridor. Following Skipton's ultimatum of the previous month, I'd gathered the unread scripts into bin bags on the floor of my room, to be distributed, after my death, by gnomes, elves or the Glasgow Police, to their rightful owners. Since I'd bargained that only one of two things could have happened – either *Celia Proust* would get the go-ahead or she wouldn't – I'd calculated that one of two sets of consequences could possibly have followed. If *Celia* were to have been given the thumbs up, I'd have garnered some much-needed kudos and therefore have bought more time to deal with the hideous script muddle. If she didn't, well, what did I care? This was my last hurrah – I'd bound off home, with a spring in my step, to kill myself, all problems solved, death or glory, etc.

In life, the thing you haven't bargained for is the thing that usually happens. In this case, it simply hadn't occurred to me that I'd lack the spine for Option B, thereby creating a fresh new complication – Option C, the consequences of which demanded that I improvise an urgent solution forthwith. Which I had done – of sorts. It had gone like this. Having staggered, bravely, through the battlefield of my own cowardice, my reward was that I must therefore read five hundred and twelve scripts by the end of the month in order to accord with the dictate of Commander Skipton. Obviously, this was a human impossibility – well, it was for this human, anyway. On the other hand, I could have managed to read at least some of that five hundred and twelve. So I had read some – thirty in all. And I'd deleted the others from my computer. But there were sixty scripts, I hear you object – that's what Skipton had said.

No, there weren't. There were sixty reports, not quite the same thing. I'd made up thirty fictitious writers and concocted three-quarter page reports on their non-existent scripts to save myself the misery of doing any more of my loathsome job than I had to. And I'd enjoyed it. I'd had more jolly fun and shown more creativity in first dreaming up, then panning my own creations than in years of sweating earnestly over the washtub of serious comedy. Maybe I'd even grown a little too playful. Skipton had been smart. Mold and Thurso? What had I been thinking of? That was sloppy – I realised that now. But, let's face it, who the hell had ever heard of places called Thwaite or Prion? I shuddered. To think I'd been toying with Ralph Bingley.

Chloe and I became an item. Which is to say we started dating on a regular basis and were soon having the obligatory talks about the importance of 'space' and 'expectations'. Looking back, I think I knew this was nothing more than a ritual minuet and that, despite her protestations to the contrary, what Chloe was closing toward was what ninety-five per cent of all single women over thirty most earnestly desired, namely a ring and a child. One night in Paperino's she even told me as much.

'You know the thing I least want in the world?' she said. 'The thing that spooks me most?'

'What's that?'

'A ring and a child.'

'Oh yes?'

'Yes. Sometimes I look at women on the school run and I'm just filled with dread.'

'Wow. Really?'

'Yes.'

'What about the other times?'

'What other times?'

'The ones you told me about – when you'll pass a playground and suddenly burst into tears.'

'That's just hormones. Ask the waiter for black pepper.'

'Waiter!'

When the black pepper hormones start to kick, women become sales sharks, men the browsing customers. This is because a woman knows she has a limited time to make her pitch before a man's interest wanders. And a man's interest always wanders. If a man is screwing a blonde catwalk super-model, it won't be long before he's fantasising about the short dumpy brunette on the Morrison's checkout who leaves the extra button undone on her overall. Equally, the man who's nightly pawing that same brunette will be secretly lusting after blonde supermodels. So, for a woman who's wrestling with her black pepper hormones, it's a matter of – *Always be closing.*

Space? Go ahead – take acres of it. Commitment? Absolutely not necessary. Believe me, sir, I'm not like those other dealers. *There is no pressure to buy at Chloe's motors.* You want me? I'm here. You don't? What the hey? So, for the first six months, the man, as potential customer, is given the full treatment. Sit back and relax, sir, take me for a test drive, sir, give me your hand, just feel this upholstery, sir, isn't that really something? *And it could be yours to own.*

Applied to Chloe and myself, this generalisation manifested as follows.

I could do no wrong. The sex, triumphant kingly sex, with just the right hint of exotic fruit to follow, had been delivered up on a platter after our second date. Not in my flat, of course – I hadn't wanted her rushing out screaming into the night so it was her flat. Chloe lived across the great divide of Byres Road, the one that still separates the reservation of grungy student rebels to the east from those pitiable upwardly mobile, Lexus-driving careerists to the west – in short, those same grungy rebels ten years on. Chloe's flat, unlike my flat, had spoken of creature comforts and pastel shades, pleasing and restful to the eye. My eye, anyway. For I'd liked what I saw and was soothed and lulled by its charms. Soothing and lulling, of course, being complicit handmaidens to the sales process. And who among us is impervious?

It couldn't have lasted, of course, nor had it been meant to. This had been a sales drive, remember? There are two points in the year at which women take stock of their lives – the annual summer holiday being one. And, since Chloe and I had never been on holiday together, I realised the age-old relationship mantra had reared up to assert its power – *I'll give it till Christmas.*

Acted upon, I'd been compelled to react. I considered my situation. Since meeting Chloe, my life had enjoyed a new stability. When I'd needed shelter, she'd been there. True, the odd cloud of domestic tedium had begun to cross our loving sun and, yes, maybe the early frenzy of the sex had cooled but only relatively – a brief step down from the lava hot. I mean one could still, metaphorically speaking, fry eggs on my stiffy.

I'd been working well too. Of course, I use the word 'well' in a relative sense – I would arrive on time and, having solved, by nefarious means, the problem of the calamitous script pile, would now read whatever writers sent to me dutifully and promptly. If one of the unlucky 482BC (before Celia) scribblers who hadn't received a response ever called me to question why, I'd simply tell them that I'd never received their script. If they'd protested that it had been sent recorded delivery and signed for, I'd protest back that I'd returned it and that it had simply been lost in postal transit. 'Simply'. Most of the writers believed me or at least pretended to. What could they prove? And, besides, I was still a keeper of the keys. If they wanted Alba to consider their future efforts, they'd better bend the knee pronto and give me, its trusted spokesman, the benefit of the doubt.

This had left only the physical problem of what to do with the seven grisly bin bags full of script evidence that continued to occupy the floor of my flat. The answer, of course, was so obvious it had taken me a while to see the wood pulp for the trees. What do you do with rubbish? Why, you take it to the dump.

I took no chances. I bribed a grumbling hackney driver with a tenner tip to drive me to the big council plant at the back end of Anniesland. As I'd thrown the bags through the hole to be forked and stacked, you'll forgive me for thinking that I had, as they say, gotten out of jail. On top of that – and maybe this was the clincher – I hadn't had a drink in three weeks.

Not unnaturally, I'd attributed this upturn in my fortunes to the influence of Chloe. Neither of us had been blind to that. The question was, would we then consolidate our union within the matrimonial state, as I knew Chloe wished us to do, or would we merely thank each other for the memory, wish the other well, then routinely slander one another's reputation till indifference or new love succeeded in erasing the last bitter traces of the past? Though I couldn't have embraced the prospect of a future with Chloe or any woman in a spirit of wholehearted yea-saying, I'd nevertheless grown accustomed to the treat of creature comforts.

I did not relish a permanent return to my glowering room and a life of hangover, spew and drunken sex with unknown partners. But nor did I yearn for the stale bed and the stifled yawn of marriage. In the circumstances, I did what most men do – I bought time by playing my joker.

On Christmas Eve, I presented Chloe with an engagement ring. Twelve hundred, if you're interested, from the Argyle Arcade in town. Enough to show I meant business but not so much that I'd suffer the ignominy of having to ask for it back should everything later fall apart. Never bet more than you can afford to lose. They say that's the trick with all forms of venture capitalism, including the emotional.

Anyway, I did the full knee-bend thing right there on her living-room floor. Chloe thought about it, then turned me down. She was 'unsure' she said, somewhat coyly. I then did some sympathetic nodding and let her sleep on it. The next morning, Christmas morning, I put on her favourite song, 'How Deep Is Your Love?' by the Bee Gees. When it finished, I asked her again.

She laughed and said, 'Yes.'

Having realised I was about to enter the middle-class Land of Cheese, it had seemed wise to cultivate a taste for Gouda.

Perhaps Chloe's doubts had been serious, perhaps not. In any case, her acceptance avoided a diplomatic incident. Such was the depth of my love that I was about to break the taboo of a lifetime and meet the parents of an *amour*. We'd been invited over there for Christmas dinner. I steeled myself for the misery of festive joy. Not only that, I was sure I'd be tested in another way. After all, I was about to meet Chloe's brother – Eric Ross, backpacker, doctor and produced screenwriter.

'Merry Christmas!'

'Merry Christmas!'

'Sherry?'

I smiled, showing teeth.

'Chloe, look at the fairy lights on the bonsai trees!'

We strained to peer through the drizzle, out at the conservatory and the fairy lights on the bonsai trees.

'Dad's idea?'

'Who else?' said Mum.

'Hey, credit where it's due,' said Dad. A large straight-backed Protestant with a lawn of obedient grey hair, Dad breathed on his nails and buffed them on the tit of his Pringle V-neck. This prompted good-natured chuckles all round – if you include a mime from me.

In my family, if family it still was, a toast to Christmas would have been viewed as some sardonic taunt and would have provoked, according to drunkenness or whim, an outbreak of scowling, retching or even violence from the assembled blood-tied captives. We might have been a small bunch but what we lacked in numbers we made up for in discontent and bile.

'Where's Eric?' Chloe asked.

'His bleeper went off a couple of hours ago. Let's hope he manages back for dinner.'

'I hope so,' said Chloe, 'because we've something to tell you.' She turned to me. 'Haven't we?'

'Yes, I said, 'we're HIV positive.'

It had been intended as an ice-breaker. It was only when the air chilled I'd realised there hadn't been any ice.

'I find that a very doubtful remark,' said Mum.

Dad, credit to him, bailed me out with a playful shove. 'Getcha,' he said.

'Eric's done a lot of work with HIV patients,' said Mum. 'Some of the stories are heartbreaking.'

'For heaven's sake, Alicia, he's only joking.'

I watched Mum consider 'joking' like it was a bedpan needing emptied.

'Excuse me, I can be rather literal-minded,' she said, grudgingly.

'Hang around this family long enough, you'll get enough material for a dozen skits!' joshed Dad.

'Say that again,' said Chloe, and we shared a knowing smile.

I didn't know what we knew. It was just one of those things the moment seemed to dictate.

'What is it you've got to tell us?'

'Alicia, you need to ask?' said Dad. 'Can only be one of three things.' He counted off the three things on his fingers. 'She's either pregnant, engaged or wants to borrow money. Now I don't mind either of the first two, but moooney . . .' Dad said 'money' in a comedy Yorkshire accent, making a prohibitive sucking noise.

'What's he like?' said Mum.

I didn't know who Dad was like but I'd had a good idea who Mum was like – Mum was Chloe, twenty-five years on. How Dad could still bring himself to clamber aboard and hump her was a mystery to me. But maybe he didn't. Maybe he paid comedy Yorkshiremen to do it for him.

'Let's just say it isn't number one or number three.' Chloe volunteered, coyly.

'In that case, congratulations,' said Dad. He kissed his daughter and pumped my hand.

'I'm overjoyed, dear,' said Mum, grimly, and she and Chloe did hugging and kissing. But Mum didn't look overjoyed to me. And Dad, though he was still swaying jovially on his toes, sherry schooner in hand, was giving me shifty little once-overs when he thought I wasn't looking. He'd already clocked I was a good ten years older than his cherished issue. And he knew I'd nothing but a verbal contract and a single series sitcom flop to my name – not exactly the young man with prospects from the shires, clear of eye and pure of gene.

More for appearances, I felt, than out of any heartfelt emotional glow, Mum began dabbing at her eyes with a Kleenex. Dad gave her a dutiful hug.

'What should we do?' asked Mum, all flustered.

'Let's eat,' Chloe said.

So we ate.

After the Christmas pud – real cream, not artificial – Chloe and Mum cleared off to the kitchen to make coffee. Dad asked me about my business and, this being Scotland, launched tentative probes to establish my religion. He'd given me the grip during the nuptial announcement and I hadn't returned it. I informed him, waggishly, that I didn't have any religion – I was Protestant. I might've been born on the same side of the line as him but I was keen to repulse any ghastly overtures of Masonic kinship.

Credit where it's due, he didn't push it. He removed his paper hat, laid aside his role of Dad and become Eric Ross Senior.

'You know Chloe's been engaged before?'

I told him I did know that.

'Paul. I liked him but Chloe decided he was a wet fucking wick.' He pronounced the g in fucking, the hallmark of superior West of Scotland breeding. 'But you're not a wet wick.'

'No? What am I, then?'

His face was flushed. He had hit the whisky though I hadn't noticed him pour. In Scotland the class system has two layers – drinkers and non-drinkers. Everything else is negotiable.

'Well, since you ask . . .' he said.

Whenever people are about to put you in your place, they never get straight on with it. First, they're got to tell you how superior their place is.

'I'm the MD of Sproat's Pressings Ltd, one of the most respected names in the flange pressing industry in the West of Scotland.' He eyeballed me for effect, daring a reaction. Not getting one from me, he gave himself one. 'And yes, it is as dull as it sounds. Stressful as hell but bloody dull.'

'You've done all right.'

'I'm well aware of that.' A tone – grain and grape. Soon he'd start bumping into things, falling asleep or be spoiling for a fight. I wasn't going to give him one of them, either.

'When you come from a background like ours . . .'

'Ours?' I said.

'Ordinary.'

I nodded. He'd surprised me.

He continued, 'In the big fun run of life, people from our class start off at the rear – we're the ones in the rabbit suits and Pink Panther outfits. By the time we reach the starting line, the race has already been won. That's why, to people like us, children are the greatest blessing, don't you agree?'

I was smiling and nodding but my mouth said, 'In what way?'

He looked at me like I was still in the fun run, wearing a jester's cap and bells. 'If you have to ask that, why are you getting married?'

Luckily, he had a head of steam up and answered his own question. 'They're our second life, don't you see?

'Yes,' I said. But I didn't see. I was my one and only life. As far as I was concerned, everything else was academic.

'When Chloe and Eric came along, I was determined they'd succeed.'

'And have they?'

'Utterly. Chloe, God bless her, not the hottest rivet in the glove but she worked hard, stuck in at Leeds and got a good place in a solid legal practice. OK, she never made the bar but . . .' he let his voice trail off, dismissively.

'And Eric?'

The voice snapped back to enthusiastic attention. 'Eric has it all. My son, the doctor – corny I know. And to think he nearly threw it all away.'

'On what?'

'Och, yon Hollywood malarkey. His head was very nearly turned. And for what? A few trashy films people didn't even go and see.'

'A few? I thought he only wrote one?'

'No, they had him bouncing back and forward like a squash ball, rewriting others. When it started interfering with medical school, I put my foot down.' Dad took a studied sip of his whisky to calm his agitation. 'The best of it is, do you know what they call these people too? The ones who fix the unworkable scripts of others?'

'Yes,' I said, 'they call them script doctors.'

'Exactly. Bloody ironic. I said to him, "Eric," I said, "take a good hard look at yourself. Do you want to do something worthwhile in life or do you want to sell popcorn?"'

'What did he say?'

Eric Ross Sr gave me an incredulous look. 'What d'you think he said? He's a doctor now, isn't he?'

'Right.' Man lost to popcorn, then.

'He made up his own mind. You can't live their lives for them, can you?'

'No,' I said, 'you can't live their lives for them.'

He relaxed, having justified himself. 'That's me and mine covered -- how about you and yours?'

'You were going to tell me about me,' I reminded him. As I said this, I thought I heard the front door close.

'Oh, yes,' he said, airily, like a lofty thinker who'd been hauled back to some mundane point. He turned and reached for a bottle of Glenlivet from the sideboard. 'The film business, it seems to me, is a world run by chancers for chancers. My Eric isn't a chancer.'

'And me?'

'Yes,' said Eric Ross Sr, 'you're a chancer, all right.' He gave a joshing chuckle to cover himself as he said this but his little businessman's eyes stayed watching, scanning me for tics and fidgets. He wasn't going to fall asleep or fall anywhere for that matter. He was an old school business-bear drunk – the sort who could keep going, without let-up, from the seven o'clock shadow in the evening till the morning shakes at breakfast. I smiled and nodded. It seemed to me I did a lot of smiling and nodding in life. When I looked up, a wispy young man wearing a snorkel parka was standing, diffidently, in the doorway. He had on medical blues and had thinning fair hair.

'Hey, about time. You'll never guess what . . .' Eric Ross Senior's new tone swooped and veered between business bear and Dad.

'What?'

Dad raised his topped-up glass. 'Chloe's engaged again.'

The young man looked at his father, then at me.

'No kidding. Again? She's a trier, isn't she?'

'What do you expect? She's thirty-two – the heat is on! Anyway, this is him – the engagee.'

'That's you?'

'Yes,' I said.

His little amused eyes squinted at me. 'I know you,' he said.

'I don't think so.'

'Yes,' he said, 'I never forget a face – not an unhappy one anyway.'

'I'm not unhappy,' I corrected everyone, swiftly, 'not now.'

'And you're getting married or just engaged?'

'Married,' I said, 'probably.'

'We'll see,' said Dad, treating me to his cheeky chuckle, 'we'll see.'

'Probably married.' The young man mulled the words over. He made them sound like something aliens did. 'My people,' he said, 'humble people, who expect nothing.'

I felt a little spasm of recognition. 'To Carthage then I came,' I said, 'burning, burning.'

'Oh, Lord, thou pluckest me,' continued the young man.

'Oh, Lord, thou pluckest me out,' I said. I started laughing to cover the fact that I didn't know any more of the Eliot poem.

'The party?' he recalled. 'South side – remember?'

'Yes,' I said.

'The dead canary? That loud girl with the long hair?'

'Karine,' I said.

'I was half asleep in the corner, watching you dance.'

'Pity. You missed a rare delight,' I said. At last – recognition. The other drunken, all-seeing eye that night – one of a pair.

'I'm Eric Ross,' said Eric Ross.

'Yes,' I said, 'I'd worked that out.'

And we shook hands, Eric Ross and I.

'You'll have a drink,' Dad said to me, as he headed for the bottle. 'Eric won't – he can't hold it.'

'I lack your gifts,' said Eric Ross Jr.

Dad appeared to let this glance off – perhaps because it was Christmas. 'Much trouble at mill?' he asked.

'No, quiet,' said Eric.

As the assembled Rosses sat chit-chatting and catching up, I marvelled at the awful intimacy of other people's families.

Chloe's mother, who'd never worked since giving her birth, was a prominent patroness of charities. 'I was offered AIDS but it was in Africa – you'd never see the benefit – so I chose cancer – well, it's closer to home – another Cointreau – I must ring Kitty,' all in one stupefying breath.

And Dad, prickly pickled, Defender of the Faith, provider of all bounty, enthroned on his Parker Knoll recliner, encased in his thumping castle, his fat balls on the dining table, draped with triumphant tinsel, daring us to deny that, yet again for another year, he'd brought home the bacon.

'You all right?' Chloe enquired, gently, putting a hand on mine.

I was startled to see the engagement ring on her finger, even though I'd bought it and put it there. Was it a loving hand? Well, mine was at that moment and so, I think, was hers. But I couldn't say if it would remain so. Women value structure above all else – above love. Marriage is the launch pad for their dreams – for men it's the crash-landing site. 'What will survive of us,' wrote Larkin, 'is love.' Not for me. Skip love, forget children or a tidy rose garden – I want words, give me words. The rest is silence.

'Yes,' I said, 'I'm good.'

'What's your mother doing today?' asked Mum.

'She's having dinner with her sister.'

'Oh, that's a relief. I'd hate to think of her sitting on her own. You must bring her over soon.'

'Yes,' I said, 'I will.'

'What did she say when you told her you were engaged?'

'She was thrilled.'

Chloe gave me a look. I made a mental note to ring the old bag and tell her. But not yet – I'd wait a while. I was engaged now but, for all I knew, I might soon be unengaged – engagements being what they were. Even if we were to marry, we might soon divorce so, all in all, it had seemed prudent to drag my feet, to see how things went, before wading in grimly with the joyous news. It was only when I'd heard the sound of cutlery going down that I remembered Eric Ross was still with us, in the corner, picking at his Christmas dinner.

'Goodness' sake, Eric, you've hardly touched a thing,' chided Mum.

'He's no scrum half,' Dad observed.

'Get you, the flying winger,' joshed Chloe.

Dad patted his paunch and laughed though it wasn't really a paunch as a working-class person would understand the term – no hanging dough of grey flab, no sagging man-tits, no wheezy rasps as a beefy arm reached out for another killer bingo fag.

'Anyone care for a walk?' asked Eric Ross.

'It's raining.'

'Don't you want any pudding?'

'It's just drizzle.'

'Let's play canasta.'

But Eric wasn't for any pudding or canasta and stood up, undraping his parka from the back of the chair.

'Looks like I'm on my own, then.'

'No you're not,' I said. 'I'll come for a walk.'

'You don't mind the rain?'

'I'm forty-one,' I said. 'I can't hang around, waiting for the rain to go off – I haven't enough life left.'

'He calls this country Sconeland,' Chloe said.

'Never underestimate a Scot,' Dad said.

'Or a scone,' said Chloe, supportively.

Dad bristled in defence of Scotland's honour. 'As a people, we've had an influence on the world, far beyond our size.'

Eric Ross Jr looked at me. 'Sconeland,' he said, 'I like that. Let's go.'

And on Chloe's face, I recall the look of tickled surprise that I, me, the declared enemy of domesticity, had made this voluntary gesture towards acceptance – that I'd begun, without prompting, to begin the process of assimilation. I was on my way to becoming family and her delight was underpinned with relief.

Of course, being a woman, she probably thought we'd talk about her but we didn't.

We walked down Craigton Road, by the golf course, the drizzle gathering on our coats like dew. Milngavie, pronounced Mulguy, is bungalow country. Uncharted sounds, a kicked stone, a sudden guffaw, attract attention there but not in the old-fashioned, curtain-twitching way of the past. These days, with a Barbie in every garden and a Beamer in every drive, the scrutiny was more direct. Every owner-occupier had a scowl on his face and a whisky in his paw and was his own guard dog. As you'd pass, there'd be a pretence of fiddling with a desk lamp or putting sixties Johnny Cash on the hi-fi but it was you, stranger, you were the one, you'd brought your guns to town and they were watching. Return the stare and the paper-hatted beasts retreated, back into the gloom to sound the alarm. Twenty years ago, they'd have been straight into the hall to ring the teacher son in Canada for reassurance. Nowadays, it was straight on the cordless, spying on tiptoe, while an alert was scrambled among the other bloodhounds in the Neighbourhood Watch scheme. If we're lucky in life, which is to say unlucky, this is where we end up.

'How come you were at that party?'

'Well . . .' Eric Ross gave the short sigh before answering that I was soon to regard as characteristic of him. 'You remember the guy with the Hilfiger shirt and the plaster on his head?'

I nodded. 'The scabby little scuzzball?' I said. 'The one who was hassling me?'

'That's the one. Well, he's a customer of mine,' said Eric Ross.

'What sort of customer?'

'It was me who put that plaster on his head. I was on A & E duty – he'd been in a fight outside a club. He invited me along to the party after my shift – as a kind of reward, I suppose.'

'Was he surprised you came?'

'Why? Nothing surprises anybody these days.' He formed a sort of whimsical half smile. 'By the way, can you guess what my nickname is?'

'Give me a clue.'

'You're in television. The clue's in the title.'

Drizzle was running down my eyebrows. 'I dunno.'

'ER,' said Eric Ross.

'Of course,' I said. I wasn't keen on telly medical dramas – everybody running about, thumping chests and shouting dosages of obscure pharmaceutical drugs at each other. But, then, I wasn't keen on anything on telly, including my own stuff.

'The producers had my agent send me a bunch of tapes,' reflected ER. 'Seems like years ago.'

'Did they want you to write one?'

He gave his head a little modest tilt. 'Three, actually.'

I felt uncomfortable. I hadn't wanted to start comparing war medals for obvious reasons. I steeled myself and feigned interest.

'Do you find *ER* true to real life?'

It had felt a bit clunky saying the RL words – normally writers, even retired writers like me and him, don't use tasteless phrases like that but I'd been stampeded into it through my own politeness.

Eric looked at me. He was the only person I've ever met who could beam, wanly. 'Ah . . . now that presupposes "real life" to be necessarily "true". But truth is naked, isn't it? And we don't like nakedness in our lives. It's indecent – we cover it over.' He shook the arms of his parka as we walked. A little spray of droplets took off like formation flyers. 'I mean we're told there's nothing more real in life than death. But even now I have to stifle a giggle whenever a patient dies on me. I want to tickle him in the ribs to wake him up. Is that very childish?'

'Not to me – I'd say it's solid medical practice.'

He gave me one of his beady looks, like he'd done at the party. 'I'm beginning to get the hang of you,' he said. 'You're one of those writers who want "no more poems about foreign cities", aren't you?'

'I dunno,' I said, awkwardly. 'If it's Prague or Amsterdam save me a seat on the bus. I'm good for a couple of sonnets.'

'It was an allusion,' said Eric Ross.

'I guessed that,' I said. 'I just didn't know what it alluded to.'

It was unfortunate. It had left a little jolt in the conversation like a traffic bump spoiling a car's nice cruising speed. I made myself speak.

'Where did you study literature?'

'Edinburgh. You?'

'WH Smith's mostly – during my lunch breaks.'

'Ah,' said Eric Ross.

'Ah,' I said.

The rain, bearable at horizontal, had turned to vertical sheets. We struggled forward resolutely for a while, heads down, wind whipping at our soaked trousers, dead set upon our stated aim of a pleasant after-dinner stroll in Mugdock Park. Finally, beaten back, we took refuge in an elderly dented bus shelter.

'Will you write again?' I asked him.

I'd shaken out my coat and had it over my knees. Eric didn't bother, he was seated next me, on the narrow bench, feeling in his rain-soaked pockets. 'What made you think I'd stopped?'

'Chloe said . . .'

'Oh, Chloe,' said Eric with a shrug. A little trickle of rain did a stuttering sprint down his nose. 'Once I qualify or the old man dies, maybe then I'll give it a proper go. It's just too much hassle to go against him right now. He was against me going out to California.'

'How long were you there?

He gave me a sidelong look. 'Long enough. You don't drink, do you?'

'Not any more.'

'The human liver can take a lot of battering. After forty, the bills start. How old are you?'

'Forty-one.'

'Ah,' he said. He'd been fiddling about with a torn envelope and a banknote.

He knelt on the damp concrete, placed the envelope on the bench and began picking open a little cling-filmed packet. He looked up at me. 'Ash on an old man's sleeve is all the . . .'

I rummaged in my mind. 'No,' I said, 'I can't remember the rest of the line.'

Oh, skip it,' said Eric Ross. And with that, he hoovered up two big lines of his own, a rhyming couplet so to speak, one up each nostril, him, Doctor Ross, right there in a dented Milngavie bus shelter.

He sniffed and wiped his snout. 'How about you?'

'No,' I said, trying not to appear shocked, 'I'm all right.'

'You won't tell Chloe, will you? Only she thinks I'm clean again.' He looked at me, imploringly.

'No,' I said, 'I won't tell Chloe.'

Somehow you don't think of a doctor being a cokehead – you assume there's something in the Hippocratic oath to prevent it – but, like he'd said, nothing surprises anybody these days. His wan smile started gathering speed and broke into a grin. Now I understood why he had been at a party full of scuttling little petty crims and dealers.

'And to think Ladbrokes were offering ten to one against a white Christmas,' he said.

I smiled dutifully. I was beginning to suspect he'd make a better patient than a doctor.

The sun peeked its milky cataract of an eye from under the stale duvet of cloud. Heartened, we walked on.

After the gloomy horror of the festive break, I'd been eager to return to the routine horror of work but, in the land of the short-term contract or, in my case, no-term contract, not even misery should be taken for granted.

'Skipton?'

'Yes.'

'What's it about?'

'He didn't tell me,' Joan said. 'He just said he wants to see you.'

We were in my Portakabin, Joan and I. 'He's seen me before, he knows what I look like.'

I could afford to be flippant – I was on top of the job. 'Notice anything strange about that in tray?' I asked.

'It's empty?'

'Exactly. Commit that sight to memory, Joan, then pass it on. I'm drawing my efficiency to your attention since I can't be sure you're taking notes.'

'Anything else?'

'Well, since you're pushing me, you could take a peek at my out tray.' The out tray was brimful of letters of acknowledgement and half promises, easily broken, to attend rehearsed readings by plodding workshop groups in Castlemilk, Stirling and Airdrie. I had left up Christmas cards from friendly writers, just to prove I knew some. Now Joan was a witness, I could take them down again.

'This card's from Alan Bold.'

'So what?'

'He died years ago. Have you been putting up old Christmas cards?'

'No,' I said, snatching it from her, 'I've been taking them down.'

The phone chirped on my desk and Joan took it without asking. 'Yes, Ally,' I heard her say. She covered the mouthpiece and murmured to me quietly, 'You'd better get in there.'

I found Skipton standing on his chair, which in turn was standing on his desk. He was trying to coax a helium balloon down from the ceiling with an unwound wire coat hanger. On the balloon was the face from Munch's *The Scream*.

I treated him to my Jay Leno impression. 'Whatever is it that brings us into this crazy business called show?'

'Shut up and hold the chair.'

I held the chair but I couldn't shut up. Well, you'd have laughed too.

Skipton explained, 'Some bugger tied it to the door handle for a laugh. Fair enough but, when I took it off, the ribbon came away and now . . .'

He made a short exclamation of anguish. 'Hold tight,' he said.

As I held tight, Skipton leapt from the chair, shouting 'Aieeee!' like an attacking Japanese in a sixties' war comic. As he sailed through the air, he thrust the wire coat hanger in a frustrated stabbing motion at the balloon. I remained holding the chair legs as he fell.

'I could've told you that wouldn't work,' I said.

'It was a long shot,' admitted Skipton, 'but at least it got me down.'

The phone sounded its little internal corporate chirp and Skipton snatched it up. 'No, it's all right, Joan,' he said into it, 'something just fell.'

He put the phone down. 'Where are you going? '

'To get some glue. Put some on a card on the end of that hanger and it might stick to the balloon.'

'Forget the balloon,' said Skipton. 'Sit down.'

I sat down. So did Skipton.

When he spoke, I forgot the balloon. 'Do you know a writer called Urquhart – Walter Urquhart?'

'Yes. Why?'

'Sheila Bing? Lachlan Elder?'

'No.'

'You sure? How about Alec Bannon?'

'I've never heard of any of those. Why?'

I was adamant but, even while I was being adamant, an awful familiarity had begun to dawn. Bannon, Bing, Elder – those had been names among the A to Es on my script index file. But were they real names of living people or fictional ones I'd invented? How come they were known to Skipton? Had their work been destroyed or merely rejected? Did it ever exist at all? Did I dare to eat a peach?

'You won't know Alec Bannon,' said Skipton. He placed his hands, palms down, on the desk and spread his fingers, like a man who's gearing himself up to say something. 'But he knows you.'

Skipton reached under his desk. He pulled out a clean white waste bag. 'Alec Bannon is a bin man.' From within the clean white waste bag, he pulled a nasty soiled black waste bag. 'And an aspiring writer. One of many.' Skipton opened the nasty black bag, flower-like, to reveal the pollen therein. 'In fact, this is his sitcom.' From a congealed lump of soiled A4 scripts, he peeled off a single soiled A4 script.

'What's it called?'

'*The Bin Men*,' said Skipton.

'Ah,' I said. I had a curious feeling of having turned very small and that Skipton's couch had grown very big.

'He'd been poking the rubbish down the Anniesland plant with a stick,' explained Skipton with restrained disgust, like he was fighting an impulse to do the same to me with his unravelled coat hanger. 'They have to sift – there might be gas bottles or toxic matter.' His face was flushed. Were those tears in his eyes? No, it was just the fierceness of his hatred, glinting under the strip light.

He continued, 'When I say "they", I mean, of course, decent people, normal people, who do their jobs properly.'

'I was doing my job,' I protested with slithering reason. 'I was sifting too.'

'You're supposed to read them first before deciding whether they're rubbish.'

I leaned forward, doing fervent acting. 'Did you read it?'

'No, Emma read it.'

'And is it rubbish?'

'Yes.'

'No further questions.' I leaned back grumpily, folding my arms, trying to look hard done by. But I knew I was in big trouble.

'Bannon wondered why he never got a response,' said Skipton. 'He thought eighteen months must be normal.'

I might've said no, three years was normal – or never – but I didn't.

Skipton drove on, 'After a search of the dump, Bannon counted six bags of unread scripts.'

Only six. A chink of light. 'How could he know they hadn't been read?'

'Many of them were in unopened envelopes.'

And again, darkness at noon.

'This is bad. If this gets out, it'll destroy the credibility of this department.' What Skipton meant, of course, wasn't 'this' but 'his' department. He. Him. King Guffaw of Laffland.

'Will it get out?' I'd sensed the hint of a reprieve. Television is a selfish business. The only unforgivable sin is no longer to be useful. If I was no longer useful, I'd be isolated like a virus. Was I still useful?

'I've given him tickets to the recordings of Scobie's show. He can sit in the gallery and watch Jasmine direct. Then I'm hoping to dazzle him at Destiny during the wrap party. With any luck, he'll be star-struck and his mouth will be hanging too far open to talk.'

'Thank you,' I said. My voice was croaky with nerves. I started to explain. 'I may've freewheeled a bit but that's in the past. I've cleaned up my act now. I'm much more . . .'

'Please.' Skipton made a 'stop' motion with his hand, shutting me up.

To my surprise, he started folding away the bag.

I didn't know what to do. I stood up.

'As a matter of interest,' said Skipton, 'just how many scripts did you junk?'

'482 – I think.'

Skipton nodded, then spoke gently, looking at his desk. 'And was one of those 482 junked scripts a gritty comedy called *Cement Wedding* by Walter Urquhart?'

'Why?'

'Walter Urquhart rang today and left a message. He said to tell you not to bother reading his script as it's just been optioned elsewhere. He was most apologetic. *He* was apologetic. And he said to tell you your father sends a regard.'

'One regard?'

'I'm just the messenger. Are you aware of who's optioned *Cement Wedding*?

'No.'

'Ken Loach.'

'No kidding.'

'Ken Loach.'

'Get away.'

'Have you seen how skinny Ken Loach is? How speccy? This skinny, speccy wee man, walking about Glasgow, bent double by principles, yet he can still go through a pile of scripts the way you eat Whoppers and fries.'

'Maybe he won't make *Cement Wedding*.'

'Maybe he won't. The point is he now has the choice of whether to make it and we don't.'

'Maybe he'll make it with us.'

Skipton's anger took on a cold, even note. 'Then it would be a co-production and not an in-house production. And we'd lose a big chunk of the budget at the front end and we'd lose a big chunk of the budget at the back end.' Skipton made to and fro motions with his arms. Together, we imagined the big chunks of budget slopping out of the two ends, front and back. 'Those are the kind of chunks that service this department and keep it resourced. And then questions would be asked of me by our superiors – like how come I didn't do it as an in-house production, when we had the chance?'

'Tell the superiors we're supporting our colleagues in the independent sector.'

'By being incompetent? You try running that one past the suits – I'll be next door with the sane people.' Skipton sat down heavily. 'I just hope to God he doesn't do it. I just hope Ken Loach doesn't make *Cement Wedding*.'

'Fuck him,' I said.

'No', said Skipton, 'no one must be fucked – not even you. We'll do this thing quietly. Maybe it won't get out but, if it does get out, I want to be able to point and say, "Look!"' He made jabbing motions at the door with his finger. '"Look, I did the right thing."'

'What do you mean "the right thing"?'

'The thing,' said Skipton, 'which is right.' He looked at me steadily. 'Clear your desk,' he said, 'you're finished.'

'Ally . . .'

'I mean it. Finito. Go.' He put his head down and started shuffling papers on his desk.

Stuck for a memorable exit line, I stood instead swaying and blinking. Above Skipton's head, the balloon still hugged the ceiling. Eventually, it would stop screaming, give itself up and wither away to die in a corner. Everyone did.

'Ally?'

'Goodbye.'

Outside the Portakabin, I was shocked to find my stuff had already been packed. A line of clean white bin bags stood on sentry duty by the side of the door. As I entered, Joan was writing a message on a yellow Post-it. She crossed a 't', dotted an 'i'.

'There,' she said.

I took the Post-it off her thumb and read aloud, 'Desk for collection.'

'That's right.'

'My desk?'

'Not straightaway – you're fine till five-thirty,' she said.

You're Fine till Five-Thirty. It sounded like the title of one of those wry memoirs by some ex-Hollywood player who's desperate to convince you he's bounced back again to the big time from pauperdom, or insanity, or both.

'Why didn't you tell me?'

'I couldn't tell you. If I'd told you, you'd have known. And, if you'd known, you'd have resigned. And, if you'd resigned, Ally couldn't have displayed his disapproval by showing you the door.'

'Displayed it to whom?'

'Nobody. It's being hushed up.'

'Then what's the point of sacking me?'

Joan shrugged. 'You never know. Walls have ears.'

I did sad nodding, trying to elicit sympathy.

'Oh and we'll need your key.'

'Who for?'

She couldn't resist a slight embarrassed smirk as she said, 'Emma.'

A spark of rebellion flared within. 'You're not getting my key. I'm fine till five-thirty, remember?' Our James and Moneypenny routine had been blasted away.

'Don't take it out on me. Emma wants her own desk, people always do.'

'You let me down, Joan.'

'Let me tell you something,' said Joan, puckering her mouth, 'you got off lightly – this could have been a criminal matter.'

'Ple-e-e-ase – you sound like Celia Proust.'

'No, I don't.' She walked away. Over her shoulder, she said, 'My dialogue's better.'

Then she left.

And I cleared my desk.

And I left my office. Although, to be fair, my office had already left me.

To sum up – I had no job, I had no income, I had no prospects, I hated everyone.

So Rule of Four then – classic joke structure.

CHAPTER THREE

I sat in the window of Tinderbox Cafe on Byres Road, my empty script bag on my knees, scaring off the passing trade with my frozen hatchet face. *The Herald* was open at the features page and a mighty head and shoulders photo of a modestly grinning Aiden Lang taunted me. 'Young Lang $yne' blared the headline. 'Big McKilling for Scots Movie Writer'. There were palm trees behind Aiden. Big girls with little shorts were gliding past him on roller blades and he was wearing Ray-Bans to shade his eyes from the dazzling sun so, yes, I supposed it might've been Largs but I didn't think so. I looked for the plusses. The bigger the photo, usually, the more undernourished the accompanying article. 'We've just had the green light,' said Aiden, thirty-six – lying toad – 'and filming has been brought forward from the fall to accommodate Angelina Jolie's availability.'

From the fall. Hah! If success ever had me calling autumn 'the fall', they could shoot me in the head and cover me over with dead leaves. They might have to if I couldn't make next month's rent. 'As a true Scot,' said Aiden, 'I'm determined to hold our UK premiere in Glasgow.'

I tore my eyes away from the paper. 'Never mind,' I told myself, 'I can compete.' I considered faxing him my own dazzling headline, from earlier. 'Desk for collection.'

When the bag slipped from my knees with a clattering 'dooff', I found myself roused from the small trance of gloom I'd entered and glanced about paranoically, wondering if I'd let out any wails or anguished groans during the temporary vacating of my senses. No arched eyebrows, nothing. These were professional people, with serious careers, talking of glass ceilings and stronger legislation against sexual harassment. I folded the paper so as to hide Aiden's triumph before returning it to the cafe's rack. To Dowanhill Street then I came, burning, burning ... Outside Starbucks, my mobile bleeped. The text read, 'Like a patient etherised upon a table. P.S. Only kidding, it's pethidine. Lve, Eric.'

Unreal city.

By Intersport, in Great George Street, I sat down and wept.

Maybe it really is a Beatley, maggotty truth and, in the end, all we need is lve. But I wasn't we – I was me. And I wasn't at the end of my life – I was in the dangerous middle.

Fcuk Lve. What I needed was succss.

I gave notice to Mr Provan.

He took the news with distaste as though to quit his lodging house were evidence of a flighty character. He counted up the entries in my rent book and made a calculation with his pen. 'Six years,' he said, sniffily. 'Miss Middleton stayed for two decades. She died or it would have been longer.'

'Goodbye,' I said and added, with noble hypocrisy, 'good luck with the book.'

'We shall see,' said Mr Provan.

Something in the brightness of his tone, in the smugness of his smooth turn-away, as if I might have been about to coax him for further details of his dismal manuscript, had me fervently wishing him dead. In wishing, I'd felt whole again. What a weight is lifted from our conscience when we return to our true, vicious little natures.

* * *

'Phup!'

The champagne cork flew off, hit the mahogany curtain pole and lodged in the braided tie-back.

'It's a sign,' giggled Chloe.

'What of? Strangulation?'

Chloe removed the cork and smoothed the curtain folds. 'Look on the bright side – you're freelance now. You can stay with me and you'll have time to write whatever you like.'

'You're right, dammit.' I sipped from the fizzing glass of life. If sounding upbeat was the price of a drink, I was downbeat enough to fake it. After abstinence, one sip of alcohol is like stepping into a sunlit room, to the Hallelujah chorus, while being caressed by handmaidens with mink mittens.

'I love you,' I said.

'Are you talking to me or your glass?'

'Don't be hurtful.'

'I love you too,' Chloe said. And we each looked into the other's smiling face for a moment longer than was strictly necessary. But that extra moment had been strictly necessary, given our circumstances – which were that we were unsure of the future and of each other yet had begun cohabiting with a view to marriage – Chloe having been the more enamoured of this prospect, it seemed, than me. We know how things will end before they begin yet still we choose to ignore the small inner voice that warns us of the mess to come. But that small inner voice is a compass and a compass doesn't get to drink champagne and smell Chanel on warm skin or watch DVDs together on the couch, on rainy Glasgow evenings.

'It's a blessing in disguise really – you hated working there anyway,' said Chloe.

'You're right – it's for the best,' I said, giving her waist a squeeze.

'We won't be like other people – we'll work at our relationship.'

We shared a short, strangely savage kiss, Chloe's lips hard and writhing on mine.

'Then we can plan our future.'

'Yes,' I said, 'we'll work at being us.' I drew breath and stroked the firmness of her bottom. Uninvited, I found my head gate-crashed by the words of a forgotten sluttish C-league movie starlet, I'd seen photographed in a Stetson with her tits out in a limo. 'I don't want to work at a relationship,' she'd said, 'I just want to have it.' That's what I call a compass.

With love tidied away like discarded clothes, Chloe and I returned to the business of living.

In television-speak nobody is ever unemployed, you just 'go freelance'.

I was freelance.

In theory, this meant I could tilt this new free lance of mine at whomsoever I pleased but, in practice, it meant sitting around life's waiting room, hoping to meet somebody who wanted to be tilted at. I'd like to report that offers flooded in and that's very nearly right if I can be permitted to fine-tune the emphasis thus – offers flooded out. I wrote to every independent company in Glasgow, Manchester and the bigger London outfits, offering my indispensable script-reading talents. Naturally, I'd skipped lightly over the dank puddle of my dismissal from the Alba Corporation and made no reference to my predilection for binning the scripts I'd been paid to read. The devil, as they say, is in the detail.

Those who bothered to reply did so in the negative. Some of them promised to 'keep my name on file'. This failed to encourage me. In my time at Alba, I'd kept names on file too, stored prudently in the waste bin by my desk. Besides, only the biggest of the independents could afford to employ an outside script-reader. And, if they were big, they were successful and, if they were successful, it was because they were run by experienced comedy practitioners who had minds of their own, supple and discerning enough to sift through the unsolicited script silt, panning for commissionable gold. These were like minds, having often quaffed and snorted, performed and scribbled their collective way from university straight up the greasy pole to television success. Producers don't know what they're looking for but they recognise it when they see it. And well they might because usually it's a reflection of themselves when younger.

Money was tight – my money, that is. Chloe's was loose and kindly so. Bills arrived and were paid invisibly; there was food on the table and warmth from the fire. My manly pride had remained awkwardly stiff throughout the early weeks of this arrangement but, with limited severance pay and a wilting credit card, I had little choice but to accept Chloe's largesse with as much good grace as I could muster. As the weeks went by, I became more adept at grace-mustering and had soon begun to do it with alacrity. Though she'd dropped no unseemly hints, I suspected that Chloe, too, had begun to notice my unexpected talent for pecuniary humility.

'Maybe Dad could help,' she ventured, once only, over the evening gnocchi.

I'd fixed her a look, like a man of moral fibre clinging to his last vestiges of dignity. 'I promise if things are ever desperate enough, I won't be too proud to ask him.'

Lacking the resources, either internal or material, to tackle the long haul of a screenplay or novel, I'd turned to the relentless short hauls of journalism. This too had not been without its humiliations. A cold call to a features editor in Glasgow had revealed her to be the former Edinburgh journo, now promoted and migrated, whose drivelling, self-regarding tosh I'd once passed, as an exercise in mischief, to Skipton. I discovered from her that Skipton, in a craven note, had ignored my treacly praise and had highlighted only my reservations, thereby ascribing her rejection to me, his trusted reader. Honour had to be satisfied and was exacted, sadistically, down the telephone. First, the journo expressed her interest in my work. Encouraged, I allowed my feature ideas to be coaxed out of me, like snails from their shells, then I listened as they were beaten to death, one by one, with the stiletto of revenge. When, over the next month, two of those same ideas turned up primped and flossed under the gleaming banner of her byline photo, I learned the meaning of the neglected word 'forbearance'.

Not long after that, I succumbed to the inevitable. I became an office administrator at Sproat's Pressings Ltd, one of the most respected names in the West of Scotland flange industry. I was no longer in thrall to Chloe's generosity and held high my head. I had no choice, my neck was in a collar, attached by a short chain to her father's fist.

For a while, I was part of a dynamic sales team. Being sluggish and uninterested, I fitted in neatly. So neatly that, following a complaint about my aptitude, or lack of it, I'd been summoned to see the Office Manager.

In his office, I'd explained my unorthodox approach to marketing – my congenital inability to sell things, my hope that clients, out of pity, might simply buy them. The Office Manager had nodded. He'd 'understood the situation'. Backstage, mutterings had ensued. Within a week, I'd found myself on the shop floor with an oily rag in my hand. Which gesture, even then, had only been for show. I polished lathes that didn't need polishing, forklifted metal units that might just as well, as far as I could see, have lain as peaceably and profitably where they'd previously rested. One morning, out of bored despair, I clocked in and headed straight to the toilets on the factory floor. Having armed myself with a cherry flapjack and a copy of *Hunger* by Knut Hamsun, I tried, by effort of will, to while away the hours until the lunchtime hooter and then, who knew, with any luck, beyond. In the cubicles, to and fro, arses came and went, rasping. I admired the wry defiance of a graffitied message carved on the cubicle door from an unknown bygone hand. 'Fuck the Moderator of the General Assembly of the Church of Scotland.' Now, theologically speaking, I didn't much care whether the Moderator was deflowered or remained forever inviolate. What I savoured was this exercise in considered futility, an absurdist statement against the tyranny of the ticking clock. Carved, I say again to you. Consider. How long would that gouging penknife or straining key have taken to impart its insolent passing message? Like Crusoe on the beach, I'd taken heart from this Man Friday's Scottish footprint. Someone else, a demented other, had known the heavy hands of a stopped clock pressing against his little life. Square flanges in round holes, what was to become of us? In a word – nothing. If we stayed long enough, we'd buckle with the heat. Here, at Sproat's Pressings, we could turn out a flange in any imprint you liked – it was easy once we'd melted the resistance of the metal.

One afternoon, I met Chloe. The cheap Albanian labour, grown cocky with numbers, leaned on their machines, munching cold meatballs with greasy hands. They whistled their appreciation with a coded gusto that skirted outright disrespect.

Chloe was on her lunch break. We walked to Costa and she pitched right in. 'I'm worried about Eric.'

'Why?'

'He's suffering.'

'Send him here to Flange World where a cheery welcome awaits all our customers.'

'I'm serious. He behaves erratically.'

'He's a doctor. Why doesn't he treat himself?'

'He does,' said Chloe, in a quiet voice. 'But you know that, don't you?' It was the first time we'd acknowledged between us, her brother Eric's little extra-curricular pharmaceutical habits.

Of course, whether she, or indeed I, knew the full extent of these habits was a matter for conjecture – hers, on this occasion.

'Some days he goes out, pretending to be at work and sits around Waterstone's reading Laforgue and Celine.'

I was surprised. 'How do you know about Laforgue and Celine?'

She looked up, sharply. 'I shop at Fraser's – they stock all the big designer names – Baudelaire, Prada, Hardy. Don't be so condescending, you arse. I've got my Higher English which is more than you have.'

'Your tongue's rather brisk, Lady Penelope.'

'I wish yours was – you haven't come near me in weeks.' Chloe said this with a gamey smile but it had surprised us both, pulling us up short. Not knowing what else to do, we steered around the subject.

'Do your mum and dad know about Eric?'

'They try to look out for him but Eric has such a fragile temperament.'

'Serves him right for being talented.'

'Could you speak to him? He likes you.'

'I hardly know him.'

'That's not important – you're on his wavelength. Mum worries but tries to keep it from Dad. He has enough on his plate with the firm.'

'Ah, yes, the firm,' I said. For spite, I kissed the breast of my boiler suit.

'Would you give it a try?' said Chloe, ignoring my brattish gesture. 'I know it's not easy for you working here but it's only temporary.'

I felt guilty. I realised I was in no small part responsible for the tight frown that was starting to characterise Chloe's brow so I said yes.

'Good.'

Chloe looked relieved as she slipped me a tenner for more lattes. 'And don't worry about the . . . you know, other business. Between you and me – we'll work it out.' She gave me a grateful little peck on the cheek. Any touching in public had become unusual between us – or private, come to that.

'Leave it with me,' I said, pocketing the tenner. 'I'll have a word with him.'

A few nights later, I entered Eric's private domain – his converted basement playroom. Above us Dad dozed on the chesterfield, glass in hand, Mum made urgent calls to charity friends across the golf course, enlisting help against the latest pandemic scourge – fat people. Lard, suddenly, was all the rage, obesity was the new famine, just as beige was sometimes the new black. Anyway, I had a word with Eric.

And that word was 'aura'.

I was staring down a hole in the floor. A switch had gone click and a bare bulb on a winding length of plastic flex had shown me a basement. 'The stairs are steep,' Eric said, 'mind your head, there's a lintel coming up.'

I minded my head and peered into the gloom.

'You sleep here?'

'Yes,' said Eric Ross.

He led me along a corridor, passing through musty chambers where small arched entrances gave way to sudden large rooms, their bare walls showing the unadorned foundations of the house. The floors were solid and dry. Box files sat on discarded bureaux and side tables – good furniture in expensive wood, stuff that was way better than the foam filled junk my own mother was probably still paying off from the seventies. A full-sized billiard table stood covered with a dust sheet and, on top of that, a ping-pong table rested, face down, kissing it. I picked up a badminton racquet and swished it a few times through the air.

'Do you play?'

'No,' I said, sheepishly, and put it down.

It was the rambling cellar of a fairly typical Milngavie villa but, to someone from my background, it might as well have been the Palace of Versailles.

'Come on,' said Eric.

I came on and slammed him accidentally in the back as he stopped by another dark entrance.

'Sorry.'

More light. Soft this time, considered light, not harsh and functional.

'Voila,' said Eric Ross.

We'd stepped into a large deep room. 'This is it – the inner sanctum,' said Eric. 'Guess what it's called.'

'I don't know,' I said.

Eric, smiling, pointed to a printed card above the door. I read 'Rat's Alley'. This tickled me. Eric was tickled that I was tickled. I didn't say but it was the careful placing of the apostrophe and the tidy black laminate frame that had amused me most. Well-brought-up people just can't help doing things nicely – even rebelling. I looked around. The walls were pale green and hung with paintings, real paintings, done with actual paint and brushes – not photographs of paintings which were the only kind I'd ever owned. There were no chairs, just two plump futons, in deeper green, positioned apart, their backrests at the same angle of languid harmony. There were books on wooden shelves and a hi-fi with a turntable and a stack of vinyl leaning in a unit. Eric Ross lived better under the ground than most people did above it. Something was troubling me.

The air was sweet with a nostalgic redolence I couldn't at first put my finger on, then could.

'This place smells like a pharmacy,' I said.

'Thank you,' said Eric.

He stepped behind what I'd taken for a breakfast bar. Actually, it was some sort of workbench – a line of wall cabinets adding to the impression of a kitchen area.

'Look,' said Eric.

He smoothly slid out a deep drawer on a rail. I'd expected to see stacked plates or Mr Muscle cleaner and kitchen rolls. Instead, vials and boxes of pills lined plastic trays, neatly signed with pop-up labels. I ran my curious hand over hypodermic needles in cellophane. I picked up a little booklet thing.

'Is this a prescription pad?'

Eric smiled and picked up a thick wad of little booklet things. 'In the past, I used them for ideas notepads. It's amazing what you can trade for grams and tabs.'

'Is that what you were doing at the party that night?'

'Do you object?'

'No,' I said.

'Quite right. We're all in the sense and sensibility business.'

He tossed the pads down carelessly and peeled a couple of Theakston's from a pack.

I picked up a vial of something. 'What's this stuff?'

'Potassium chloride,' said Eric. 'Be careful – it can do you in.'

'Why's it here?'

'I'll tell you when I know you better. Here – stick to beer.'

We stuck to beer, leaning on our futons, listening to T. S. Eliot on the turntable reading, what else, 'The Hollow Men' in his horrible droning voice.

'I've got *Four Quartets*,' I said, 'the EMI recording – I'll bring it over sometime.'

'Do that,' said Eric but he didn't sound keen. I got the impression he liked his Eliot one-note, dark and empty, like early punk, with no way out, no bigger picture. Eric turned the disc and I felt my heart sink. We started listening to 'The Fire Sermon'. I watched Eric's lips move and his eyes take on a faintly stricken look as he mouthed the lines, 'We think of the key, each in his prison. Thinking of the key, each confirms a prison . . .' Then he caught the look on my face, smiled self-consciously and went, 'Blah blah, blah de da, blah.'

Being a gifted writer, he'd improvised the blah blah bit, right there on the spot. Da is in the poem though. Fuck knows why. To bail them both out, him and T. S. Eliot, I said, 'I'm here to have a word with you. I'm supposed to give you a friendly talking-to.'

'Please do,' said Eric. His fine fingers fiddled with something small. He leaned over. 'Meanwhile, try this.' He gave me a small square of paper.

'What is it?'

'Lysergic acid diethylamide.'

'Acid? You mean *that* acid?'

Eric nodded. 'Industrial strength – 60s' strength. Not these pissy little modern teabags.'

I told him I was the wrong class. I told him the nearest I'd come to a state of Brahma was a bag of chips and a wank.

'Relax,' he said, 'you owe it to yourself. I'm taking one.'

'I can't – I'm working at Sproat's in the morning.'

'What better reason?'

We looked at each other.

'Go on, you're perfectly safe. You're in the presence of a doctor.' I watched as Eric put a tab on his tongue. Then I did the same.

And that's how the 'aura' word had come up.

My aura was violet – Eric told me so. 'The most vivid shade of violet I have, at any time, ever seen.'

Eric's aura, I recall, was green and I told him so.

'I know,' he said, 'hence the walls.'

Then he put his finger to his lips and said, 'Sshh. No more words.'

Having disposed of words, we were as one. Class, colour, creed and kind did not exist. Neither did futons and we sat, our backs propped against the green brick walls, our useless legs splayed before us, looking at each other beam. Brothers, sisters, failed suicides, fellow assholes, I bring great news from the rear of the cerebrum – light exists. Perhaps nothing else does.

We giggled with great glee, silently, inwardly, endlessly – you had to be there.

'If only it could be like this,' I thought, 'if only life could mean life and not just simple useless living.'

'I know what you're thinking,' said Eric.

'I know you know,' I said and, as I said it, I noticed the soles of Eric's shoes said 'Ecco'. And, for a moment – or maybe it was an hour – all was, if you'll excuse the term, harmony. I had been sick, I realised, and now was healed. I had lost my way but had now come home. If I'd looked in a mirror at that moment, I knew I would have seen *me* looking back – not the distorted caricature I had become. To enable me to glimpse this new improved won-derme, I moved my leg and, as I did so, a broom clattered to the bare wooden floor, shattering everything, including the moment.

If you went to uni in the sixties, chances are you know these sensations already. But bear in mind, your ways are not my ways – my ways are the ways of the tucked-in shirt, of the bargain-bin Merlot and of the casual loafer. I was a man of aftershave, not Aftershock.

After light, we crept from the house, Eric and I, and walked a long, long way. We still spoke of light, though, and of the many ways we might capture it and let its glitter filter through the slug word globules we strove, as writers, to make our slaves but which were not our slaves, rather our elusive dancing masters. Oh, word notes, rapt and pitiless, speak of precious light which makes all dumb and sightless by first dazzling us with its blessed stellar gaze.

Anyway, we said shit like that. Then we bought crisps and Twixes from Singh's in Maryhill Road.

When I got home – no, I'd been home, you know this, you've been on the house tour round the rear of my cerebrum – when I got back to the place where I lived, Chloe said, 'Well?'

'Well what?' I picked up her newspaper and pretended to read. The FTSI 100 danced like shoals of playful dolphins before my eyes.

'Where the hell've you been?'

'Having a word with Eric.'

'Till this time? What did you talk about?'

'Nothing.'

'I don't understand.'

'Neither do I. But we had a word and we said nothing. Now let's get back to bed.'

'I'm doing my best for you – you know that.'

'I know you are.'

'And so is Dad yet you're blaming him for what? For giving you a job?'

'I'm not blaming him – I'm blaming me.'

'I don't understand you.'

'Shouldn't we at least wait till after the wedding before you hit us both with that line?'

My fiancée's face flushed, like I'd slapped it.

My fiancée said, 'I can be cruel too, you know.'

But I wasn't listening. And a lover should always listen when a woman uses seven words where normally she might use a thousand.

Sitting on my fabric beanbag, I knew, instinctively, what I ought then to have done. I should have torn myself free with a mighty wrench, declared my independence, packed my bag and flounced off home to mother. One day, I'd find yet another room, make another even fresher fresh start. Maybe then, when

I'd given up hope, I'd meet a maiden, a simple shop girl, perhaps, or seamstress. But I'd met simple shop girls before – Karine for one – they were howling mental cases, spoiling for a ruck.

'Chloe, come out of the bathroom.'

'Go away.'

'I love you.' The love word – when the cards are sticky, play your trump. Never fails.

'Grow up. Then go away.'

OK, sometimes fails. Play another trump. 'Come on.' Weaselly intonation, implying apology, regretted words spoken in passion. 'We'll talk – we'll work it out together. We've a future to plan.'

'You don't want a future. And I'm not sure I do either.'

'Chloe, we need to talk about the wedding.' Marriage – my biggest face card.

'Don't be ridiculous. There's no prospect of our ever marrying.'

'Chloe.'

'I mean it.'

'Not the wedding then – you choose. We'll talk about whatever you want.'

A pause.

'Chloe?'

'OK.' I heard her rise from the edge of the bath. 'But I don't want to hear any more talk about weddings.'

'The subject's dead, I promise – off the menu.'

She came out, looking tired and long-suffering, and I perked us both up with some coffee.

Ten minutes later, as I was spooning in a touch of demerara, Chloe said, 'You want to get married? You mean it?'

I looked over at her. 'Yes,' I said. 'I mean it.'

'We can make each other happy,' said Chloe.

'I know we can,' I said.

Happy – I made a mental note to look it up in the dictionary.

CHAPTER FOUR

I hear you're getting married,' said Denis Rourke.

We were having lunch in the Cul de Sac. I say 'lunch' – a small green salad apiece and three bottles of Chardonnay. My skinny wallet had hoped I'd muster the sense to stop at two.

'Who told you that?'

'Morag. I bumped into her.'

'Where, in your bedroom?'

'It's not like that. She's sweet. We're friends.'

'You mean you're too bored to screw her.'

'It's prudent. These days you can't take chances. You have to keep your exes on message or they'll stitch you up in "Surveillance", maybe even the Sundays.'

'What's "Surveillance"?'

'*Daily Mirror* – Celebrity Hotline. You know, "Spotted – Denis Rourke, wearing a Rainmate, queuing for a bus in Maryhill Road".'

'You'd suit a Rainmate.'

'Agreed. Be damaging though. An image like that gets around, I'd never wave a nine-millimetre in *Taggart* again. Might as well be dead.'

'You were dead in *Taggart*. They binned you for a better corpse.'

'I've been binned from better shows than *Taggart*,' said Denis. 'By the way, did you hear about Walter Urquhart?'

I braced myself for the bad news of more good news for Walter Urquhart. 'What about him?'

'He's dead.'

'What?'

'Suicide.'

'You're kidding?' I thrilled, deliciously, the way one does.

'Cross my heart. Pills. Neighbour found him two days ago, stinking up his armchair.'

'That's mad. He had a script in development.'

'Tell me about it. He'd promised me the part of the socialist brickie. I've been doing tantric yoga to get myself in the right headspace.'

'Couldn't you just have worked with some real brickies?'

'What am I? Sir Christopher Wren? Fuck that.'

'What'll happen to *Cement Wedding*?'

'Binned. Too problematic. Dead guys can't do rewrites.'

I didn't understand. I couldn't comprehend. 'Why would anybody kill himself when he had a script in development?'

'You saw him. He was deeply ugly.'

'Yes but he had a script. In development. A real live film on the go – with Ken Ordinaire.'

'There's more to life than movies.'

'No, there isn't.'

'True. But you hardly knew Walter. Sad bastard. Always looking for love. Not smart like us.'

'Like you – I'm getting married, remember?'

'Course you are. Where you living these days?'

'Chloe's flat.'

'Where you working?'

'Chloe's dad's factory.'

'Wow, you must be really loved-up.'

'It's not a career move, Denis.'

'Did I say that? No offence, but you've got to *have* a career before you can move it anywhere.'

My eyes did wounded dignity.

Denis grinned. 'And take that flush off your face, I've been there. Believe me. Here's one sentence you'll never hear from any actor's lips – "No wife of mine is going out to work."' Denis laughed. He was feeling relaxed. He was speaking to someone less successful than himself.

'OK, better go,' he said. 'See you at the premiere, yeah?'

'What premiere?'

'Don't be like that. I thought writers were generous.'

'What premiere?'

Realisation dawned, embarrassing us both – but chiefly me.

'Aiden hasn't sent you an invite?'

'No.'

'Oh.'

I shuffled a bit. 'It's not his fault,' I said. 'I've moved house. I'm not working at Alba any more. How would he have found me?'

'Same way he found me.'

'You've spoken to him?'

'Yes. Well, not him – his agent. Aiden's in LA till the end of the week. Relax – it's just an oversight. I'll speak to him.'

'You got an invite?'

'I told you, I spoke to his agent.'

'You haven't got an invite either, have you?'

'Leave it with me,' Denis said. 'Jeez, some people.'

So I left it with him. And he left the bill with me, like it was fair exchange.

I stood outside the Cul de Sac, looking up and down the lane.

My head was mad with drink. The cobblestones were bleak with drizzle. Meeting Denis had helped fill the vacuum of my stolen day off. A few more hours of illicit boredom and I could return to my partner and be legitimately bored. 'You should go home now,' I said aloud, as though I were some helpful stranger giving myself sound advice. 'Turn back, leave well alone.' But my shoes, as always, had a mind of their own. When you're desperate and somebody gives you a dice, what have you to lose by giving it a throw?

Ahead, through the trees, lay Fortress Alba.

I decided to storm it.

Two hours later, I was sitting on a bench in the Botanic Gardens. Sober. Bleary from the comedown. The living room of my soul, trashed and scorched. On the upside though, two scripts, in folders, lay across my lap.

Looking back, what happened in that couple of hours started everything.

Here's how it went.

'Hi, Alex, how you doing? Looking good – you been working out?'

Alex, the old one-legged doorman, had looked at me in a quizzical fashion. His job was to inspect your security pass. He knew me by sight, though, so I'd wrong-footed him by being pleasant, at speed. While he was still deciding whether to throw me out or give a matey chuckle, I was through the swing doors and into the bowels of the building.

'Yo, Rufus! How was Guam?'

'Hot and black.'

'Just the way I like it, ha ha!'

On I sped along the corridor, ignoring Rufus's look of discomfited surprise, the acrid stink of stale alcohol from my lunch with Denis wafting behind me like aftershave. Adjust the give-away voice volume. 'Hi, Ellen – hi, Isobel. Keeping busy?' Slit-eyed glances from the two gnarled telly crones with their red and blonde hair helmets. They'd seen the likes of me before. The trajectory of a loose cannon may be unpredictable but, by the laws of media physics, it may only move down. I threw open the door of the main office and tossed an imaginary hat on to a non-existent stand.

'Hello, Moneypenny, I'm back!'

Moneypenny's desk was empty. The office though was crowded; new, strange young faces occupied desks tilted at unfamiliar angles to accommodate the crush of personnel. Somebody laughed, nervously. Taking a deft mental account of the situation, I said, 'You were only supposed to blow the bloody doors off!' I was being ironic at the expense of irony itself. Any fool could see that – me, for one. But the new young people didn't care about such finely crafted distinctions – it just wasn't funny, that was all.

The door of Skipton's office opened, rescuing me. Joan appeared, a short white pillar of scripts in her hands.

'My, what a surprise! What are you doing here?' She dumped the scripts heavily on a desk corner.

'Seeing Ally,' I said, 'got some news for him.'

Joan seemed puzzled.

I headed her off. 'Department's busy, I see.'

'It's all go. We've had the green light for a sitcom series and our first full-length feature. We've a lot of new faces.'

I beamed out at the new faces. 'Hi, guys.'

Not a flicker. 'I've been starting a few fires myself, Joan,' I said, 'to chuck some irons into.'

'Well, that's all anybody can do. No offence but could you put that script down please – it's confidential.'

I tossed the script back on the pile, watched it skim off, picked it up off the floor and smoothed its creased pages. I assumed a casual tone. 'So what's the full-length feature?'

Joan slid the script pile deftly, safely along the desk.

For some reason I twirled imaginary mustachios and said 'And, more to the p-p-p-point, what dashed blighter has written it, what?'

Joan's face flushed on my behalf, not hers. She gave me a look.

I felt cold sweat dripping from my armpits. 'Don't worry,' I said, 'didn't mean to put you on the spot. I expect I'll read the gory details in the papers after the seasonal launch.'

Matter finished, Joan smiled, put her headset on and stared at her computer screen. 'What time's your appointment with Ally?'

'Ah . . . well.'

'Only he didn't say you were . . .'

'I'm not,' I said. 'It'll only take a minute. I'll just go in.'

'You can't just go in.'

'It'll be all right. I'll just go in.

'No, don't.' She tugged off her headset – too late.

Skipton was standing in the middle of the room, knee slightly bent, neck inclined at an awkward angle, his arms stiffly enfolding a girl. His mouth was on her mouth. It looked to me less like he was kissing her than trying to inflate her. The girl had a bare midriff and sawn-off cargo pants. Skipton removed his mouth from her mouth and looked at me. 'Knock, knock,' he said.

'Who's there?' I said.

'You – but not all there, evidently,' said Skipton. Then he added, 'You remember Emma?' They uncoupled, still holding hands. 'Emma now has your old job.'

'She's welcome to it if it comes with those strings attached.'

Emma didn't look fazed. Skipton and I watched her as she sat down and crossed her legs. Then Skipton said, 'In case you're thinking of spreading poison, this is all above board. I've left Jane in a mature way and worked out good access arrangements for the children. Emma and I now share a small mews house in Kilmacolm.'

'A love nest,' said Emma, giving me a cold look. She'd picked up a yellow highlighter and was fiddling with it. She was already bored and impatient for me to leave.

'What do you want?' Skipton demanded. 'I'm expecting Scobie in a minute. His sitcom got the green light.'

I should have obeyed the red light that the mention of a green light had prompted. But I didn't. 'Green light?' I said. 'You don't get any green light for poxy telly. You get the nod, then they sling you some tenners.'

'You're pushing it. I'm going to have you thrown out of the building.' Skipton said that – my old friend and colleague, Ally Skipton. He reached for the phone.

'Don't,' I said.

He looked at me.

'I've got some news for you,' I said. 'Good news.'

'You've written *Celia Proust*, the sequel?' said Emma, without looking up.

'*Cement Wedding*'s been cancelled.'

Skipton and Emma looked at me, blankly. 'What are you talking about?'

'Walter Urquhart's dead. You know – the writer? Suicide.'

They were still looking at me. 'That news is two days old,' said Skipton. 'I hope you have an and?'

I didn't have an 'and'. I'd only brought a 'please' which I hadn't wanted to mention. It went like this – 'Please will you give me my old job back, please?' To fill the hole, I blurted out, 'Dead men can't do rewrites.'

'The rewrites are already in,' said Skipton, in a voice now as bored as Emma's face.

'I did them,' said Emma. 'We hope to shoot in the autumn when the funding is in place.'

I was confused. 'What about Ken Loach?'

'Option didn't stick. Slow with the money. Fatal hesitation. Fuck him – we moved faster.'

'That's our good news. Now what was yours?' asked Skipton.

My knees seemed to buckle. Things were moving too fast. 'That's all,' I said in a croaky voice.

Skipton perched confidently on his desk. 'Walter Urquhart was up for grabs – he didn't have an agent.'

'No,' Emma said, 'he negotiated his own contract.'

'I bet he did,' I said. 'I bet he negotiated whatever you chose to give him.'

'I warn you, don't be unpleasant,' Skipton said.

'He was only too happy to sign,' said Emma. 'To some people, it's about more than just money.'

Skipton nodded concurrence. 'The film will go out with his name as joint exec producer.'

'As a tribute,' said Emma.

'Yes,' said Skipton, 'It's not like we're complete bastards.'

They shared a little laugh.

'This is a first for Ess 'n' Em Productions,' Ess said, flashing Em a proud loving glance. I could see the whole dynamic of their relationship in that glance.

'Was there anything else?' said Emma.

'Yes, go fuck your . . .'

But Skipton was on me, steering me expertly by the elbow. 'I'll see you out,' he said.

At the door he made an announcement. 'A moment, everyone.'

'Everyone' meant anyone who wasn't talking into a telephone or faxing a document or photocopying a shooting schedule. Young fresh faces, fresh compared to mine that is, looked up.

'Take a good look at this man,' said Skipton. He pointed to me.

I gave a little wave, out of drink.

'I don't know how he got in here, since his security pass was long since withdrawn, but he is no longer welcome in this department. If he attempts to return to this department or indeed to the building, you have my authority to call security or the police and have him removed. Is that clear?'

All the people at their desks said that this was clear. Skipton turned to me, like I was a stranger or a beggar – or, worse, a failure. 'You will leave the building, please,' he said. He was looking at me but it was live theatre for his staff, his audience. 'You will not come back. I don't want to catch you here, ever again.' He turned away, went back to his office. Shut his door.

'You have to understand,' said Joan, showing me out of the department door, 'things change.'

I nodded. The door shut.

Outside, I walked quickly away. I turned a corner. Out of sight, I leaned against a garden wall and tried to stop shaking. Couldn't stop shaking. The thing about rage, even impotent rage, is that it has to go somewhere. Needs a target. Greater the rage, bigger the necessary target – has to be bigger than the rage itself, else the rage is futile, worse, ridiculous. More ridicule was not what I needed right now. Knowing this, realising this, I started to calm. Calm, I started to walk. I didn't know where.

Follow my feet. They knew. My shoes have always had an instinct all their own.

When I found myself near the corner of Otago Street, I stopped. Walter Urquhart had lived in Otago Street. I took out my mobile and phoned his number, the communal pay phone, hoping his landlady would answer.

She did.

Because Walter Urquhart had paid by the week, his rent was overdue. This meant that Mrs Langella, his landlady, was stuck with losing money. Mrs Langella didn't want to seem hard, she explained, as she wheezed her way upstairs, me following behind at a respectful distance, but Walter's sister Sandra, who'd had to come over from Canada, had pledged payment only till after the funeral and, well, a room can take time to let out, can't it?

Sometimes you're lucky, sometimes not, so it might as well be viewed now as Mrs Langella was stuck with losing money, though money isn't everything and she didn't want to seem hard. She stopped, mid wheeze, to canvas my opinion. 'Do you think I'm hard?'

'No,' I said.

'Good,' she said. 'I don't like it but business is business.'

'My sentiments exactly,' I said, professional to professional.

The sagging armchair Walter Urquhart had died in was facing the open window. There was a mop in a pail by the open door and a box of Flash on the dressing table.

The door was wide open so I walked right in. 'Do you mind if I take my time?'

'It's only a small flat,' Mrs Langella said. She hesitated but was keen to let so had taken the hint and shoved off. While I looked around the room and its tiny kitchen, I could hear Mrs Langella downstairs on the pay phone making arrangements for a council rubbish collection. When he was alive, I had known nothing about Walter Urquhart – now he was dead, I knew everything. Because I could, I leafed through his chest of drawers, the way one does, disturbing pants and vests, looking for personal secrets or little wedges of folding money set aside for rainy days but Mrs Langella had probably already done that because business is business. In the dusty utility wardrobe, I found a couple of jackets on wire hangers, including the denim one Walter Urquhart had usually worn because he'd thought it made him look young and bohemian. In a breast pocket I found one of my own business cards but no money, apart from small coins, and no secrets.

On his cheap Ikea-type desk sat a diary. It was black with a red spine and gold embossed lettering. The lettering said 'Knox & McKimmey, Chartered Accountants Ltd.' I picked it up and slid it down my waistband.

On the shelf above his desk, I located what I'd really been looking for, the few box files containing works completed and in progress. In one marked 'Correspondence' was a letter of encouragement from Ken Ordinaire about *Cement Wedding*. There had been two other positive-sounding letters from Festival Films and Gimlet Productions about scripts he'd submitted called *Smoking Gun* and *Love Letter Blues*. Let's see, had they returned those scripts or retained them? I perused the print for the magic key, the only two words that matter a damn on any letter of rejection, no matter how thickly the syrup of praise is spread – 'however' or 'unfortunately'.

Add to those the more informal 'The trouble is . . .' because that's how Festival Films had phrased it, before urging Urquhart to rewrite. Gimlet, too, had urged rewrites. This was significant. I knew from experience that you didn't urge a resubmission unless you felt the script truly had something to offer – otherwise what you ended up with was duff writers sending you endless versions of the same script, each one bad in a different way. On the other hand, neither Festival nor Gimlet had, at this stage, formalised their interest by optioning the scripts. In the immortal words of Quentin Crisp, 'You know they mean it when they pay your fare.'

Once again, Walter Urquhart was up for grabs.

I found *Smoking Gun* and *Love Letter Blues* in the W. I. P. file. I pulled them out and stuck them down my rear waistband. I already had the desk diary down my front so it was hard to squeeze the scripts, even flat, over my arse.

I was in the act of struggling to button up my weirdly bulging jacket when Mrs Langella spoke, startling me.

'You have chance to look around?'

'Yes. It's a very nice room – small yet compact.'

'You want to take?'

'Let me think about it.'

'Is a nice room – go very soon.'

'I know. There's somebody walking around out there now with his name on it. Doesn't even know it yet.'

'Not you though?'

'I'll be in touch.'

Mrs Langella sighed. 'OK.'

I took a last look around the room. I wanted always to remind myself of its wretchedness. This was how most writers died – ignored to death. Not forgotten – how could they be, when they'd never, in the first place, been remembered?

At the street door, I let myself out. The landlady didn't bother to say goodbye. She'd known I was a time waster.

So there I sat in the Botanic Gardens, the two scripts I'd stolen from Walter Urquhart on my lap, wasting the last of that time before I might return home for dinner and Chloe. I already knew what I wanted to do with the scripts, which was why I'd taken them from Walter Urquhart's room. The diary, though, had been sheer prurience. I stood at the top of Byres Road, outside the Post Office, and leafed through it, looking for references to myself. Finding none, I slung it in the bin. *Smoking Gun* – not a bad title; but *Love Letter Blues* – that would have to go. A recent article in *Variety* had declared 'Blues' in a title to be 'seventies redolent'. And since seventies retro had been done to death, the choice for a budding screenwriter was simple – spend a billion dollars rebranding retro into re-retro or else, duh, lose 'Blues' from his title. And you never knew, if Urquhart could knock it off once with *Cement Wedding*, then why not again?

One day I'd be a somebody.

Even if that somebody wasn't altogether, strictly speaking, me.

CHAPTER FIVE

'Sam and Morag will be bridesmaids. I've asked them.'

'Uh-huh,' I said.

We were in the bathroom, in different stages of readiness. Chloe was in a slip, doing her eyes. I was waiting to use the underarm deodorant.

'You've no objection?'

'If you've already asked them, what's the point of my objecting?'

'Don't be like that. If you'd rather call it off . . .'

'So call it off.'

'I wish you'd told me. I've just asked Sam and Morag to be bridesmaids.'

'Jesus.'

'It's you – you make me insecure. You never want to talk about our wedding.'

'It's not for months.'

'Just the same . . . There's a gift list under the fridge magnet on the door of the chest freezer. If you have any ideas, make a note.'

'I will – I'll make a note. Now hurry up. We can't be late.'

'I'm excited. We haven't been out in ages – and to a premiere . . .'

I slid my hand over the curves of her satin slip.

Chloe turned and shaped for me to kiss her so I did. Her breath was garlic and toothpaste.

She attempted a vixen temptress look. 'We're not that late. We could squeeze in a wee cuddle, if you like?'

My stomach squirmed slightly. A 'wee cuddle' plus garlic. Hold me back.

'Let's save it for later,' I said, doing unconvincing randy sea dog acting.

'OK.' Chloe applied a few more strokes from a tiny brush, turned. 'There, do you like my eyes?' She fluttered them at me, as if a few dabs of black dye had the power to cancel out the bad things.

'I love your eyes,' I said, 'they cancel out the bad things.'

'I like that. It's a nice thing to say. You mean that?'

'Yes,' I said. 'I loved you the first moment I saw you. And I love you now even more than I loved you the first moment I saw you.'

'What bad things?'

'There are no bad things. The bad things melt away.'

'That isn't an answer. They have to be there before they can melt away.'

'There are no bad things. I adore you.'

'That's an easy word to throw around.'

'Not for me.'

'You mean it?'

'Yes.'

Urgh. Bitch. Shut the fuck up and get ready.

Bob Hope once joked that he left England when he realised he'd 'very little chance' of becoming king. Woody Allen once joked that his interest in crime varied according to how successful he felt. Joe Orton once joked that there was no such thing as a joke. I thought these things as we hung around the foyer of what used to be the Odeon but was now Cineworld in Renfield Street. We were trying not to gawp at the famous people.

'Look, there's Aiden!'

'Don't point. And that's not Aiden – it's a fat slob with a smirk.'

'I thought it was Aiden.'

'Aiden isn't here. He won't come.'

'It's his big night.'

'Wrong. It's *our* big night. His big night's next week at the London premiere in Leicester Square.'

After the screening, crowds milled around the bar. There hadn't been a bar years ago when I'd queued alone for *Eraserhead* and *Days of Heaven*. Small-time Scottish producers in dark linen suits, with dark turtlenecks and cropped hair, were holding earnest conversations with other small-time Scottish producers in dark linen suits with dark turtlenecks and cropped hair. Everybody adjusted their specs and hitched their shoulder bags, hinting in modest voices about big things just up ahead. Young actors, with mussed hair and rising profiles, found themselves approached by PR girls with dreary friends whom the actors would tolerate till the praise ran out.

Older actors stood about dying for a fag, looking tetchily nervous, both encouraging and dreading the approach of a dark linen suit, with yet another steaming turd of a project-in-development which might, who knew, with enough star names and Lotto money, be born and quickly die, buried in the shallow grave of straight-to-DVD, having yielded enough spondulicks to provide for a year's school fees, with possibly enough spare change for a tummy tuck for the wife.

Amid the sneerers and liggers were the unemployed collectives, an 'unfortunately' of writers, a 'me' of actors, all hunched and stricken, with rueful mouths and downcast eyes, seeing the night as a character test that each had been doomed, individually, to fail. Just as Aiden's film had been destined to succeed. Or so I feared.

'Didn't I tell you, didn't I say I'd get you on the list?' Denis Rourke came up behind, then around me, tickling my waist and winking a big flirty one at Chloe.

'Ta,' I said.

'There's no need to gush. So go on – what did you think?'

'I thought it was interesting. But flawed.'

'Yeah, I liked it too. It's a bastard isn't it? He'll be insufferable. But, then, so will we.'

Chloe laughed. Denis liked her laughing. 'You're looking very glam tonight, Chloe.'

'Thank you,' Chloe said, then to me, 'I hope you're taking notes.'

I felt a twinge of sexual jealousy, which was an inconvenience since I was already struggling to keep a lid on the hissing vat of professional jealousy that was bubbling within me. To change the subject I said, 'Did you know that *Cement Wedding*'s got the go-ahead?'

Denis's face froze. 'Who from?'

'Alba.'

'Alba? Who's casting?'

'It's already been cast.'

'It's been cast?'

'So I hear.'

'I didn't get a call.'

'Ah.' A solid jab. Pain in his eyes. Point to me.

'You'd have thought I'd get a call. I was promised the socialist brickie.'

'Things change. Mistah Urquhart – he dead. Speaking of which, did you go to the funeral?'

'I meant to. Something turned up.'

'A job?'

'A pub.' Denis's sunny face shadowed. Cloud gathered. 'Anyway, it wasn't my responsibility to go to his funeral. Let the fucker who got the socialist brickie go to his lousy funeral, God rest him . . . who got the socialist brickie, by the way?'

'I can't remember but he was definitely a fucker.'

'That's all that matters. I want a vodka before the free bar runs out.' He turned and went.

'Nice to see you again, Denis,' called Chloe.

Denis didn't answer.

'What's up with him?'

'Actors,' I shrugged, perking up.

My goading of Denis had offered me small recompense for the flaming spear in my heart – 'Executive Producers Liam Neeson and Aiden Lang.' Right there, on the closing credits. Just as 'Written by Aiden Lang' had been on the opening credits, over steamy shots of Angelina Jolie soaping her silken skin in the shower. No script doctors then. No additional bearers of the writing baton, no relay, but a solo race to glory. The plot was tight and it worked. The jokes were punchy and worked. The characters, OK, the characters were . . . what? Aidenesque? This film was not bad. In Scottish terms, that made it more than good – it was a triumph. I'd watched the audience watching the film. To be in an audience is to be demeaned. Their up-tilted heads, slack mouths, the benediction of the celluloid glare exalting Aiden, making him big out of our collective smallness.

'Are you all right?' Chloe asked on the taxi ride home.

I tried to shape words with my mouth but could not speak.

'Don't measure yourself against Aiden,' she comforted. 'I don't care if you never write another word.'

'I do.'

Once home, I locked myself away to gather my thoughts.

'Come out of the bathroom,' Choe called.

'No.'

'What are you doing?'

'Planning our wedding.'

'Do it out here where there are no sharp things.'

'Soon.'

Eventually, with Chloe in bed, I emerged. In the bathroom I'd offered up a silent, hopeful prayer that Aiden's film might flop hideously. Tomorrow, I'd send him a congratulatory card.

Next morning, in the prefab shop of Sproat's Pressings, the staccato blast of drills had rattled even muffled ears. Electric cranes whined overhead then clanked their chains and hooks as loads slammed ground-ward, resting. Stolid men in boiler suits hit mighty cylinder lids with clanging hammers. Between bouts of banging, they'd break for a piss to talk in rasping bantering voices about the Hoops or the Gers and who was or wasn't a shite player, their lines of allegiance drawn along the religious divide. And, if it was a long piss, perhaps they'd extend their bile to include *Big Brother* on that Channel 4 and whether it was or wasn't a shite programme, their lines of allegiance drawn this time along the generational divide.

Seated in my favoured cubicle, I felt like some creepy father confessor, my task to listen, never counsel. The two scripts I'd stolen from Walter Urquhart lay across my lap, freshly read, the question of their merit now resolved. Shite or not shite? Emphatically the latter. Doable or not doable? Emphatically, at this stage, the latter.

It was all there – the inciting incident, the turning points, the beats, the three-act structure. Urquhart had done his Robert McKee screenwriting course, plain to see. I'd known this to be true, having seen him do it for myself three years earlier at the STET building on Dowanhill Road. Showily amused, I'd watched as Walter, head down, complimentary biro moving diligently across complimentary pad, had compiled the notes from the guru's wisdom that had helped lead him and, therefore, me to his suicide and my possible rebirth.

The stories themselves were serviceable. Both were psycho-
logical thrillers so he'd done his market research too. Of course,
the trick with those things is to keep them plausible, as far as
you are able, then gather speed and frenzy before finally, in the
third act, waving goodbye to all common sense and lifting off
like a ski jumper to land safely in the arms of another feel-good
Hollywood ending. Which was what he had done with both
scripts. So what I'm saying is that, although I'd stolen Walter
Urquhart's work and hoped to sell it on, I was also slightly
embarrassed by it as I'd also felt it to be somewhat beneath me.
Does that sound ungrateful? On the other hand, pragmatism
told me that Walter Urquhart had made sensible choices. With
those sorts of script, engine is all. That's what they always told
you. Screenplays are structure, they'd say. Engine is all, they'd say.
So you'd give them engine then they'd say very good, you have a
plot that works but where's the character, the texture? We miss
the colour. Where is the yeast? We are yeast cravers – let there be
yeast.

I'd thought I'd been good at yeast – until *Celia Proust*. Now I
didn't know. In the end, as William Goldman famously
remarked, 'nobody knows anything'.

I wasn't even sure about that any more.

Luckily, I knew somebody who was wise enough to know as
little as William Goldman.

'Actually, it's more difficult than you'd imagine getting a hold
of a little snort.'

'But you're a doctor.'

'A junior doctor – I can't even afford to run a car.'

'Serves you right for having expensive habits.'

'Habit. Please. It's more reassuring as a tidy generic singular.
Come on, come on.'

It was raining and Eric had his parka hood up. He'd just put
in a twelve-hour shift at the Western. We stopped by the lights in

Dumbarton Road, waiting for the green man. Turning traffic from the Byres Road filter lane spat black puddle water at us. The right turn up Byres Road marked the demarcation line, broadly speaking, between the Hillhead pubs and the Partick pubs, the Hillhead pubs being regarded as more upmarket. A lot of staff from the hospital would turn off right for The Living Room or the converted church that was Cottier's. Eric, for reasons of his own, preferred to avoid the Hillhead pubs.

'Working at different hospitals makes it easier and harder.' He took a small sip from his Red Bull and put it down. 'You're moonlighting so they're not going to see you again. On the other hand, because they're not going to see you again, the nurses play by the book and won't trust you with the key to the controlled drugs cupboard.'

'So what do you do?'

'I rummage,' Eric said. 'In a hospital, you can always find a reason for being wherever you are – looking for case notes . . . whatever.'

I took a sip from my spritzer and glanced around. The bar was choked with middle-aged men in baseball caps and too-young trainers, swearing and drinking pints. No one else among this clientele would have drunk a spritzer. Not men, not women, not dogs. Gay dogs, maybe. I came to the point. 'So what do you think?'

'I sympathise,' Eric said.

'You could do more than that. You could work on them for me. Script-doctor them.'

He looked pained. 'I don't do that any more.'

'At least read them then and tell me what you think.'

'I don't want to. You might be offended.'

'Believe me,' I said, 'I won't be offended.'

Eric pulled a rueful face and picked up a script from the table. I watched as he read the title page. '*Smoking Gun*,' he said, 'by

Ivan Rugg.' He flicked through the stapled wad of pages. 'Why that name? Why not use your own name?'

'I don't like my own name,' I said.

'When did you write it?'

'My name, you mean?'

'No, the scripts.'

'I might change my own name.'

'That's not what I asked you. Are these scripts out of your bottom drawer?'

'What makes you say that?'

'If you want me to be honest, I may as well start now.'

'No,' I said, 'they're both new works.' Which was true. Just not new by me, that's all.

Eric put down *Smoking Gun*. He picked up *Love Letter Blues*. He said, 'There was an article in *Variety* recently . . .'

'"Blues" in the title,' I said. 'I know – I might change that.'

'If you know, why did you call it that in the first place?'

'Just read the scripts. Would you do that for me?'

'Don't be so nippy.'

'Then don't you be so nippy.'

Eric rubbed his eyes, shrugged. 'Maybe it's me,' he said. 'I've been stuck with cancer cases all day.'

'I don't know how you do your job.'

'It has its compensations,' Eric said. 'Put your hand in my pocket.'

'What?'

'Just do it. Be discreet.'

I did it. I was discreet. I felt a small glass shape. 'What is it?'

'Morphine.'

'Won't they miss it?'

'Why? It isn't missing. Officially it's been used on a lymphoma case. Unofficially, the lymphoma case got an injection of water and I got this.'

'You can't go on this way. You're bound to be caught.'

'Only two more years then I'll be a registrar. If I stay, Dad'll support me – if I quit, he won't. Simple as.'

'What will you do when you've qualified?'

'Write. Remember Flaubert? "Writing is a dog's life . . ." '

' "but the only one worth living." '

We picked up our drinks and sipped in silence.

'Flaubert's father was a surgeon,' I said.

'Yes,' Eric said. But he wasn't listening, he was thinking. Finally he said, 'I'll do it – I'll read your scripts.'

'You will?'

'On one condition.'

'Name it.'

'You don't know what the condition is yet.'

'Just name it.'

Eric reached into his battered leather document case.

'What's that?'

'A script. A new one. I've just finished writing it.'

I was taken aback. 'I'm taken aback,' I said.

He held out the wedge of A4 in its clear plastic jacket. 'Go on.'

'You want me to read it?'

'Yes,' he said, 'that's the condition.' His fretting face looked youthful when he smiled.

I took the script and read 'An original screenplay by Eric Ross.' I was puzzled. 'Why no title?'

'Gimme.'

Eric took the script from its folder, took out a pen and started printing something in block letters. 'If this screenplay is ever published,' he said, 'I want it to look like this.' He passed the script back to me.

'Green ink?'

'Symbolism,' smiled Eric Ross. He jabbed his pen at the script. 'Good title, uh?'

I read his good title. 'Looking at the Stars.'

'I haven't mentioned it to Dad for obvious reasons.'

'Sure. How about Chloe?'

'No, don't tell Chloe either – she might ask to read it and, well, that could be a problem.

'Why?'

'You'll see when you read it.'

'OK, I won't tell Chloe.'

'In that case, we have a deal. Agreed?'

'Agreed. Cheers.'

And we were. We were cheered. At least I was. I walked home through the slashing rain, not caring. The uneven pavements sloshed my shoes. 'Let it rain,' I thought, 'I can't get any wetter than I already am.'

I turned my key in the lock and shivered as the warm glow of the flat engulfed me. Shaking out my coat, I could hear laughing voices from the living room. I thought of my old room in Cecil Street and smiled with something like relief as I realised how much my life had changed.

'Hello, Sam. Hello, Morag.'

Chloe smiled, didn't say hello.

'We were just leaving,' said Sam.

'You don't have to,' I said, 'stay and have a drink. Chloe, let's have a drink.'

'We're having a drink.'

'Have another – let's raid the wine rack. Three Chilean reds for a tenner in Shivram's Bargain Den and you know what? *It's not bad.*'

Sam smiled – even Morag fractured her face. At a dip in the evening, women like a slightly drunk man around for sport. Chloe went off to fetch the hooch while I went into my comic turn as 'inebriated but good-natured male who wedges his foot in his asshole for the entertainment of others'. The appreciation of my audience soon instructed me that this was a role I could inhabit without any uncomfortable overstretching of my acting ability. In comedy, the line between being laughed at and laughed with can, at times, be a fine one. To a drunk man in his own living room, there is no such distinction – no lines are fine, all are pleasantly blurred. By the time Chloe had returned from the kitchen, I was wearing Sam's hat and talking about penis envy. I eyed the drinks tray. 'Where's my drink?'

'In the teapot,' said Chloe.

Before I could retort, she headed me off and started in about a legal paper she'd read – human embryo cultivation, its ramifications, legal and ethical. A real crowd-pleaser. 'We can't keep rolling back the frontiers of medicine,' Chloe was saying, 'then expect the law to play catch-up. There must be harmonious conjunction. *Festina lente.*' What that meant in plain English was that every legal shark in the water had sensed another fat killing and was waiting for the human rights boat to throw them meat.

'Yadda, yadda,' I said.

Chloe looked at me. 'What?'

'Blah, blah, yadda, ya . . .'

I was swaying slightly. I was still wearing Sam's hat. I didn't want to talk about harmonious conjunction and was making my objections clear. I'd wanted to talk about chicks and dicks. So did Sam and Morag. I could see it in their faces.

'What would you know about the subject?' Chloe said. 'Pray enlighten us.'

Pray? How could I be engaged to anybody who said 'pray'?

'Take Sam's hat off.'

'No, leave it on,' Sam said.

'Yes, leave it on,' agreed Morag, slyly. She'd sensed something bad impending – humiliation or rancour or both – and was gleeful.

That night, the noise of my own snoring woke me or maybe Chloe had given me a shove – I don't know. I do know that one minute I had been enjoying a pleasant chortling dream and the next I was awake and sensing tension in the stillness of the room. 'You awake?'

'Yes,' said Chloe. She was lying on her side, turned away from me. I detected trouble. To test the mood, I stroked her arm, then her leg, then I started to get interested as my hand travelled up and I began to lift her nightdress. 'Don't,' she said.

I stopped. I groaned and snuggled up closer. 'OK,' I said, 'cuddling is nice too.' I slid my hand down to rest on her hand, delicious warm, delicious heat-scented woman, her back shapely in my hollow, delicious.

I heard Chloe's voice say, 'This isn't really working, is it?'

My heart chilled. My hand on Chloe's hand squeezed for reassurance. Realisation dawned. 'Where's your engagement ring?' My own voice had become vigilant, attentive. The alert had been sounded and we were on the parade ground, tense before battle.

'I took it off. It's been off all night. You never noticed.'

'Why'd you have to keep testing me? You know I love you.'

'And I love you. But marriage is a practical arrangement as much as an emotional one.'

'What's that supposed to mean?'

'You think I like having to pull in my reins, buy grotty Chilean red from Shivram's whatsit . . .?'

'Bargain Den. Things'll change. I won't always work in the factory. Just lighten up.'

She let me run my hand up her thigh.

I said, 'Maybe you should speak to Sam and Morag.'

'I did.'

'What did they say?'

'That's personal.'

'Tell me.'

'They told me to dump you before it's too late.'

I stopped stroking.

'What?'

'Sam likes you but thinks you're a lost cause. Morag thinks you'll drag me down.'

Chloe removed my hand from her hand, swung her legs over to the floor and scrunched her feet into her slippers.

'Those treacherous crows – they sat here laughing.'

'Nobody twisted your arm to make a fool of yourself.'

'I entertained them at my own expense. I told them stories about my past.'

'I know you did. I don't like it when you tell stories about your past – it accentuates the differences between us. Am I supposed to spend the rest of my life smiling gamely while you turn your life into an anecdote that I can't share?'

'You pick your moments to have a row.'

'It isn't a row – it's a process. I'm sorry if the crossroads in our relationship has come at an awkward social hour for you.' Chloe took a sip from the Evian bottle she kept at her bedside. 'I can't sleep. I'm going to take a Sominex.' She picked up her pillow.

'Where are you going?'

'To sleep on the couch – I think it's best.' But she didn't move. Maybe she'd planned to whistle and have the couch come to her.

The penny dropped. I picked up my pillow. 'I'll sleep on the couch,' I said.

'For tonight,' said Chloe. 'Then tomorrow you should go back to your mother. That's if she exists. All this time and I've never even got to meet her.'

'Don't push me,' I said. I tried to keep my temper but couldn't. On the way out, I said, 'Those two slags – they were supposed to be your bridesmaids.'

'They're more than that – they're my friends.'

'I thought they were my friends too.'

'They are. They're trying to help us both before we make a big mistake.'

'You're insane listening to them.'

'They've only confirmed what I'd refused to accept. That you and I are very different people.'

'You're being unreasonable.'

'Time will tell.'

And she shut the door.

'What did *The Herald* say?'

'"A fine film – Lang has taken on a Hollywood genre at its own game and won."'

'Only "fine"? That's faint praise. That's praise for the aspiration, not the achievement. What about the nationals? What about *The Guardian*?'

'*The Guardian* liked it,' said Denis Rourke. ' "Quirky", they said, ' "with unexpected twists and turns".'

' "Quirky" – that's a word they use for geniuses and amateurs. And Aiden's not a genius.' We were in Denis's living room. I'd poured the last of the wine I'd brought. 'Do you think Aiden's a genius?'

'What was his post code?'

'G11.'

'That's F-band council tax – the real geniuses are in G12.'

I started to cry, suddenly, then stopped.

'You can stay here a couple of nights,' Denis Rourke offered.

'Thanks,' I said, 'I'm all right.' Through my sobs I managed to ask, 'Did Angelina Jolie go to the premiere in Leicester Square?'

'Don't you read the papers? She went everywhere.'

'With Aiden?'

'Of course not with Aiden. She's done a hundred films, she's met a hundred greasy writers.' Denis gave me a joshing prod with his foot. 'Anyway, who shags writers? You remember the old joke?

About the ambitious starlet who was so dumb she slept with the writer?' Denis grinned.

I didn't grin. I'd never liked that joke – it was probably a writer who'd made it up, playing the self-effacement card to charm the drawers off that same starlet.

'What happens, Denis? What becomes of ageing actors?'

'They turn into Benny Lawrie.'

I shuddered and pressed on. 'OK, how did Benny Lawrie turn into himself?'

'Benny and his wife have this bric-a-brac shop,' explained Denis. 'Not a real shop – a stall in one of those arsey west-end church conversions. The idea is that Benny runs the stall when he's not in acting work. Only, at some point, nobody quite knows when, the stall started running Benny, not the other way round. Anyway, a year ago, Elouise Neath . . .'

'Under Neath's sister?'

'Under Neath's sister – God rest him, the booming fuckwit. Anyway, Elouise went in and, in the course of conversation, told Benny about this new job she had in a Brian Friel revival. Not boasting, just excited – the National, a tour, profile, work for a year, the lot. You know what Benny said?'

'Congratulations?'

'Worse than that. He gives Elouise this grisly smile and goes, "It would take more than that to tempt me out of retirement."' Denis looked at me, his face beaming like a sprite. '*Tempt me out of retirement!* Can you believe that? I mean, since when did he retire? Did you see any BAFTA tributes?'

'No.'

'Me neither. Hadn't worked since *Jungle Book* at the Citz when he was a monkey with a magic wand and you know how long ago *that* was. "Tempt me out of retirement." The self-delusion is *astounding!*' Denis tee-heed delightedly, then stopped suddenly. 'That's what happens to ageing actors.' He took a draw at his roll up then balanced it on the lip of the ashtray. 'Mind you, we're all grateful for that line. Probably use it myself one day when I'm sitting on the Sunshine Coach in my rubber underwear.'

I stood up to go. 'By the way, do you still see Morag?'

'No.'

'Good.'

'Why?'

'Because now I can tell you she's a rabid hound with a poisonous mouth who should be muzzled and put to sleep.'

'Nah, you've got Morag wrong.'

'I haven't.'

'She's just . . . intense, man.'

She's toxic.'

'So are you but she's got a flat and 30k a year.'

'Ah – and there we have it,' I said.

'Have what?'

'The case against you, the accused. You're doing with Morag what you accused me of doing with Chloe – being cynical and using her as a wage packet.'

'It's not like that.'

I pulled on my coat and did a Southern lawyer voice. 'I have no further questions at this time.'

'You're going? Don't go – stay.'

I shook my head. 'I'm OK – I've found a place.'

Denis looked at me. 'Listen,' he said, 'I know you. All these little things inside, these wee demons swarming around . . .' He made worms of his fingers. 'Eating you up.'

'Not me,' I said. 'I'm cool.'

'Cool. Listen to him.'

I was at the door – I was finished with listening.

'Nobody's cool,' said Denis Rourke. 'Everybody's a square, deep down.'

I shut the door.

Next day, ensconced in my toilet cubicle office at Sproat's, I read through Eric's script. Once I'd read it, I went back immediately to the beginning and read it through a second time, just to be sure. I sat thinking things, feeling things, before a sharp rap at the door brought me back to what passed outside myself for reality. 'Harry Potter, you in there?'

'Yes.'

'Get your arse up the office – old man wants to see you.'

I did so. I got my arse up the stairs to the office but the old man quickly marched it down again. Straight out the office block we went and on to the factory floor. 'What's this I hear about you and Chloe?'

'You'd better ask, Chloe,' I said, like a stoic gallant.

Dad grunted. 'We're in luck, Fevsi,' he called out in passing, 'another eighty thousand pressings for Walthamstow.'

'Great stuff, boss.'

Fevsi, some kind of Eastern European, gave a cheery thumbs up, like a serf who loves his master.

'Pick that glove up.' Dad was talking to me.

I picked up the gauntlet and dropped it into the cup of a welding mask. We walked on, past the skulking eyes of workers who'd suddenly grown more diligent, less shouty, now that Dad was about. Every few paces, I'd be instructed to move a grease drum or re-park an iron trolley. I understood it to be a display of power for my instruction and the entertainment of the watching ranks.

'I can see both points of view,' said Dad or Boss. 'Chloe's and yours. This isn't the job for you – you're operating below capacity. That's spilled tallow on the floor – give it a wipe. And I can see Chloe's. I'm not saying she could have her pick but marrying a labourer from her father's factory floor ... well, name of goodness, that's hardly the chef's special, is it?'

'I won't always be a labourer.'

'You're right there – I don't carry passengers.' He pointed to a tool bag with his foot. I pushed it under a workbench, tidily.

He shook his head, like a man who's at a loss. 'I was going to give you my "young people today" speech but look at you – you're not even young.'

In my elderly doddering way, I nodded acquiescence.

Dad continued, 'All the same, she's very fond of you and life's not all about filthy lucre.'

'I'm very fond of her,' I said. 'I love Chloe.'

I felt Dad's irritated tangle of disgust and humanity. We stopped walking and were back at the office block. Dad fixed me with a look, his eyes veiny from the strain of fifty-one per cent ownership. 'Eric's fond of you too. That boy is my life. My children are my life. Not my wife, not this factory – they're just fucking hard work.'

'I appreciate your frankness.'

'Frankly, you should. Take a hard look at yourself. You need to get your life sorted.'

'I will,' I said, 'I'm working on it.'

A matronly woman in a navy skirt suit had been standing discreetly, with an invoice that needed to be queried. She stepped up to Dad and they queried it together. As they did so, I touched the script under my overall to remind myself I still had an inner life. Then I drifted away to lose myself in the factory, till siren time.

That night, I rang Eric several times on his mobile from the men's hostel where I was staying. After the third ring out, I left a message. At six-thirty next morning, my new ringtone of choice, 'The Ride of the Valkyries', chirruped from my mobile over the crunch of dry toast and muttering semi-derelicts.

'Sorry to ring so early,' Eric said, 'I'm on my way back from work.'

'I'm on my way there.'

'Yes, I guessed – the horror, the horror.' And we both tried to laugh.

It dawned on me that this was how dreams die, crumbling slowly, day by day, through sheer fatigue. 'I've read your script,' I said.

'And I've read yours. Can you meet me at the house tonight?'

'Not tonight. Can we do it when your parents aren't around? The Chloe business, you know.'

'Yes, pity about that. I'm sorry.'

'One of those things.'

'Have you spoken to Dad?'

'Yes,' I said. I didn't elaborate. I left a conversational hole, hoping he'd fall into it. He did.

'OK . . . how about Thursday? I'm on an early shift, the folks are at a charity fundraiser.'

'Thursday's good,' I said.

'You all right?'

'Yes,' I said. I pocketed my phone, tried another spoonful of hostel porridge but felt sick.

What if I should change my mind between now and then?

A nudge from an elbow interrupted me. 'I wouldn't flash that phone in here,' a gaunt stubbly face murmured. 'You're asking for trouble.' I nodded.

I stood up and scraped my breakfast leavings into the bin, dropped my cutlery into one basin of hot water, my dirty plate into another.

I couldn't change my mind.

What would I change it to?

To Thursday then I came, burning, burning.

CHAPTER SIX

'Do me a favour,' I said to Eric Ross, 'get pissed with me.'

'That bad, uh?' I poured red wine in big glugs into the tumblers Eric had provided.

'Are you and Chloe still in touch?'

'No,' I said. 'But it's all cool, it's cool.'

I leaned back on Eric's futon, trying to seem relaxed, taking big swallows of wine, though it might as well have been Ribena – I wasn't tasting it. 'How about you, Eric, is love on the horizon?'

He looked surprised. 'Nothing,' he said, a bit wistfully. He went on, 'I think the trouble for me is that women have turned into people and who wants to fuck *people*? They're too damaged. Not only hollow men, hollow women too.' He took a deep pull on a thin joint.

'Maybe your job's made you think like that.'

'I hope not,' Eric said, breathing out. 'Like I say, I've still another two years minimum.'

He offered me a drag. I shook my head.

'Quite right,' he said. 'Filthy habit. Best keep our minds clear till after we've talked.' He gave me a professorial look. 'Good writing isn't a popularity contest.'

He waved both scripts in the air and started right in. 'I liked both of these,' he said, '*Smoking Gun* and whatsit?'

'*Love Letter Blues*. I'm glad.'

'Up to a point.'

'Ah.' I topped up the glasses – mine first, then his. I used two hands, to keep the bottle steady and hide my nerves.

'The thing is you've a very odd writing style – at odds with your personality. I can almost smell the sweat on the structure. As if you write with your elbows tucked in.'

'You're saying they're not really good scripts, just worthy?'

'Don't be defensive. Worthy has its place – but on the small screen, not the big screen. These are small-screen plays – telly plays with aspirations. They're too safe.'

'I was hoping you might develop these aspirations. Make them, what, unsafe?'

'Me?'

'Yes, you. You could work on these scripts – my scripts.'

He sighed, exasperated. 'I've told you I can't do that.'

'If I sold them, I'd pay you.'

'You know it's not about that.'

'Joint credit – your name first.'

Eric looked startled. 'That's . . . very generous but it's not that either.'

'Please,' I said.

'Look, don't put me on the spot. My absolute priority is my need to qualify.'

'Mine too,' I said.

But Eric didn't hear. He nipped his joint and placed it carefully on the lip of the ashtray. 'In a couple of years, I can climb back into the writing ring again. If I try to straddle both worlds now, I'll end up like last time.'

'Last time?'

Eric did rueful with his eyebrows. 'Psycho ward. Six weeks. Nervous exhaustion. Nice ward, though.'

'Private?'

'Thank God. That's flanges for you. If they're not helping you into a nervous breakdown, they're helping you out of one.'

'So you're saying you won't help me?'

'Don't put it like that.' Eric looked pained, began fidgeting in his chair. 'I only want to work on my own stuff. That's why I turned up my nose at American telly.'

'Would you like to rephrase that?'

'OK. Turned my nose down.' A moment of levity.

I sent a fresh lick of dark Burgundy into his glass.

'Do you have any acid left?' I asked.

He looked at me.

I shrugged. 'You know what they say. Converts are always the worst.'

Eric shrugged too. 'Couple of tabs in the drawer. Help yourself. Not for me though, I'm knackered.'

'What time are you expecting your parents back?'

'Round midnight. Mum's making up a golf four in the morning. You sure you're all right? Is it the Chloe thing?'

'I suppose. That's why I wanted to get pissed.'

'Fair enough. In that case, we'd better get on with it then.' He raised his glass. 'Cheers,' he said. And he gave me his youthful smile.

'We haven't talked about your script yet,' I said.

'*Looking at the Stars*? Well, what did you think?'

'I've only one question,' I said, 'then I want to drop the subject.' I composed myself then asked the one question. 'Would you give it to me?'

'Give it to you? You mean like *give* it to you?'

'Yes.'

'The script? My script?'

'Not give. A swap. Like comics, you know, when we were kids. Well, like when I was a kid.'

He looked a bit stunned. His lower jaw was hanging slightly.

'Go on,' I said, 'two for one. I'll give you *Smoking Gun* and whatsit, the other one.'

'*Love Letter Blues*. That's crazy.'

'Isn't it just? All the same, is that a yes?'

'You're strange tonight. No more acid for you. You're not serious. Are you serious?'

'I liked your script,' I said.

'Good.'

'I liked two things especially about it . . .' I paused, like a man who's trying to concentrate his thoughts. Actually, I was checking out where Eric kept his laptop. I noticed it, flap up, resting carelessly on the cushion of a rickety cane-backed armchair.

'First,' I said, 'I liked the comedy.'

'You liked the comedy?' Eric looked pleased. 'I'm relieved. You're a comedy man. What else did you like?'

'I liked the murder. I loved the murder. It's a "how-to-do-it". Who was it said, "Audiences love how-to-do-it."'

'George Roy Hill. You liked the murder?'

'Good murder. Effective murder. Simple. Is it true though? I mean, would it work like that, the way you describe?'

'Of course.'

I gave him a doubtful look. Eric took the bait. He waved his glass, almost sloshing his wine. 'Give me some credit,' he said, 'I'm a doctor, aren't I?' He mopped the dribble from the rim with his finger, licked it. 'Well, almost.'

'All the same, Eric. Could you maybe . . .'

'What a stickler – typical script-reader. OK, I'll tell you . . . but between ourselves?'

I nodded agreement.

'I know it works because I tried it out . . . the procedure . . . on next-door's cat. There.' He sat back, waiting for a reaction. 'Are you horrified?'

I didn't say anything.

He went on. 'Just nicked the moggy – Tigger his name was – hid him under my coat, tried it out, ran a blood test, nothing.' He looked at me, evenly. 'If you're interested, Tigger's buried in the long rough near the fifth on the Clober golf course.' He smiled. 'Are you sure you're not horrified? Go on – at least tell me you're shocked.'

'I'm not shocked or horrified,' I said.

'How disappointing.' He leaned back and scratched the back of his head. 'Anyway, how about you and Chloe? Or shouldn't I ask?'

'You can ask . . . I really wish you'd trade me this script.'

'You like the script?'

'It's not a bad script.'

'Good. I'll have to sit on it a while. Till I qualify. Two years, maybe three. Four years tops – it'll soon pass.'

'That's much too long. The shine will go off it.'

He looked pained. 'What else can I do? It's an exhausting process. Rewrites. Meetings. Wrangles. Apart from which, you've doubtless noticed, it's more than a bitty autobiographical. I mean, for fuck sake, if I was still in medicine and this were to come out, questions would be asked, you with me?'

I was with him.

I watched carefully, as Eric Ross made himself more comfortable, folding his legs under him, in an untidy yoga style. 'Like I say, I just don't have the time.'

'You won't swap then?'

'Are you serious? You're serious. No, my work is myself, my writing is me – we can't just swap souls.'

I looked at him long and hard. I was giving him every chance to change his mind.

'Pity,' I said at last. And meant it. 'Can we get drunk now, please?'

'I'm not much of a drinker,' said Eric.

'I know,' I said, 'but I am.'

And we shared another bottle.

When his eyes looked a bit heavy, I asked Eric if it would be all right to put something calming on the hi-fi.

'Sure. Whatever.'

To the tender bombast of Dylan Thomas reciting 'A Child's Christmas in Wales', we chatted some more and drank some more until, finally, over 'Fern Hill', Eric's head had begun to loll. And, by the time 'Fern Hill' had rolled down the valley to become 'Do Not Go Gentle into that Good Night' (Caedmon Volume I TC 1002), Eric Ross had fallen asleep.

I remained where I sat and finished my drink. As I've said, I was giving him every chance. He might've have woken up at any moment but didn't. I rose, went to the pharmacy drawer and pulled it open. I looked back at him, to check. I took out the things I needed. The vial, a needle in cellophane. I tried to break open the cellophane as quietly as possible. I stress he still could have woken up but didn't. I filled the pump from the vial, the way I'd seen them do in the films – the ones we both loved, Eric Ross and I. Although, of course, being a doctor, Eric had received his doctor's training properly, at medical school, not from the Odeon, Renfield Street, like me.

I approached him, holding the needle in one hand and the acid tab in tweezers with the other. Once again, I stress *he could have woken up at any time.* His head was to the side and he was snoring gently, mouth enough agape for me to feed in the paper tab with the silver tweezers. It rested between gum and cheek and, because gum and cheek were warm moist places, the tab would soon dissolve. Then I stood looking at him, the hypodermic in my hand, poised. 'Eric,' I said, softly, 'Eric?' But would he wake up? Wake up not would he.

I paced around the futon, like a snooker player lining up a shot. I'd thought I might have to risk tugging at an ankle when

I'd watched him fold his legs under him earlier but the dusty sole of a navy blue sock was showing sufficiently for my needs. I decided to risk an attempt with the needle. So I risked an attempt with the needle. I aimed it two toes in – from the little toe, that is, not from the big toe. There's too noticeable a gap between the big toe and the next toe – a pinprick might be spotted on the pathologist's table. At least that's the way Eric had explained it in *Looking at the Stars*, quite the best, the brightest, the most scurrilous and well-written script, incidentally, I'd been privileged to read in some long lean years.

As I'd told Eric himself earlier, it wasn't bad.

But I digress.

Aiming between the second and third toes and making sure that the point was tucked away and discreetly hidden, I carefully sank the plunger in, my thumb feeling its pressure push the needle into his foot. Then, with its release, I brought it back out of his foot. This time, Eric Ross did indeed open his eyes. When I saw his eyes open, I started back and hid the needle that was in my hand.

'Where are you going?' His voice was thick, cotton-woolled with wine and sleep. He smacked his lips and swallowed.

'I was just going,' I said.

'I'll see you out,' said Eric Ross. And he tried to rise. But no movement came.

'Eric?'

Eric Ross was still sitting looking at me, frozen in the act of still sitting looking at me. I waved my hand in front of his eyes. I thought about tickling him under the ribs, as he might have done himself, if our situations had been reversed. 'Eric?' I said. But he didn't shout 'boo' or 'fooled you' like you or I might have done because his eyes were sightless eyes, unlike your eyes or mine. So I supposed, far from his seeing me out, I'd actually, in the deeper sense, seen him out.

Anyway, I took a crumpled Tesco bag from the pocket of my coat. I dropped the used hypodermic into it, then the glass I had drunk from. I wiped down the wine bottles and replaced them on the table where they'd stood. I wrapped the vial of potassium chloride in a couple of Kleenex and dropped it into the Tesco bag.

I took the vinyl record of Dylan Thomas off the turntable, slotted it back into its sleeve and replaced it in the nondescript pile under the unit. 'Do Not Go Gentle' might have seemed like a giveaway, some sort of veiled precursor of suicide. I didn't want that. I wanted no suspicious circumstances – I wanted plain, honest to goodness death by misadventure. With even half a gram of luck, he'd look like one more of that endless legion of desperate fuckwits whose weary, overworked hearts pack in owing to the cumulative effects of their dangerous daily indulgences. I walked across to the rickety cane-backed chair. The light of Eric's laptop was on. I pressed for his script folders. Nothing. A herd of thoughts stampeded round my brain before I rounded them up and pressed for his documents. A spatter of figures appeared, drug names, hospital business. And finally a title. *Looking at the Stars*. Summoning it up, I read, 'Screenplay. Final Draft.' I pressed the edit key, highlighted, and cut big swathes of Eric's final draft. The remainder, I banished to the Recycle Bin. From the Recycle Bin, I chased what was left of *Looking at the Stars* into the long grass of his hard drive. I switched off his laptop at the mains, covering my bare hand with my sleeve before I did so.

I turned my attention to a little pile of CDs in a smoked plastic container. I opened the container and flicked through the CDs, looking at their labels. There were other examples of Eric's work there but I wasn't tempted – one was enough. I found the disk with the hand-written label reading *Looking at the Stars* and put it in my pocket.

After all that, I stood, scratching my chin, wondering what else I had to do. I was like a man who's off on holiday and didn't want to find himself halfway to the airport before realising he'd forgotten to turn the iron off.

I suppose I must have stood there, desperate to get away yet at the same time scared to leave, for, oh, quite some time. When I could think of nothing else to do, I plumped the seat of the futon I'd been sitting on and smoothed its back. I pulled on my coat. I picked up *Smoking Gun* and *Love Letter Blues*, folded them and put them in the pocket of my coat. I was actually halfway out of the door when I realised I'd forgotten the most important item. I had a brief spasm of panic, like murderers do in bad films, before I saw what I was looking for. I leaned over and held Eric's wrist. With my free hand I slid the hard-copy script of *Looking at the Stars* from his grasp.

I looked at him for a last moment. 'Well,' I thought, 'it's his own fault. *He could've woken up at any time.*' But he hadn't done the sensible thing – he hadn't woken up in time.

If he was right, the potassium chloride would leave no trace in his bloodstream.

If he wasn't right, then on his own head be it.

'Either way,' I thought, 'my hands are clean.'

And I climbed out of the basement and turned off the light.

CHAPTER SEVEN

Speaking of hands, I couldn't help noticing, at the funeral, that Chloe's hands were pale.

I remember watching Chloe, the strain perhaps or the chilly autumn day draining her of colour. My clean hand had taken her pale hand and squeezed it, gently, just enough, for reassurance, as she'd stood at the church entrance alongside Mum and Dad, accepting and giving succour to assorted family drones and crones. Curious how selfish the weak are, how they can never remove the blinkers of their own need, even for an instant, even when three open wounds in sombre clothes stand stricken before them, offering pale, formal hands in token of the endless years of regret and guilt that lay ahead.

'Why? Why?'

I'd mouthed the words, bewilderedly, shaking my head just enough for public consumption, as Eric's polished mahogany casket, expensively inlaid, had made its way from hearse to hands, from hands to shoulders, from shoulders in silent shuffle, apart from the odd scrunch of gravel under patent leather shoe, onward into the open mouth of the church.

'I don't know why. We'll none of us ever know,' said Dad, his voice satisfyingly cracked and quavering. He remembered he was grasping my hand and let it fall.

Chloe wore black. A simple black dress, bought for the occasion. 'Too much pain,' she said with simple black grief when I looked at her with my sensitive suffering eyes.

I didn't linger. I hovered around outside only long enough to mumble my clumsy condolences. As I entered the church, the organist was clumping out the last chords of an ill-advised 'Moonlight Sonata' as he warmed up his fingers for the later hymns. I made my way into the pews and picked up an order of service booklet.

In front I could hear two young men, doctor types I assumed, discussing Eric in low voices. 'Guy was an arse,' said a fin-haired man with stubble and a belly, 'only ever a matter of time.'

His colleague was less convinced. 'All the same, no vomiting – that's unusual.'

'OK, it was unusual,' shrugged the fin-haired man, 'but so what?' He spoke behind his order of service booklet to mask his agitated tone. 'Amount of stuff that dingbat was emptying into his system, organ failure was inevitable.'

'I know, Caleb, but no vomiting . . .'

I'd been trying to listen. The organist struck up an intro for a familiar hymn, forcing me to strain my ears.

'Forget vomiting – he had it coming.'

'Maybe you're right.'

'Course I'm right. The silly bastard, he can rot in . . . *Jesus, our help in ages past, our . . .*'

I was pleased and relieved by their informal diagnosis confirming, as it had, the verdict of the Coroner's Office – 'Misadventure'. Result then. Let's hear it for Jesus, '*our help in ages past . . .*' I was so grateful, I actually sang along. After which, it was time for the three most boring words in the English language –'*Let us pray.*'

And, by God, did we not. After prayers, I was called upon by the minister to make the reading I'd wheedled Dad into allowing me to give. I kept a discreet eye on Chloe as I intoned 'In My Craft or Sullen Art' by Dylan Thomas. I'd selected this poem not because it was fitting, especially, but for its pompous euphony and actory cadences which, through the wondrous entanglement of echo and grief, make banal sentiments sound seductively profound. Dad's breathing was open-mouthed and rapid, I observed. Every now and then, Mum would touch one of his pale meaty hands as they rested on his knees. I wanted Chloe to be moved by the power of my delivery but the visual evidence for such had been inconclusive, comprising only of her forlorn stare and the odd wipe with a Kleenex at a dew-dropped nostril.

Later, at the cemetery, after the lowering down of the coffin on its heavy straps and after more dry words lost on the damp wind, I hung around making small talk to bores, hoping to catch the eye of Dad or Mum, someone with the ear of Chloe, who might help nudge us back into our previous, uncomfortable, comfortable, coupled status. Of course, the one person I hadn't looked to for help with this had been Chloe herself. I glanced about, feeling nervous, the tang of the turned earth sour in my nose, fearing that the key players might be whisked off to their private gathering before I'd had the chance to make my play, befriend them anew and somehow inveigle myself back into the easeful shelter of their wounded family.

After all, crudely speaking, the Rosses were now a man short and here was I, a forty-one-year-old helpless urchin, eager to leap from the poor house back into Chloe's bed whilst bearing fresh tendrils of surrogate joy to her grieving parents. The fact that I'd murdered her only brother, their only son, was an unfortunate blemish I wished to airbrush from this homely, hope-filled, portrait.

Thinking of Eric made me look at his grave. I eyed the fingered crevice of the disturbed earth and, to my curiosity and shame but mainly curiosity, felt the thrill of his talented bones tingle my belly. Strange. You'd have thought, as indeed did I, that, with such delicious detachment, I'd have made a better writer. Perhaps I was too close to my own detachment to be objective. In any case, I'd made a better writer dead, which was, in itself, a lateral form of self-improvement.

'Thanks for coming.'

I turned startled and saw Chloe's face, pinched with cold, attempting a smile.

'I wanted to come,' I said. 'I liked Eric.'

'I know you did.'

Nothing more. I lobbed in a further oily gobbet. 'I'll never forget him.'

No response. Was that in itself a response? The way she held my gaze had me momentarily unnerved. I watched the mania of withheld pain threaten to dance its devilish jig across her features. Did she know? What did she know? I considered an instinctive gesture of support, but didn't want to overplay my hand. Untalented creatures, such as myself, can't afford the luxury of clear conscience. I risked the raise of a tentative arm and, affecting a faraway look in my misty eye, began rubbing, soothingly, the black shoulder of her soft wool coat. She neither yielded nor resisted. 'Chloe, dear,' called Mum, gently. Chloe tensed a little, inclined her head, nodded faintly over her other black shoulder. I removed my tentative, soothing, rubbing hand and waited.

'Yes, Mum,' she said, slightly phlegmily. I felt her place, rather than slide, her arm around my waist. 'Coming?' she said.

'Who's coming? How many?'

'Two,' said Chloe. 'Both of us.'

Thrilling inwardly, I retained outward calm. Resolved now, Chloe lowered her eyes and steered me, with purpose, toward the forgiveness of the open door of the shiny black limousine. As I loped, gingerly, over the squelching sod, toward the stricken, curious faces of her peering family, I knew we were lovers again.

* * *

Six months later, Chloe and I were married.

And our wedding day? God bestowed his Protestant blessing of warmth and early spring sunshine. We held our reception in the function suite of the Grosvenor Hilton at the top of Byres Road, then, for fun, took more snaps at the photographer's insistence – 'The light is glorious!' – across the street in the Botanic Gardens. Mum and Dad wrinkled their faces in the sun, the pain of grief thawing briefly for this little bud of future hope.

'If only Eric could have been here,' Mum said.

'He is,' I assured her, gently, 'he's with us in spirit.'

She melted, giving my hand a squeeze, a small gesture of gratitude – me family now. Dad's big shadow shaded me, a sundial signalling a slightly crooked noon.

'Thank you, Dad,' I said, 'for today and for the honeymoon.'

He shrugged, shook his head absently, thanks not being what he was looking for. What then? One child left, what else? Reassurance?

'Can I ask you a straight question?' he asked.

I felt a flutter at my entrails. What does he know? Suspect? 'Of course,' I said.

He steered me a few feet into privacy. Behind him, outside the Botanic Cafe, a Wall's sign wafted creakily in the breeze.

'What is it?'

His big businessman face became a mask of glaring concern. 'I want to ask . . . you're not . . . a drug user, are you?'

'A drug user? You mean like a junkie?'

'Like a junkie. Like Eric. God rest him. You're not like Eric?'

Relief. So that's all. 'No,' I told him, 'it's all right. I'm not like Eric. I'm clean.'

'It's just the drink then?'

'Just the drink – not even that these days. I don't know if Chloe told you but I'm writing again.'

'She did,' he said. 'She told me. Any joy?'

'Yes,' I said, 'I've had a bite.'

'Really? You've had a bite?'

'On a screenplay.'

'On a screenplay? Who from?'

'America.'

And he looked at me, all bereft and bittersweet. 'Of course,' he said, 'America.'

'It's early days,' I said.

'Even so – America. America.'

'I'd never have done it without you, Dad.'

'It's only money.'

'It's bought me time. The time to write the screenplay.'

I could see what he was struggling not to say. But what with the darkness of his recent loss and the brightness of his daughter's wedding day, he couldn't deny himself a momentary wallow in the warm murky pond of parenthood. 'Maybe I should've bought Eric time instead of demanding that he finish his studies.'

'Eric wanted to finish his studies.'

'He did?'

'Yes,' I said, looking him straight in his wounded eyes, 'he told me so himself.'

'He said that?'

'That's what he said – more than once.'

I don't know if he believed it but it was what he needed to hear. Dad gripped my elbow. 'That's a comfort,' he said.

I gave him a homely smile.

'What's it called?'

'What?'

'Your screenplay.

'Oh. I've called it *Looking at the Stars.*'

'Good title.'

'You like it?'

'I like it. Best of luck – I'm behind you all the way, son.'

'Thanks, Dad.'

And Dad turned, walked away.

I allowed myself a deep breath. As I did so, I felt Chloe slip her arm in mine. She was out of her wedding dress and into her smart new going-away civvies. 'It's good to see him smile again.'

'It's good to see you smile again,' I said.

Chloe smoothed her hips. 'You like my new outfit?'

'I'm a lucky man,' I told her and meant it.

In other words, a perfect wedding day. Did I mention one tiny blemish? As the car taking us to the Scottish Borders paused at lights on Byres Road, a wasted-looking figure caught my indolent eye. Did I mention dread? He stopped by the car and tried the door.

'Who's that?' said Chloe, unnerved.

I didn't answer.

Beating his fists against my window, the man began to shout my name.

'What's he doing? What does he want?'

'He's a dosser – what do they always want?' said our driver.

'I'm sick, I'm dying,' shouted the dishevelled man.

'Beat it,' shouted the driver.

'Look at you, looking at me,' the man's voice rasped, a scream of scorn. 'You're just a lousy thief.'

'Drive on,' I said.

'I can't, the lights are against me,' said the driver.

'Thief! Thief!'

'Drive on.'

'I would drive on if . . .'

As the driver spoke, the filter light showed its green arrow and he scrunched gears, cussing softly in his hasty getaway.

'My God,' said Chloe, 'my heart is pounding. Feel.' She pulled my hand to feel her thudding heart. 'He seemed to know you. Did he know you?'

'I've seen him about. He hangs around the pubs.'

'He knew your name.'

'Yes,' I said.

I might have added that he should have known my name since it had been he who had given it to me. But of course I didn't tell her the dishevelled man was my father. I didn't tell her for much the same reasons that I hadn't invited my mother to the wedding – at least not until two days before the event, when I could be sure she'd be too insulted by the tardiness of the invitation to attend. There'd been enough ghosts, enough worlds colliding, for one day.

Put simply, I had now traded up to a more nurturing set of parents.

'Why did he call you a thief?'

'I don't know,' I told Chloe. And I didn't know. And, though I tried to forget my father, he troubled me.

We honeymooned at Stobo Castle. Dad hinted that he'd used his influence and connections to land us this exclusive venue but I suspected that, like everyone else, he'd just emptied his wallet on to the reception desk. The walls of our room were pink wallpaper and the duvet covers blue gingham. It was like sleeping in a box of Edinburgh Rock. The staff seemed to outnumber the guests and would hover like close fielders in a cricket match whenever we'd appear for breakfast or hit the bar in the evening.

This was the other Scotland – car-sticker Scotland. This was Alba, Scotbrand the Brave, embracing an image our politicians and media commentators nowadays loved to peddle – an image that people from my background saw as a big lie and one we shouted loudly to deny the gruesome, dispiriting truth. Which was why people from my background tended to die, gruesomely dispirited, in gutters. I, on the other hand, no longer dispirited, boasted a glass of Macallan, a pretty, if earnest, wife of good breeding and a father-in-law who now subsidised my ambitions out of guilt. So what if, in the bowels of the kitchen below me, a pitiful clan of underpaid lackeys slaved wretchedly for our dining pleasure? Who was I – or Eric Ross – to disturb the universe? An uneasy truth, from an easy chair, looks only ridiculous.

'Are you happy now?' Chloe asked.

'Blissfully.'

At night, when I hauled the big floral curtains shut, we'd see black hills through drizzle. When we opened them in the morning, I'd see green hills through drizzle. You can transform all the castle turrets you want into sauna rooms, you can chop your moat into a dry dock and make it a twenty-five-metre heated swimming pool but, no matter which way you cut it, it's always Sconeland. When the whisky wore off, I still wasn't a somebody – I was a nobody with better furniture.

'What's wrong?' asked Chloe on our last night, after more drink, more sex. 'You seem restless.'

I didn't answer. I was opening out the fax message that had been pushed under our door.

'What's that?'

I sat on the edge of the bed, my fat white towelling robe feeling grand, like a toga.

'Good news?'

'I think so,' I told Chloe.

'Then why so cautious?'

'You've married a man of experience, young lady,' I said. 'I'm always cautious.' But I couldn't stop a big grin starting up.

'Go on, let me see.' Chloe held out her hand but I teased her, making her lunge for the page because she was naked. She sat crossed-legged on the bed and pushed a hunk of dark hair behind her ear. She read aloud. 'Meeting soon. Keep diary clear next fortnight.'

'Look at the heading,' I said.

Chloe looked at the heading. 'Winters and Daly, Westwood Avenue, Los Angeles.'

'Fantastic,' she said but she didn't say it in such a way that it needed an exclamation mark.

'What's wrong? I thought you'd be pleased.'

'Will you be gone long?'

'As long as it takes,' I said, with rather too much eagerness for my new wife's comfort.

She looked at me.

'Not long,' I said. I gave it a moment then capitulated lamely, 'You can come too if you want.'

Chloe looked at the fax. 'Your agent's David Shenson.'

'Yes,' I said, 'he's American but he handles a few British clients.'

'I know,' said Chloe, 'he was Eric's agent.'

'Oh,' I said, 'do you mind?'

'I don't mind,' said Chloe, 'but I'd rather not come.'

As I slipped a comforting arm around her shoulder, she shivered. 'It's alright,' I said, 'I understand.'

'I know you do,' she said.

I guided her gently down and opened my dressing gown, making it our blanket.

'I so miss Eric,' she sobbed.

'So do I,' I said. And I did, even though I'd killed him. I allowed a brief interval for decency, before gently hinting that Chloe's hands guide me inside her.

'I love you,' murmured my wife, her trusting fingers aiding my intrusion.

'I know,' I said, 'and I want to say thank you, thank you, thank you.'

Badness is its own reward.

CHAPTER EIGHT

A week later, at Glasgow Airport, I climbed the magic ramp that led to the boundless skies. I carried a script case, wore a new linen jacket, fresh cotton trousers and a beatific inner glow.

I had arrived, I was at Departures.

The fates, it seemed, were smiling on me. Or was it at me? Browsing among the books in WH Smith's, I was almost reassured to experience a small familiar pang of bilious envy. There, in the 'Local Interest' section, between the flailing tartan dancers and the assorted garish volumes of couthy urban patter, it sat, *Where We Live Now* by Hugh S. Provan. Flicking through the illustrations, I recognised Cecil Street and that distant desperate time. On the back jacket, Mr Provan's scrubbed face beamed like a Lotto winner. I shivered, chucked pages over him, like soil on a coffin, and laid him to rest where he belonged, among the also-rans. And thus it was that, following a three-hour security scare, I was borne aloft at last, at long last, through, then above, that great grey bin-lid of cloud, Scottish sector, that darkens our dearest dreams and keeps us all cowed and runted.

> And, oh, my brethren, the light, such light, my brothers, my sisters, come see, come see!

Sixteen hours later, my pungent clothes were sticking to me, my back ached and my plastic lenses seemed to be boiling in my eyes. After a long nit-picking session at the immigration desk, every other hostile sentence of which included the lengthy threat of expulsion, the bad-tempered white male official finally allowed me into the land of the free. I looked for the carousel. I picked up my bag as it circled, sad and alone. Welcome to Los Angeles. Hispanic chauffeurs held up cards of greeting for the lucky few. I'd vaguely imagined that somebody – Aiden, maybe, or David Shenson or a team of cheerleaders fronted by Roy Rogers on Trigger – might have come to welcome me. After all, I was talent – I'd come bearing the secret of fire. But, as I looked around, I could sense the to and fro of other fire-bearers in Ralph Lauren casuals with expensive shoulder bags, better travelled than mine.

I felt a little daunted. Here I was in Heaven, California, to talk to God's representative on earth, its Supreme Holiness, the Film Industry. I steeled my resolve by demystifying the business, reminding myself that this was just another working town, that's all. I made myself think of it as Sheffield and that here I was, another salesman in cutlery, in town to show off his new teaspoon. I felt better as I waited in the Hertz queue. And better still as I thought about *Looking at the Stars*.

In his brief e-mail, Aiden had recommended the Jacey Gardens on Franklin Avenue. Sitting in my hired Fiat – or Wendy as I quickly christened her – I looked for Franklin on my street map. From LAX, it was an easy drive for a competent driver. I was not a competent driver, however, and my journey proved a predictable six-honk adventure. The Gardens were a complex of apartments, in motel layout, squaring a communal swimming pool. The Mexican concierge, Raul on his badge, showed me to my first-floor quarters. When I saw they were roomy and bearable, with private balcony and open-plan kitchen, I felt a sudden energy rush. I dumped my bags on the bed and immediately scurried back out into the street, looking to buy wine and groceries.

Big Batmobile cars, muscle-boy El Caminos and prissy flower delivery vans hissed up and down the street. I looked around for pavement, fearing that someone, perhaps the bad-tempered immigration official, might have rolled it up and taken it in for the night. There was pavement all right but it was a thin and grudging token sidewalk, like a disabled ramp in a rundown department store. Except there was no department store – or, indeed, any other kind of store, no matter how far this thin-lipped, mealy-mouthed pavement rolled out its sullen welcome. I trudged back into the complex, suddenly tired. I bought a packet of Oreos from a vending machine and fell asleep on the bed, among my bags, before I'd even opened it.

I'd like to report that I was massaged awake next morning by the sun on my face and the gentle chirrup of small birds. I was not. Instead, I was roughed to consciousness by a squall of shrieking argument. Did I dream it? I hauled myself to sluggish feet and stood looking at my stupefied self in the mirror. The imprint of my holdall handle had formed a neat arc on my cheek. I poured water into a glass. There it was again – a man and woman, hammer and tongs, through the thin wall. What's the time? 4.05. Day or night? Dark. Must be night. Was that crying? Yes, crying. I put my ear to the thin wall and listened.

'You're a loser,' she was shouting, 'your agent is full-cream shit – he's a garbage man.'

'Give it time,' the man was barking back, tetchily, 'give him a chance – he's working.'

'I'm glad somebody is – you sure as hell aren't.'

'I'm going to change agents. I'll dump him – once he finds me a job.'

'You've been saying that for how long? Months.'

Something fell. Did something fall? A clothes rail, an ironing board? Anyway, she quietened down.

'Our luck will change,' said the man, determinedly, 'we have talent.'

But she wasn't to be mollified. 'That's what everybody says.'

'We aren't everybody.'

'Everybody says that too,' said the woman.

He must have been tired trying to soothe her because he swore and said, 'Shut up.'

This settled things.

I lay out on the bed, thinking about sleep. Then the man started up again.

I heard him say, 'I'm not a quitter – I'm never giving up.'

And the woman chimed in with a spot of sobbing but they were quiet sobs. And the man fell quiet, maybe lulled by the sobbing. And eventually, everything turned quiet.

But not me, I was wide-eyed and tense.

'Good morning, sir.' The Mexican concierge, Alfonso on his badge, indicated a table off the foyer, laden with coffee and doughnuts. 'Every morning, come fresh for you.'

'Not today.'

'Is included in the price.'

'I'll have double tomorrow.' I was walking fast. I was late already.

Though I knew next to nothing about Los Angeles, the little I did know was that you didn't keep people waiting for meetings. They kept you waiting since they were always more important than you were – even the unimportant people were more important than you because they knew, or might know, the important people and you knew no one and knowledge was power and power was meetings ... or meetings about meetings. I'm telling you this but you already know it, having absorbed it all, as I had, through the universal cultural osmosis of celluloid.

The Winters and Daly agency occupied the tenth floor of an unusually tall building on Westwood. Not Westwood Avenue, just Westwood – you see, I was getting the hang of it already. I parked Wendy without incident and walked through the art-deco style revolving door.

'Hi, I'm sorry I'm late.'

She checked an appointment page. 'You're not late – you're expected. David's ready for you. I'm Tess Schwartzenbuch – hello.'

She offered a porcelain hand. I wondered whether to shake or dust it. American Wasp, a smile to swoon for, but that wholesome sterility, like she'd use cake tongs to toss you off.

'Please come with me.'

I Glasgow-shuffled after Tess Schwartzenbuch, trying to appear urbane. What had I expected? I don't know but not this dazzling feast of marble and smoked glass.

'You had no trouble parking your car? I left your name at the gate.'

'No, the gate was fine. Thank you.'

'My pleasure. Please come on in.'

And I came on in. And we went up in a lift. And David Shenson stood up. 'David Shenson,' he said. I recognised his picture from the trade papers but managed to stop myself saying so. He was mid forties and balding. He wore a shiny grey lightweight suit and looked like a TV divorce lawyer. The Hollywood Hills beyond a tinted wall of glass formed his personal office mural and above those hills was the frieze of a dazzling blue sky. Here was a man who could position a desk to impress.

'What a pleasure,' said David Shenson, giving me his hand.

'I hope so,' I said, trying out my modest smile.

David Shenson gave me a dry look. 'Let's find out, shall we?'

The pleasantries over, he swung open a door marked 'Conference Room'. As one, around thirty men and women, all in suits, stood up around an immense boardroom table.

'Who are all these people?' I asked, dry-mouthed.

'Agents,' said David Shenson, showing teeth. He pulled out a chair at the head of the table and motioned me to sit.

'Good,' he said, sitting down next to me. 'Now let's get to know each other.' As he shot out a measure of stiff indigo cuff and silver links, I smelt a faint waft of cologne. I watched David Shenson make a steeple of his hands, then topple it on to the desk.

'Questions please,' he said.

As one, the heads leaned forward.

Two hours later, I was sitting in a sidewalk cafe opposite Book Soup on Sunset.

'Don't call it Sunset,' said Aiden, 'call it the Strip.' He took a sip from his espresso. 'How did your meeting go?'

'I'm not sure,' I said, straining above the traffic. 'He made me meet all the agents – I don't know why.'

'It's a meat market,' said Aiden, 'and you're the meat.'

'How do you mean?'

'You'll get a call soon and one of them will want, or have been told, to represent you.'

'David Shenson represents me.'

'That's not the way it works. David Shenson doesn't represent just anybody.'

'He represented Eric Ross.'

'You're not Eric Ross.'

'No,' I said.

Aiden seemed distracted, unaccountably irked. 'Eric Ross had the touch but he blew it, stupid prick.'

'You didn't know Eric,' I said, speaking up fearlessly for the man I'd robbed and murdered.

'No – but people I've met knew him. And they're people who know. And what they knew is that he had the touch.'

'The gift of fire?'

'There is no gift of fire – there's just a knack, a touch. The gift of fire is something we imagined back there.'

'Back home?'

Aiden looked at me sternly, like I'd used a taboo word. There was something resolute in his look. He damped it down with a shrug. 'To have the touch and throw it away . . . Jesus.'

'You know Eric died?'

'Yes. He had the touch.'

'And Walter Urquhart?'

'He didn't have the touch – he didn't matter. There's no sense rushing to die. We can die anytime – we're all on a ticking clock. But to have the touch and trash it . . .' He looked beyond me, restlessly.

'Are you waiting for someone?'

'No.' He drained his little cup. 'Let's move on.'

And we walked down the street, the strip, Sunset Strip, on Sunset Boulevard, Hollywood, California, me and Aiden, from wee Glasgow, together in the choking air.

In the Virgin complex, we sipped lattes. Aiden seemed to summon up something within himself – pluck, perhaps. 'What did they say about your script?'

'They liked my script. They think they can sell it.'

'They always say that. Did they mention names.'

I dropped a few names. 'Lumus are interested.'

Aiden didn't react.

I elaborated, 'They're an arm of Warners.'

'No they're not,' he said, 'they're a pinkie on the hand.'

I must have looked disappointed. Aiden relented. 'But the hand's on the Warners' arm, I grant you.' We looked at the huge shiny posters for *Legally Blonde* and *The Lord of the Rings*.

'How about you?' I said. 'I was at your premiere in Glasgow – your film worked well.'

Aiden took a breath. 'Moderate business in Europe, which means no business at all. Didn't make the complexes here, which killed us. So . . .' Aiden smiled maturely, relaxedly. 'It was a great calling card – it bought me time. I've been working on something new.' While he was smiling, I watched his fingers peck in agitation at the table surface. 'Did he say anything about a timescale?'

'Who?'

'Shenson.'

'He said I'd need a lot of patience.'

Aiden nodded, wisely. 'Yes,' he said, 'that's the way it works.'

I didn't understand. 'How? How does it work?'

'You'll learn,' Aiden said. 'Out here, it's every man for himself.' He looked at me, grimly. 'Next stop development hell.'

On the way back, I stopped off at Ralph's for groceries. I bought tinned soup and wine, a Superdanish for comfort and a cigar for novelty. As I swung into the drive of the Jacey Gardens, a paramedic van was parked at a careless angle, hogging two spaces. I parked as best I could and walked upstairs. On the landing, outside my door, two paramedics, a man and a woman, were unsnapping a foldaway stretcher. When it was unsnapped they went into the apartment next door, the one where the fight had occurred the previous night. I was curious and hung about, fussing with my key to buy nosey time. The paramedics reappeared with a groaning man. They helped the groaning man on to the stretcher. The man was mid thirties had lank dark hair and was wearing a blood-spattered T-shirt over a pot belly. Printed on the T-shirt was 'Never give up'. He was bleeding profusely from both wrists, which were bandaged.

'I'm not going home,' he kept repeating, 'I'm never going home.'

'You are home, sir, you're home already,' the woman paramedic kept saying, by way of reassurance.

'Yes,' said the man paramedic, 'we're taking you to the hospital.' He squatted down over his end of the stretcher and counted aloud. 'One, two . . .' And, on a silent three, the two paramedics lifted the stretcher.

'You know him?' The man paramedic asked me.

I shook my head.

'Bobbie?' Shouted the man on the stretcher at the door of his receding home.

'Bobbie's coming.'

'Bobbie?'

'I told you she's coming. Excuse us,' said the woman paramedic. 'Better give him a shot,' she said and they all bundled past me towards the lift, the elevator. 'Calm him for the examination.'

A good-looking woman, maybe mid thirties too, must've been Bobbie, appeared in the doorway of the apartment. She was wearing a smart striped blouse with denim shorts, like she'd been caught in the middle of either dressing up or toning down. She had some small packets in her hands. 'Here take these,' she said, 'he's diabetic.'

'Bobbie?'

'Yeah, she hears you, sir, Bobbie hears you. He's diabetic, you say?'

'Yes,' Bobbie said, pushing some hair behind her ear, 'you won't forget?'

'We won't forget.' They had him down again, the paramedics. They were squatting, probably giving him the shot.

He started singing, a bit of Spandau Ballet. 'Gold, always remember your so-ul, you've got the power to know, you're indestr . . .' Seeing the hypo, he stopped singing, started whimpering. 'I hate needles.'

Bobbie was holding both hands over her mouth in a fatigued gesture. Her hair was long, frizzed-up, crinkly fair and her eyes were watery and heavy. I'll say this, it didn't put me off.

'Never give up, sugar,' shouted the man on the stretcher. He had one fist clenched and his other hand was trying to point to the message on his T-shirt. His voice was a sort of woolly wheeze; I suppose the shot was starting to take.

'I won't,' said Bobbie, 'I'll never give up.' She blew kisses on her hands. Her face was freckled and so were her legs. I could see her legs because I was interested enough to peek. The denim shorts were sawn off just the right side of decency – like the ones foot-ballers wore in the seventies. Two lean, tanned shapely American stems but bony knees, though, which gave her a slight tomboy air. The bell light pinged and the stretcher started to shrink into the elevator. Bobbie turned to me.

'That's number three,' she explained, 'his third try at killing himself.'

'Never give up,' I said.

'If only he could succeed at something – at life or death, anything at all – then it would be all right, then I could go home. But not him. He won't go home, so I can't either.'

'Where's home?'

'Chickasha, Oklahoma.' She looked at me, with hopeless optimism. 'You know it?

I shook my head. The bell light pinged again. We both looked at the lift, the elevator, as it started to go down.

'I guess it goes with the territory.'

'What is his territory?'

'Lorne's a writer, I'm a singer. I say singer – I'm an office temp too. I do a lot more clerking than singing, I'll say that much. You?'

'I'm the same as Lorne.'

Bobbie looked at me, sighed. 'Honey, I hope not,' she said.

And we went into our apartments and shut our doors.

I was huddled in my armchair, munching fearfully, the pouches of my cheeks filling with consoling Danish pastry, when the phone rang.

'Hello?'

A flat voice spoke. 'Hi, this is David.'

'Hello, David.'

'You survived the meeting.'

'Is that a question or a statement?'

He laughed his flat laugh. 'No, no, break it down into dialogue. You should have said – are you asking or telling me?'

'Just tell me what to ask, David.' I was still raw from the pitch-forking he'd given me, straight into the agent herd.

'You Scottish, so spiky, I love it.' It was his first oblique reference to Eric Ross. He continued, 'Now please listen, I have an important message for you.'

He told me the important message. When he'd finished telling me the important message, he said, 'You clear on that?'

'Yes.'

'Nancy loved your script. I love your script. It reminds us both so much of Eric Ross. What happened to Eric?'

'He died. Drug overdose.'

'Figures. Eric was fragile. You're not fragile?'

'No, I'm spiky.'

'OK, spiky, you have the ditails?'

'No but I have the de-tails.'

'Make us love you – see you soon.'

'I hope so, David.'

I put the phone down and picked up the pastry. I wasn't sure what had just happened and I needed someone to interpret. I put down the pastry and picked up the phone.

'Hello, Aiden?'

Aiden's voice sprang to attention. 'Yes, this is Aiden Lang speaking.'

'It's just me.'

Aiden's voice slouched, at ease. 'Oh.'

'Who's Nancy Roff?'

'Nancy Roff?'

'Yes.'

'Ex-casting director. Widow of Lester Daly. She's president of the company that may or may not want to represent you. Old Hollywood, medium powerful, why?

'She wants to represent me.'

Silence. 'Aiden?'

'I heard you. She personally wants to represent you?'

'Yes.'

'She doesn't represent anyone. That's not the way it works.'

'I know, I feel terrible.' It had been a long time since I'd had leverage enough to put Aiden on the back foot. I could hear the telly in Aiden's apartment – which is to say his agent's secretary's sister's apartment, whose rental was nearing its break clause – could hear the smooth purr of a game-show host sliding another dejected loser off the set.

'She wants to take me to a party.'

'Nancy Roff does? Where?'

'Pacific Palisades. Is that posh?' The turning knife. I knew how posh it was. I'd have to borrow an iron from Raul to give my linen jacket a once-over.

Aiden tried to put a shrug into his tone. 'It's solid. Mainstream Hollywood – Tomland. You know – Hanks. Cruise. The really cool people live further up the coast. What's the address?'

'I don't know. I'm being driven. Anyhow, I just thought I'd let you know.'

'You did right. We should help each other.'

'Be seeing you.'

'Do something for me,' said Aiden, quickly.

'What?'

'When you get there, call me.'

'Call you?'

'Give me the address of the party. I'll get a cab and stand outside. See if you can get me in.'

'I thought out here it was every man for himself?'

'It is. That's why I'm asking.'

'Leave it with me,' I said.

I felt bad for Aiden – he'd tarnished himself. If only he'd had the foresight to murder someone, as I had, he wouldn't have needed to beg.

I got to the Winters and Daly building at six. In the reception area, Tess Schwartzenbuch, in long shorts, was swishing a sheathed tennis racket through the air. 'Goodness, a writer on time? That's something.'

'I mightn't be good but I'm punctual.'

She'd eased up – maybe I'd passed a test. One way to find out.

'You play tennis, Tess? I used to play. Maybe we could meet for a . . .'

Outside, a car horn sounded. Tess laid her racket between the handles of her sports bag.

'Always be punctual. Nancy would sooner fire people than wait for them. This way, please.'

'Sure.' Something in her tone told me we wouldn't be meeting for a game of anything. Ever.

We were both standing looking at a Jaguar, an XJ something, I don't know, maybe fifty-grand worth of car. A middle-aged woman was sitting at the wheel.

'This is Nancy Roff, our president,' said Tess.

'A minute.'

Nancy Roff didn't look up, remained tapping at her electronic diary. She was what? Sixty-something? Her hair was set but soft – not old-woman hard – and more white than grey.

'OK.'

She looked up – no face-work horrors, no geological layers of make-up, old eyes, yes, but a young mouth, lipsticked boldly in recognition of its own prettiness. 'You like the car? It's British.'

'I know,' I said, 'so am I.'

'I like British things – I'm an anglophile. What do you think of the colour?'

It was a muted gold colour – muted for LA, that is. 'I like it.'

'You like it? I'm not sure. Know why I bought this car?'

'No.'

'I liked its fanny. Get in.'

I got in.

'Have a good party,' waved Tess, all peaches and cream again. Nancy Roff grunted, drove off. 'You like her fanny?'

'Tess's?'

'She's from Connecticut. Moneyed family. Well educated. Proper. I thought proper would appeal to my English, you know, my British clients. But a tight ass is a tight ass, right?'

'It's still a nice fanny.'

'You're wasting your time – she won't give out. I have a strict rule – DFT, Don't Fuck the Talent, too many complications. You want to talk about your script?'

'You think you can sell it?'

'Do I . . . wait a minute.' She sniffed the air. She stopped the car. 'Have you been smoking?'

'No.' I remembered the cigar. 'Yes.'

'Jesus Christ, how many a day?'

'None a day – one a decade. Two if I'm on a roll.'

'Get out of the car.'

'What?'

'Get out. Get out.'

I did as I was told. All fingers and thumbs, I clicked off my seat belt, got out of the car. The lights were green. Drivers were lining up behind us. They began pulling out, honking and swearing at me.

'No, no,' Nancy Roff was saying, 'I have to rethink this entire relationship.'

'I'm standing in the road. Couldn't you rethink it later?'

'When I've rethought, you mightn't have a later.'

'I won't have a now if don't let me back in the car.' I was shaking and angry. It would make a nice quirky anecdote – if I lived.

'You promise you'll stop smoking?'

'Yes.'

'You mean it?'

'I mean it. I don't smoke anyway. But I promise I'll stop.'

'Get back in the car.'

I got back in the car.

'What other vices do you have that might waste my time?

'None.'

'You a junkie, a drunk?'

'No.'

'This is why I stopped representing people, they always let you down.'

'I haven't let you down.'

'Same old same old.'

'Listen, I smoked a cigar – half a cigar. If it helps, I'll throw the other half away.'

She was shaking her head. 'Eric Ross let me down. Blow. Tears. Pills. I want to be a doctor. Well, be a fucking doctor. But be a script doctor. He had the touch. But I didn't have the stomach. They break your heart, honest to God. I had to save myself. I passed him back to Shenson.'

I gave her a look. 'I'm not Eric Ross.'

'No.' She looked straight back at me. 'He was younger. And better looking.'

'Not any more he isn't.'

'But you've got the touch. You promise you'll value it?'

'I will, I'll value the touch.'

'Then maybe you've got a later'

I re-buckled my seat belt. 'You think you can sell my script?'

'I don't have to sell your script. A fool could sell your script. I want your script made into a movie. That's not the same thing. That's what tonight is all about.' She turned the fan on, full belt. 'Let's go.' And we went, shooting across on amber's last blink.

We drove up a straight road till we reached some residential areas. Then we began to snake up some hilly streets. We were heading into the Holmby area. It occurred to Nancy that maybe some small talk was in order. 'That's Mapleton Drive, where Bogart used to live.'

'With Lauren Bacall?'

'With Mayo – his third wife. She stabbed him.'

'No kidding.'

'In the back. He stood bleeding on the telephone – know who he called first?'

'The hospital?'

'The studio.' She glanced at me. 'You like that story?'

'Yes.'

'Sure you do. That's the kind of lurid junk that brought you here.' She bumped the Jag up on to the narrow kerb and applied the handbrake. 'Get out.'

'Again?'

'No, we're here. Get out.'

I got out, stood shiftily by her side, while she fought stiffness, attempting spry. 'I've got a hip,' she confessed.

I took it as a hint and gave her a helping grip by the elbow.

'Don't do that,' she growled, brushing me off, 'never do that.'

There were cars up the long drive, cars with fannies, fannying out along the kerb. In the house, I could see people busying about with plates and glasses. Catering staff – nobody else. 'Where are the guests, Nancy?'

Nancy frowned. The door opened. Under the narrow-rimmed porch of the house, a man in a dark suit appeared.

'Where is everyone?'

'You're invited?'

'Yes.'

The man in the dark suit gave Nancy a discreet once-over, clocked the Jag. 'You're just in time,' he said, 'everyone's out back.' He spoke into a walkie-talkie. 'Two more coming out back.'

Out back, in a fountained garden, striped by miniature poplar trees, a middle-aged woman, the hostess I assumed, was standing under a small rippled awning. She was making a speech at a microphone and holding a big shiny coffee-table type book. People in expensive clothes were standing attentively, watching with homely expressions.

'This book about both our grandmothers has been a labour of love, for Brod and for myself.' She glanced acknowledgement.

At her side, Brod – black Armani, white hair – thought about looking bashful but beamed proudly instead.

His wife continued, 'And its launch, at our home today, is made possible by the wonderful people at Bulgati.'

At this, Nancy sucked her teeth, causing a faint stir.

'Bulgati have kindly provided not only tonight's hors d'oeuvres but the champagne. Bulgati have . . .'

I leaned in, whispering to Nancy. 'Who is everyone?'

'I don't know – I don't recognise anybody.' She fumbled in her Vuitton handbag, purse, rooted among a clutter of invitation cards and pulled one out. 'Fuck.'

'It's been a wonderful journey, publishing our own book, our own baby, and Brod and I have . . .'

'What's wrong?'

'Wrong party.'

'Wrong party?'

'You heard. Let's go.'

She started elbowing a path though the guests, me following. 'Excuse us, excuse us.'

'And, later on, in the Bulgati tent . . .'

Nancy stopped. I could sense it coming.

'Brod and I will be . . .'

'You cunt!' screamed Nancy. 'It's Bulgari – Bulgari!'

Everyone looked at her.

She looked straight back. 'I'm sorry but, when you have a stone in your shoe, you have to shake it out, right? Goodnight.'

We hurried back down the drive, Nancy panting and cursing. In the car, she took out an asthma inhaler and took a couple of toots. 'Why didn't you tell me it was the wrong party?'

'I didn't know,' I said. 'I've never been here before.'

'Ignorance is no excuse,' she said. She gave a concessionary little grunt, though, then she put her foot down and we drove like hell.

We made the Palisades party – posh-cool – though I couldn't see what all the rush had been about. People were mingling, relaxedly. A younger set, less android casual, face stubble, jeans even.

'Where have you been?'

'To the toilet,' I told Nancy.

'To the bathroom. Tip back your head. Discreetly.'

I did my best. Nancy squinted up my nose. 'Now show me your gums.'

I peeled back my lips, made like a horse.

'You're wasting your time,' I said, 'I inject up my ass.'

'That would account for your accent. Let's get a drink – you've people to meet.'

'You like this house?' asked Nancy as we waited for our mineral waters.

'Out here we call them homes,' I corrected, folksily. 'It's OK.'

'It's OK enough to set you back eight million dollars.'

'Carbonated or non-carbonated?'

'Non,' said Nancy to the waiter, answering for us both.

I looked around – smaller house than the one in the Holmby Hills. The style looked like it had been ordered piecemeal from a catalogue – pastel walls, big white sofas and blue Ali Baba vases. The vases troubled me. I expected muggers from Compton to spring out of them, waving automatics – silver automatics, of course, to complement the colour scheme. Out on the lawn, I could see people by the pool, lounging, sitting, eating crackers, sipping Kir. It was like a Seurat painting – except for the 'Armed Response' signs on the lawn and the security guards.

Nancy saw me gazing around. 'You're impressed,' she said, 'but there's one thing they never get right over here.' She tugged my elbow, stomped her foot on the floor. 'You see this?'

'What?'

'This.' She stomped again, her foot making a substantial noise. People looked, idly. She didn't care. 'Fitted carpeting,' she said. 'In Britain, carpeting is vulgar – it would be Italian marble, right?'

'You think so?'

'Don't you?'

'No, I would say parquet.'

'Parquet?'

'Yes – in my experience.'

She gave me a long stare. I felt uncomfortable. I had the feeling her stare was reaching out across the ocean, back to Cecil Street and was examining my so called experience, rooting among my broken food cabinets and desiccated floor cloths.

'No,' she said, finally. 'Maybe in Gorbals, not in Holland Park. Here's your drink – let's get busy.' And she cut her already familiar swathe through the room, her elbows working like the blades on Messala's chariot. 'You see that woman over there?' she said. 'Don't look.'

I looked. 'What about her?'

'You think she's attractive?'

'Why?'

'That's Barbara Boyle, president of the ICF. People say she looks like me, only younger.'

'Yes, a little,' I said.

'Which? A little younger or a little like me?'

'Both.'

But I wasn't looking at Barbara Boyle – I was looking at Martin Landau talking to Ian McKellen. As I watched, a little flutter of women gathered by Ian McKellen and he turned to speak to them. Martin Landau was smiling. The women didn't go away. I saw Martin Landau flick off his smile and head for the consolation of the open French windows.

'George!'

'Nancy!'

George and Nancy didn't bother to kiss-kiss. Instead, Nancy tugged me by the jacket, breaking me into the ring of narrow-waisted men who'd been talking amiably to George.

'George, I want you to meet my brilliant new protégé.'

George, my height, trimmer, looked me over. 'He has wonderful eyes,' he gushed. 'Expressive – his eyes alone will make him a star.'

'He's a writer, George.'

'I wondered,' George said. 'He's sort of grey and podgy.' Having garnered his group laugh, George turned to me. 'I hope I haven't hurt your feelings?'

'It's OK,' I said. 'I hear you're not important so it doesn't matter.'

'This way,' said Nancy tugging me on, 'there isn't much time.'

She made me sit under a Hockney-type painting of young men in Ray-Bans, flexing their torsos under a palm tree. She was locked in earnest conversation with a grey-haired woman around her own age.

Nancy's arms were waving and the woman's head was nodding. I knew I was the subject under discussion. Every so often, I looked away in case they wanted to have an admiring peek at my grey podge. A few feet to my left Andie MacDowell was smiling sweetly and carping about the food. I got the impression you could have cut her leg off and she'd pick it up, put it in her purse and continue smiling and carping. A female minder, possibly his agent, had steered Ian McKellen toward the door. I watched him negotiate his exit, making charming jokettes, blowing kissettes, giving wavettes. Nancy stepped into my eyeline and started clawing the air, her way of motioning me over. The grey-haired woman had gone.

'Yes, Nancy?'

'You know who that was?'

'Who?'

'Yvonne Mulgrew. She has budgets for television.'

'But we're here to sell a screenplay.'

'We're here to find you work. You have ideas for television?

'No.'

'Find some.'

'What about the screenplay?'

'Where's Ian McKellen?'

'Heading for the door.'

She looked to the door for confirmation. 'OK,' she said, 'hold this.' She gave me her glass to hold. 'I didn't want to do it this way but I have to do it this way.'

She turned, arrowed herself toward a small discreet gathering in the corner of the room. I watched her detach a tall, politely bewildered man from his wife and speak to him intently. It was obviously a no-holds-barred, naked hard sell. I saw the man look over in my direction. I tried to help my case by flexing from within, attempting to emit a glow of writerly gravitas. While I was emitting, the lights started flicking on and off madly. Our hostess, a preserved stick insect in tailored slacks, was twiddling the dimmer switch.

'OK, that's it,' she was saying, 'if everyone could leave now please – it's over.'

Nancy came panting back, looking flustered. 'OK, we're fixed,' she said. Her hands were shaking. She took a furtive toot from her inhaler and sneaked it back into her bag. 'And not a moment too soon.'

'Why was it? What's going on?'

'Ian McKellen has left the building.'

'So what?'

'That's who she threw the party for.'

'Who?'

'Her. The hostess. The lizard at the light switch. Whoever she is.'

'You mean you don't know her?'

'Who'd want to know her? She's a Giacometti in slingbacks. Cunt. Let's go.'

We went. On the way out, Nancy said, 'Wait.'

She disappeared into the kitchen, dumped her purse on the island and started rooting around, opening cupboards.

'What are you doing?'

'I want a good look at everything she's got.'

Hefty security men watched as we walked down the driveway. Should Nancy have strayed any further out of order, they might've kicked our ribs in but, instead, they wished us impeccable good-nights – all except one who, it turned out, wasn't a security man. He stepped out from some foliage by the entrance, startling me.

'Hi.'

'Hi,' I mumbled. 'Have to go – sorry.'

When we were in the car, Nancy adopted a tone of icy polite-ness, 'Who was that?'

'Who?

'That man – I saw him earlier. He was standing on the

driveway, making small talk with the gardener, trying to work himself up to the porch.'

'I don't know.'

'He knew you. He kept trying to catch your eye. Come clean.'

I came clean. 'All right, he's a friend – a writer. His name is Aiden. He wanted an invite to the party.'

'And you gave him the address?'

'Yes.'

She looked at me, hard-faced. 'When?'

'When I was in the toilet, the bathroom.' I showed her my mobile phone, like a guilty schoolboy.

She was still giving me her Jack Palance look.

'You want to drive us into the desert,' I said, 'so you can order me out of the car again?'

'That won't be necessary,' said Nancy. She started the car, drove a little then stopped. She turned off the engine for emphasis. 'Never do that again,' she said.

'He's a friend,' I said.

'Change your friends. Never be friends with anyone less talented than you are yourself. They suck you down.'

'You think so?'

'It's human nature – that's the way it works.' And she started the car again. 'The Jacey's on Fairfax – I'll drop you on Beverly by the complex.'

'The Jacey's on Franklin.'

'You prefer to walk?'

'No.'

'I'll drop you on Beverly – I'm up off of Coldwater.' She started the car and gave a little scornful hiss. 'A cunt like that living on the Palisades.'

And we drove away.

On the way back, Nancy was silent except for the occasional

bitter comment she'd direct at other road users. Because it was dark and we were nearing the end of our night's adventure, I thought some intimacy might be in order so tried asking her about her past life, her husband.

'We divorced,' she said abruptly.

'Was it acrimonious?'

'The marriage was acrimonious – the divorce was good. We did it the wrong way round.'

'Do you still see him?'

'He died. He was a dear sweet man and he died. We should have done it differently. But, if we'd had another chance, we'd have done it all just the same because we were young and, when you're young, you're going for a certain thing and, even though you suspect that certain thing isn't worth it, you go for it anyway because that's how you're wired.'

'I see.'

'I wish I knew then what I know now.'

'What do you know now?'

She was silent – didn't answer. Maybe that was her answer – silence.

I waited for her to ask about me. But she didn't. I think she knew about me. I think she'd had me nailed as a type, right from the off.

As I got out, Nancy reminded me about Yvonne Mulgrew. When I reminded Nancy about the screenplay, she grew tetchy. 'I wasn't the one sitting on my fanny at that party,' she said. 'You know who that man was I was speaking to,' she said, 'just before we left?'

'No, who?'

'Vice President of Paramount.'

'No kidding.'

'You're not impressed?'

'Why should I be? Everyone I've met in Hollywood is a vice

president. It's a courtesy title – it doesn't mean a thing.'

'Did I use the indefinite article? Did I say "a"? He's *the*.'

'Seriously?'

'Yes. He promised me he'd read your script personally.'

'Why would he do that?'

'He knew my husband in the old days.'

'I see.'

'You see nothing. You have no gratitude or appreciation.'

'Thank you, Nancy.'

She grunted, wound up the window. I heard her muffled voice say, 'They break your fucking heart.' Then she drove away.

I got out my street map and found Franklin. On the way back, ravenous, I bought some KFC from Chico, a vice president of fries.

And that was it shot, my first day in Hollywood.

CHAPTER NINE

Next morning, eleven o'clock, I met Aiden for coffee.

'So how was it?' he asked.

'Interesting.' I tried to suppress my big Huck Finn grin but couldn't. 'Last night I hardly slept a wink,' I gushed. 'All these impressions kept flooding through my mind. The agents gave me the third degree. But I think Nancy will work for me. I really feel something could happen out here.'

Aiden fidgeted in his chair, mopped a coffee blot with his napkin. 'It's always like that on the first day.'

'Is it?'

'Always. They lay on this big energy fest to impress you, assure you they're on the case.'

'I see. I didn't realise.'

Aiden rose, blocking my sun. He reached for a plastic fork and sat back down to his Danish. We were at a sidewalk table in a Santa Monica cafe.

'Agents want you to think they have their fingers on the pulse,' he continued, 'but it doesn't work that way. The way it works is that, once in a while, they just get lucky and the pulse hits them on the finger.'

Aiden forked some fruit goo, chewed, ruminatively.

'I'm sorry about last night,' I said.

He swallowed. 'Forget it. I've been to a thousand parties.

They're a waste of valuable writing time.' He pressed his fork down too hard, snapping it. 'Shit.'

'I'll get you another fork.'

'Skip it. So who was there?'

'Where?'

'At the party.'

'Well, let's see . . .'

'No, wait, don't tell me . . . Minnie Driver.'

'No.'

'Martin Landau? Andie MacDowell?'

'How did you know?'

'They're always wheeled out. Jeff Goldblum?'

'I didn't see Jeff Goldblum.'

'You will. Anybody looking at us?'

'No.'

He picked up the Danish and took an ungainly bite. All morning, our eyes had flicked up and down the Promenade, looking for girls or film Brits, anybody who could gratify us more than we could gratify ourselves.

'Be careful of stars,' Aiden counselled in a pastry-muffled voice. He pouched some currants to facilitate speech. 'Unless they light up a studio, they're black holes – they suck a project down. Don't take their money unless you have to.'

'I won't,' I said.

'I'm only telling you what it took me months to discover.'

'I know, Aiden, I appreciate that.' Even though I knew and appreciated that, I could feel the helium of optimism hissing out from last night's balloons every time he spoke.

'Anything else I should watch out for?'

'Me,' Aiden said. 'If you hear about any more parties, let me know.'

'Even though they're a waste of valuable writing time?'

'I'm festooned with valuable writing time.'

'OK,' I said. 'But it's a two-way street. If you get any invites to parties . . .'

'Naturally. Which brings me to my next point.'

'Which is?'

'Wait. Volkswagen.'

'V or W?'

'W.'

We watched intently as another ten-a-minute blonde girl crossed the precinct. Ten-a-minute here – one month in Cecil Street. She was carrying a lilac workout bag. Much female sportswear forms only the common V on a woman's genital area – hence Volks. This blonde, however, was wearing thin shorts of pink gingham, tight enough to display the full and much rarer W formation of her pressed region, greatly admired by discerning males, especially of the podgy grey, writerly variety. She disappeared into Ultrahouse and the spell was broken.

'Uh. Where were we?'

'Your next point?

'Forget it.' Aiden slid his Police shades down from his fore-head, jabbed them up the bridge of his nose. 'The only point that matters is that are thousands of Brits out here. Thousands. Know what they call this place? Santa Margate. Most of them are no-hopers sitting around the Brit bars with pints of Harp, waiting to see last week's Ipswich Town match. If you're going to survive out here, you've got to avoid them.'

'That shouldn't be hard.'

'But it will be,' said Aiden. I could see his eyes watching me from behind the shades. 'You don't know anybody here. And you'll go a long time without the phone ringing.'

'You think so?'

'Snuggle up, get ready. I told you yesterday. Welcome to development hell.' He saw the look on my face and laughed.

My party balloons were all flat. On Santa Margate sands, I could connect nothing with nothing. 'What happens now?'

'This,' Aiden said, raising his half-empty coffee cup. 'And this.' With a sweep of his free hand, he incorporated everybody on the Third Street Promenade – shoppers, drinkers, bums and wannabees, the shole shebang. Aiden said, 'Somebody should open up a cafe chain out here and call it "Nada".'

'Nice one.' I don't know why but I felt suddenly sick from the heat. I stood up.

'Where are you going?'

'Think I'll head back. I've stuff to do.'

'Want to browse in Midnight Special?'

'No, I'll head back.'

Aiden stood up to say goodbye. 'Remember,' he said, 'to survive out here, you've got to have a strategy. That's the way it works.'

'You're right,' I said. 'I'll think about that.' But I didn't have to think. As I walked along the beachfront to the car park, I already had a strategy – to ditch anyone who had the power to burst my pretty balloons . . . starting with Aiden.

When I got back to the Jacey apartment, the red message light was flashing on the phone. I pressed 'listen' and Tess Schwartzenbuch's android voice said, 'Hi, this is Tess. You're not here. I've tried your cell phone. If you get this, please ring the office. Thank you so much.' I took my mobile phone out of the dressing table drawer and looked at it. The screen said '3 missed calls'. A second voice, tinny and deliberate, sounded from the room phone. It said, 'Listen carefully. This is David Shenson. The time is 11.05. If you are not in my office at Winters and Daly by two o'clock, then you may climb back into your nasty little hire car and paddle it all the way back to Scotland, do you understand? There are adults working at this agency and you are wasting their time. That is all.'

It was two-fifteen. I was standing in David Shenson's office, sweating, breathing hard.

'You didn't take your cell phone with you when you went out?'

'No.'

'Why not?'

'I didn't think I'd need it. I thought I was in development hell.'

'You have to sell a script before you can be in development hell.'

'I realise that. I was being cocky.'

'First spiky, now cocky – I begin to wonder if you're listing your qualities or naming the seven dwarves.'

David Shenson had his door open and his feet up. Everyone could hear us. 'Anyway,' he said, 'no matter. You're fired.'

'What?'

'Fired.' He smiled and affected a Brit accent, 'Sacked.'

I thought of Eric Ross's funeral. I thought of Eric Ross's script.

'David,' I said, 'I have a dwarf name for you.'

'Please leave.'

'Want to know what it is?'

'I warn you, don't say another word.'

'Cunty.'

David Shenson took his feet off his desk, leaned forward, feigning incredulity. 'Mister, are you in the suicide business?'

'If you're going to work me over,' I said, 'I'll take it – I've got it coming. But one thing – do it in private.' I shut the door. 'You're an agent – you're not in the chorus line of *Showboat*. There are adults here – don't waste our time.'

David Shenson looked mildly surprised. 'Spiky, this is a small culture. I could finish you in this town. Do you realise the size of the chance you're taking?'

'Not me – you. I've written a great script – I'll write others. You're the one who's taking the chance. Ask Nancy. Ask Yvonne Mulgrew.'

'Who?'

'Mulgrew! Mulgrew!' I gave him a triumphant look – I hadn't managed one of those since I'd filched that twenty out of Karine's purse. 'And, when you've done that, ask the Vice President of Paramount.'

David Shenson sighed, looked at me, pityingly. 'Spiky, if you'd played your cards right, you could have asked the Vice President yourself.'

'What do you mean?'

'Tess dropped off your script at his home this morning and he read it on his way to work. He wanted to take you to lunch. Why do you think we were calling you?'

I looked at him, dumbly. I'd had a lunch meeting with the Vice President of Paramount? All I could think to say was, 'That's not the way it works.'

The door opened. Nancy stepped in. In the flooding daylight, she looked like a psychotic Doris Day. She stared at me. 'Did you fire him?'

'Yes,' said David Shenson.

'Good,' she said. 'I had one favour to pull and I pulled it and he threw it back in my face.'

'They break your heart, Nancy,' said David Shenson.

'Tell me about it.' Nancy turned to leave.

'Nancy, wait,' I said.

'Wait? For what? You disgust me. Why should I wait around to be disgusted?'

'Please, I was up all night working on a script.'

Nancy puckered her mouth, grunted.

'For Yvonne Mulgrew,' I said.

Nancy looked at me with wary eyes, the mouth still set in pucker.

'Who is this Mulgrew person?' asked David Shenson.

'She has television budgets,' I said. 'And I have a television script. And you know I'm good. And you know I can write.'

Nancy and Shenson looked at each other.

'What's it called?' asked Nancy.

'*Smoking Gun*,' I said.

'Good title,' Nancy said.

'Yes,' agreed David Shenson.

'Gimme.' Nancy held out her hand.

I opened my script bag and handed her a clean hard copy of *Smoking Gun*.

'I'll read it later,' she said and left the office. Which left me with David Shenson.

'Well?' I said.

'Well what? You'll never get another meeting with Paramount, mister. You blew that one.'

'He liked the script though. He must have. It stands to reason.'

'Yes,' admitted David Shenson, 'it stands to reason.'

'What happens now?'

'Now?' David Shenson stretched his arms, gripped the outer edges of his desk, a great beast of prey smiling gleefully. 'Now you go home and wait,' he said. 'And you wait. And you wait.'

I saw things clearly now. 'I blew my chance of development hell, didn't I?'

'You said it.' He stopped being a beast of prey and sat up straight and busied himself with other people's scripts. 'Now please step outside.'

I stepped outside.

'And shut the door.'

I shut the door.

I lay on my bed at the Jacey, making noisy slurps through a straw from a can of Dr Pepper. I made noisy slurps, therefore I was.

Aiden had been right about one thing – I needed a strategy. You needed the pretty balloons, sure – they're what kept you buoyant, still feeling you could succeed – but a strategy was ballast, otherwise you just drifted on, directionless, until you crash-landed someplace, out of your own control. The trick was to see the obstacles coming and have the ability to steer around them. I considered the pros and cons of balloon life – buoyancy versus ballast. If pure buoyancy was having my film made, what was the countering ballast? The answer had to be 'What happens after that?' And what happened after that was that I'd most likely turn into Aiden, who was one step ahead of me in the balloon race. Aiden now lived in a perpetual state of agitation since his one and so far only film had come and gone. The lease on his apartment was running out, he was living on his capital and the pressure was on him to come up with another saleable script. If he ran out of money before he came up with a saleable script, what would he live on? Wouldn't the immigration authorities start prodding him in the back? After all, there were plenty of honest to goodness American bums over here so why would they need to replenish their stock with a Scottish strain? OK, I asked myself again, if deportation was balloon drift, what then was the countering ballast?

The answer, plainly, was citizenship. If you were a citizen, they couldn't throw you out. If you were a citizen, you enjoyed the inalienable American right to bear arms, wank to Buttman videos and generally waddle around until somebody shot you or wired your jaws shut to stop you gorging yourself to death on muffins. If you were serious about working in the film business, you had to be uninterruptedly in LA. How, then, did one attain citizenship? My musings were interrupted by a gentle knocking. I checked routinely for untoward items and opened the door for the maid. Only it wasn't the maid.

'Oh, hi,' said Bobbie.

'Hi.'

'Lorne and I were wondering . . . we wanted to ask you a favour.'

'How is he? How is Lorne?'

Her bust looked nice through her jumper. She had a small waist.

'He's good. He's right next door. You want to say hello?'

I was wary about the favour. Hadn't I just advised myself not to become involved with time-wasters? 'I would,' I told her, 'only it's difficult right now.'

'Please.'

'I can't. I'm busy working on my . . .'

I heard a voice, Lorne's, shout out, 'Bobbie?'

'Yeah,' Bobbie called back, 'I'm asking him but he says he's busy.'

'Busy on what? He's watching Montel, I heard it through the wall. Tell him it'll only take a minute.'

Bobbie smiled gamely. 'That was Lorne.'

'Yes,' I said.

Bobbie cocked her head. There was something endearing about Bobbie. Obviously, with Lorne, she was in a difficult situation. Still, she'd kept her smile, her buoyancy.

'So you want to come in?' It was a statement. We were both cornered. What else could we do?

I nodded. 'Let me turn off the television.'

Their apartment had the same dimensions as mine but looked smaller. There were two of them, of course, and they'd lived here longer, acquired more clutter.

'You like American beer?' asked Lorne.

I was sitting on the two-seater settee. I looked up. 'Yes.' Lorne had given me some lyrics to read. I was reading them.

'It's piss. I prefer Belgian. But it's too expensive.'

Bobbie handed me a Coors. 'Thank you, Bobbie,' I said, using her name for the first time. She tore the ring pull off for Lorne.

'Careful with that,' Bobbie said.

'I know, honey,' Lorne said. He looked at me. 'You like my lyrics?'

'Yes,' I said, 'you know the human heart. Your work is universal.'

'Universal, yes, I've lived, I've covered the waterfront,' Lorne said. 'Did you recognise yourself from the lyrics?'

'Yes,' I said.

'That's because we are all one spirit.' When he said this, Lorne looked at Bobbie and winked.

I put down the A4 pages. I'd recognised myself all right and I'd recognised Lorne. He was that most hideous manifestation of the writerly will to live – the untalented stayer. I'd recognised this because I too was untalented. But, whereas I'd taken desperate steps to solve the hideous paradox of that unspeakable conundrum, Lorne's slovenly will lacked sufficient focus to kill anyone, even himself, except, apparently, on paper with the blunt instrument of his own dreary lyrics.

'I'd sing you something on Bobbie's guitar but you see how I'm fixed.' Lorne held up two stoic wrists in thick hospital bandages.

'Which sort of brings up the favour we want to ask.'

I took a sip of cold Coors. 'What is it?'

Bobbie was sitting cross-legged by Lorne. She said, 'I have a gig tonight at the Orange Grove – it's a bar in Silver Lake.'

'Oh?'

'Bobbie can't drive – normally I drive her but . . .' He held up his wrists again.

'We sold our car this morning to cover Lorne's medical costs.'

'And the rent. Don't forget the rent.'

'It's not just me. The rent's both of us, honey.'

'I know that, sugar,' Bobbie said. She squeezed his hand, instinctively. Lorne winced – a little theatrically, I thought.

'Sorry, hon.'

'Would you drive Bobbie?'

'Drive her?'

'Maybe he's busy.'

'Doing what? He's new here – he'll pick his toes, go to the movies. He can do that any time. Would you, friend?'

'What would I have to do?'

'Just drive her.'

'To the bar?'

'Yes, to the Orange Grove.'

'That's all?'

'That's all. And maybe stay for the gig. Make sure she gets paid.'

Bobbie looked awkward being talked about like she wasn't in the room. 'If he just drives me, Lorne.'

'But you get nervous, honey. Bobbie gets nervous. These places can be rough.'

I felt a faint alarm bell. 'Rough?'

'Not rough.'

'Not rough. But I worry,' Lorne said. 'It's a late gig, you get a bunch of guys with beers . . . You know what I'm saying?' He held up his wrists again. 'What could I do with these? Fan them to death?' He laughed.

'We'd pay you, of course,' Bobbie said. 'We'd ask someone else but . . .'

'But we don't know anybody else. We're hicks, like you.' Lorne looked at me, guy to guy. 'Come on, you've got a car, you've got wrists, you're a writer. I'll do the same for you when you try to kill yourself.'

'Lorne.'

'I'm kidding, honey. What do you say?'

I shrugged, smiled, nodded. 'OK,' I said, 'we hicks have to stick together.'

'All-right,' Lorne said. And, as Bobbie and I looked at each other, he pulled down on an imaginary train whistle and did one of those 'woo-woo' whoop things.

At the agreed time, I knocked on the door. I'd studied my maps and Silver Lake represented a less adventurous driving challenge than its name suggested. Bobbie slid out of her apartment, trying to be quiet. She bumped her guitar in its case on the doorframe and muttered, 'Shoot.'

As she shut the door softly behind her, I got a whiff of fresh perfume and liked it. 'He's sleeping,' she whispered. 'He's still sort of weak.'

'Yes,' I said. She was dressed in a black turtleneck sweater with a short denim skirt, black stockings, boots. Her long hair was combed as straight as it would ever be. A thought struck me. 'Don't you have a costume?'

'I'm wearing it,' Bobbie said. She dropped her keys into her bag, picked up her guitar by the case-strap and shouldered it. I must have looked surprised. 'Who did you think I was – Calamity Jane?'

On the drive to Silver Lake, Bobbie smoked two cigarettes. 'Cars and toilets, that's the only safe havens left.' She flicked her ash into her cupped hand, scattered it out the window and, as she did so, she talked about Lorne. How he was a wonderful talent. How it was unfair to judge him now he was going through a bad time. I wondered if she was chattering, keeping me at bay, in case I made a move on her.

'It's his faith,' she said. 'It isn't easy – his faith puts him in an awesome bind.'

'What faith? What bind?'

'I'll tell you later.'

'Tell me now.'

'Listen to the songs – if you're smart, you'll get it. Now take a left and then a right and we're there.'

There was no parking bay at the Orange Grove so we found a lot around the block and walked back. At the door, a man in a Timberland lumber shirt asked us for a cover charge. 'I'm performing,' Bobbie said, hitching her guitar for verification. He considered a couple of chalked names on a wallboard. 'Well, you're not The Clowns of Columbine so I guess you're Leanne Calvera?'

Bobbie nodded.

'One second, I'll get Marty. Hey, Mart.' He went to speak to Marty.

I looked at Bobbie. 'Leanne Calvera?'

'I know. But Bobbie Binkley sounds like a stripper.'

'It worked for Bobbie Gentry.'

'Don't confuse me.'

'Marty will take you backstage,' said the man in the lumber shirt.

'Thank you,' said Leanne Calvera. But it was Bobbie Binkley who squeezed my arm.

'Wish me luck,' she said.

I sat at the bar with my complimentary Schlitz and looked around. My four-year-old guidebook described Silver Lake as 'the coolest district in LA'. I felt out of place and uncomfortable there so I supposed it may well have been true. The Orange Grove looked like Corporate Bohemia to me – not the rundown dive on the prairie road I'd fondly imagined. After an hour, it began to fill up. Waitresses lit the artfully melted candles on the carefully distressed tables for the dining couples and big, clean-limbed middle-class boys began to spill out of shiny jeeps that they bumped confidently up on to the sidewalk. They were here for the Clowns of Columbine – not Leanne Calvera. Though, when Leanne Calvera's denim skirt rode up on the high stool she'd been provided with, they fluttered attentively and then, when she adjusted it and started singing, they talked again among themselves. I suppose to them she just looked like their good buddy's shapely mom.

Early on, Leanne sang bittersweet songs of thwarted love with a catch in her voice. I recognised some of Lorne's lyrics. Some of Leanne's later songs were more bitter than sweet and, when she sang those songs, she took the catch out of her voice and those were the songs and this was the Leanne that I preferred. When she finished her set, Leanne tipped an imaginary cowboy hat and left the stage to sarcastic applause and the bleeping of tills. The Clowns of Columbine, who'd been setting up their gear behind Leanne as she sang, filed moodily back on stage to stomps and cheers.

Their singer was into their second number, a bittersweet song of thwarted love, declaimed in a deafening whiney voice, when Leanne appeared beside me at the bar. She said something but I couldn't hear it over the Clowns. I watched Mart count out fifty dollars from the till and lay it on an open accounts book. As Leanne signed for her money, I understood why she'd changed her name – it was Leanne Calvera who took the insults up there, not Bobbie Binkley.

I knew the feeling. When you're somebody else, you're free.

We didn't drive straight back. Bobbie's nerves were jangled from the gig so I suggested we follow the signs for the lake, which wasn't far away. 'I liked your singing,' I said, to get it out of the way.

'Thank you,' said Bobbie. She took a sip from her bottled water.

'You should be in Nashville.'

'Bobbie gagged on her water. 'Listen, you any idea how many singers there are in Nashville? Whole lot more than there are writers in Hollywood – that's a fact.'

'Not like you.'

'All like me. My age, my look. It's Stepford Wives with spurs out there. Stetson Wives.'

'No,' I said again, 'not like you.' I didn't follow it up – just let it hang there. I saw a sign saying 'Picnic Area' so wheeled the car off the road and bumped over dry cracked earth till we were overlooking the lake. Then I stopped the car. 'Anyway,' she said, 'if you'd listened to the songs, you'd have got it. Like I told you earlier.'

'I did,' I said, 'I got it.'

'What did you get?'

'You sing bad songs and good songs. The bad songs are Lorne's – I know because he showed me his lyrics.'

'That's cruel. And the good ones?'

'Yours.'

'Wrong,' she said. 'They're all Lorne's.' She took another sip of water, dabbed her lips on the back of her hand.

I frowned. 'Maybe I didn't get it after all.'

'It's easy. His old songs have steel balls, his new songs are cheese balls. It's his faith, like I told you – his faith is a thorn in his flesh.'

'What is his faith?'

'Just regular Buddhist, like everybody else. When he first came here, he walked every day to the Hsi Lai Temple in West Covina. He used to study at the Cimarron Zen Center with Leonard Cohen. Lorne's a big Cohen fan.'

'It doesn't show in his music.'

'Ah,' Bobbie said, giving my cheek a little tweak, 'now you're getting it.' It was the first time she'd touched me. Maybe Oakies too were uncomfortable with touchy feelings the way we still were in Glasgow.

'You're saying the good songs were written before he got religion, the bad ones after?'

'Now you've got it,' Bobbie said. 'I've been with Lorne, off and on, since I was twenty-two. He's abused alcohol for years.'

'That why he's diabetic?'

'Didn't help. Back home, he had a car smash, left him a mess. In hospital, he saw visions.'

'Lorne saw visions?' I tried to keep the tone out of my voice.

'Yes.'

'What kind of visions?'

'Just visions. Angels, you know.'

'Boring old angels? That it?'

'He wasn't offered a menu. There wasn't any Visions Royale or anything. Lorne just got the regular kind.'

'With no fries or beverage?'

'With no fries or beverage, wise ass. Anyway, they turned him spiritual. He took the angels as a sign – that's why we came out here. And it helped, his faith definitely helped.'

I thought of Lorne with his congealing wrists, singing ancient Spandau Ballet songs on a snapaway stretcher. 'Yes,' I said, 'I can see that.'

'But it came at a price. It put out his fire, it killed his creativity.'

'No kidding?'

'He's written nothing worth a damn since. His agent's given up on him.'

'Couldn't he do something else?'

'People like Lorne don't do something else.'

'No,' I said. 'I'm with him there.' And I was, I was with him there.

We sat small in the darkness, in the little interior light of the car, looking out at the black hole where the lake was supposed to be. I thought for a moment. I said, 'It looks like his faith hasn't so much saved Lorne's life as prolonged it, dragged it out here into limbo-land.'

'Yes,' Bobbie said.

I felt my eyes give a beady squint. 'And you with it.'

'Uh-huh,' she said, 'and me with it.' And this time it was her who let it hang there.

Bobbie opened the car door. 'Careful,' I said, 'there's grizzly bears out here.'

'Grizzly bears, where'd you get that from?'

'My guidebook.'

'Ma gyde byook,' she said, mimicking my accent. It sounded cuter than it looks on paper.

I stepped out of the car and walked towards her, the ground bone hard and uneven beneath my loafers. 'I can't see the lake,' she said, leaning over a rail. 'It's too dark.'

We both leaned on our elbows, looked down. 'It's down there,' I said. 'We'll just have to take it on trust.'

'So you say. You're the one with the guidebook.'

'I need a guidebook. But you live here.'

'Nobody lives here,' she said. 'The Jacey is a waiting room. We all sit around, hoping one day we'll hear our names called.'

I slid along the rail, letting my arm brush her arm. 'If Lorne's Buddhist,' I said, 'what does that make you?'

'Nothing,' she said. 'I'm not anything. How about you?'

'Me neither,' I said. 'I'm nothing too.'

She turned, leaned her back to the rail. I did the same. We were looking up at the stars – big, full-fat American stars, swirling milky brown above Los Angeles, a diamante brooch that lay dropped or discarded in the desert.

'Do you have stars in Glasgow?'

'I don't know. I never looked up in Glasgow.'

'They must have all the answers. They've seen it all before.'

'No,' I said, 'the stars are dimwits. Just dead light.'

'I don't care,' she said, 'It's still my favourite kind.'

'Yes,' I said, 'mine too.' I left a little pause for punctuation. 'That's why we're both here.'

I leaned off the rail, stepped in front of her. 'I think we've covered the stars,' I said.

'Yes,' she said. 'What'll we do now?'

'I could consult the guidebook.'

She saw the guidebook in my pocket. She took it out of my pocket, threw it over the rail. 'Some things aren't in the guidebook,' she said.

I leaned in close, peered over her shoulder. 'You'd think at least it would have made a splash,' I said.

'What?'

'The guidebook.'

'I think I heard a splash.'

'You heard it?'

'I think so.'

'I didn't hear it.'

'A little one,' she said. 'But it was definitely a splash.'

And I kissed her.

On the drive back, we were hot, sweaty. I drove chivalrously fast for Bobbie's sake.

'By gosh almighty, I needed that,' Bobbie said.

'Me too. Think he'll be suspicious?'

'How would I know? If we're talking usual, he drives me – remember?'

I could see Bobbie next me, fussing with her make-up in the vanity mirror. I marvelled that, no matter how agitated a woman is, her hand is always steady when there's a lipstick in it.

'Will that do? It'll have to do,' she said. She put her make-up bag away, brushed invisible grass off her denim skirt for the trillionth time.

'We're late back,' I said. 'What'll you say?'

'I'll say sorry I'm late back, hon. Now slow down unless you want us both seeing angels.'

I eased my foot off the petrol, the gas.

'He'll probably be drunk in his chair like when I left him,' Bobbie said.

'Drunk. Broke. Diabetic. He's quite a catch.'

'You missed bipolar.'

'Don't we turn off here? I think we turn off here.'

I swerved the car fast. Bobbie screamed, instinctively hugged her guitar case. We halted sedately by the sidewalk. 'Sorry,' I said, 'wrong turning.'

Bobbie, shaken, straightened up. 'If I was bored with your driving, I'd have let you know,' she said. 'Up ahead.'

I steered up the street, rummaging in my jacket as I drove, found my mobile and turned it on. I remembered I'd turned it off in the Orange Grove. 'My agent warned me always to keep this on.'

'They all say that,' Bobbie said.

'Does yours?'

'No.'

'Does Lorne's?'

'Lorne's won't answer his calls. Hey, where you going? Take a left.'

I took a left. Green and red strip neon, at once harsh and feeble, spelled out before us 'Jacey Gardens'.

I drove to the back of the building, over strewn garbage from burst bin bags, looking to park the car. Burger cartons scrunched under the tyres as I halted by the wheelie bins.

Bobbie sat looking ahead at the high, cemented wall of the yard. Some bricks were exposed from where the garbage trucks kept nudging it. 'Home sweet home,' she said. She didn't move.

I didn't speak. I had the mobile to my ear and was listening to my messages – my single message. When Bobbie made to get out of the car, I took her wrist gently, stopping her. 'Wait.'

'What?'

'What happens now, Bobbie?'

'Nothing. We had an itch, we scratched it. Nothing happens now.'

I thought about ballast and about balloons. I thought about the green card I needed and decided to say something big – a big bold dangerous thing that would stay with her, that would shake her up and make her take me seriously and not see me just as a fling to be dismissed because her boyfriend hadn't touched her in God knows how long. I wanted to see if I could make an option out of Bobbie. So I said to her, 'Leave him – leave Lorne for me.'

'What?'

'You heard.'

'That's crazy.'

'You're right,' I said, 'it's crazy anywhere else but not out here, where we are.'

She gave a little gasping laugh to emphasise my craziness. 'You're putting me on.'

'No, I'm not.'

'We don't even know each other.'

'You know all there is to know about Lorne. That make you want to stay with him?'

'Lorne and me won't always be here.'

'No, they'll throw you out when you can't make the rent.'

'That's insulting. I'm going.' But she didn't move. 'Anyhow, what makes you any different?'

'I'm blessed,' I said. 'I've got the touch.'

'All writers say that.'

'Even Lorne?'

'Even Lorne.'

'Paramount says it too.'

'What?'

I spoke slowly, making it more of a moment for all of us, for me and her – and, of course, for Lorne since he wasn't here to hear it for himself. 'That was a message from my agent,' I said. 'I have a meeting with the Vice President of Paramount . . . about a script of mine . . . a film script . . . a script for a film.'

'A film script?'

'Yes.'

'You have a meeting with Paramount about a film script?'

'Yes.'

'All-right,' she said but her tone was subdued. She looked at me, looked away, stared at the cement wall. She was taking me seriously. Why wouldn't she? She was stuck in Lorne-land and here was I, a mad cavalier with a rope ladder, a Paramount rope ladder, declaring his impulsive love. She started breathing quicker. I could see the rise and fall, under her austere black turtleneck, of tiny panicky waves. 'And you're asking me to leave Lorne?'

'Yes.'

'Why?'

'Because we're right for each other. I sense it – so do you.'

'Jesus Christ.'

I looked at her, honestly, frankly. If I could only get her on my hook, I was thinking, I could chuck her over the side if and when I landed a bigger, better fish.

'My-oh-my! Now I've heard it all.' She pitched forward laughing, then sort of rocked to and fro, still laughing to herself. It was a little discomfiting but I sat quietly while she did this, giving her plenty of reel, till she'd calmed from the hysteria of the evening and started collecting her thoughts. When she was composed, she ran her pinkies under her eyes, blinked rapidly and said, 'OK, here's what it is. There's something you don't know about Lorne. Six years ago, way before the car smash, he was diagnosed with MS.'

I nodded. 'He just gets cuter and cuter.'

'They say in another five years he could be in a wheelchair. Don't you understand?'

'Pretty much,' I said. 'Since you'll be the one pushing it, you must understand even better.'

She looked at me like I was the Jacey's resident fleeing Nazi. Her eyes were wide, her open mouth trying to find what words next to say. I resisted a strong urge to pull that mouth to mine. But this was a cold thing, a power thing, so it had to come of its own accord.

'I can't leave him,' Bobbie said. 'I'd never forgive myself.'

We gazed up through the dark at the squares of window, their light cold and yellow like an illness. 'I'm all he's got.'

'Think about it,' I said.

We looked at each other. I thought about the green card I needed – maybe she thought about the rent she couldn't pay.

'I'm sincere,' I told her.

'So you say.'

I took her hands and we sat in silence, me caressing them.

After a long time of this hand touching, Bobbie sighed and said, 'Well?'

Then we stepped out of the car, picked our way through the garbage and went in.

Back in my apartment, the message light was flashing. I pressed 'Play' and sat by the phone, listening. David Shenson's voice said, 'Spiky? You there? I'll try your cell phone.' The next message said, 'OK, I've left a message on your cell phone. You have the message. It's out of my hands. It's your career, Spiky, your life – it's up to you.' Through the wall, I could hear Lorne's muffled stretch and yawn as he woke up, bleary, in his armchair. The message machine spoke – 'Message three.' A woman's voice – a strange squeaky accent – said, 'Hi, it's me. You still haven't called. I just wanted to make sure you were . . .'

I jabbed a button, stopping Chloe.

I sat wondering what to do. I knew I should call my wife. I picked up the phone. Two or three times I picked up the phone, swithered each time and put it back in its cradle. If I spoke to my wife, her voice might waken me from my dream. Once awake, you never get a dream back again, do you?

I put my ear to the wall and listened. I could hear Bobbie's voice arguing with Lorne.

I felt better.

CHAPTER TEN

At ten-forty-five next morning, I was sitting in the car with the windows down.

I'd come early, so I could drink it all in.

'Jonesie, hey, Jonesie.'

'Why, if it isn't Miss Desmond.'

'Where's Mr de Mille shooting, Jonesie?'

'Stage eighteen, Miss Desmond.'

'Open the gates, Jonesie.'

'Sure, Miss Desmond.'

I entered the Paramount Building by Melrose, just like Norma Desmond and Joe Gillis had in *Sunset Boulevard*. As I drove Wendy up to the barrier, that was the dialogue that was in my mind. No doubt it would have been in your mind too but, since I was the one who'd robbed and murdered a man to get this far, you'll forgive me if I hog my own limelight.

The entrance to Paramount wasn't gates like in the movie – it was a barrier.

I gave my name to a security man in a pale blue shirt and he checked for me on his list. I was sweaty from nerves – he was sweaty from the heat. He had a line round his hair where his hat had been. If this meeting didn't go the way I hoped, I'd be wearing something similar myself as I stood behind the counter of Burger King.

'Thank you, please drive on through and pull up – I'll direct you.'

I did as asked and a valet guy parked my car while the security man gave me a map of the studios. 'The Ball Building is to the left.'

He ringed the Ball Building on my map and pointed left. I thanked him and walked off right.

'You're going the wrong way.'

'Don't worry – I know what I'm doing.'

Map in hand, I ambled along 4th Street past de Mille and Sturges. On Avenue P, I headed past the Lubitsch Building then on beyond Props and the Cabinet shop. There was nothing exciting to see there so I turned into Avenue L, down by the Crosby Building, then took a right past the Water Tower that stands up beyond Zukor.

It goes without saying that the presence, if not the ghost, of Eric Ross walked alongside me at all times on my exquisite prom-enade, which I suppose, not wishing to be melodramatic about it, was a walk of death. Yet I felt, as they say, no ill. If his ghost had walked ahead of me and not alongside me so that I could actually have seen it, I would, without doubt, have felt differently. Luckily, this didn't happen and I did not see the ghost of Eric Ross. Merely felt his presence. And I could live with a merely. I don't know why I felt him but never saw him. Perhaps in Los Angeles, which is bright and hot, ghosts disappear in the sun.

On Avenue A, I stopped and took some deep breaths. I folded away my map, carefully, in case things went badly and I needed a souvenir. In quick succession, I walked past the Swanson Building, the Wilder, the Lasky, walking further than I needed to so that, yes, finally, I could stand with something like reverence looking up before me at the Hope Building. They call them Buildings but they're really only glorified, white painted office units – they're just names.

What I'm saying is some things you have to drink in, squeeze dry and savour, while you have the chance because, life being what it is – whatever it is – that chance might never come again. Once I'd glutted myself with gawping, I doubled back and stood outside the Ball Building. I smoothed my jacket, binned my gum and then stepped into reception and whatever fate had prepared for me.

'How was he?' asked Tess Schwartzenbuch.

'Who?'

'The Vice President of Paramount.'

'I don't know – I didn't see him.'

'I thought you had a meeting with the Vice President of Paramount?' She looked alarmed. 'Didn't you go?'

'Of course I went.' It came out grumpy.

Tess went glacial. 'The term "of course" is inappropriate,' she reminded me. 'You didn't go last time. I myself had to apologise on behalf of this office.'

'Nancy apologised on behalf of this office.'

'My role was to undertake the pre-apology.'

'What pre-apology?'

'The pre-apology to the First Assistant of the Vice President's Secretary, then to his Secretary in person. If the ground had gone unprepared, then his Secretary might have stalled the call indefinitely – the call for the apology proper. Why is that amusing?'

'It isn't amusing – it's insane.'

'We none of us make the rules but it pays to observe them. I should try to bear that in mind if I were you.'

'I will – if I'm here long enough.'

'Indeed.'

She picked up an internal phone, flicked her warmth back on. She looked at me, put the phone back down. 'David will see you now.'

I went up. Shenson was sitting at his desk, eating lunch. He had his jacket off, his shirtsleeves rolled up. 'I have an extra bagel,' he said. 'You want it?'

'No.'

'It's cream cheese.'

'Still no.'

'I ordered two in a moment of weakness. Then I remembered I loved myself.'

'Maybe you'll love me too one day, David.'

'That's what we're waiting to find out. You want some water?'

I shook my head. 'You're being nice. Have I got cancer?'

'If you had cancer we'd want fifteen per cent of it. Who'd you see at Paramount?'

'I don't know. Eve la Due.'

'Eve la Due is at Paramount? She was at Fox 2000. You sure you went to the right studio, Spiky?' He looked at his extra cream cheese bagel, waveringly.

'Yes, I was at Paramount.'

'You know, with *your* track record . . .' He gave a little laugh, went serious, binned the bagel untouched. 'What'd she say about the script?'

'She loved the script.'

'Of course she loved the script. Or you wouldn't have been there. She give you any notes?'

'She asked about the murder.'

'She didn't like the murder?'

'No, she liked it. She wasn't sure it could be done that way.'

'What'd you tell her?'

'I told her it could. I said I'd researched the murder thoroughly.'

'Good boy.'

'I said, if she was still in doubt, maybe we could find a guinea pig.'

'I could think of a few.'

'So could she. She mentioned your name.'

'Eve la Due is a cunt.'

'She was laughing.'

'That's different.' David Shenson coughed, flexed his fingers. 'Audiences love "how-to-do-it".'

'Yes,' I said.

We sat silently for a moment. 'David?'

'Yes?'

'Why am I sitting here?'

'We're killing time. Nancy is on the phone to Paramount. Trying to find out how your meeting went.'

'I'm telling you how it went. I was there – I was in the room.'

'Sure you were. You're in this room too – that doesn't mean you have any idea what's going on, does it?' He looked at me. 'Do you?'

'What?'

'Have any idea what's going on?'

'No.'

'Well, what's going on at this moment is that your future is being decided.' He poured some Vittel water into a paper cup. 'If all goes well, I'll get up from this desk and give you one of my big special hugs. That'll mean you've made me love you.'

'What if all doesn't go well?'

He did ruthless Hollywood agent acting. 'I'll still get up. I'll shake you warmly by the hand and remind you that you're a genius of the highest order but that the world is run by fools. I'll tell you to pay no heed because I and all at Winters and Daly are working tirelessly on your behalf and that success is just around the corner.'

'Does that mean what I think it means?'

'You got it. The moment you leave this building – you're history. Which is to say you'll no longer exist. We'll delete you, your dreams and all your endearing little foibles from our data banks.'

'Gee, Dad,' I said.

'I'm not kidding,' he said. 'Stand on the sidewalk and watch. Ours isn't a revolving door by accident. As you walk out another set of foibles shambles right on in.'

'That's the way it works, right?'

'You can laugh.'

'I'm not laughing.'

'Believe me, Spiky, this isn't England. No offence but here we have an industry – there you have a cottage industry. I meet people who would kill, literally kill, to be where you're sitting now.'

'I know you do,' I said.

And I did – I knew.

David Shenson calmed down. 'Have you seen *The Lord of the Rings* yet?'

I wasn't listening. My future had been edited down to a tiny decisive exchange. 'So what I'm waiting for is a yes or a no, right?'

He leaned forward on his desk. 'What you need is a yes. Everything else is nowhere. Sorry.'

I nodded.

He remembered he was a ruthless Hollywood agent. 'Actually, I'm not sorry – it's just business, simple as.'

I could hear Nancy's voice outside barking orders. She didn't knock as she entered the office.

'I should've knocked.'

'We don't want you to knock, Nancy,' said David Shenson. 'We're all ears – what's the word?'

'Well . . .' Her voice was phlegmy. She spotted the Vittel bottle. 'Can I have some of that water?'

Shenson poured some into his own empty cup, proffered.

Nancy threw down a copy of *Looking at the Stars*, took a long drink of water. Finally she said, 'There's a position.'

'No word?' I said. 'Just a position?'

'You want to hear the position or don't you?'

'Shh,' said David Shenson, looking at me. 'He wants to hear the position.'

'Well, it's simple,' began Nancy. 'The reason Paramount are moving so fast is that they have to spend money.'

'Why?'

'It's a tax thing,' said David Shenson. 'Will you shut up and listen?'

Nancy gave a small belch and continued, 'They've got five million sitting offshore which they've managed to move from their mainstream operation over to their independent arm – which, incidentally . . .' She jabbed me with her finger in the back. 'Is why you saw Eve la Due and not the Vice President.'

David Shenson said, 'Wasn't Eve la Due at Fox 2000?'

'That was Eve Lanois,' said Nancy.

'Will you shut up and listen?' I told David Shenson. I mimicked his accent. It might have been the last point I ever scored off him so I figured what the hell? They were both looking at me. I said, 'Is five million pounds . . .'

'Dollars.'

'Dollars. Is that enough to make a film?'

'Yes, a small film – for their independent arm.' Nancy took another sip of water, binned the cup. 'Sorry, did you want that cup?'

'No, I'd finished,' said David Shenson. 'There's a bagel in that bag – I haven't touched it.'

'What's on it?'

'Cream cheese.'

Nancy did throwing up her arms in horror. 'No way! What? I'd never dare.'

David Shenson frowned. 'Eve la Due is black. Can she green-light a project?'

'Not yet,' said Nancy, 'but, in time to come, I think she will – I think she'll be the first.'

'You think so?'

'Wait and see,' Nancy said.

I listened to them chatter but they were veering off course. I wanted someone to talk about the big question, my question. Nobody did so I geared myself up. 'Is that the position?'

'Yes, that's the position.'

I felt that strange capricious thing, that exhilarating flutter of heart-in-the-mouth that normally precedes a prolonged misery. 'And is there a word as well as a position?'

'Yes,' Nancy said, 'there's a word.'

I looked down at my shoes – old faithful, thieving, murdering shoes. I looked up. 'What's the word, Nancy?'

'Well . . .'

I glanced at Shenson. He wouldn't look back at me. He was rummaging for something in a low desk drawer – his hanging judge's black cap possibly.

'The word is maybe,' said Nancy.

Shenson stopped rummaging.

'Maybe?' I said. 'Is that good?'

'It's not as good as yes but better than no,' said Nancy. She tapped on the office window, motioned. The door opened. One of the junior agents came in holding a silver tray with a bottle of champagne and some flute glasses. A few of the other agents dribbled in behind her.

'I thought this called for a celebration,' Nancy said.

'But it's only a maybe,' I said.

'I know,' she said, 'but this might be as good as it gets.'

The cork popped out with a polite Californian 'phut'. I decided I'd run with it. Nancy bossed the agency – if she was happy, that's what counted. I made myself look all smiles.

Probably because it was his office, and I was tangentially his client, David Shenson decided to be elated. 'Stand up,' he ordered.

I stood up. He came toward me. 'It was only a maybe,' I said.

'Maybes are what we live for,' said David Shenson. And he gave me one of his big special hugs, allowing me a brief whiff of cream cheese and stale cologne.

I still hadn't heard about *Smoking Gun*. I decided to strike while the iron was tepid. 'Nancy, have you spoken to Yvonne Mulgrew?'

'I was coming to that. I spoke to her yesterday. She likes the engine. Says it has a decent engine but plodding dialogue. She'll put it on the list for their discussion group. Champagne, anybody?' Nancy proffered the bottle.

'Not me – not alcohol.'

'Or me.'

'Nor me.'

'Nobody? Nothing? You pussies.' Nancy looked around disgustedly at her agents. 'It's his big day – he has a maybe.'

'And an engine with plodding dialogue,' I reminded us all. That touch of gallows humour perked up the mood a little.

'Well at least let's do the thing with the glasses,' badgered David Shenson. He made everybody pick up a flute from the tray.

'OK. One, two, three . . .' ordered Nancy.

And they did. The agents, senior and junior, Nancy and David, did the thing with the glasses, which meant pinging their flutes with a fingernail so that they all made a sustained zinging tingling noise.

OK, it doesn't sound much. But it was 'The March of the Toreadors' to me.

Down in reception, I looked to seize my moment. I stood at the desk flushed with the confused confidence of having been pinged at by powerful Hollywood agents. Tess Schwartzenbuch let me wait while she oozed her brand of nasally android velvet down the phone. I decided Connecticut must be the Chalfont St Giles of America. I got the feeling she was stringing it out to exasperate me. Or maybe I was just over-eager to proclaim my triumph. Finally, she said, 'Hello again, I hear you have some news.'

'Yes,' I said, 'Good news. Excellent news.' I beat a little tattoo on her desk with my hands. 'Would you do something for me, Tess?'

She looked wary, kept smiling. 'Go on.'

'Would you ring *The Herald* newspaper in Scotland for me?'

'*The Her–ald*? I don't know that journal.'

'You don't have to know it. I just want to tell them my good news. About the film, you know.'

'Your good news? I heard it was a maybe.'

'That's right. I wanted to tell them about the maybe.'

She looked doubtful, wrong-footed. I realised I was asking her to breach some sort of protocol. I turned folksy, trying to appeal to the hick in her. 'I wanted to share it with my people . . . my countrymen, you know?' Yes, I actually said countrymen. Like we all lived under pelts in tepees, with goats, singing mouth music. And nobody did that in Scotland, only Gaels – and then only in documentaries and if the money was right.

'What's the problem?'

'You don't have a film. You may never have a film.' She wasn't wrong-footed. She was clear now. 'So I don't think I can do that.'

'This agency represents me. That's what agencies are for.'

'I know but your project hasn't been signed and sealed. If we release the news and the film doesn't happen, it'll reflect badly on this agency. It protects you too.'

I couldn't argue with her logic but did anyway. 'I'll protect me,' I said, trying a new tack. 'Let me ask you something. How many people live in the United States?

'Why?'

'Never mind why – just tell me.'

Tess considered. 'I guess around what? Two hundred and fifty million?'

'Right,' I said. '*The Herald* is Scottish. You any idea how many people live in Scotland?'

She folded her hands on her desk, sighed. 'I have no idea – twenty, thirty million?'

'Under five million. You know how many of that five million read *The Herald*?'

She sighed. 'Like I'm dying to know.'

'Around a hundred thousand people. You know how many of that hundred thousand people will read the features page of the paper?

She sat, stiffly, looking straight ahead. Forget breeding and education, she had the sullen glare of a scheme kid in the English room being lectured by a demented supply teacher.

'No more than twenty thousand,' I enlightened her. 'And, of that number, maybe only a tiny fraction will read it right through to the end.'

Tess saw her opening and pounced. 'In that case, why is it so important to you that I make the call?'

I leaned my elbows on the desk, spoke quietly, intensely, from the heart. 'Because that tiny fraction are all the bastards I want to fuck.'

We'd reached an impasse – she wanted to scratch my eyes out, I wanted to punch hers black and blue.

Nancy walked past. She'd jammed a plastic stopper in the champagne bottle, saving it for the next hack with a maybe. 'What's the problem?'

Tess adopted a martyred air, woman to woman. 'I'm being asked if I might call the Scottish press to tell them about the film.'

Nancy took in Tess, then me, without breaking stride. In two looks she'd weighed up her checks and balances. 'So do it,' she said. 'Now.'

'Yes, Nancy.'

Tess picked up the phone like it was a steaming turd.

'Thank you, Nancy.' I called.

'Writers,' huffed Nancy and stepped into the relentless brush and sweep of the revolving door.

Within an hour, *The Herald* had rung back and I'd done a lengthy self-satisfied interview, just as I'd always dreamed of doing, all the way from my suite on the summit of the Big Rock Candy Mountain, down along the zinging wires to Sconeland.

But Tess was right. No matter how heartily I gorged myself on the marvellous gift of me or, to be more accurate, the thefts of the gifts of others, *Looking at the Stars* was still, and perhaps would forever remain, only a maybe – unlike the murder of its creator, which had been green-lit, signed and sealed. And lacked only an audience.

In the Jacey Gardens, I lay on my bed and thought about the future. Both my futures – the balloon future and the ballast future. The balloon future airily foretold that I'd remain in America, become a successful screenwriter and dance along an unbroken nimbus line, garnering fame, wealth and the love of women as I went. The predictive criteria the balloon future used for postulating its theory were admittedly sketchy but wistful longing and self-delusion seemed prominently to the fore. The ballast future, on the other hand – or the realistic future as I couldn't help thinking of it – seemed confirmed, rather than suggested, by a leaden jumble of indisputable facts that fate had piled up to form an immovable, daunting monolith. To pick randomly from the monstrous pile, I was a thief and a murderer and I was dependent financially on the father and sister of the man I had stolen from and killed. My heart and head told me that I would be found out, vilified and punished. My heart and head told me this because they were, like me, Scottish, and, in our culture, Sconeland culture, that was the way it usually worked for hearts and heads and people like me.

Speculations of defeat keened at my entrails and I thought longingly of the dancing nimbus life I'd lose even though, truth be told, I'd never really had it. That's balloons for you – when you've been up in one, you can never forget the view.

My spirits were raised by the sound of movement in the next apartment, Bobbie's apartment. I heard their door open and a moment later a ring on my bell. I jumped up and speedily binned or tidied the more desolate of my debris, before giving the room a quick toot with my Eau Sauvage aftershave spray.

I kept the smile on my face but my heart sank.

'Hi,' I said.

'Hey,' said Lorne. He wasn't smiling. 'Can I come in?'

I nodded.

He came in, stood, looking around. 'Nice place.'

'Same place as yours.'

'Mine's for two – yours is for one.'

I let it pass. 'Like some wine, Lorne? Coffee?'

'No wine, no coffee,' Lorne flatly said. He wouldn't sit down either. He picked up my car key, rudely looked at the Hertz fob and put it back down. 'I hear you had a meeting with Paramount?'

Maybe that was it. Professional envy. I soft-pedalled. 'Oh, sure. But you know what these things are like.'

'No I don't,' he said, abruptly. 'I've never been to a meeting with Paramount. Tell me what it's like.'

It wasn't professional envy. Or, if it was, it was tied up with something else – the other bigger thing he'd come to confront. 'How'd it go?'

'Very well,' I said. 'Pretty good.'

I knew he'd report back to Bobbie about our conversation – the one we were on the cusp of undertaking – so I wanted Bobbie to receive a heroic report of my conduct so as not to lose faith in me. I started to explain to Lorne in exciting detail how the meeting had gone and what my agents had said and about the quirky pinging fingernail thing and I suppose I laid it on medium to treacle. Not that it mattered because Lorne wasn't listening. As I was telling him these things, he had stuck a cold grin on his boozy face and I watched him take something from the pocket of his grimy jeans, slowly, slowly, as I spoke. At first I thought it was a pale blue hanky but what man keeps a pale blue hanky? And it was when he started winding it, playing it around his knuckles and fingers, that I saw the tiny white lace bow and recognised the pale blue thing as Bobbie's panties from the night before and that's when I stopped talking.

'You've stopped talking,' Lorne said. 'Go on.'

I went on but of course I couldn't take my eyes off these panties. He turned them inside out, giving them, and me, a look of mild scrutiny. He began picking little white flakes of cum off the gusset and I felt my face go red. 'Bobbie have a good gig last night?'

'Yes,' I said, 'it seemed to go really well.'

'That's not what she said.'

'No?'

He gave me an even stare but I saw his hard-guy grin tremble at the lower lip. 'Bobbie and me have been through a whole lot together, friend – more than you'll ever know.'

'I do know,' I said. 'She told me what you'd been through.'

His eyes gave a little flutter, hovering briefly between self-pity and surprise. 'She tell you I'm a spiritual man now?'

'She told me all about you, Lorne.'

'That I was above fleshly pleasures and all its sordid adherents?' I watched him pick a little more gunk off.

'She told me you were impotent, yes.'

I'd passed straight through guilt without stopping. I'd decided, if it came to it, I could take Lorne. He still had thick brown plasters on his wrists. Like he'd said himself, what could he do? Fan me to death?

'She tell you about how I passed out on Mount Baldy? About how that was when they first knew I had MS?'

'She didn't tell me that.'

'My religion is a great comfort to me.'

'Yes, I can see that.'

'Wonder what else Bobbie didn't tell you?'

'Or you, Lorne.'

He gave a snorting laugh. 'No, I know all there is to know about Bobbie.' He held the panties between thumb and forefinger, gave them a disdainful jiggle. 'She had these off and in the laundry bag a little too quickly for my liking.'

I watched him scrunch the panties, push them back down into the pocket of his jeans. He'd wanted my attention on that because then I didn't see his free hand take one of those flashy, movie crack-dealer, silver automatics from behind his back and point it at my face.

'Lorne, don't be silly.'

'In case you're in any doubt,' Lorne enlightened me, 'I've used this weapon before. It took off a candy salesman's kneecap in Flagstaff, Colorado and some toes and the ball of a foot in Liberal, Oklahoma.'

I didn't doubt him. I didn't ask why the kneecap had been removed, or what a psychotic warrior drunk was doing in a town called Liberal – I didn't do anything. I just remained very still. And Lorne remained pointing the gun into my curious, horrified face. If it would have helped my cause, I would have broken down and blubbered or pissed myself – anything to give Lorne the victory he needed. But the nervous system, I discovered, goes into shock at such moments – mine did anyway – and I could no more have pissed myself than wrestled the gun from him with a slick movement and knocked him out with a single punch like Humphrey Bogart in a noir movie. I could have begged for my life, though, like Bob Hope in a *Road* film. I could have managed that and more for Lorne, with gusto, had he demanded it. But he didn't demand it – just kept pointing his gun and staring.

Eventually, fearing that we were at a conversational impasse and that he might shoot me as a sort of crazed punctuation mark, like in a Laurence Sterne novel, I risked a question. 'What do you want me to do, Lorne?'

'Stay away from Bobbie. Keep your worm in your pants. Leave her alone.'

'I will – I promise you that.'

'Fucking spitball.'

He jabbed the gun at my face for emphasis. I jumped, dutifully. Satisfied, he grunted. He tipped the barrel up so that it was pointing at the ceiling. He kept his finger on the trigger.

Because the atmosphere had cooled, I couldn't help asking, 'With respect, Lorne – no offence – but why did you get me to drive Bobbie? Why did you bring us together?'

Lorne let my words sink in. He straightened himself up to his full medium height, gave a sort of showy, fighter's hitch of his shoulder. 'That needn't concern you,' he decreed.

I realised he was enjoying himself. He had loosened up into his cameo role as Crazy Lorne, Widowmaker of the New West. He gave his belt buckle a little tug over his beer paunch, 'That is between me and my creator.'

'I'll do whatever you say, Lorne,' I assured him.

Lorne jack-knifed and gave a schoolgirl giggle. For a moment, he did actually seem psychotic. 'Will you now? Will you really?' He started waving the gun around the room, pointing idly at things – lamp stand, socks, window blinds. For the first time, I realised he was more drunk than sober. 'There's one more thing I want.'

'What's that?'

'Leave.'

'You want me to leave the Jacey Gardens?'

'I thought I liked you. But I don't. I smell something off of you. You're a bringer of bad news.'

I shuffled. 'It's the only news I've got.'

We looked at each other – drunk to spitball. He said, 'Bobbie and me were here before you came. We'll be here after you've gone.'

I felt a harsh painful intrusion and realised he'd jammed what would fit of the gun barrel into my ear.

'Speaking as a fellow writer,' Lorne said, 'wouldn't you agree this is a significant experience?'

'Yes,' I said.

'If I don't pull this trigger,' Lorne said, 'you've got yourself an anecdote.' He wiggled the gun about in my ear. 'And, if I do, then I've got myself a ballad.'

'I'll go,' I said. 'I'll leave end of the month, promise.'

'Thank you.'

He removed the gun. He made me lick the end of the barrel clean. 'Ear wax,' he explained.

Lorne seemed a man of complicated pleasures.

I rang Chloe that night to get it out of the way. I told her all my news in a gabble – the film, the parties, the *Herald* article, all of it. Everything, of course, except screwing Bobbie and being threatened with an automatic weapon by her jealous boyfriend. After some initial frostiness, she succumbed to my apparent enthusiasm – which was to say my genuine enthusiasm. It only came out hollow because I was telling Chloe. As I spoke to my wife, I realised she was the living embodiment of everything I associated with home and the simple truth was that I didn't want to go back there.

Not ever. My marriage was a prison, my small country its exercise yard. I belonged here, sitting in the desert, dreaming of miracles. Despite everything, America was still a big place, with wide fences. The deluded, the deranged, the demented – each of us could nurture, unmolested, our unique talent to its fullest flourish. Lurid flowerings, maybe, and scents that didn't suit all tastes but I, for one, was drawn like an insect to its seductive petals.

Chloe broke the silence. 'I saw Denis today.'

'Oh, yes?'

'Aren't you jealous?'

'Is he working?'

'Yes, in a call centre.'

'A call centre? Fuck.'

'He was upbeat, though. He's up for a part in *Prime Suspect*.'

'Did you tell him I was in Los Angeles?'

'Yes.'

'What'd he say?'

'Nothing. Why didn't you invite him to our wedding?'

'I don't know.'

'He was hurt.'

'Did Denis say that?'

'No.'

'Then how do you know he was hurt?'

'It was the way he didn't say it.'

'He say anything else? Apart from not saying he was hurt?'

'Yes. He said at least things can't get any worse for him.'

'Yes they can. They could move the call centre to Karachi. Hello? You still there?'

'I'm here. When are you coming home?'

'I'm waiting for news.'

'How long will you wait?'

'I don't know. I'll keep waiting. I'll go on waiting. It can't be long now.'

'I miss you.'

Silence.

'Hello?'

I couldn't say it. I just couldn't say to my wife, 'I miss you.'

I put the phone down.

For the next couple of days I sneaked around the apartment, trying to keep out of Lorne's way. I kept hoping for Paramount to ring, or Winters and Daly, but nobody did. The writer's life is like that. When somebody says 'soon' to a writer they don't mean a day or a week, they mean three months, maybe six, and before you know, a project's drifted on for years, unpaid, before the call is finally made and his script is dumped in a shallow grave, then shovelled over with thin praise, tales of bad timing and hard cheese. And that's if you're one of the lucky ones. Not necessarily talented, just lucky. There were plenty of talented people working in call centres. There were others too, like Denis Rourke, me too perhaps, if Eric Ross were to prove in death no luckier as a writer than he had been as a doctor. 'When I was young,' went a quote I once heard from some anonymous grizzled hack, 'I thought I could perfect the work and life could fuck itself. Now that I'm older, all I have is a fucked life.'

I was older. I didn't want a fucked life. That much, I hoped, was avoidable.

The next day, I gambled and made a phone call.

Bobbie's voice said, 'Hello?'

'Bobbie, it's me . . .'

I felt her go tense, adjust instantly, the seamless way that women can. 'No, I think you've got the wrong area code – that's the old area code, three ten.' In the background I could hear Lorne, thrumming Bobbie's guitar.

'Can you meet me tomorrow, one o'clock, at the Coffee Bean on Westwood?'

She didn't miss a beat. 'I know, it's confusing, no problem.'

I hung up the phone, put my ear to the wall. Silence. Maybe Lorne had stopped with the guitar and started thrumming Bobbie instead. Maybe Bobbie liked being thrummed. Who could say for sure? These were people – anything was possible with people.

I knew that better than most.

CHAPTER ELEVEN

The traffic shushed on the junction of Olympic near Westwood. Nice traffic, well-bred traffic, sifted through a finer vehicular mesh than Glasgow's. I watched dainty deli vans, Coffee 2U, Porsches, big square Mercs, big flat Caddies, all class, tail to tail, whether old or breath-suckingly new.

'I've missed you.'

'I've missed you. I didn't think you'd call.'

'I had a gun in my ear where the phone should be.'

Bobbie stirred the ice in her cola with a straw, smiled. She said, 'A person could wait their whole life to say a line like that.'

'Not if they're an acquaintance of Lorne. Or, more especially, of you.'

'He gets jealous.' She used a girly smile to take the edge off it. She lifted her glass but didn't sip, just held it in her long fingers for the cool feeling. 'He tell you about the salesman's kneecap in Flagstaff, the toes in Liberal?'

'Yes.'

'That bother you?'

'Is it true?'

'I don't know. He says it is. I'm not exactly going back there and find out.'

'I like your hair.'

'Thank you.' She touched her naturally bushy, trying-to-go-straight hair. 'I'm telling you because you may as well know everything.'

She had on a grey silk blouse with dark skirt and a little more jewellery that I recalled from last time. She'd made an effort to look good, which was risky. I told myself, if I heard the sound of hooves, I'd duck. It would be Lorne on a mule, trying an Oklahoma drive-by.

'He gets off on you being with other men, doesn't he?'

Bobbie rolled weary eyes. 'He doesn't only get off on it – he actively promotes it. You know that.'

'What's he get out of it?'

'Not what he wants, that's for sure. Lorne thinks the more fucked-up he is, the more he'll have to write about. It doesn't work that way. He just hates himself and drinks more.' She frowned, gave a little breathy laugh, sipped her Coke.

'Then he sits down in a lotus position with a four-pack and a six-gun, looking for peace?'

'You got it. Amen,' Bobbie said.

I wanted to ask her but hesitated – I was needled, I wasn't sure I could deal with the answer. Anyway, I asked her. 'What do you get out it?'

She gave me a challenging look for my insolence. 'What do I get out it? What do *you* get out of sex?'

'An empty.'

'I get a fill. There now – everybody's happy, wouldn't you say?'

She didn't look happy though. She watched the traffic rumble past us, all around and up and down. 'I have to watch my time,' she said and took hold of her bag strap. 'I'm doing a reception shift over in the Holiday Inn at Fullerton.'

'Hey,' I said.

She looked at me.

'I wasn't trying to put you down. Are we going to fall out every time I ask a question?'

'Depends on the question.'

'How about the answer?'

'What? Am I sitting an exam paper here?'

'No, an audition.'

'What's the role?'

'My girlfriend.'

She gave me one of her looks.

'And, before you ask,' I said, 'I'm serious.'

'Yeah, yeah.'

I was grinning in a slippery way to cover the fact that, this time, I *was* serious. The thing about the hook is you never realise it's inside you until somebody gives a tug on the line. Bobbie was a bigger fish, a more alluring fish, than I'd thought. She had behaved in a thoroughly sleazy, duplicitous and reprehensible manner in order to assuage her own base needs. As a man, how could I do other than respect her for it? Like all men, I only valued women who had the capability to hurt me. And I'd realised now Bobbie could.

She didn't react, took another sip of Coke. I could tell she'd thought about things since the other night. Drawn back a little. But out of what? Self-protection or insufficient interest? I didn't know for sure – all I did know was that she'd put on more jewellery.

That was when she came out with it. 'My guess is you already have a girlfriend.'

'No, I don't,' I protested.

'Yes, you do,' she said. 'I heard you talking on the phone.'

'When?'

'The other night – I had my ear to the wall.'

I gave her a mature look.

'Don't gimme that face – I bet you do it too.'

I didn't answer. 'I don't have a girlfriend,' I said. And that was when I came out with it. 'I have a wife.'

Bobbie leaned back in her chair, looked skyward, exhaled. 'I knew it,' she said. 'I sensed it all along.'

'Nobody falls out of a clear blue sky,' I said, reasonably. 'We all have baggage.'

'Baggage, sure – but a wife?'

'I'll leave her.'

'Yeah, I've heard *that* one before.'

'Not from me you haven't.'

'I've heard that one before too.'

She laughed for the first time. It was as though the impediment of my marriage had now freed her from the responsibility of pursuing, and possibly failing to find, future happiness in her own life away from Lorne. I watched her watching the other diners. What was it I saw in her? Looks? Sure, no question. Too skinny legs, though. And that hair – looked more like a village tribeswoman in a pencil skirt than any office temp I'd ever seen. But life, though, big life and a spirit fluttering inside, trying to soar away and fly before it was all too late. Just like me. Anyway, that's what I saw. Maybe others, the other diners, wouldn't have seen that at all. Maybe all they'd have seen was some podgy-faced guy and a fading blonde trying to put a little kick back into their lives with a trashy affair. Let them think that. Who were they to measure our true worth? They didn't know the real us. They'd never met Leanne Calvera or Eric Ross.

'I wasn't judging you,' I said, continuing my thought process out loud.

'What?'

'Before. I don't care who you've been with or what you've done. I've done things too.'

'What things?'

'Bad things. Chances are I'll do more bad things to get what I want.'

'What do you want?'

'I'll start with you.'

She lowered her eyes, pursed her mouth. She looked up. 'How did your meeting with Paramount go?'

'They have a budget. They think they're going to make the film.'

'It's been green-lit?'

'Nearly. Maybe.'

'Maybe, uh?'

'Look at me,' I said. She looked at me. 'Forget maybe. When it gets made, I want you to be at the premiere – on my arm – as my woman.'

And she smiled and blushed. Well, what woman wouldn't smile and blush at that?

Saying confident things to Bobbie stimulated me. When you play hide-and-seek with your emotions, you can rush into rooms you never knew were there.

Bobbie leaned over her glass, concentrating to find words. 'You know I can never leave Lorne. He needs me. I told you that.'

'Find a way,' I said.

'What way?'

'Which ever way it takes.'

'I don't know what you mean.'

'Sure you do.'

A fish truck had stopped at the lights. Huge, it dwarfed the more routine stretches, making them look silly. The throb of its engine passed straight through our bodies and jittered little espresso cups on their saucers. In the cloying heat, moisture dribbled down the flanks of the truck from its contained sealed units on to the baking street. I laid my hand on the table for Bobbie to touch it.

'Trust me,' I said.

There's a thing about writing duos – in the best ones, they form, between the two of them, a third person who can achieve greater things than either of those two writers could ever aspire to achieve on their own. Without that union, that lucky fateful union, those writers, those half-formed, toiling wretches, would struggle on fruitlessly to wither and die.

I didn't want to ask Bobbie any more questions about her past. I didn't want to hear about lunging candy salesmen or horny truckers or think of Lorne dogging in the bushes, stroking his Glock. I'd been under stones like that myself. I'd glimpsed the light now and was trying to creep out. Bobbie was swamp life, just like me. I wanted her to crawl out of the pond and into the sun with me.

At last, Bobbie touched my hand.

'Here are your tuna melts. Sorry they took so long.'

We looked up. It was the waiter.

We'd ordered melts, you see, and finally they had come.

Over the next couple of days, Bobbie and I took greater risks to see each other. She lied to Lorne about more shifts as a receptionist and I'd pick her up outside the Coffee Bean. We spent time driving up through Holmby Hills into the Santa Monica Mountains, where we'd stop the car, open the doors wide like bat wings and sit, listening to the hissing silence and watching the heat rise off the arc of the road. Another day, we set out early for Zuma Beach. This was crazy – our time together was short and the PCH becomes horribly choked but we were filled with the tawdry mania of illicit lovers so there we stood, among the whirring Sonys and clicking Nikons, trying, as instructed, to spot for whales. That's to say I spotted for whales and Bobbie watched for Neil Young. I never saw a whale and Bobbie didn't spot Neil Young. We had a shock together on the way back to the car, though, when we thought we saw Lorne basking under an ice-cream parasol, eating a pizza slice. Disaster felt only ever a step away around the wrong corner.

'Maybe I should talk to him,' I said.

'You can't talk with him,' Bobbie said. 'It's too late for that. You could only talk with Lorne if you weren't a threat.'

'What's it take to be a threat?'

'I have to like you,' Bobbie said.

She unzipped my fly.

When Bobbie liked you, you knew you were liked.

On the way back from our trysts, I'd drop Bobbie a few safe blocks from the Jacey Gardens, well away from any temples of calm from which Lorne might suddenly appear, cursing and blasting his .22. Once I'd parked the car, I'd take the stairs not the elevator, hoping to avoid Raul or Alfonso, and enter my apartment near to silently, leaving the Yale lock open on its snib. Minutes later, Bobbie would appear and I'd lock the door properly, quietly, behind us. Through the wall, we would hear the television or Lorne's thrumming – sometimes both – as we made love on the floor or on the couch but not in the bedroom as we were unsure if Lorne would be able to see into the bedroom were he to lean way out over his balcony. With myself inside Bobbie, I knew I was in love but then I'd catch my face in the mirror and think, 'What am I getting into here? What about my wife?' And I'd ask myself, 'Is this one more love that might quickly die – like with Chloe?' Then I'd think, 'And what about the green card? Wasn't that supposed to be what this is all about?' And I didn't know the answer to this because I'm a born liar and my lies are thorough and seep all the way down to my core so that, even with us liars, there are some things we have to go through, we just can't second-guess ourselves. The question then was whether this thing with Bobbie, this dangerous thing, was worth going through at all, what with the deadly bumpy road that lay ahead, but, in truth, it was out of my power now – I was no longer sniffing around but held within Bobbie's world, inside her and gripped, for better or worse. Moving in our rhythm, I hoped she felt the same way, thought she felt the same way, but how can anybody tell anything and for how long, even me or her in our sweating throes, pumping, close to joyful tears?

One thing, though. Maybe it was the mountains or the whales or even Neil Young but I felt something opening up – a sort of fissure through rock, along which our momentum poured. I wanted to say so as we dressed, nervy fingers on buttons, hopping into socks, but I just couldn't bring myself to – a word like fissure seeming right for the description but wrong for the occasion. She'd just have laughed and we couldn't risk a sound, not anything, even at the height of our heat, for fear of being splattered by a wronged Lorne.

All the same, a fissure it was – a breach in the rock of our mutual prisons, formed by the storm of this momentum and along which we must now gamely paddle, pioneers, forging new rivers down to old oceans, like others, the many great millions of confused souls, who, down through the rotten, lovely history of coupledom, had long since done before us. Anyway, I'd think poetic stuff like that but maybe I was only trying to gloss over bad shit coming.

'You have everything?' I'd whisper to Bobbie. 'I'll let you out.'

'Wait. I'll check one last time.' And she'd lift her skirt.

'I came over you – I promise.'

'All of it – not any of it inside me?'

'Not any inside of you – you know that.'

'I know that but . . .'

'I know,' I said, 'I know.'

And I did – I knew. Not only were we rounding Cape Horn, we were using Bobbie's panties as a mainsail. Before she left, we'd hug. 'What'll we do?'

'I've told you,' I'd say, 'we'll find a way.'

'What way? If I can't leave him?'

'There's always an answer.'

'I can't just abandon him. He loves me.'

'Then ask yourself – what's the answer, the way?'

Everybody pretends that love is pure. But love isn't pure and it's a crime against nature to think that it is.

I'd listen at the door before opening it. Bobbie would tiptoe out with her shoes in her hand. She'd walk a flight downstairs, put the shoes on then she'd turn around and come click-clacking back up again, singing along the corridor breezily, house keys jangling, and, right through the wall, all in a fevered minute, she'd be inside her apartment with Lorne. And maybe Lorne would say, 'Why, hello, sweetheart,' in a sarcastic way and maybe he wouldn't say anything in any way. You never knew. One way or another, we were all of us on our toes.

There are two great arenas in life, the personal and the professional. Like most people I'll strive, with as much fortitude as I can muster, to do battle with any challenge on either front. At such times, the remaining front, the non-combatant front – personal or professional – becomes a source of consolation, of respite from the trials of combat. Strength may be renewed during times of peace but what if, through one of life's occasional freakish misfortunes, battles must be fought over two fronts, simultaneously, without respite? What strategy can there be then, except survival?

'Hello, David.'

'Hello, Spiky. Why are you here?'

'I wondered if there was any news – about the film?'

David Shenson flicked up his rimless reading specs, looked at me, blankly. 'News?'

'Yes.'

'Let me ask, do you have your cell phone on?'

'Yes.'

'Is it ringing? Is it playing "Yankee Doodle Dandy"?'

'No.'

Is it showing my name?'

'No.'

'What does that tell you?'

'That there's no news.'

'That there's no news,' said David Shenson, flatly. He flicked down his specs, resumed reading.

I knew it had been a mistake to turn up uninvited at Winters and Daly – I had gone against my instinct. I had been fraught, though, out-psyched on the professional front by the unblinking stare of continuous silence, out-muscled on the personal front by the horrible exhilaration of impending disaster. As if to confirm my bad tactical move, Tess Schwartzenbuch was missing from the desk and the relief girl made me sit in the foyer with the deliverymen and messengers while she checked out my status with Shenson.

'Is Nancy around?'

'She's in Reno with Tess,' said Shenson, 'at a seminar on production contracts.'

'Maybe I could wait.'

'Did you bring a sleeping bag? It finishes Friday.'

'Maybe I should go.'

'Good suggestion – I'm glad you made it.'

I needed something before I left the building – a morsel of hope, the tone of optimism. Give me the tone – I'll make my own morsel. 'David . . .'

'I don't know.'

'What?'

'I have no answers. You're looking for reassurance. Reassurance – there is none.'

'You're a cunt.'

'And you're an asshole. The distance between us is short but significant. Go home, Spiky.'

'This game is hard.'

'Of course it's hard. If it was easy, everyone would be doing it.'

'Everyone is doing it.'

'That makes it harder.' He flicked on his caring tone – anything to get me out the door. 'Go home. Play golf. Take positivity lessons. We'll call you if there's any change.'

Descending the cool marble stairs of Winters and Daly, I felt hot and rattled. Some mental shift was in progress, a loss of buoyancy, I dreaded my outlook gliding down to the old familiar barren fatalism. As I smiled my polite goodbye to the anonymous receptionist, it occurred to me that this was how hope died too, like dreams die – a revolving door brushing the shoulders, a rush of noise and heat from the sidewalk, then the gradual shrinkage of that walk away from the building, down and further down, until you disappeared forever, back under the black stone you'd struggled so hard to crawl out from under. That's if you were lucky. That's if your faithful secure old black stone was still waiting.

'Hello?' I'd barely heard my mobile ringing under the soundtrack of my own reverie and the traffic hum. 'It's me,' a woman's voice said. I hesitated. There were two mes in my life now – Bobbie and Chloe.

'Bobbie,' this me said helpfully.

'Bobbie, what is it?'

'Where are you?'

'Outside the Jacey – I'm about to drive in.'

'Don't come in,' said Bobbie, urgently, 'keep driving.'

'What?'

'Go around the block. I'll meet you there.'

'Bobbie?'

'Just do it. Keep the engine running.'

I did as I was told. I steered Wendy into the Jacey forecourt, around the building, past the wheelie bins, back out and around the corner. I'd just pulled up and put a stick of gum in my mouth when the car door opened and Bobbie got in. She had a red scarf over her face.

'Drive on,' she said and crouched down below the window.

I laughed. 'What's going on?'

As she looked up, I saw her eyes fat and blue above the scarf. There was a long angry graze on her forehead.

'Drive on,' she said again.

I drove on.

In the parking bay in front of Dom's Big Bites, I stopped.

'What happened?'

'Nothing happened.'

'Did he do that?'

'You can't go back to your apartment,' Bobbie said. She was holding the red scarf in place, over her mouth.

'Let me see.'

'No,' she said, 'look away.'

I looked away. An exhausted-looking black woman was loading boxes into a dusty hatchback. Her fat kid in gold chains was hip-hopping beside her.

I could hear Bobbie pull down the vanity mirror. She gave a squeaky whimper. 'Oh no,' she said, through lips that didn't sound like they could move much, 'he's broken my teeth – he's bust my caps.'

'Who's bust your caps? Lorne?'

'Look away.' She tugged the scarf back up again, quickly. 'OK.'

I wanted to kill Lorne. I wanted to tear him apart for busting my Bobbie's caps. I scrutinised the graze. The skin was broken upward in a trailing line, like a Nike tick. 'What did he hit you with, Bobbie?'

'With the gun.'

'He pistol-whipped you?'

'You surprised?' Bobbie looked at me with her purply-blue beaten-up eyes. Her voice was amused, couldn't help it, under the red scarf. 'Wouldn't you say that was psychologically consistent,' she drawled. 'For Lorne, I mean – wouldn't you say that?'

Like I said – spirit, you can't buy it.

I thought of Lorne's wrists, still bandaged. 'I'm going back and take him apart,' I said.

'You can't do that,' Bobbie said.

'Yes, I can. You think I couldn't take Lorne?'

'It's not that. He'll shoot you. He's told us both he'd do that.'

I thought of the candy salesman's kneecap in Flagstaff, the unknown toes in Liberal. I calmed down. 'Did he find out about us?'

'Yes,' Bobbie said.

'How did he find out? Did the agency call when you were supposed to be at work?'

'No,' Bobbie said, 'it wasn't that.'

'What then?'

'I told him.'

'You told him?' I was . . . well, thunderstruck. I didn't understand. 'I don't understand,' I said. 'You told Lorne about us?'

'This morning – it just came out.'

'Why?'

'I don't know why.'

'Go on,' I said.

'We were having breakfast. I heard you leaving your apartment. Lorne was eating a bowl of Cheerios. He looked up and asked me what date it was. I told him the second. Next thing he started into cussing and swearing.'

'I know why,' I said. 'I told him I'd be out by the end of the month.'

'You got it,' Bobbie said. 'That's when he started to add it all up in his head. And he asked me outright if I was still seeing you. And, for some reason, maybe crazy, I told him that yes, yes I still was.'

'You told him that?'

'I'm sorry,' Bobbie said. 'I've been going out of my mind.'

I put my arm around her. 'Don't blame yourself,' I said. 'It's not your fault. It's the situation – it's too much for us.'

'I couldn't see a way out,' Bobbie said. 'I thought, if I was honest, something might happen. To change things for the better.'

'There, there,' I said. I understood now. It was like me turning up uninvited at Winters and Daly – pure desperation.

'You didn't shout? You tried to reason?'

'I tried,' Bobbie said, 'but I was on the floor with a cereal bowl stuck in my face – that's how I got this cut brow.' She leaned forward, fingering her scalp. 'My hair stinks from the milk and there were Cheerios in it. I picked them out – can you see any that's left?'

I fingered her scalp, looking, but Cheerios were there none.

When Bobbie looked back up, the red scarf had come loose, stayed down, looped at her chin. Uncovered, I could see my lover's broken smile.

'There's only one way to change things for the better,' I said.

'Don't.'

'I'm going back to the apartment.'

'You can't. He'll blast you. He'll hear you come in.'

'If he shoots me, he shoots me.' I started the car. I was aflame with passion. Strategy was out the window.

'The hell with any green card,' I thought. 'The hell with it.' It was as though the prospect of another murder had cleansed me, had revealed my heart's true desire.

'You mean it?'

'Yes,' I said. I released the handbrake, gunned the accelerator to drive off. 'It's him or me.'

'Don't,' Bobbie yanked the brake back up hard, pitching us forward.

'Bobbie,' I said.

'You can't.'

'If I don't go back to my apartment, where else can I go?'

She went quiet.

'Bobbie?' It dawned on me that the beating had concentrated her mind – she'd been thinking things through in its recent aftermath.

'Home,' she said, finally, 'I think you should go home.'

Another one – first Shenson, now Bobbie, everyone was telling me to go home. I looked at Bobbie.

'You're saying it's over? Between us?'

'You're not listening,' Bobbie said. 'I'm saying just go home.' She had a resolute look about her – a grit.

A horn sounded behind us – the exhausted woman in the dusty hatchback. I moved the car over from blocking the exit of the parking bay. I was confused. 'What about my clothes?' I said, limply.

'Give me your key.'

'What key? My apartment key?'

'Not unless you live in your car.'

Bobbie held out her hand. I gave her my apartment key on its big plastic Jacey Gardens fob.

'You sure you know what you're doing, Bobbie?'

'I'm sure.' It might have been me sitting behind the wheel but it was Bobbie driving us now.

'Book a flight,' Bobbie said, 'then message me on my cell phone. I'll bring your clothes to the airport.'

'If I go, I'll come back' I said.

Bobbie looked at me, didn't speak. Stayed looking at me.

'I mean it, Bobbie,' I said.

'What's happening with your film?'

'I don't know,' I said. 'Who knows? Everything's up in the air.'

'Things will change,' Bobbie said.

'You think so? They'll change for the better?'

'Who can say?' Bobbie said. 'Time will tell.'

'Yes,' I said, 'that's the way it works.'

She opened the car door. 'I'll walk back.'

She got out, shut the car door. No goodbye, nothing. I opened the door, leaned out. 'Bobbie?'

She didn't answer, didn't look back. Head down, she kept walking. To what, I didn't know. I flicked up the car indicator, turned the other way from Bobbie, wheeled right. What to? I didn't know that either.

Seemed like, every way I turned, I was in development hell.

I drove down to Santa Monica, rang Aiden's number. I left a message but he didn't get back. Maybe he was out of town or maybe he was worried that I had more good news to pour into his empty bucket and he didn't want any more of someone else's joy slopping over the sides, whatever. That night I slept in the car in a parking lot close to the beach.

Bums begged at the windows and I couldn't quite see the ocean – which seemed about right.

At LAX the next day, I saw Bobbie again. I was standing under the Departures sign like we'd agreed and she came toward me wheeling my bags on a trolley. She was wearing her short denim skirt and her black Leanne Calvera turtleneck.

After we'd hugged, I asked, 'How was Lorne?

'Asleep.'

'He let you come?'

'Hell, I wasn't going to wake him up to ask his permission. Besides, why wouldn't he? You're out of my life and his hair – that's what he wants, isn't it?'

'He won't ever get what he wants,' I said. We turned, looking out at the palm trees and the cabs for hire. I'd managed a flight on Continental through Chicago and a queue was gathering at the check-in desk. I asked her if she wanted coffee. She shook her head.

'I'll be back,' I again told Bobbie Binkley.

'You say that now – when you're here. But, when you get home, you won't know for sure.'

'In that case, you won't know for sure either,' I said. 'You won't know if you want me to come back.'

'No,' she said. 'I guess we're both shooting the rapids.'

I could see people glance at Bobbie's battered face and at me. I could see what they were thinking, that wife-beating didn't square somehow with my deck shoes or the copy of *Time* I had under my arm.

'One thing,' Bobbie said.

'Yes?'

'Whatever you do, whatever moves you make, you do it for yourself, understand? You don't make any moves on my account. No way. Because I'll be looking out for me and no one else. Just me.'

'Sure,' I said, 'we're big boys and girls – we're adults.'

'I've never met an adult in my whole life,' Bobbie said, 'apart from my mom.' She wheeled the baggage trolley round so the handle was pointed toward me.

'I'd like to meet your mom.'

'No you wouldn't – she's old and ugly. Oh and there was a message for you.'

'What message?'

'On your machine – from your wife. Cleo?'

'Chloe.'

'Uh-huh. She says she'll meet you at the airport.'

We looked at each other.

'Yes,' I said, 'I should call her.'

'Sure,' Bobbie said. 'Do it now if you want to – go ahead.'

'I don't want to do it now.'

'Why didn't she call you on your cell phone?'

'Because I left her a message when I knew she'd be at work. Then I turned my mobile, my cell phone, off.'

Bobbie gave an unpleasant little smirk. 'You turned off your cell phone? To your very own wife?'

'I don't want to be with my very own wife,' I said. 'I want to be with you. You know that.'

She went quiet.

Then she said, 'I hope so.'

There are many needles and barbs around our hearts and, when we lay our hearts bare, we see why we need them. I looked at the time on the departure screen. 'I'd better check in,' I said.

'You want me to wait?'

'No,' I said.

I took her in my arms and held my lover close and tightly. Then I said, 'OK,' and we both pulled apart.

'Hey.'

I turned to look.

'Next time you see me, I'll have my teeth fixed.'

I nodded. 'Next time you see me,' I said, 'I'll have my life fixed.'

The trolley wheels were slippery over the shiny floor. No matter how I steered, they didn't seem to go where I wanted.

At the desk, the check-in girl asked 'You're travelling to Glasgow via Chicago?'

'Yes.'

'Did you pack your bags yourself?'

'Yes.'

It dawned on me, of course, that I hadn't. I realised I'd have to make damn sure that I unpacked my bags myself. I marvelled at how quickly, out of survival, we think in future tenses.

* * *

The bumpy descent through the cloud blanket into Glasgow woke me from my fitful doze.

Chloe met me at the gate. There had been a delay at LAX and a security alert at O'Hare so that, all told, I was five hours late in arriving. Maybe that's what accounted for the coolness of her manner. I was still in California shirtsleeves as we hurried through the rain, under the low dark lid of Glasgow sky, across the street to the car park. When we'd negotiated the roundabout to the M8 and were safely on the motorway, she started in. 'Didn't you get my messages? Why didn't you answer? Why didn't you call?'

I made a big thing out of the last-minute nature of my travel arrangements, the frantic pace of life out there, the interminable script meetings with Winters and Daly. 'You know what it's like – you remember – I'm sure Eric used to fill you in.'

At the mention of Eric, she let it go – maybe not that, maybe pushed it aside, saving it up for another time but soon. That's how it felt to me. Then again, I wasn't exactly a disinterested spectator where the subject of Eric was concerned.

'Watch out.'

She braked hard, swerved left, on to the exit for the tunnel.

'I wasn't thinking.'

The outraged toot from the wronged driver receded down the motorway.

'Calm down,' I said. 'It's all right.'

'I am calm,' she said. And so she was. And she'd been thinking too.

Chloe dropped me at the flat but didn't come up. 'I have to get back to work,' she explained. 'The delay with your flight meant I had to juggle a couple of things.'

'I'd like to juggle a couple of things,' I said. I felt obliged to come on all horny for safety's sake.

'I can't,' Chloe said. 'Later.'

'Later' helped put my mind at rest.

In the flat, I made tea and went through the mail. I realised I'd switched a lamp on even though it was summer and 4 p.m. I drank half the tea but couldn't finish it. I felt spaced out and vaguely nauseous.

On the dining room table lay a copy of *The Herald*, open at the features page. It was the interview I'd given down the phone. My face, from ten years earlier, *His 'n' Hers* sitcom time, grinned back at me. The article size was smaller than Aiden's – maybe by a column. I blamed the staid library photograph for this – it just didn't say pizzazz. All the same, I approved of the headline, its black print gleaming satisfyingly under the lamp where I read it – 'Birth of a Hit – Medical Romcom Will Be a Howl'.

I read the interview through a couple of times, first as an appetiser then as a main course, then twice more after that – for pudding and coffee. In short, I glutted myself on me. My early struggles, my native wit, my gift of tenacity, that sort of thing. It was all approving, there being nothing yet to judge but my own proud Scottish fortitude – I'd had a film green-lit; I had two other projects in development. It was exaggeration about the green light, of course, and hokum about the projects in development but nobody cared about that, including me. I'd received my reward of attention and the paper had been allowed first dibs to the latest embodiment of that most potent of ethnic fables – the braw local laddie who conquers Hollywood.

I had arrived, I was a McPlayer. My place card at the Spirit of Scotland Awards, between Kirsty Wark and Sharleen Spiteri, was all but written. To cement my celebrity, I must be sure to play the game. I'd wear a kilt to my premiere and in every interview I gave, I would take care to spout endless reams of ingratiating guff about the fictitious plethora of world-class Scottish talent over which all Hollywood remains agog and in a constant state of stupefied amazement. Follow that up with a snap of myself beaming encouragement to a horde of baldy kiddiwinks in some hospice and I would be a made man. Such is the game that Mc-Players play. I pictured Ess and Em seething in their rented Alba office or, ski caps in hand, doing the rounds of the film fund agencies, trying to scrape together enough bawbees to make *Cement Wedding*; yet another of those scabby-dog, allegedly admired, unwatched, grey-skied, semi-improvised Caledonian junkie pluke fests that made you feel you'd just spent two hours queuing in the fish shop, waiting for the chips to fry.

Not for moi. Hooray for Hollywood. Here comes the sun.

I climbed into bed, stuffed full from the banquet of me. A moment later, I realised I'd forgotten something and climbed back out again, cursing. I'd remembered my bags. I forced myself to unpack everything, all of it. I didn't want to risk Chloe coming home and doing it for me, while I slept. I'd half expected to find some keepsake from Bobbie, a photo perhaps, peeking out coyly from a shirt pocket or maybe some whimsical message on a cupid card but there was nothing – just clothes and books and shoes. I got back into bed and was quickly asleep. I dreamt of voices, though, whispering. I woke up just as quickly and listened to cars, shushing through the Glasgow rain. Something had made me uneasy and I realised what it was. With the publishing of the article, I felt as though all my crimes were exposed now – not only my ego. But it was as if some long-hidden part of me was now somehow in the public domain and visible.

In short, I felt the paranoia of celebrity and was afraid.

CHAPTER TWELVE

'Mum and Dad have invited us over for lunch on Sunday.'

'That's nice. I'd like to go for lunch. I want to tell Dad all about Hollywood.'

'My father's been very good to you.'

'I know he has. I owe Dad everything. Pass the marmalade.'

Chloe passed the marmalade. 'You slept for twelve hours straight through last night,' she said.

'Not straight through,' I told her, 'I woke up a few times. Disoriented. Didn't know where I was – if I was awake or dreaming. You know that feeling?'

'I know it.'

I smeared my toast, mister fresh and breezy. 'Your side of the bed was cold.'

'I wasn't on my side. I slept in the other room. To give you peace.'

'I got peace.'

'You didn't sleep though.'

'I slept, just not straight through.' I took a casual bite of toast. 'You read my article in *The Herald*?'

'Yes,' Chloe said.

'How did I sound?'

'It was accurate. You sounded like you.'

'Is that good?'

'I'm no judge,' she said. She looked at me. '*Smoking Gun*? *Love Letter Blues*? Those your latest projects?'

'Yes,' I said.

While I was trying to weigh up her tone, she said, 'Your father read it too.'

'What?'

'Your father – the article.'

'I'm not with you.'

'Yes, you remember.' Chloe dragged her knife along the butter, skinning up a thin yellow shaving. 'That man on our wedding day – the one who lunged at the car – that father – him.'

'You spoke to my father?'

'He called me a few days ago. After he'd read the article. I agreed to meet him in the Metro Cafe.'

My molars continued to grind and my throat to swallow but I wasn't tasting anything. All I could think to say was, 'How did he get our number?'

'From your mother.'

'They're not in touch.'

'Oh yes they are. You didn't know?'

'No.'

'You should. Your father said your mother told you he'd been in touch. Did she tell you?'

'Yes.'

'Then why lie? What's your problem?'

'My mother hates my father.'

'No she doesn't. Your mother changed her mind. She likes your father now.'

'She likes him now?'

'Yes.'

'I don't get it.'

'He came back. Your father came back.'

I fumbled with this proposition. 'You mean my father came back to my mother?'

'That's the one. That's the kind of back I meant.'

'It doesn't make sense.'

'Yes it does – it makes perfect sense. When he walked out, did that make sense?'

'No.'

'Now he walks back in and fixes it. It's perfect. It's business as usual.'

'After thirty years?'

'Why not?' Chloe gave a sort of brittle shrug. 'Things change.'

'I know things change,' I said. 'I know.'

We sort of let that settle between us. Then Chloe said, 'It was the wedding. You didn't invite them to the wedding. Rejection brought them together.'

I watched her try to raise the coil of hard butter. It dropped from her knife on to the table. She tried to jab it, gave up and lifted it with her fingers on to her plate. She wasn't in any mood for niceties. 'You know your father has cancer?'

'Yes.'

'You know he wanted you to get in touch?'

'Yes.'

'Yet you never got in touch?'

'No.' There was something about her tone – a solicitor's tone, here over our comfy toast and marmalade.

Before her tone could harden further, I decided to become indignant. 'Who are you? The cancer police? So what if I didn't get in touch with my own father?'

Chloe nodded to herself. 'Maybe that's it. Maybe that's why he wants his revenge.'

'What revenge?'

She took a breath. She clasped her hands, unclasped them, drummed her fingertips together, agitatedly. She took another breath, a sort of preparation, then she said, 'Right.'

I watched her dive down, pick up her sculpted Gucci shopper from under her chair, surface and lay it on her lap.

I thought I might risk a bewildered chuckle. 'What is it? What's going on?'

She didn't answer. From inside the Gucci shopper, she took a small Reiss bag. From inside the small Reiss bag she pulled out a tightly folded newspaper. Chloe gave me a resolute stare as she unfurled the garish Scottish tabloid and threw it across the table. 'Page seven,' she said.

I picked up the paper. I made a thing of wiping butter off the back page, from a picture of Hampden Park. I found page seven. On the bottom half page was a photograph of an emaciated man with a bald head – my father. The colouring was bad – he had pink eyes and looked startled, like he had been surprised coming out of the make-up trailer for a kiddies' comedy sketch show.

A byline read 'Corpse Blimey!' Then, smaller, 'Top Writer Stole from my Pal – claims angry cancer pop'. I assumed this to be the relevant item of interest. So I read the relevant item of interest in full. I closed the paper. I kept calm, watching Chloe as she twitched with grievance.

'You know who showed me *that*.'

'No, who?'

'Our senior partner, Mr Joseph.'

I nodded. I didn't say anything. I might have asked what Mr Joseph was doing reading *that* – if it's tits you're after, might as well buy the *Sport* and have done with it. But I didn't ask and it didn't matter. The damage had been done – for Chloe and for me.

'My firm is named in that article. Mr Joseph is named in that article.'

'He's clean,' I told her. 'It's a private matter. That's all your Mr Joseph says – that it's a private matter between you and me and my father.'

'I am named in that article.'

'Yes, I saw that.'

'You saw that?'

'Yes.'

She nodded to herself a bit more. 'Did you do it?'

'What?'

My wife looked at me, spoke very deliberately. 'Did you steal *Smoking Gun* and *Love Letter Blues* from that dead man, from Walter Urquhart?'

'No,' I said. I realised I was now involved in a card game for high stakes. I matched Chloe's twitching outrage and raised her my bristling contempt. 'It's a filthy disgusting lie,' I said.

'Honestly?'

'Honestly. And I'm stunned that you could even ask me that.'

She considered for a moment. 'All right,' she said, 'I believe you.'

'Good.'

I clenched my jaws. I folded my hands in front of me in a forthright manner.

Chloe allowed herself little yielding. 'In that case, why do you think your father said it?'

'I don't know,' I said.

'You need to ask him.'

'No.'

'If you don't ask him, I will.'

I thought about this, about my wife and my father chumming up to dissect my personality. 'All right,' I said, 'I'll ask him.'

I finished my tea and stood up from the table. For the first time in thirty years, I went off to look for my father.

* * *

It took a while. There were three bookies along that one small stretch of shops near my mother's house. As I waited, I thought about the quotes from assorted media types I'd seen in the scuzzy tabloid story. Skipton, now apparently a 'stalwart of the industry', had been prominently to the fore. 'It's an unpleasant claim,' he'd declared, gleefully, 'but sometimes, in our business, ideas overlap – the world today is a homogenous culture and we're all subject to the same influences.' He was covering his bases, as usual, in case there'd be any unseemly issues raised over *Cement Wedding*, a project which he himself had plundered, albeit legitimately, from the same Walter Urquhart. I felt dispirited. It didn't matter what I achieved – murder, infidelity, theft – there was always someone waiting to drag my efforts at self-improvement back down into the mire.

He came out of Ladbrokes. He was wearing the same shabby black Crombie coat he'd had on that day, that afternoon when he'd come galloping up to my wedding carriage and started pawing at the windows. I was clutching the crumpled tabloid. I wanted to run across the road and start hitting him with it. I couldn't do that, though – he'd only have sold that story to the press too, the way he'd sold the last one. I watched him vanish into a greengrocer. When he came out, he had a bunch of blue flowers in one arm and, to my surprise, my mother on the other. Her share of the blood money, I assumed. I stepped into the doorway of Somerfield where they couldn't see me and waited. When they crossed the street, I slipped in behind them, following at a distance.

I had been, what, twelve, when I'd last seen them together. Now, thanks to the wonderful human gifts of loneliness, self-pity and vengeance, they'd conspired to reunite themselves. Coming over on the underground from the west end, I'd read my father's interview over and over. As I walked behind him, I could hear his griping voice in my head. 'My illness came as a shock,' explained the plucky lymph-gland victim, speaking exclusively to this newspaper. 'Walter had been helping me put my tax affairs in order when he died. He dreamed of writing success. He often spoke of his projects to me – that's how I recognised his titles instantly. Imagine my horror when I opened the paper and read that my own son was bragging about those same titles as his own work.' 'Imagine my horror'? So I did. I imagined about a grand's worth. 'He didn't even invite us to his wedding. His mother and I are hurt and disappointed.'

The hurt and disappointed couple were nearing the tower block. I'd had it in mind to slip in through the fire exit and surprise them as they entered the lift. If I'd done that, then, within a minute, we could all have been sitting in the same living room, a family once more. Tea might have been taken. And, after tea, the easy slippage into recrimination as inevitable harsh words were uttered and our collective wounds, ancient and recent, either bared or flourished, according to whim or temperament. And, after tea and wounds, the lurch into grudging silence, followed by more tea. And, with the second brew, the pleas for tolerance, for the quelling of old fires, over caramel wafers, in the name of family love. But fires are proud things – they go out when they want to, not when they're asked. If I'd gone in to my mother's house, I'd have been tempted to shake my father's hand, been coerced into shaking his hand, out of gooey working-class sentiment, just because he was dying. And, by the time I'd come out, he'd have tapped me for twenty. He'd be dead in a year – I'd never get it back.

No, I'd keep my own home fires burning, burning.

What I'm saying is that I didn't surprise my parents. Instead, I sat on the low wall by the car park, thinking things out. Older now, I could understand my father's reasons, even admire his spirit in having left my mother – the flight from turgid domesticity, from the weary thankless grind of tax returns and sweaty shoes. But leaving to do what? To stagger in a tethered circle round the Glasgow pubs, then to return, thirty years later, to where he started from, old, defeated and skint. And to the woman he started out with, my mother – that Madame Butterfly of the council high-rise, who never stopped pining, fag in paw, for the return of this mouldering heap of bones with his baldy coat and whisky breath.

I heard the voice of Eric Ross intone beside me as I sat, 'My people, humble people who expect nothing.'

Truly, they deserved each other. But, though their toxic scumland slop of fags and spunk would always ooze from my every pore, I didn't deserve them, oh no. They'd run their race, handed on the genes, life's baton; it lay in my hands now.

I walked back to Cessnock, still smarting from the article. I'd rise above my father's vile and petty lies, even though they were true. Resolved, I binned the tabloid and walked down the hole in the street to the underground. At Hillhead, I walked back up from the hole in the street and across Byres Road into Antipasti.

'Did you see your father?'

'Yes.'

'Did you speak to him?'

'No.'

'I don't understand.'

'I saw him but I didn't speak to him.'

'You mean you're letting him off? After what he did?'

'Yes.'

'I don't understand. You should sue.'

'I don't want to sue my father.'

'Litigation would clear your name. I'll speak to our libel lawyer.'

'It's a one-off story. If I sue, it becomes an issue.'

'Let it be an issue. It would clear your name.'

'Would you forget my name? It's my name, if I want it uncleared, that's my business.'

'It's my name too or have you forgotten?'

The cafe tables were too close together. We tried to quit arguing for etiquette's sake but it was hard as both our danders were up. We compromised by bitching in quieter voices.

'I don't understand why anyone wouldn't want to clear their name. To me, it doesn't make sense.'

'Look, let him get on with it. He has his life, I have my life.' I took a big agitated forkful of carbonara, shovelled it into my mouth. 'My lives,' I might have corrected – all three of them, wife, lover and corpse, all on the same tangled plate. I say I might have corrected but didn't. I wasn't given the chance.

'Who's Bobbie?

'What?'

'Bobbie B.'

My non-shovelling hand gave my pocket a discreet squeeze. No phone.

'There was a missed call on your mobile. Her name came up.'

'Her? How'd you know it's a she? Bobbie could be a man's name.'

'Spelt with an I, E? Is he a cross-dressing gay man?'

'No.'

'Then she's a she. Who is she?'

I should have been on the back foot but something started up in me. Anger nudged me forward on to the front foot. 'Wait a second. My phone was off.'

'It was not. It was on.'

'Off. You turned my phone on.'

'I did not. Your phone has a code – I couldn't turn it on.'

'You know the code. It's easy.'

'I don't know why you need a code. Only people with secrets need a code.'

'I don't have any secrets.'

'You're right there because, if you did, I'd find them out. I'd find your secrets out.'

I looked at my wife. Her chin was set, just like her father's. Tears were gathering, there was a smear of coleslaw at the corner of her mouth. I wasn't bringing out the best in her.

Or me.

I had a mistress I couldn't forget. And I wife I didn't love.

I suppose I was a divided man.

As we stepped out of Antipasti, we were shouting.

It didn't get any better. We occupied the same bed but didn't have sex. On the Saturday, Chloe went to meet Sam and Morag for one of her girls' nights out or, as I preferred to think of them, strategy meetings. Alone in the flat browsing though obscure channels, I caught something called *Celebrities and their Shoes* before it occurred to me I might permit myself a boys' night out. I washed, changed my shirt and buffed my good Grenson brogues.

Rounding the greasy cobbles of Ashton Lane, I could see that things had moved on. Two new bars had sprung up, big and bright bars, pleasant and spacious-looking, one on top if the other. There were white ropes and doormen to be negotiated before anyone could get into these bars. And people, all young, were queuing to get in. I'd been young myself when I'd first come to this lane. Over the last fifteen years, its bars had nourished me, feeding me with fights, friendships, affairs, relationships, heartaches, disappointments, trysts and dalliances – and enough one-night stands to wring my ball bag dry, each and every one of them gratifyingly grubby and delicious. Women, partners all, pure and rancid, flitting bedfellows of the dissolute night, wherever you are now, my vagabond cock salutes you. I stood, thinking this and taking in the moment, both admiring and daunted by the fresh colour and light of the lane, thinking what all older people think – that change happens in jumps, not steps.

Then I lugged the door open and my cleaned and buffed shoes climbed the familiar, sloppy, piss-scented, red-tiled stairs of Xenia. It was dingy, as always. The same jaded eyes lifted from the same half-turned heads but what the eyes registered failed to animate the faces. So much for my celebrity, then – or even my notoriety. With new life in other places, the old crowd had thinned, like hair. No Aiden, no Walter Urquhart. When I asked the young barman whether Denis had been in lately, he gave me a puzzled look and had me describe him to a colleague, an old-timer of eleven months' service. Nobody knew anybody any more.

I stood at the bar, sipping my Highland Spring. At a table, far end, I noticed an attractive woman and a man stand to leave. The woman had dark hair, soberly cut, stylish but subdued, not red and long the way it used to be. I noticed her figure, fuller at the hips now, the black skirt worn long and loose hoping to fool, as she pulled on her coat. As she smoothed the collar, I saw her nice new shiny wedding band. The man was way older than the woman – maybe fifty. He wore serious specs and a crumpled business suit and his belt was fastened tight to throttle his gut and try to make the woman swoon with desire. I didn't think she'd seen me as they'd gone out, leaving the narrow doors swinging. She must have, though, because she came back in again, alone, took my spritzer from my hand and emptied it over my surprised head. Then she turned and walked out again without a word. It was another sign of the times – the old Karine would have called me a cunt.

The barman gave me a napkin. As I wiped down, I told myself I'd have her again, though, Karine, when the timing was right. When she and her new man grew tetchy with each other and divorced, as they would, Karine would diet, grow her hair back to red, then she'd head out on the trawl again with her friends. She would be loud and soused, as we all were after a let-down, seeking out new damage under the banner of love. That's the way it worked. Everything here would repeat itself, over and over, and we'd only stop when we were dead.

Still, at least she hadn't asked for her twenty back.

When I came out of Xenia, I walked over to the quiet of the car park and tried ringing Bobbie. Her cell phone was turned off and I didn't know what to think. So I thought everything, the way a troubled person does. I didn't risk leaving any message on her voicemail. She too had a wounded partner nursing a grievance, just as I had.

Chloe came back late that night, maybe one o'clock. I hadn't been sleeping so I got up when I heard the door go and made us each a cup of tea. We sat at the dining table, a vase of dried flowers between us, sipping. Chloe was drunk, her head lolling to and fro as she negotiated the cup on its saucer. She was in an odd state – a kind of morose giggliness. I asked her where she'd gone with Sam and Morag but she hadn't gone anywhere, they'd sat in Sam's flat and drunk wine. It had been a celebration evening – Sam was pregnant.

'Isn't that lovely news?'

'Yes, lovely.'

Sam's husband was a gem it turned out, completely devoted, he'd kept them all plied with Sancerre and jokes. Sam hadn't drunk anything, only water, being careful now, what with the baby. Then Sam's husband had gone out with his friends, she didn't say where – maybe to be completely devoted someplace else. Who could tell with gems? That's when they'd talked, the three of them, a real good-old girly talk, just like old times, all about what they wanted out of life. And about what they didn't want. And about how to get rid of those things they no longer wanted.

'Sam and Morag are my closest friends – I can tell them anything, anything.'

I took this to mean she'd told them everything, everything.

'Did they see my article?'

'Sam saw the nice one in *The Herald*, Morag saw the disgusting one in the tabloid. I don't want to talk about the disgusting one.'

'I'll bet Morag did.'

'You're wrong. Morag was shocked. Morag had to ring Denis to ask if it was true.'

'Why'd she ask Denis? Why didn't she ask me?'

'Morag is close to Denis – she isn't close to you.'

'Since when is Morag close to Denis?'

'Since his flat was repossessed for his defaulting on his mortgage repayments. It was a difficult time. She was there for him.'

'Sure she was.'

I pictured Morag being there for Denis. I imagined a dying wildebeest with a Halifax payment book in its paw and a vulture with a sour face and a long-ago dumped fiancé's engagement ring through its beak, hovering over the wildebeest, waiting its moment.

'Denis is living with his parents now. He didn't tell you?'

'No.'

'Some friends you've got, who don't tell you anything.' Chloe began to look a little ill. 'My friends warned me about you – they all did.'

'I know,' I said.

She put her cup down clumsily and it toppled over in its saucer, spilling. Chloe didn't care. She leaned forward till her brow was resting on the table, in the tea puddle. Chloe looked like a bludgeoned woman bleeding camomile from the forehead.

'I didn't listen to them,' my wife kept moaning, 'I didn't listen.'

She went quiet. I sat for a minute then I made myself get up. I went to the kitchen and came back with a cloth. Chloe seemed to be asleep. I lifted her head up by the hair and wiped the table dry.

She wasn't asleep. Her eyes flashed open. 'But I'm listening now,' my wife said.

CHAPTER THIRTEEN

The weather for the Sunday was set to be cloudy but mainly dry with possible showers. As the Rosses were a family in need of an uplift, I accentuated the positive in this assessment and suggested lunch in their conservatory, to jolly us all along.

I laid out the cutlery on the white wrought iron garden table while Dad sat vacantly by the roaring Gas Miser, gripping a big glass of supermarket blend, not his usual malt. He looked shrunken somehow, deflated, the way older people do when you haven't seen them for a while.

Chloe was in the kitchen, helping Mum with the braising and chopping, so I took the opportunity to paint an enthusiastic word picture to Dad of my Hollywood business trip. I described how hectic things had been over there, how it had been no picnic, but that I was teetering on the brink of seeing all my endeavours bear wonderful golden fruit. He listened without really taking this in, just smiling vaguely and nodding, looking, from time to time, a bit pained. Perhaps he'd been thinking about himself as a young man. Perhaps hearing my youthful energy and boyish fresh-faced promise had made him wistful, wishing he could live his life all over again.

More likely, though, he'd heard all this stuff before, from his own son Eric, whom I had murdered for profit and gain. Watching Dad in one of his potholes of silence, I thought of an image from the poet Neruda that seemed somehow to fit Dad's state – 'like a shoe without a foot'. No doubt, Neruda had been speaking about one of life's great issues – love, perhaps, or feet – when he'd thought that image up. Whatever. My concern was that Dad should sense a return on his investment – after all, he'd funded me out of his own guilt over Eric and I wanted him to go on funding so it followed that it was a useful thing if Dad's guilt was poked occasionally with a stick, as it could only be to my benefit. Us poets, Neruda, me, we had to be tough.

Mum came through, carrying a big slab of brown meat on a silver dish.

'OK, it's ready.'

'Smells wonderful, Mum,' I told her.

Nobody else said anything.

Over lunch, Dad made a startling announcement. 'I'm selling the factory,' he said.

We waited for him to elucidate but he didn't until Mum prompted him. 'You've been made an offer, haven't you?'

Dad nodded. 'That's correct. If my co-directors don't buy me out, there's an offer on the table from a Frankfurt company. They want a foothold over here – our Albanians are cheaper than their Turks – and they've the resources to upgrade and modernise. They think . . .'

We waited dutifully for more but he wasn't going to give us any more. It was as if his interest in the subject had been a car that he'd stalled on the road and he couldn't be bothered with all that restarting the engine malarkey and instead had decided to sit idly at the wheel thinking his private thoughts. We, the other traffic, taking our cue, began driving around him.

'Good idea. Take a sea cruise,' Chloe advised.

'Yes, buy a holiday home,' I said, rallying to the cause of good cheer.

Mum smiled, tolerantly. 'It's been a difficult week,' she explained. 'We finally cleared out Eric's den.'

'I'd been putting it off,' said Dad.

We left a little respectful silence in memory of Eric's den.

'So many drugs – it was like a dispensary,' said Mum, gamely, fighting shame.

I chuckled. 'Yes, that's what I said.'

Chloe gave me a sharp look. 'You've been to the den?'

'Yes,' I said, 'once or twice.' I'd been taken aback by her tone. 'You know I've been to the den.'

'You told me you'd been there once, not twice.'

'It might have been once, it might have been three times, I can't remember.'

Mum came to my rescue. 'Yes, Chloe, what does it matter? It's immaterial.'

'It's well seen she's a solicitor,' said Dad. He'd managed a joke. He smiled, pleased with himself. Seeing him perk up, Chloe didn't push it. I was unnerved a bit, though, I can't deny.

Mum and Dad looked at each other. 'Shall I ask him or will you?'

Dad said, 'You do it.'

I shifted position, making my cane chair creak. 'Ask me what?'

Mum looked at me. 'You and Eric had a lot in common – we know that. Eric's books are down there, his music – if there's anything you want, then . . .'

'Take the lot, clothes too,' urged Dad.

'Don't be silly – Eric's clothes wouldn't fit him.'

'It's him or Oxfam,' Dad said, flatly.

'If there's anything at all, just say . . .'

So I did, I said, 'I could be doing with a laptop.'

Following the embarrassing allegations in the tabloid, Eric's laptop had worried me. What if it were to be poked about with – the screenplay for *Looking at the Stars* dredged up from it somehow? Then again, I reassured myself, who would do the poking? Only a suspicious person. And why should anyone be suspicious? All the same, with the laptop in my possession, I could relax.

Mum looked embarrassed. 'The laptop . . .'

Dad fidgeted in his chair. 'That's awkward,' he said.

'Why?' I asked, innocently.

'The police have it,' Mum said.

You could say this perturbed me.

Dad took up the story. 'Eric had been ordering pharmaceuticals on his laptop, using the hospital account numbers and pass codes. The police are going over it for details.'

'I see,' I said.

Mum squeezed Dad's hand, for mutual comfort.

I was aware of Chloe's eyes on me. 'You look a bit pale,' she said.

'And you look a bit red. So what?'

'They're finished with it now,' said Mum, brightening for my benefit. 'You can have it when they return it.'

'Tell them I'll collect it,' I said. 'It'll save everybody's time.'

'No you won't,' Chloe said. 'I'll collect it.'

We all looked at each other.

'What's got into you?' asked Mum.

'They won't give it to him.'

'Yes, they will,' I said. 'They'll give it to me.'

'No they won't,' she said. 'You're not a close relative.' She leaned forward in her chair, turned to her parents. 'He's not a close relative. I'm blood family and I have authority. I know how the procedure works because I'm a solicitor.'

Dad looked at Mum. I could see they were taken aback. 'Well,' he said, 'that's us told.'

Mum saw us to the door. As I was about to step into the car, she gripped my elbow. 'He's forgetting things now,' she said. 'Did you notice?'

I told her I had noticed. Mum had seemed strangely pleased. Thrilled, even. And why not? A whole new world of good works might be about open up, right there on her own doorstep. Charity would begin at home. The circle would be unbroken.

'Well, that was nice,' I said to Chloe on the drive back.

But she didn't answer.

I'd heard nothing from Winters and Daly. Nothing from Bobbie. After the brush-off I'd received on my last visit, I didn't want to ring the agency. I told myself things were out of my power, that what would be would be – those sorts of platitudes. It was easier to heed my own counsel over this, a professional matter, as I knew an established process was under way, that a protocol would have to be observed which would, at some point, for better or worse, proceed toward the resolution I both craved and dreaded. With private matters, affairs of the heart, there were no such assurances. Hearts were manic, unpredictable things, docile when asleep but dangerous when roused, like Alsatians on taut leads, dragging small children behind them. Lorne had a heart. He'd savaged Bobbie with it. Perhaps that was why I'd heard nothing – once bitten, twice shy. Who could tell what hearts might do?

I was in Tinderbox, thinking these things, when my phone rang.

'Hello?'

'It's me.'

It was Chloe.

'Where are you?' I asked.

'I'm at Partick Police Station. Could you come down?'

'To the police station?'

'Yes. It's about the laptop. Eric's.'

'What about Eric's laptop?'

'There are some forms. I haven't time to wait around. Could you sign them and collect the laptop?'

'I'm not a close relative.'

'You don't have to be – I was wrong.'

'I don't have authority.'

'Do you want Eric's laptop or don't you?'

'Yes.'

'Then come down to the station. Ask for DI Paul Redfern. Have you got that?'

'Yes.'

'Who do you ask for?'

'DI Paul Redfern.'

'That's right. He'll be waiting.'

'OK.'

So I did, I went down to Partick Police Station. And I asked for DI Redfern. And he was – he was waiting.

He led me along some short corridors, choked with policemen in clean white shirts and heavy polished shoes, to a room in the bowels of the building.

And, in that room, Chloe was waiting too.

'What are you doing here?'

'I had time to stay after all – I just found out. It was too late to ring you.'

'Sit down,' said DI Paul Redfern.

He was about the same age as Chloe, tall and clean of limb, corn-fed, like her, not battery-reared like me. Eric's laptop was on the table in front of him. Chloe busied herself, making notes in her diary. I noticed, as I was doubtless supposed to, that something else was in front of Redfern – a copy of my script, on nice yellow A4 paper. I could read the title on it upside down. 'Looking at the Stars,' it said, with my name in bold black type. I decided to ignore it.

'Where do I sign?

He looked puzzled.

'For the laptop,' I said.

Chloe looked up from her notes. 'It's been signed for – I've done that.'

Redfern looked to Chloe. Now that she'd piped up, he seemed unsure who should take the lead. Chloe stepped in. 'Paul was an old friend of Eric's, weren't you Paul?'

This seemed news to Paul. 'Not so much a friend really,' he explained. 'My brother Caleb was at medical school – Eric studied there with him.'

I nodded, looked at them both. Whatever they'd cooked up together had been at the last minute – they hadn't even got the easy stuff straight.

'Terrible business, isn't it,' said Redfern, 'such a shock.'

'Excuse me,' I said. I tried to make it look like the staggering thought had just dawned on me. 'Is this an interview?'

'No, of course not,' said Redfern.

'Then why are we in an interview room?'

'We're just having a chat,' he said, 'about a mutual friend, who's sadly departed.'

Detective or not, he didn't seem comfortable – he had no clear focus, no momentum. I gained the impression he was acting under duress.

'The police experts went through Eric's computer,' Chloe said, driving matters on. 'They found things on the hard drive.'

'Things?' I said.

She'd lured me down here to lean on me. She and this big bullock of a cop, they were going to intimidate me with their skilled, highly trained, middle-class professional minds.

'Oh my God!' I said. 'You mean like kiddie porn?'

'Don't be insulting,' Chloe said. 'Of course not!'

'Why of course not? We don't know the truth about anybody these days – even brothers.'

'Or husbands.'

'Now who's being insulting?' I did indignant bristling. 'Eric was a weedy little guy with no girlfriend who lived under his parents' floorboards,' I said. 'How socially maladjusted is that?'

'You're despicable.'

'Let's calm down, shall we?' said Redfern. 'It's a fraught time.'

I didn't want to calm down. I wanted a rough house. If Chloe was calm, she'd be more incisive. I didn't want her incisive – I wanted her inflamed. I wanted Redfern to assume a different role, to have his hands full as a referee keeping the domestic peace between a warring couple.

'There wasn't any child porn,' Redfern said.

'What things, then?' I said. 'Go on.'

'A script,' Redfern said.

'A screenplay,' Chloe went on, 'entitled, specifically, *Looking at the Stars.*' Using her no-nonsense, successful career-woman's Mont Blanc ballpoint, my wife pointed at the hard copy of the said screenplay.

Redfern, taking his cue, riffled its edge with his thumb.

'Yes,' I said, 'go on.'

'That's it,' Paul Redfern said, 'There are questions over the authorship of that script.'

I looked at him blankly. I wanted him feeling it was a silly matter, the authorship of a script. I wanted him reminded that he was a cop, a beefy lad, used to manly stuff, stabbings and eye gougings and the wicked ways of big bad men. Not silly, womanly things. The authorship of a script – kids' stuff.

'What are you asking me?'

He gave me his professional stare. 'I'm asking if you stole that script from Eric Ross.'

'No,' I said.

'Then why does your film script have the same title?'

'Because Eric gave me that title.'

'He gave it to you?'

'I liked that title. I admired it. Eric said I could have it. "I won't be needing it for a long time," he said. "Take my title with my blessing."'

'He said that?'

'Yes.'

Paul Redfern looked at Chloe to see if she was satisfied. She wasn't.

'Some of the dialogue is identical,' she said.

'Well, it would be, wouldn't it?' I said. 'I asked Eric to work on some of the dialogue for me. Specifics. He was a medical man, wasn't he? I needed his expertise. Isn't that reasonable?'

Redfern didn't say so but I could tell he had to agree.

Chloe didn't agree though, Chloe became even more exercised. 'Don't tiptoe about,' she told Paul Redfern. 'Cut to the chase.'

He looked at her. 'Are you sure you want to repeat what you said to me within a police station scenario?'

'Yes,' my wife, the solicitor, said.

Paul Redfern nodded. He turned to me. 'There's a murder in your script,' he said.

'Yes,' I said.

'And there's a murder in Eric's script.'

'So what?'

'The murder method used in each case is unusual and identical. How do you explain that?'

'Easily,' I said. But I couldn't explain it. Nor could I explain why they didn't simply whip out a copy of Eric's script, compare it with a copy of my own script and say, 'There you are – completely copycatted. You're fucking nicked, my old beauty.' Then it dawned on me. They couldn't do it because they didn't have one. They only had a copy of my script, provided by Chloe. They didn't have a copy of Eric's script, taken from his laptop. Obviously the hard drive had yielded only bits and scraps.

Under the circumstances, I said the best thing I could have said because it happened to be true. 'Eric gave me that murder.'

'He gave you the murder?' Chloe pulled a gawping face. 'He gave you the murder as well as the title?'

'Yes.'

Chloe threw back her head, did incredulous mocking laughter. 'He's priceless,' she said, 'absolutely priceless.'

She rocked in her chair, clapping her hands. I watched her distorted features. She was doing courtroom stuff, trying to give the impression of a person who's finding something so implausible she can't keep her face straight. But her eyes told a different story. My wife's eyes told me that she hated me.

She composed herself. 'Tell Paul why, just why the hell Eric would write your entire bloody script for you. Tell him that, please – we're dying to know.'

Paul Redfern nodded but he didn't look like he was dying to know. He was starting to look like I wanted him to look – a busy man, with a heavy workload, having to devote valuable time to yet another wronged wife with a petty grudge. Fair play to him, he plodded on. 'Why would Eric do a thing like that?'

'Well . . .' I began.

'Eric wouldn't do it, would he, it doesn't make sense.'

'Chloe, please,' pleaded Redfern.

'He didn't write the entire script . . .' I said, 'just the murder.'

Redfern's flagging interest pricked up. 'But we know he had used that murder method in his own script. Why would he give it to you?'

'Simple,' I said. I looked Chloe in the eyes. It was easy to look people in the eyes when you were telling the truth. 'He wasn't absolutely sure about the method of dispatch,' I said. 'It was all very well on paper but he didn't know if it would work in real life.'

'So he offered it to you?' Redfern asked. He flicked though my script. He'd located a page flagged with a paper clip.

'Yes.'

'And you took the method, even though it might not work in real life?'

'I'm less picky,' I said. 'Not being a medical man.'

Redfern nodded. He wasn't a medical man either.

I continued, 'It sounded plausible – that was good enough for me.'

Redfern skimmed over the flagged page, looked up. 'And have you done any research, subsequently?'

'No,' I said.

'So we still don't know if the murder would work in real life?'

'You tell me,' I said, 'you're the experts.'

Redfern arched his eyebrows, closed the script. I could tell he was ready to close the subject too.

Chloe wasn't ready though. She leaned forward, out of her chair. Her hands gripped the edge of the table as if to keep herself tethered and not float away or throttle me. Her face was close to mine. 'I've asked medical experts,' she said.

'Oh, yes?' I said.

'They said it would work.'

'Did they now?'

'Shall I tell you what I think?'

'Go on.'

'I think that not only *could* it work but that it *did* work.'

Redfern leaned over to touch Chloe's hand. 'Chloe, don't,'

'Don't patronise me.' She pulled her hand away.

'Don't say something you'll regret later – that's all.'

She shook her head. 'The only thing I'd regret is not saying this.' She turned to me. 'I think that not only could that method work, I think it did work.'

I looked startled. 'On whom?'

'On Eric,' my wife said. 'I've been thinking about this night and day.'

'Obsessions are dangerous,' I said. 'They must run in your family.'

'I think you injected Eric with potassium,' she said, 'like in the script. I think you killed my brother.'

Redfern took a deep breath.

'There,' Chloe said, 'I've said it.' She gave an odd little laugh of triumph or something. She sat back down, looking satisfied.

I allowed many emotions to play across my injured face – some of them even genuine.

'I take it you're denying this allegation?' said Paul Redfern.

I found myself holding a note of hurt disdain. 'Sorry – that was an allegation? I thought it was a plot device. I thought we were still talking scripts.'

'It is an allegation,' Chloe said, defiantly.

'Oh, yes,' I said, 'based on what evidence?'

'Based as yet on no evidence. Based on . . .'

I finished her sentence for her, 'A woman's intuition?'

'A sister's intuition,' she spat the words out. 'And a wife's intuition.'

I turned up the thermostat of my scorn. 'In that case, there's only one way to find out,' I said. 'Why don't we dig Eric up?'

'Don't think I haven't thought of exhumation,' Chloe said, 'I've discussed it already.'

'I'll bet you have,' I said, 'over Sancerre and nibbles with Burke and fucking Hare – sorry Morag and Sam.'

Paul Redfern was mulling it over. He risked saying something. 'How would that help?' he asked Chloe in a wary voice. 'Digging him up?'

'It's about truth,' she said. 'Knowing the truth would bring me peace.'

'How about your Dad?' I said. 'Would it bring him peace too? A spot of midnight gardening, a bit of repotting in the boneyard?' I was still doing bristling acting.

Redfern gave me a look that said, 'Calm down.' He went on, 'If this method works, as the experts say it would, we wouldn't find anything in his bloodstream, would we?'

'Exactly,' I said. I kept my voice down. 'And, if it didn't work, it couldn't have been that method that killed him anyway.'

'So how would that help you, Chloe?' asked Paul Redfern, gently.

Chloe rounded on him like it was his fault now, not mine. 'I don't know!' she said. 'But it would.'

The phone bleeped on Redfern's desk. He answered. 'Keep him restrained,' he said into the receiver. 'I'll be right there.'

'I may well pursue this,' Chloe said. 'I'll go through the Home Office.'

'If I were you, I'd forget the Home Office,' I told her. 'Take it to Hollywood instead – they'll love it.'

I was ready to crank the argument up still further, just in case, all the way if necessary, but Chloe didn't take me on. She was quieter. Something inside her was wilting. She looked at me. 'From what you tell me, Hollywood already does.'

Paul Redfern wasn't listening. It was just a husband and wife scoring points. He was already on his feet, thinking about the familiar world of proper crime, of drug barons, car thefts and drunks resisting arrest. He handed me Eric's laptop. 'Enjoy,' he said.

He gave Chloe a wan smile. She didn't smile back.

Outside, Chloe and I stood on the pavement, facing each other.

'Satisfied?' I said.

'How can I be,' she said, 'unless you tell me the truth?' She gave me a challenging look. 'Tell me the truth,' she demanded.

I didn't answer.

She hurried across the street to her car – our car.

I shouted over. 'Can I have a lift home?'

She acted like she hadn't heard me, started the car.

'Chloe.'

I trotted across the street before she could drive off and spoke to her through the open window. 'You seemed very pally with him,' I said. 'Paul Redfern. He certainly waived a few rules for you, didn't he?'

She didn't answer straightaway. 'I was engaged to him before I met you,' she said. She went on, 'He was a dick then and he's a dick now.'

My wife gunned the engine and, without indicating or even looking, pulled out and drove quickly away.

I looked at the laptop.

'After such knowledge,' as Eric might have put it, 'what forgiveness?'

That night, feeling a sudden nostalgic yearning for love, I rose from the couch and climbed into bed. Wrapping Chloe in my arms, I attempted a tender kiss but had to abandon this idea when she woke, jumped up and fled naked to the bathroom, wailing. When she wouldn't open the locked door, I kicked it wide in manly fashion but I didn't find her floating face down in a tub full of her own blood, as I'd rather melodramatically thought I might. Instead she was sitting calmly on the toilet seat, texting Sam and Morag.

She looked up at me. 'Tell me the truth,' she said.

'I've told you,' I said again, 'I didn't do it.'

'Yes, I expected you to say that.'

I considered this. 'All right then,' I said, 'I did do it.'

She considered this. 'The trouble is I expected you to say that too.' She shrugged. 'So you see my dilemma,' she said in conclusion. And she bowed her delicate head with its dark lustrous hair and resumed tapping. Sitting there naked on the pan, my wife struck me as looking like the woman in that painting by Vermeer – one of the young woman sewing. Only she was not sewing this time but texting, and not by Vermeer but reworked somehow by Francis Bacon – if you get my meaning, if there was any such painting. Which perhaps there should be.

Anyway, the marriage was over.

For both our sakes, I tried to quit the flat as speedily as I could but the whirl and clunk of changing times had severely dented my options. My mother, that faithful, faithless, hideous old standby was now living with my father in a state of rekindled bliss in their cramped, high-rise, fag-fugged love nest across the Clyde. Denis's flat, that west-end mission for errant semen, that party pen for slumming husbands, for wronged women on the pull, that mute witness to a thousand evenings of tone-deaf choristers singing 'Losing My Religion', was now under auction and had sheets of corrugated iron for curtains.

Swallowing what passed for my pride, I pitched up on Mr Provan's doorstep and asked if he had anything spare to rent. The strains of Vivaldi's *Four Seasons* on Classic FM made for nostalgic listening as he retreated within his dark warm lair to confer with his sister. After some murmuring, he loomed back out of the gloom and announced in a firm voice, 'I'm sorry but I'm afraid there's nothing doing.'

I nodded and was already halfway down the path when he hurried after me, slipping me his latest slim volume. 'It was the mince on the ceiling,' he explained. 'It did you no favours.' Then he scuttled back indoors to the plunging strings of 'Winter'.

Trudging down Cecil Street, I looked the book over – *Room to Breathe: Poems of a Hillhead Landlord* by Hugh S. Provan. Touchingly, there was a twenty inside. I pocketed it and binned the Breathings.

Having exhausted my limited list of possibilities, I steered my feet toward the inevitable. I stayed in the Homeless Men's hostel – same one I'd domiciled myself in after our last break-up. I thought about Chloe. About how, when I'd first met her, I'd been bobbing about on life's cold indifferent ocean etcetera. And how, after she'd helped me into her lifeboat and nursed me back to health, I'd kicked her over the side and rowed away, whistling merrily. Still, that's how it is with us sensitive, creative types. Perhaps I'd pen her a limpid sonnet and posterity would record that all ended well. But would posterity know I'd penned it on her murdered brother's laptop? Posterity is literature's stately home. In Glasgow, our stately home is Barlinnie. So, basically, sod the limpid sonnet.

My tenure at the hostel ended abruptly one night when I awoke in the early hours to find a grizzled crack hound attempting to remove my mobile phone from under my pillow. I hit him hard in the face and was told to leave. This I did without qualm. Nobody would be allowed to steal my mobile, nobody. My phone afforded my only possibility of escape, a frail tendril along which sustaining droplets of hope dripped, keeping me half-alive and waiting. I dropped my under-sheet and thin blankets out the window, walked past reception and picked them up from the pavement outside.

Six bleary nights later, crouched unsleeping under a frail cardboard tepee on the Kingston Bridge underpass, my faith, my bad faith, my hollow ruthlessness, call it what you will, was finally rewarded.

'Hello?'

'Hi, Spiky, how goes it?'

'Who is this?'

'Now don't hurt my feelings. Who else calls you Spiky? Are you still there?'

'Yes, David, I'm still here. What is it?'

'Are you sitting down? You should sit down for this.'

I looked around. A man of standards, I was, indeed, seated. Some, less formal, lay lined along the wall, like human grouting. Others, no slaves to decorum, lay soaked in their own piss, clutching bottles and moaning. A toothless creature, a fellow wit and ironist, lay sprawled in a tangle of limbs warbling 'The Bonnie, Bonnie Banks of Loch Lomond'.

'Yes, I'm sitting down. Why?'

'I'll tell you why,' David Shenson said. 'Because I have some news for you.'

And he told me the news.

And my battered old twisted heart did gladden.

A couple of days later, Denis came to see me off at Glasgow Airport. He was flabby and his features had thickened. He looked like his own unsuccessful sponging brother might have looked – if he'd had one.

He managed a smile though.

'I didn't know if you'd come,' I said. 'I heard you were annoyed I didn't invite you to my wedding.'

'No matter,' he said, 'here I am for your divorce.'

He took out a packet of Superkings, looked about awkwardly for No Smoking signs. Not seeing any, he lit up.

'So,' he said, 'another good man bites the dust.' He took a draw, looked me over. 'Literally, from the look of you.'

'I've been financially embarrassed,' I said, 'but I trust an improvement in circumstance to be imminent.' There was a chance our meeting might turn into an anecdote and I was going for a note of languid stoicism. Giving my head a scratch, I noticed an earthy pong and made a mental note to buy some underarm deodorant, soon as I became ridiculously wealthy.

'Who told you about the break-up? Chloe?'

'No, Morag.' Denis had the decency to look a bit shifty on the mention of Morag's name.

'Morag wouldn't give me your parents' number when I rang her,' I told him. 'I had to get it from Billy Givens. She went into this hissing rant, said I was an evil influence on you.'

Denis was peeved. He looked me over, archly. 'Clearly evil isn't as good as it used to be,' he said.

This being our last meeting, I'd hoped we could share a nice bilious five minutes about how loathsome an article Morag was but Denis staked out his territory.

'She's a nice girl,' he insisted. 'It's you – you see the worst in everybody.'

'Denis, she called me a murderer. Your girlfriend broke up my marriage.'

He shrugged. 'If a marriage can't stand the odd allegation of murder, it isn't worth having.'

A cleaner in a fluorescent jacket pointed to a sign. Denis extinguished his Superking.

'Will you marry Morag?'

'Only if I have to.'

'Will you have to?'

'Depends. I'm up for a part in that soap – *River City*. It's my last chance.'

'What if you don't get it?'

'I'll cut my throat.'

'What if you do?'

'I'll cut my throat.'

We shared a little smile. But our eyes were flitting now, each over the other's shoulder. Already, we were rewriting the inner tale of our passing lives, had begun tweaking and revising our character lists, each busily reducing the other, in our own eyes, to occasional bit-part player. The show would go on. We would run and run, to nowhere, until we stopped.

I held up my boarding pass, my ticket receipt. 'Thanks for this,' I said. 'I'll wire the money back by Western Union, soon as they pay me.'

'No bother,' he said, 'you can do the same for me some time.'

'You never know.'

'No, we never know,' said Denis. He puckered his face. 'But we usually do.'

And that was it. No hugs or handshakes, we just grunted, politely, like Scots do, these Scots anyway, and I watched him walk away.

Finally he turned. He had to ask, his one last chance, so he asked, 'Tell me,' he said, 'are you really a thief and a murderer?'

'Yes,' I called to him.

He nodded, smiled. 'That's what I thought,' he said.

We stood, at a loss for a moment, then he reared up, doing the Lone Ranger on an imaginary Silver. 'Adios, amigo.'

I watched the escalator slide Denis Rourke slowly down to Sconeland. Outside, the sky was glowering. If he hurried, he might cheat the rain on his way to meet Morag. I'd never learned to cheat the rain.

I picked up my bag.

CHAPTER FOURTEEN

When I arrived at LAX, seventeen hours later, following security alerts at Schipol and O'Hare, I had nothing – no luggage, just a stuffed Asda bag and the shirt, well, the three shirts, I wore on my back. No hire car this time ready to whisk me to my spacious, if frill-free, apartment complex, complete with shared pool, freckled broad and resident Buddhist psycho. If I wanted a gun stuck in my ear this time, I'd have to stand on the sidewalk and wait, like everyone else.

In my pocket, I had eighteen dollars and fifteen cents. I could eat or take a cab. I chose a cab – I could always take a bite out of Shenson's leg later. When the meter hit eighteen dollars, I told the cabbie to stop right there – I'd walk the rest. When I tipped him my last fifteen cents, he was so overwhelmed he didn't even thank me and drove off immediately to splash it around town.

It was still early morning when I arrived, Asda bag in hand, outside the entrance to Winters and Daly. I sat down on the step and dozed lightly until the morning cleaners arrived in a little van. They huddled round me in a group looking dubious but I showed the head cleaner, Rochelle on her tag, a script with my name on it. I pulled out my passport from an inner shirt to confirm and, after dropping some names, I was allowed to wait in reception. I took out a book of Jack London short stories to pass the time with but the time passed anyway because I dozed off, seeming to surf on deep rolling waves of sleep. I woke to find someone shaking me by the shoulder. When I looked up, Nancy Roff, David Shenson and Tess Schwartzenbuch were standing over me.

'Hello, Spiky,' Shenson said. He glanced at my bag. It was spilling underwear, books. 'And who are we today? Jack Kerouac?'

Nancy picked up my book from the floor where it must have fallen.

'Ah, Jack London – nearly right,' said Shenson.

Nancy passed the book to Tess and she pushed it carefully into my bag. Even through my fuddled state, I noticed she didn't dare wrinkle her nose. Everybody looked fresh, showered and crisply laundered. Evidently, I didn't.

'What is it, adopt a germ week in Scotland?' asked Nancy, wiping her hands.

They all stood over me, beaming. Through the natural good-will of shared commercial interest, they had built this small comedy moment for me, had done everything right, had developed a situation, reinforced it and were now standing around waiting expectantly for the final flourish of the punch line. I could have said anything, whatever, it wouldn't have mattered a damn, the discharge of tension would have made it funny.

'Well, say something – even if it's only to call me cunty,' said David Shenson.

But my mouth wouldn't work, I couldn't answer. I had just woken up, you see.

Somewhere, I could smell coffee.

An hour later I walked out of Winters and Daly holding a cheque for thirty thousand dollars. In my shirt pocket, which is to say my innermost shirt pocket, was a rubber band holding five hundred dollars more from petty cash. In a month, we'd be shooting *Looking at the Stars*. On the first day of principal photography, I'd pick up a further thirty grand. Nancy had Tess charge a cab and take me to the Marriot Courtyard on Olympic Boulevard. On the way there, I saw a branch of Ralph's. I had the driver stop. I went in and bought some deodorant. I felt I could afford it.

Over the next two days, with clean hair and money in my pocket, came the confidence to think again of Bobbie. I'd had a film green-lit, I was no longer an abstract emotional difficulty from across the ocean. I was back here, successful and in the flesh – surely that would help us clear the tangled path of love? If love it was and if the path was still mine to clear . . .

I went down into the foyer of my hotel to make the call, not wishing to do so from my room – if it didn't go well, the room would be tarnished by the association of failed romance and I'd have to move. Even in the foyer, I hesitated about making the call, fearing it might be untimely and place Bobbie in jeopardy with Lorne. But I steeled myself, hand shaking, heart pumping, and did it anyway.

And it rang. It rang and rang. I walked around the block then tried again. I checked the number, twice, three times, obsessively, and kept on ringing. But the phone just rang out – no message facility, nothing. I wondered what to do. I thought about tracking down Bobbie's temp agency to find out where she might be working – that's if she was working. But there were dozens of temp agencies in the phone book and she switched all the time. And, even if I stumbled on the right one, they'd be unlikely to give out details to a stranger. The easiest thing, which is to say the hardest thing, was to risk Lorne's wrath and go back to the Jacey Gardens.

So I did.

I paid off the cabbie a little way down the road and walked up. For some reason, I was tiptoeing. The lobby seemed smaller and seedier than I'd remembered it. A young oriental guy I didn't recognise looked up from a Chinese newspaper. Or maybe it was a Korean newspaper – I don't know, being ignorant of the ways of the east. He smiled, pleasantly.

'Hi. You want help?'

'I think so,' I said. 'I'm looking for Miss Bobbie.'

'Miss Bobbie?'

'Yes.'

He stopped smiling and looked suspicious. It occurred to me he might think I was looking for a hooker, so I elaborated quickly.

'Miss Bobbie Binkley and Mr Lorne . . . I can't remember his second name. But they live on the first floor. Could you please check if they're in?'

'Not in. Not live here.'

'Not live here? You're sure?'

'Sure.'

'They do live here – I know that. Could you maybe please check the register?'

'Sure, do that.' He got out a ring binder, opened it, ran his finger down a list. I tried to read the names upside down, checking with him, just in case.

'No, nobody that names first floor.' He checked again. 'Nobody that names on building. Sarry.'

'Are you sure?'

'Sure, sure. You see?'

He turned the binder around, so I could run down the columns of typed names.

'See? Sarry.'

'I don't understand. They were here not long ago.'

'Ah, people here come go all time, all time.' He spun the binder back. My confusion reassured him and he went back to smiling pleasantly. He'd been sizing me up because of the questions. He seemed to decide I was a harmless hick, not some troublesome local stalker.

'You American?'

'No, Scottish.'

He switched himself off, turned out the lights.

'English.'

He sparked to life again, all smiles. 'Ah, English, yeah. England like Korea. People stay. Here, America, people come go all time. All time, come go.'

I was at a loss for a move. I remembered Raul. 'What about Raul?'

'Raul?'

'Yes, the other concierge.'

'Other concierge?'

'Yes, the one who isn't you,' I looked at his badge, 'Chou Tao.'

'Ah, Raul. Oh, he gone. He come go too. Everybody here LA come go all time. All time.'

'Can I go upstairs?'

'Upstairs? Why?'

'To check.'

'What, what? No live here.'

'Please. Just to check.'

Chou Tao thought for a moment. 'OK. I best come too.'

He came too and we walked up the stairs. On the first floor landing I could hear television sounds from an apartment, my old apartment. I hesitated. He looked expectant. He was ready to knock.

'That one?'

'No, next one.'

He walked the few steps along the corridor. I loitered by the stairs while he knocked on the door – I didn't want to risk Lorne springing up from a lotus position and strapping on his hardware. Though Chou Tao kept knocking, nobody answered. He stooped down and peered through the letterbox. 'Come see,' he said to me, gesturing.

I hesitated.

'Is all right, not anyfing howwible,' he guffawed happily. 'Come see.'

I came. I saw. I pushed back the rusting box flap and looked on through to nothing. A furnished apartment, that's all. Stripped of life, cleaned and ready to rent. Nothing.

'What you think?'

'I don't know. What do you think?'

'Gone away looks like.'

'Yes,' I said, 'gone away looks like.'

He saw the look on my face. He looked sad for me. 'Is people – they come go all time,' he shrugged.

'Yes,' I said, 'people come go all time.'

Soon after that, I moved into a small one-bedroom apartment up off the downtown road. The initial exultation of having had a film green-lit had settled to the familiar routine of waiting, in silence, trying to occupy my time. Though the rumble and clamour from the Hollywood Freeway was constant, I had a little balcony so there was always the consolation of sitting with my feet up, contemplating eternity while being irritated by next-door's TV set. The mountain road wasn't far away and the mailman, Troy, told me that, at night, you could hear the coyotes howl. I listened on many nights but never heard a coyote so much as clear its throat. All I ever saw or heard was the receding tail lights of single men in open topped cars with their laughter echoing to me from the distant valley. Maybe 'coyote' was local gay code.

One morning, I was hovering by a corner news-stand wondering whether to blow eight dollars on a two-day-old *Sunday Telegraph* when my phone rang.

Without preamble, Nancy's voice said, 'We need to have lunch. Have a shower, comb your hair.'

'I have no hair. I've grown old and bald through waiting for this call.'

'Good – you'll look distinguished. And wear a jacket.'

I made my way to Winters and Daly and Nancy drove us to Santa Monica for lunch. At Shutters on the Beach, her Jag was valet-parked.

'We have a table booked,' Nancy told the head waiter or the footman, whatever, some smart-looking guy who glided rather than walked.

'Nancy Roff – we're celebrating.'

'Way to go. Now was it 1 Pico or Pedals?'

'Pedals.'

'This way please.'

As he led us through to the cafe, Nancy turned to me. 'The bigger the budget, the better you eat. If you want 1 Pico, next time write in a few laser weapons and get George Lucas to direct.'

'I will.'

We sat down and took bread rolls from the proffered basket. Casting for *Looking at the Stars* was well under way, Nancy assured me, and I wasn't to worry about a thing.

The wine waitress appeared. She asked my choice. 'Wine or water?'

'Wine.'

'Forget it – he'll have water.'

Over lunch, Nancy again explained that I wasn't to worry about a thing because it was all in good hands.

'Who's in it?'

'New people – bright young things.'

'How bright? How young?'

'Questions later – I'm giving you the details.'

The crucial hospital scenes, the bulk of the interiors, would be shot in a disused school building near Pasadena, Nancy explained. The other interiors could be shot on the lot.

'On the lot.' I stifled a gleeful smirk. That was big adult film talk. I did an inner handspring but outwardly nodded, affecting the seasoned indifference of the hardened pro.

I'd neither met nor heard of the director but he was young, naturally, hot and somewhat of a performer himself. I'd like him, Nancy assured me. He was all for 'verisimilitude' – just like me. I asked Nancy, as my agent, mentor and Lord Protector, for assurances that he'd be faithful to the script.

'Of course he'll be faithful to the script – he loves the script.'

'He won't change it?'

'Why would he change it? He loves it. Why would you ask that?'

'I've heard writers say they've bad experiences.'

'Only bad writers have bad experiences.'

'So he likes the script?'

'He loves the script – that's why he's doing it.'

'And I have your guarantee he won't change anything?'

'Who can guarantee? Change is inevitable. Look at me – I have a plastic hip. Change is adaptive – a part of life. Ask Charles Darwin.'

'OK, to sum up, he might add a plastic hip and Charles Darwin but that's it – I have your guarantee?'

'Would you take a verbal guarantee?'

'Yes.'

'Nothing on paper?'

'No.'

'Then you have my guarantee. Relax, I'm joking.'

'I'm joking too – I'm just not laughing.'

I had come too far, been through too much – I was nervous about any changes.

Nancy tried again. 'Look, put it this way – you wouldn't go into a department store and buy a pair of blue pants then, when you get home, try to turn them into a pair of green shorts, would you?'

'No – but I'm not a movie director.'

'Neither am I. You're right – they're nuts. Just pray he doesn't cast Stallone. Ask me why.'

'Why?'

'You remember that stuff when you were a kid – Alphabetti Spaghetti?'

'Sure.'

'That'll be your script when Rambo's finished with it. Now eat your salad and cross your fingers. All you can do is hope.' She laughed.

I realised I'd never seen Nancy laugh. I laughed too. Why not? I was a screenwriter. I'd written *Looking at the Stars*.

The night before PP began – that's principal photography to you (and, for that matter, to me) – I sat out on my balcony with a bottle of Cabernet and read the script again. I hadn't read it in weeks and, on completing the standard 120 pages, I felt oddly depressed. Not because I didn't still think it good – I did. In fact, that's what had depressed me. I knew in myself that, if I were to write as well as my talent would possibly allow, I still couldn't write half as well as Eric had written in *Looking at the Stars*. It beat me hollow – there were no two ways about it. I may have killed him but his work left me for dead. It was better than anything I was capable of, no matter how hard I might try.

But, and here's the rub, was it the best Eric was capable of? We'd never know. Even if he'd lived, it's possible we still would never have known. Very probably Eric Ross would have sniffed and jabbed his ability, if not himself, into an early grave. Eric's talent was strong but the vessel that held it, weak. Which is where I had come in. I had liberated the talent by smashing the vessel. Eric, as an artist, would have understood that. If he'd been alive, he'd have thanked me for killing him. Not everyone on this earth has the will to make a thing happen, the thing they most want, to have it, to do or die. But I had. I'd killed a man in a Glasgow basement and now here I was in Hollywood about to touch the stars. And it was when I started thinking these thoughts that I stopped being depressed about the gleaming magnitude of Eric's mighty star and began feeling good about my own dear little twinkle.

Of course, the wine helped.

The next day, PP day, I walked into the offices of Winters and Daly and walked out again clutching my second thirty-grand cheque. In keeping with my new tradition or superstition – I've never been clear on the difference – I walked into a branch of Ralph's intending to buy some more underarm deodorant. It's fair to say that, if I hadn't done this small thing, my life might well be different from what it is today. As I queued at the till, a local daily newspaper reminded me of Lorne's surname.

Tippits. Lorne Tippits – that was it. I knew this because a small photograph of the same Lorne Tippits was on the front page of that paper. Not top, not hogging any headlines – the main story was about local fury over electricity failures – but there, stuck to the side, was Lorne, grinning out in his characteristic way, struggling at the same time to look both spiritually mellow and manly mean. I picked up the paper with shaking hand and read the story. Lorne wouldn't be doing any more grinning, it transpired, because he was now deceased – the deceased Lorne Tippits. Turn to page six for more. I was all fingers and thumbs finding six. When I found it, I had that rushing sensation in the ears you get when your body is fuelling itself with adrenaline, ready for take-off. There it was, halfway down the column, Bobbie's little picture. Below the picture, it just said, 'Accused: Lover Binkley'.

Accused: Lover Binkley.

You've read these stories, every paper carries them – the squalid little tales of the working poor. 'Suspicious circumstances. Neighbours told of fights. Daytime drinking. Money worries.'

The intricate web of life reduced to bullet points on a stringer's byline. 'Four-day trial expected. Judge Beth Harding presiding.'

Accused: Lover Binkley.

I felt jealousy and confusion rising in me.

So far as I was concerned, Bobbie was nobody's lover but mine.

The trial was in Santa Monica and a cold wet fog had hung around off the bay all morning. There were no film-star misdemeanours to grace the famous courthouse – just cheats and rapists and poor folk with guns, the extras who make up the numbers in between the celebrity drunk drivers and the sexy palimony cases involving the rich and famous.

I'd already missed the first day of the trial but turned up early on the second to make sure of a place in the public gallery. After queuing in the drizzle, we were admitted to an outer chamber where we were all of us passed through a metal detector. The Binkley trial was in Courtroom Four B. I walked, two at a time, up the stairs, in between the two security officers on the doors. There were already people in the front row – senior citizens, mostly, but also some straggly-haired ghouls and some couples with rugs over their knees and inflatable back supports, there to make a day of it.

Some were trying to hold the good seats for others but I wasn't having any of that. I moved a white raincoat and put it back on a big black woman's knee. She said she'd complain. 'So complain away,' I said but I said it politely – I didn't want to be evicted by security. The cast came in and took their places, ready to speak their lines and begin. I looked for Bobbie, couldn't see her and then I did. She was between two women police officers. I must've missed her when I was murmuring at the raincoat woman. Bobbie had no make-up on, her hair was tied back and she was in saggy women's prison greens. All the same, on seeing her, my heart, as they say, stood still.

Judge Beth Harding came in and we were told to rise. Then she sat down and told us to do the same. And everybody sat – except me. I remained standing. There, front row of the spectators' gallery, in full view of the judge and jury, of the attorney for and of the attorney against and, most especially, in view of the prisoner at the bar or whatever they called the bar in America – the bar, possibly. At first, Judge Beth didn't see me and neither did the prisoner at the bar but the security officers did and one gripped me by the elbow and whispered for me to sit. I didn't sit though and Judge Beth looked up.

'Could you please be seated?' she said.

When she said that, everybody looked up – all the players on the floor – and so did the prisoner at the bar. Despite the localised fuss and rumpus, I remained standing with my hands held up, like the Pope giving a benediction – only he tended not to whistle and stamp, like I was doing, when he did his benedicting. Then again, his Holiness, to my knowledge, wasn't in love with Bobbie Binkley.

'One second more,' I begged of the officer as I remained looking at Bobbie and she at me. With my look, I wanted Bobbie to know that I was there for her. I wanted to send a message that I'd stand by her if the worst happened, if she was sent away, even though I knew I probably wouldn't stand by her, not for long anyway, because life's not like that. In fifteen to twenty, she'd be old and ugly like her mom and I'd be long back to my bad old ways but, even so, it was important for me to convey that message and for Bobbie to understand it and receive it into her heart because we were on a new path together, a bumpy road, and the journey we were undertaking demanded our utmost endeavours so maybe, just maybe, we could do it hand in hand, all the way, despite everything.

Anyway, that's what I hoped my look conveyed.

'Come with me, sir.'

The security officer escorted me out on to the street. Once there, he was not so polite. 'Get a freaking life,' he advised.

'I will,' I promised. 'Not yours, though.'

He made as if to hit me and I hurried back to my borrowed production unit car.

As I started toward Pasadena, the fret was still rolling off the sea but, as I drove, I started to outstrip it. By the time I arrived at the disused school, the day was baking hot and the unit had broken for coffee.

I could see the director emerging from the school, the hospital building. He was with his DP, his director of photography, whom he respected totally and with whom he'd worked on many projects – in fact, they suggested each other for projects, so great was their mutual respect. I picked my tentative way between the trucks, the trailing cables, the men with walkie-talkies who eyed me curiously for I was that strange grey lizard, the writer, the only man on set whose time wasn't on a meter, who had already been paid, whose task was already complete, yet who'd still turn up on set each day to do nothing, except hang around, looking worried, until the sun went down. I continued between the bright folded brollies and the make-up bags, trying to head the director off before he made the catering bus. By the time I got there, the director was listening to a joke told by the leading actor. When they hit the punchline, they went 'aw-right' and high-fived. It was that kind of production and they were that kind of people – which is to say not my kind of people.

But I was the writer. And these were my mountains and this was my glen.

When I asked the director how it was going, he told me great. He threw his arm around me, telling me they'd got some really terrific stuff, juicy stuff, stuff with life and yes, verisimilitude, that kind of stuff. I couldn't help noticing he was steering me away from the leading actor. You wouldn't know the leading actor, incidentally, I didn't know him and it was my film. But he was a friend of the director. And the director was also an actor – just as the leading actor, I soon discovered, was also a sometime director. They'd started out as comics together, way back, maybe five, six years ago, way back at the Comedy Store, back then. The director was a film school graduate – as was the leading actor. I listened as the director stitched himself and the leading actor into the great living pageant of comedy history.

Paramount had got them just at the right time, the director assured me, just as they were breaking out of the indies but before they'd been 'blanded out' by the mainstream. I hadn't wanted to prejudge and, as I listened, I tried to draw a bead on him, the director, to crystallise the vapour of what I was being told.

Finally, I said 'Who's your favourite comic actor?'

'John Belushi.'

'Not Woody Allen? Not Billy Crystal or Ben Stiller?'

'Nope, John Belushi every time. Food fight, food fight! Aw-right.'

That night I rang the editing suite off Lexington and asked to view the day's rushes.

'No problem,' the editor said. To cover himself he added, 'Hold on a second, I'll just clear it with Herr Directore.'

I heard a brief mumbled discussion then the editor repeated his invitation. 'No problem – come on along.'

The editor was alone when I arrived. When he'd heard I was coming, the director had quickly absented himself, the editor told me, and had headed off to Dan Tana's to eat. The editor sat me down alone in an adjacent office and slotted a tape into the VCR machine.

'My brother-in-law is a writer,' he muttered, sympathetically, and went quietly out.

I watched the tape through. I sat there, trying to choose a word that would best encapsulate my state of mind. I settled on 'horrified'. I made myself calm then watched the tape again. This time I noted a subtle change to my mental condition. Now I was 'numbly horrified'. When I'd finished watching the tape a second time, I went through to the editor's office.

At the console, he looked up from his bran muffin. 'You look pale,' he said. 'Would you like some water?'

'I'm always pale – I'm Scottish. Are those the best takes?'

The editor thought for a moment. 'Well, that's hard to say,' he said. 'The actors never seem to do the same thing twice.'

'Or say the same thing twice,' I said.

'No,' the editor agreed. He looked up at me, smiling hopefully. 'Maybe that's the joy of it.'

But it wasn't.

The following morning, I queued again outside the Santa Monica Courthouse but they remembered me and wouldn't allow me in. I made a rambling speech on the sidewalk, invoking my civil rights and it appeared to be holding some sway until someone realised I wasn't an American citizen so didn't have any civil rights. 'OK,' I said to the security officer in charge, 'at least tell me one thing. How do you think it's going in there?'

'In where?'

'The Binkley case.'

'What the hell's the Binkley case?'

'Court Four B.'

'Oh, Court Four B? Lady with the freaky hair and the busted teeth?'

'Yes,' I said. 'Help me out here. You've seen all kind of trials. How do you think it'll go for her?'

'Who can say?'

'If you were a betting man.'

'I never bet on human life.'

'Break a rule.'

'You press?'

'No,' I said, 'I'm not press – I'm her boyfriend.' I felt myself blush as I said this.

The Security Officer eased up a little. 'Look, boyfriend,' he said, 'you've seen that jury. There's people on those benches I couldn't guess their sex, let alone how they're going to vote. There's uglies on those benches and munchkins, there's people with false limbs and hair, there's a man in there with double hearing aids wearing matching tie and socks – who can tell what frightening hang-ups these terrible strangers have? All I can tell you is that, in my experience, it's a lottery, my friend – seven times out of every ten, a lottery.'

'Thank you.'

'I wish you all the luck in the world.'

'Could I get in to say hello?'

'No. And, if you attempt to do that thing, you will be arrested. And, if you resist arrest you will be shot down – we will shoot you down. Do you understand?'

'Yes.'

'Have a nice day, sir. Be good to yourself.'

Back in the car, I took out my phone and rang Winters and Daly. 'Put me through to Nancy,' I told Tess Schwartzenbuch.

'Nancy's in a meeting – she can't be interrupted.'

'Sure she can – interrupt her, Tess.'

The battering ram of my tone worked – being cold and angry enough to wrong-foot Tess and have her do my will. Through my anger, I made a mental note to use the same tone and make her play tennis with me. Once through to Nancy, I made a formal complaint about the work of the director and of the leading actor, specifically concerning their cavalier attitude toward the script, my script.

'It's the first day, they'll settle down. They're nervous.'

'They're not nervous. Nervous people don't improvise scenes.'

'They're improvising scenes?'

'Yes.'

Silence.

'Nancy?'

'I hear you, I hear you. Listen, you have to grow up.'

'You're saying I'm a child?'

'I didn't mean grow up, I meant open your mind. Film is a collaborative medium – accept it. That's the way it works.'

'Not on this script it isn't,' I told her. 'This script has cost me too much.'

I ended the call. Having made my formal complaint, I drove at speed to Pasadena where I then made a more informal complaint to the leading actor. It was so informal I had him by the lapels and was shaking.

'Please take your hands off me.'

'You're ruining my script!'

'If you remove your hands, we can talk.'

We were on set in a side ward. A sign above the bed said 'Infectious Disease'. I hadn't thought there should or would be such a sign above the bed and said so to the set designer. Set designers are nice people and this one apologised, referring me to the leading actor.

'I need it there,' the leading actor explained when questioned, 'I have a great sight gag I want to work in.' He turned and called to the props guy, 'Which reminds me, where's the melon and the surgeon's saw?'

At which point, I laid my hands upon him.

'I'm telling you, take your hands off me.'

'No,' I said. I shook him again.

'Stop!'

I gathered my senses, removed my hands. I was doing the shaking now.

'I'm sorry,' I said.

'Never touch me – EVER – AGAIN.'

'I won't,' I said. 'I apologise.' I composed myself. 'This script means a lot to me.'

The director appeared with the DP. They'd been in the corridor, working out shots for the next scene, but obviously someone had alerted them to the commotion.

'What's going on here?' the director asked. He was wearing a catcher's mitt.

'We're having an artistic discussion,' I said.

'What about?'

'He put his hands on me,' the leading actor said, 'but it's OK.'

'He put his hands on you?'

The director's voice and manner had turned cold. He remembered he was wearing the catcher's mitt. Obviously this was indicative of the mood of good fellowship that had prevailed on set before I, Beelzebub the writer, had arrived. Now the mood was different and the director took off the catcher's mitt and tucked it under his arm, like a staff baton.

'Why did he put his hands on you?'

'He said we're ruining his work,' the leading actor said. 'Both of us.'

'He said that?'

They turned, as one person, to look at me. 'He apologised, though,' the leading actor said.

'I did,' I said, shuffling. 'I apologised.'

The director looked around the crew, called out, 'Is that right, everybody   did he apologise?'

Everybody looked at each other just to be safe then voices started mumbling that, yes, I had indeed done that thing.

Because I'd apologised and, therefore, given ground, the director risked an authoritative touch on my arm. 'Come to my trailer,' he said.

In the director's trailer, I watched the new day's rushes on a small monitor. When they'd finished, he leaned back in his chair and looked at me.

'Well, what'd you think?'

'They're awful,' I told him truthfully. 'They're worse than yesterday's.'

'You don't like today's rushes?'

'You're ignoring the script,' I said.

'No, I'm not – your script is my bible.'

'Really? Really?' I took my crumpled shooting script, his bible, from on top the monitor and opened it at the scene we'd just watched. I leaned over him. 'Look,' I said, 'here's what the bible says in that scene.' I dragged my finger up and down whole speeches. 'It says this and this and that. The leading actor didn't say any of it. Not one line. He made stuff up. Junk.'

The director looked up at me. 'He's tailoring the dialogue to his own needs.'

'What about my needs?'

'He's your star, your money. He knows his talent better than you do. We're obeying the spirit of your script, not the letter.'

I thought of Eric. His dead eyes, his Ecco shoe soles. 'The spirit is in the letter,' I said.

The director sighed and shrugged. He was at a loss. 'Man, I don't know what to tell you,' he said. 'Film is a collaborative medium. You need to learn to leave your ego at the door.'

'Along with my self-respect?'

On a film, the director is king. When a director says film is a collaborative medium, he's only saying that to marginalise the writer and patronise his crew. Because they want to please him, his crew will parrot the director's words like a mantra. But let any producer try and change a single frame of a director's work without his consent and you'll find out very quickly just how collaborative a medium is film. The director will squeal like a stuck pig.

This director, my director, spread his arms to heaven, signifying hopelessness. The artistic discussion being over, he stood up, pulled his catcher's mitt back on. 'Take my advice,' he said, 'try to rub along with people. You'll have a longer career.'

He started for the door. I got there ahead of him, blocking his way.

'Listen to me,' I said, 'the guy isn't an actor – he's shit on a stick. And you're sucking it out of his arse.'

'I wouldn't tell him that. He knows people who kill.'

'So do you,' I told him. 'Only you're such a numpty, you don't even know you know that.'

Numpty? Yes, I said that – I said 'numpty' in Hollywood.

The director bristled. At least I'd had a bristle out of him.

He couldn't beat that for an exit line so I let him pass.

I arrived at the courthouse early the following morning. It was the fourth day of the trial and a verdict was expected imminently. A large gathering of press photographers and news reporters was clustered around the entrance. The morning was already hot and most of the paparazzi were in shirtsleeves with bulky Nikon bags on their shoulders and expensive flash cameras poised at their chests. The news reporters were smartly dressed, though – the men in sober suits, the women in those gaudy television skirt suits that no woman would ever otherwise wear in real life. I stood across the street, away from the hubbub, watching, waiting. After twenty, maybe thirty minutes, there was a sudden stirring. I heard a shout of, 'Here she comes!' and the posse surged around the doorway. A blonde female appeared, doing fearless yet vulnerable acting, flanked by men in suits, trying to protect her.

There was shouting all around as the photographers fought and jostled for their pictures. 'Over here!' 'Have you a statement?' Stuff like that. Her name was Zalome, spelt that way with a zee.

Her tiny criminal misdemeanour had squalled up suddenly and was now being widely reported on the showbiz channels. Two years earlier, she had been a prize on a reality television show. Fat ugly men and dwarves had fought each other for the right to date her. Now she was medium famous for being medium infamous. Every so often, she had to do something outrageous so her market value would be kept buoyant and she wouldn't have to go and work in the Hollywood equivalent of Gregg's, selling pies to workies.

Zalome shouted a few brief words about justice and God into the mics that were thrust at her. People were shouting over her voice. 'What's she saying?' 'She's saying she's relieved it's all over.' 'Yeah but did she do it? She did it, right?'

Having said her piece, Zalome stooped low to climb inside the limo that had slid up outside the entrance. When the limo drove off, the news crews did too, with the press boys and girls running off to their cars and motorcycles. The older men in suits tried to remain statesmanlike as they hung around the sidewalks waiting for lifts in logoed vans and their female peers held their stiff hair in place then ran with click-clacks for the best possible seats when those vans arrived.

And then the courthouse was caught suddenly bare like all the Christmas decorations had come down.

Around two o'clock, a city garbage truck appeared in the street and began trawling slowly, slurping up the brushed-out sludge and foam coffee cups from the gutter. It crawled past the courtroom entrance like a slow yellow curtain and, when it had passed, three female figures were revealed in a little tableau. A short dumpy old woman stood to one side, clutching her shiny Sunday handbag in thick hands, and, on the other side, a severe-looking woman in a white coat, a nurse it looked like, had her arm around the shoulders of a frail-looking woman – Bobbie's shoulders. Because I saw no security officers gripping her or prison vehicle waiting, I knew that Bobbie stood there a free woman.

'Bobbie.'

She looked at me when I called.

I ran across the street toward her. 'Bobbie,' I said, standing before her, my love, my own dear heart.

The old dumpy woman positioned herself between us as a shield – she must have thought I was press. 'I'm her mom, mister. Who are you?' she demanded.

'Bobbie will tell you who I am,' I said.

'No, she won't,' said Bobbie's mom.

'It's true,' the nurse woman said. 'She can't speak.'

'What do you mean?'

Bobbie tried to say something.

I watched her. I urged her on, empathising with her struggle, my own mouth silently uttering the things I thought she wanted to say. In Bobbie's mouth, clucking, spitty noises formed in lieu of words. I grew alarmed. 'What happened?' I shouted. 'Was it Lorne? Did he cut her tongue out?'

'Why would Lorne cut her tongue out?' Bobbie's mom asked.

'I don't know. He's from Oklahoma.'

'I'm from Oklahoma – I've never cut a tongue out in my life.'

'I'm sorry.'

'Forget it. We're used to ignorance. No, what's happened here is she's a dummy – she's been struck dumb.'

'Bobbie's lost her voice?'

'The shock,' the nurse woman explained. 'She went into trauma while awaiting the verdict. Judge had to recess the court for ninety minutes.'

Bobbie's lips moved again. She gave a sort of rasping gasp before wilting from the frustration of the effort.

I took her in my arms and held her – I held my true love tight. 'Will she get her voice back?' I asked the nurse woman.

'I sure hope so,' the nurse woman said, 'but I can't say. Maybe, though, maybe in time.'

'You hear that Bobbie?' I said. 'Well, we have time now.'

I looked at Bobbie. 'Isn't that right, Miss Calvera? Miss Leanne Calvera.'

And finally, I got a smile.

I drove Bobbie and her mom to the bus station so they could journey back to their home in Chickasha where Bobbie would be staying till she'd recovered from the trial. On the way there, I took a detour and bumped the car up on to the sidewalk outside the Winters and Daly building. 'Wait here,' I said to them. 'I won't be long.'

Minutes later, I was back behind the wheel.

Bobbie gave me a quizzical look.

'Just something I had to do,' I explained.

And I had, I'd needed to do it. Nancy had urged me to wait, to see how the film turned out but I'd been insistent.

'Writers,' she'd said in bitter conclusion, 'it's self, self, self all the way – every one the same. They break your fucking heart.'

I was sure a private bit of Nancy had been sneakily reassured, though, by having her heart broken one more time. As an ageing woman in a youthful profession, she'd had her instincts approved and endorsed yet again. This was, of course, poor compensation. Despite her best efforts at promoting me, I, her latest protégé had, in Nancy's eyes, committed professional suicide. I'd demanded that my name be removed from the credits of *Looking at the Stars*.

I was so disgusted over what they've done with my script that I'd disowned it. Sure, I'm a murderer, a liar, a thief, a philanderer but, hell, I still have principles.

I sat around the apartment for a few weeks, not knowing what to do with myself and wondering what would happen when the money ran out. Now and again, my lofty principles would chafe at me like a hair shirt but, though there were moments of weakness, like when I'd see *Looking at the Stars* mentioned in the trade dailies, I never went back on my word. The thing that kept me going was waiting for Bobbie to get well.

When she was as recovered as she was ever going to be, Bobbie took the bus once more and came back out west to live with me. Things, though, were far from sweet. Having no voice, she couldn't be Miss Leanne Calvera any more or even Bobbie the receptionist and soon she took to drinking. Worse, I took to joining her. We had become two people cast adrift on an ocean of our own making and that's a fact.

One beautiful morning, staggering back from the liquor store, I dropped a bag with six bottles of Sonoma red, splat on to the sidewalk. I was scraping the glass shards and splinters with my foot into the gutter and clutching an advertising board, a piece of street furniture, for balance. Clean people, in crisp clothes, on their way to work, were giving me a wide berth, stepping out into the street in avoidance of this stinking, sinking drunk.

'Hello,' I was shouting to nobody, 'hello.'

I slumped down on the kerb, feeling dizzy and sick from the heat. That's when I noticed the advertising board, the one I'd used as my Zimmer frame. 'Mrs Filtner,' it said, 'I Teach Deaf Sign.' An arrow pointed to a narrow slit doorway between a second-hand vinyl store and a Chinese acupuncturist's.

I'd passed that sign board what, maybe fifty, a hundred times yet, somehow, till that moment, had failed to remark it.

We both of us went to deaf and dumb classes, Bobbie and I, and learned some basic sign language. It equalised us and, yes, I believe it helped draw Bobbie out.

We could each sign simple sentences together like 'Look, a bus.' or 'This movie is interesting but flawed.' Under protest, I had Mrs. Filtner, an old Jewish widow woman, teach me sign for, 'You have great tits.'

As I say, it helped. There was something else, though – a block, a great black stone, sitting at the heart of Bobbie. One night, I had a brain wave – it just came to me or me to it, whichever. I went over to Bobbie and took the TV remote out of her left hand, the glass out of her right hand. I placed an exercise book on her lap with some pencils.

'Bobbie,' I said, 'I want you to write me a story.'

I leaned over her. She looked puzzled.

'You know what I mean – a story. Are you with me?'

I looked Bobbie in the eye and I'll say this, she was with me, she knew what I meant.

I didn't push her and it took a while. Finally, one night while I was sipping camomile tea on the balcony, Bobbie came out and handed me some handwritten sheets torn from the exercise book. I thanked her and she went in. She sat down with her back to the French windows so she didn't have to watch me read.

It was a romantic story, a tale of love-torn turbulence and illicit trysts, of dashed dreams and of hopes rising from the ashes. Though the names had been changed and the story was related in the third person, I recognised it to be a thinly veiled account of what had brought Bobbie to trial in the courthouse at Santa Monica – in short, the story of Lorne Tippits' last night on this earth.

If I refer to the two protagonists as the Hero and the Heroine, it's for reasons of literary shorthand. Basically the Hero was a diabetic drunk, prone to violence. The Heroine, occasional subject of that violence, was obliged, twice daily, to administer insulin via intravenous injection unto the Hero, he being, as Heroes often are, too drunk, lazy and incompetent to administer it unto himself.

Eventually, the Heroine had, unbeknown to her lover who we'll call 'Lover', gotten the Hero good and drunk one afternoon then injected him with a massive dose. When, finally, the Hero had dropped, comatose, on to the floor, the Heroine had placed a Ralph's grocery bag over his head in order to speed his demise. This task completed, she'd then removed the grocery bag, pulled on her coat and skipped off on the interstate bus to visit her mom who, by coincidence, lived in Chickasha, Oklahoma. The Heroine's intention had been to return two days later, discover the body and claim that the Hero must have died accidentally, by his own hand, having given himself a wrong dose, a lethal dose, while blind drunk. Unfortunately, the Concierge, who we'll call, for name's sake, Raul, had been in his tiny office eating a tuna and onion sandwich and had glimpsed on the CCTV screen the Heroine leave and could recall the approximate time of her going, this having being confirmed when the CCTV footage had been later consulted, routinely, for accuracy. The two times – the time on the tape at which the Heroine had actually left the building and the time which she stated she had left – did not correspond. The garbage bins out back were searched and a discarded needle had been found inside a Ralph's grocery bag. There were some telltale signs of vomit in the bag. These things, coupled with the Heroine's generally anxious demeanour, had raised questions with the authorities and, though the evidence was circumstantial and the police work unenthusiastic, those questions had led to a trial.

And, ultimately, at long last, to her acquittal.

I put the story down and rubbed my eyes. It had been a strong piece of work – and moving. I thought about what I wanted to say. Then I stepped back into the house.

I sat down and told Bobbie straight. 'Frankly,' I said, 'as fiction, this disappoints.'

She moved her hands to swear at me but I motioned for her to stop.

'Listen to me,' I said. 'I used to read scripts for a living and it's my view that this one of yours is unsuitable for publication.' That's what I told her. I didn't even sugar-coat things with a 'however' or an 'unfortunately'.

I stood up, motioned for her hand and led her into the kitchen.

'It reads like facts, Bobbie,' I said, 'and facts just don't add up to a satisfying story.'

That said, I took a matchbook from the drawer and together we burned the pages in the sink. 'You got it out of your system,' I said. 'Now forget about it.'

And she put her arm around me.

I ran the tap and together we slewed the blackened wisps of carbonised paper down the plughole and into the drain.

This incident marked a turning point. It seemed to help Bobbie my knowing, at last, the facts of her criminal fiction. Gradually, the drinking days dwindled and the guitar started coming out of its battered case for thrumming.

About a week later came a call from a lawyer's office in Grady County. Bobbie's mom, Theadora, had dropped dead from a brain aneurysm.

Bobbie blamed herself, of course, feeling that either the wrath of the Almighty or the strain of the trial, perhaps both, had precipitated the demise. Personally, I blamed cholesterol – all Bobbie and her mom had seemed to live on being home fries and ribs. Whatever the cause, I had a strong sense of being all that Bobbie had left.

With my dear one still unable to speak, I phoned the *Express-Star* newspaper in Chickasha and paid for a tasteful announcement. Then we travelled back for the funeral where I delivered the oration. Being a traditionalist at heart, I recited 'In My Craft or Sullen Art', just as I'd done at the funeral of Eric Ross.

Afterwards, small-town people with crumpled ties and drawling voices stepped up with tears in their eyes to pump my hand – they'd been so moved – and, though, to me, the poem is as false and garish as a Halloween mask, the words do make a lovely noise on the air.

Theadora Binkley had occupied one of a cluster of small wooden houses up behind North Sixteenth Street, in what time had turned from respectable homes for working people into a clapped-out enclave for welfare cases and trapped senior citizens. The heavy encroachment of the Standridge Utility Vehicle Dealership spoke of a municipal impatience to redevelop. We spent a couple days there, gutting the house. We emptied drawers and sorted clothes into different bags, either for binning or for gifting to the leukaemia charity shop downtown, next to Bag-A-Donut. In the damp cellar where Bobbie remembered, as a child, stacking wood that smoked like stink when you lit it, we found mouldy old cardboard suitcases that fell apart when opened.

Inside were stained ancient letters and dozens of bills marked 'paid' in faded ink. Down the side of Theadora's recliner television chair, I found pairs of big old woman specs in cases that I'd take out and try on when Bobbie wasn't looking. Bobbie only kept some paste jewellery for herself and the wedding ring, of course, and a cookie tin that held photographs, including some that showed Bobbie's father Ray, in his GI Joe uniform and later on in his dungarees and work shirt before the cancer took him.

At Theadora's funeral, Reverend Hulliksen had recommended a local dealer, Frank Alvaro – Maximum Frank – who, he said, would give us the fairest price possible for the furniture. All three rooms' worth, including the walnut veneer bedroom suite with matching chiffonier, her mother's pride and joy, fetched the princely sum of ninety-four bucks. It was only later we learned that Maximum Frank was related to the Reverend H. by marriage, which confirmed to me what I've always thought about small towns and people with slow mouths and so-called warm hearts.

That was it, though. We left the drapes up against vandals and handed in the keys at the lawyer's office, next to Goody's Family Clothing Store on Ponderosa drive, pending settlement.

The day before our flight back to LAX, a weird feeling came over me, kind of ardent, and with my hands I asked Bobbie to take us out by the playing fields and farms that skirted Chickasha, this town in Grady County where she'd been born and raised and where she had played as a child, in that distant time before Lorne, dumbness, shot-off toes, the groping candy salesman and, yes, before even me.

I drove the Hertz car north-west along 44 then took the cut-off heading to Pocasset. I was looking for a place to stop, where we could throw open the doors against the singing heat, as in our old courting days, only short months previously, when we'd stolen time to be together. There was more traffic than I bargained for so I took a left at a dirt road leading to some farms. There were grain silos up ahead and far off the noise of working machinery so, at the first passing place we came to, I parked the car and we got out and stretched our legs. Crickets chirped and you could smell manure on the air. A dried-out tuft of hedgerow gave way to a little metal gate. I tugged it open and we walked along the thin track that skirted a field of ripening crops. I don't know what they were – alfalfa or artichokes maybe. What the hell did I know or care? Bobbie was walking up ahead. She had on her denim skirt, the tanned stalks of her legs bare, her arms freckled, her hair as thick and vibrant as any crop or flower.

I caught up with her, taking her by the arm.

She looked at me, sort of puzzled.

'This is the place,' I said.

I guided her down, right there on the path skirting the crops, the alfalfa, the artichokes, and that's where I took her. Yes, I did, I took my stricken Chickasha baby right there on Tom Joad's parched and dusty blanket. She gripped me hard with her legs, I think she'd begun to understand. There was so much hurt and darkness in us, we had to make some light somehow.

I was so sure that, on the flight back, I turned and said to Bobbie, I said, 'If it's a boy, Bobbie, I want him called Eric.'

Looking at the Stars appeared some months after Theadora's funeral. Its release had been delayed and then some because it had to be cut and recut again which is never a good sign. It came and went in a week and the critics buried it deeper than Bobbie's Mom. 'Crude comedy' and 'Dire drivelfest' were more or less representative of the general tone of collective opinion.

For myself, I didn't much mind. It's the untold story behind that movie that I value. I go over it all in my mind sometimes. With scripts, it's different. No matter how good, they almost always disappoint, the stories seldom catch the life that's out there, the life we can never hold even as it slips through our fingers. I suppose there's no harm in trying, though – like I say, it keeps writers off the streets and out of harm's way.

One day I received a call on my cell phone while Bobbie and I were out collecting driftwood at Big Sur. It was Nancy. Yvonne Mulgrew had got back – they'd sold the other script, *Smoking Gun*, as a pilot to Warner Television. Nancy said Warners wanted to buy me out with a flat fee but this gave me a hunch and I told Nancy to skip the fee, all of it, not a thin dime, just hang tough to the format rights and we'd take a big slice off the back end if it went to series.

Those turned out to be smart words. We're into series three, thirteen shows a season, and that's how I bought this spread, off the back end of the deal.

If you were out here now, about a mile off the fork road east side of Tucker, you'd see the hand-carved words on the burnished cedar wood sign above our home saying 'Smoking

Gun Ranch'. Maybe you've seen our show, *Prospect Valley*, over where you are and maybe you haven't. Maybe you've seen it without even knowing – it's that kind of television. It has bright colours to dazzle the British eye. I offered Aiden a job writing an episode and he was cool about it. In fact, he was so cool he was stone cold and to this day hasn't ever returned my call.

Early on, my father tried to mount a legal action, backed by my wife Chloe, who was acting as his solicitor and on behalf of the man I'd reputedly plagiarised, Walter Urquhart. Having no choice, I'd buckled on my legal armour and prepared to fight back with expensive vigour to clear my fair name. Luckily, my father's tumours had the commendable comic timing to bag him before the matter could attain sufficient head of steam so I didn't have to do anything more than sit back and count my money. I'm always waiting for Chloe's next move – I guess with that one I won't ever sleep till I die. Some things you just have to live with.

As I write, Bobbie's fixing lunch and humming a song of Lorne's – one of his early good ones from the old days before Buddha kicked in. With her teeth nicely fixed and recapped my dear heart looks herself again – I guess we've Muley to thank for that.

I've no green card, though – Chloe won't divorce me, out of badness I guess, so that makes me still an alien. Anyway, no fences – I like it that way. One thing, it kind of makes our little girl a bastard but that's OK – a healthy child should grow up holding grudges.

We christened her – what else? – Leanne Erica Theadora. I want this kid of ours to flower, to blossom and, yes, to be a writer. Sometimes, when I pin her by the shoulders and stare into her shrewd green eyes, I think I can see that in her. Maybe I'll abuse her to make sure she's good and fucked up enough to write a startlingly fresh first novel. When I make jokes like that, Bobbie gets mad and throws stuff. Maybe it reminds her of Lorne or maybe she too believes there's no such thing as a joke. Either way, what Bobbie lacks in vocabulary she can make up for with the clatter of earthenware.

I'll say this much, though, things are good. Love has changed my life – the unspoken undercurrent of its to and fro, its benevolence informing our humdrum daily chores.

When I look at my family, I bless the day I committed murder.

To get out of Bobbie's hair, I'll maybe sit with a book.

Out on the stoop, by night or day, I'll read stories to our little Leanne. Sometimes I'll recite 'To a Mouse' by Burns, in a rolling guttural burr – she likes that. The strangeness of the Scottish words on the air combined with the familiarity of those tiny creatures seems to draw her in, to mesmerise her. When I'm done, she'll make us comb the scrub all around the house looking for creatures to pour her human understanding on. We take sticks, though. We're not fools – there are snakes here.

Maybe Bobbie will join us after supper and pick at her guitar.

'This is a big country,' I like to say to my daughter, 'but words are bigger still. Reading books is like looking for driftwood at Big Sur, sweetheart – you never know what you'll find there.'

Sometimes my daughter listens to me, other times she's too busy with her pink hand-mirror, the one with the tinted rhinestones her momma gave her to adore herself in. When the time comes, I'll have a fatherly talk with her. I'll sit my little Leanne Erica Theadora down and speak to her. I'll do so lovingly, earnestly, from the heart. 'Sweetheart,' I'll say, 'there is nothing you cannot achieve in life – no goal is beyond you, so long as you are prepared to pay the price. But it's a big price. If you don't have that big price, then it must be extracted from others. Without compunction. But there's a bargain here that must be honoured – great work must follow. If it doesn't, then the sacrifice of all has been in vain and your life is forfeit. Death or glory, sweetheart, that's all there is. Everything in between is hanging around for the chips to fry.' When the time comes, that's what I'll tell my daughter. But right now, she's playing with her dollies. She'd better make the most of it, though. She has competition on the way – a sister. We had the scan done yesterday at the clinic in King City.

Women.

If I were to reach up to my nearest bookshelf now, I could show you a battered, much travelled copy of *Love Letter Blues*.

I keep a few things around to remind me of who I used to be.

And of whom I have become.

I am no longer me. I'm bigger now.

It's how I cheat the rain.

God bless America.

Or anything.